BEING VARIOUS

Also available from Faber

BEING VARIOUS

New Irish Short Stories

Edited and with an introduction by
LUCY CALDWELL

FABER & FABER

First published in 2019
by Faber & Faber Limited
Bloomsbury House
74–77 Great Russell Street
London WC1B 3DA

First published in the USA in 2019

Typeset by Typo•glyphix
Printed and bound by CPI Group (UK) Ltd, Croydon CR0 4YY

ISBN 978–0–571–34250–1

FSC
www.fsc.org
MIX
Paper from
responsible sources
FSC® C020471

2 4 6 8 10 9 7 5 3 1

for English teachers, everywhere
for libraries, fighting the good fight
and for bookshops, most of all No Alibis

Contents

CONTENTS

Introduction

One rainy afternoon just before St Patrick's Day, my husband and I walked from our current home in Whitechapel to see an exhibition at London City Hall. As we took turns pushing the baby's buggy and trailing our three-year-old on his scooter, we slipped into the grooves of a conversation we often have these days, about where we might live, if and when our accumulated drift of London years is no longer sustainable. We talked about the sunshine in Sydney, where one of my sisters is; of my cousins in Canada. My parents considered emigrating before I was born; the ghost of my imagined Canadian self flickered in and out of vision. We talked about Europe – Andalucia or Tuscany or Berlin – and I pointed out that whilst the children and I would be okay, with our Irish passports, my English husband would need to rely on spousal rights after Brexit. And we talked about Belfast, of course, a conversation we've been having with varying degrees of intensity for years.

My phone in my pocket was abuzz with a stream of banter from my family WhatsApp group about the imminent Ireland rugby match and the Grand Slam and the Triple Crown; a separate, far more sombre conversation with my mum was about the ongoing trial of the Ulster rugby players accused of rape. I wondered aloud about the Ireland we'd be moving to, if we ever did move back (or, from my husband and children's point of view, move). Meanwhile, our children sing Bengali nursery rhymes and celebrate Eid, and even without ever setting foot in Ireland, their own children will be automatically eligible for Irish citizenship by dint of mine, one quarter of their grandparental make-up. One eighth, if you take into account the fact that my mum was born in England; though set against this is the fact that Belfast is the place she chose to come to, and that, besides, her own family once hailed from Cork.

I often wonder how Irish my Cockney-born children will feel, or feel entitled to be. My son at two, solemnly watching the progress of the construction site opposite our flat and admonishing his visiting Grampy: 'It's not *tar*, it's taow-ah.' My daughter with her anglicised Irish name. The tug of my complicated relationship with the place I'm from, its eddies and swirls and undertows, cross-currents.

The exhibition, called *I Am Irish* and curated by Lorraine Maher, is a series of portraits by the Jamaican-born photographer Tracey Anderson, celebrating mixed-race Irish people aged from one to seventy-five. It intends to address, the accompanying literature says, the lack of representation of the Black Irish experience, and to question the concept of Irishness. For Maher, growing up in Carrick-on-Suir in Tipperary in the sixties and seventies, there wasn't anyone else around who looked like her. For the best part of her life, she explains, she didn't know that there were any other mixed-race Irish people.

She grew up with folk constantly questioning her Irishness and casting doubt on whether she belonged.

As I moved from portrait to portrait, the patronymics – Power, Fitzpatrick, Behan, Griffin, Ní Eochaidh, Costello, Kelly, Walsh, McGowan, Keogh – were a roll-call of Irishness. A middle-aged woman was standing in front of one of them, crying. I thought about how far Ireland has come in my lifetime and how far it has to go.

What makes a writer Irish? is the question that has enervated and energised me for the whole of my writing life.

I was born and grew up on the island of Ireland, yet never called myself 'Irish' until I'd left.

I sit at my desk in London, yet still find myself calling Belfast 'here'.

I hold both UK and Irish passports and neither of them tells the full story; I feel apologetic and fraudulent to varying degrees, depending on who I'm with, or where I'm going, whichever one I use.

Who is more Irish: a writer born in Ireland who moves and stays away, or a writer born elsewhere who chooses to come – and there's that 'here' again. A writer born in what is technically Ireland, in the 'island of' sense, but who chooses to identify with 'the mainland'? A writer born outside of Ireland to parents who keep it alive through songs, St Patrick's Day and waking up in the wee hours to watch the rugby? A writer born in Ireland to parents from elsewhere, who constantly has to answer the deathly question, 'No, but where are you *really* from?'

*

All of this was to the forefront of my mind as I put together this anthology, the latest in the series begun by David Marcus. Ireland is going through a golden age of writing: that has never been more apparent. I wanted to capture something of the energy of this explosion, in all its variousness. The crime writing that's come from the North, the closest we've had to a way of questioning and dealing with the past. The new strain of magical realism coming through. Young Adult fiction, where some of the thorniest questions about feminism and bodily autonomy are being addressed. The new modernism, with its linguistic pyrotechnics and emotional urgency. Writers at the height of their powers turning the full beam of their attention to subjects that have long been unspoken or dismissed or taboo, with a ferocity and unsentimentality that's breathtaking. Writers who are truly the inheritors of Bowen and Trevor and O'Faolain, telling twenty-first-century stories with effortless elegance and grace.

I wanted to look, too, at where the new ways of Irish writing might take us. The fresh narratives, perspectives and multiplicities that are coming from immigration to a place so long and persistently defined by emigration. The brilliance of the voices we have can blind us to those we're missing. I would love to read, in future iterations of this anthology, stories by Polish-Irish, Syrian-Irish, Traveller voices. Stories about the Venezuelan friends my parents met through Duolingo who came to Belfast after having to leave Caracas at short notice and in peril. Of my son's friend's grandmother, who came to Belfast in the fifties from what was then called British Guiana. We are all the lesser for not having these stories in our common cultural experience, and I hope we're

4

at the verge of such new voices beginning to come through, or at last to be heard.

After much deliberation, I took as my starting point the Good Friday Agreement, deciding to focus on writers who've begun to publish since then. Recently celebrated and newly imperilled, the Good Friday Agreement changed everything for my generation. Suddenly, psychologically, we were free to experiment with and to embrace pluralities – contradictory ways of being. The milestones in contemporary Irish literature come thick and fast from then. The founding of the *Stinging Fly* magazine and its publication of Kevin Barry's *There Are Little Kingdoms*, the influence of which cannot be overstated. The #WakingTheFeminists movement, which asked, loudly, where our women's voices were, on the national stages and in the national tapestry. The work by historians such as Catherine Corless and activists such as Colm O'Gorman, bringing buried and hidden stories into the public domain, and keeping them there. The more recent publications of Sinéad Gleeson's beautiful and important *The Long Gaze Back* and *The Glass Shore*, both published by another formidable small press, New Island. This pair of sister anthologies redefined the Irish writing landscape, restored neglected women writers to the canon, and led to more conversations about whose stories are missing not just from the pantheon, but from our quotidian lives.

All of the stories in this anthology are new, commissioned especially. It will be of no surprise to anyone who knows me that the balance is two-thirds female, one-third Northern. Two-thirds born in Ireland, two-thirds currently resident. The youngest writers are in their twenties, but it's not just youth which is new: some of the best writers represented here are in their forties, fifties and sixties and only just beginning to publish.

This anthology, and many of its individual stories, ask, again and again, questions about contemporary Irishness which, like those I ask on a personal level, cannot be answered, only further complicated. But I hope that most of all it is a celebration – in the words of Louis MacNeice, words which are the closest I have to an article of faith – of 'the drunkenness of things being various'.

Lucy Caldwell, 2018

How I fell in love with the well-documented life of Alexander Whelan

Yan Ge

By the time Alex Whelan became part of my life he had already died. However, it was not until much later that I became aware of this fact.

I met Alex at a meeting of the Foreign Movies No Subtitles (FMNS) group. The date was 2 March. The movie was *An Autumn Afternoon*. The meet-up place was Eoin (the organiser)'s studio off Meath Street. And the fee was 8 euro per person (with a glass of red/white wine).

When I arrived the movie had already started. I stooped and sneaked in, taking a seat at the back. Alex was sitting right beside me but we didn't talk for the duration of the whole movie. Only when it was over did he turn to me and ask for the time. I checked my phone and told him it was 9.15.

'I like the song they sang at the end,' he then said. 'What do you think this movie is about?' 'It seemed the old man was about to die so he arranged a marriage for his daughter,' I said. 'I don't think so,' he disagreed. 'I think he liked that hostess woman and the daughter decided to get married so her dad could find his own happiness.'

'Wouldn't that be too much of a twist?' I frowned.

'It wasn't straightforward anyway,' he admitted. 'But isn't that what Japanese culture is about? The forbearance and the elusive love.'

'I don't know much about Japanese culture.' I gave him a smile.

'I'm Alex,' he grinned.

'Hello, Alex,' I said.

'What's your name?' he asked.

So I told him my name and briefly coached him on the pronunciation. Then he asked me what it meant. I in turn elaborated on my factually tedious name. To respond, he said it was unbelievably beautiful and I nodded humbly to accept yet another round of applause for my culture and my smart-arsed ancestors.

It was all cliché. We then talked about the weather (wet and changeable), the place he came from (Kilkenny) and how long it took to drive there from Dublin (an hour and a half), among other things.

'How long have you been in Ireland?' he asked me at a certain point.

'Would you believe me if I told you I'm actually from Tipperary?' I said.

He laughed loudly. 'You must be kidding me!'

He checked his phone, saying he needed to head to Vicar Street to join the lads and he wondered if I had any plan.

'I need to go home now,' I said. 'It's too late.'

'It's not ten yet.'

'Long way to Tipperary, you know,' I said, and picked up my satchel bag.

He wheezed.

8

'Add me on Facebook, will you?' he asked me before I left. 'The name is Alexander Whelan.'

'Sure,' I nodded and walked out of the door.

Apologies if I have challenged your attention span and I admit the dialogue above isn't particularly interesting. However, I had to show it in full detail because it was the only time we spoke. I'll go through the crucial part of the story very quickly now. What happened was:

On my way back to the apartment I added Alex on Facebook and it was approximately 10.30 p.m.

When I got home, my roommate was in her bedroom, having left some tortilla chips and hummus on the coffee table. So I sat down, had some food and lingered on Instagram for about an hour before I went to the bathroom to pee. It was almost 12 a.m.

I had eaten too many tortilla chips and hummus to sleep. So I went back to my bedroom to work on my thesis/wait for the food to digest. I stared at the Word document for about twenty minutes and went to YouTube where I watched some old Chinese TV series for about three hours.

Eventually I decided to get ready for bed. I went to the bathroom to wash up and got caught up by a test (Which *Game of Thrones* Character Are You?) and sat on the toilet for another thirty-five to forty-five minutes.

Then I lay on my bed, browsing through my phone to allow my day to sink in. It was 4.47 a.m. when I got the notification from Facebook. Alexander Whelan accepted your friend request. Good man, I thought. I wanted to click into his page and maybe send a message but I was too tired so I put my phone down and fell asleep.

The next day I woke up around noon. I was running around and doing whatnot for about five hours during which I routinely checked my phone every three to five minutes but there was no message from Alex.

I decided to PM him when I was preparing dinner, heating up a Tesco soup and buttering two slices of brown bread. So I went to his Facebook page and that was when I saw the posts coming up on his wall. *R.i.p. Alex. My heart was broken when I heard the news,* one person posted. *R.I.P. Bro. Have a good one on the other side,* another one went. And many others.

It was 6.10 p.m., 3 March. I learnt from his Facebook that Alex had died that morning. There was an accident and he was sent to St James's Hospital and died there at 6.15 a.m.

I almost dropped my phone into my carrot and coriander soup.

It wasn't the first Cyberdeath I'd experienced. But this one also took place in real life. Or did it? I spent the whole evening questioning the authenticity of this news. Could it be a prank played by Alex and his friends?

This was how I pictured the situation:

Alex: So I just met this girl. She is kind of cute.
Friend A: Oh yeah?
Alex: She is Chinese. Actually I'm not sure. She said she's from Tipp. But she looks Chinese and her name sounds Chinese.
Friend A: Well, if it looks like a duck and swims like a duck . . .
Alex: Hey! . . . Wait, she just added me on Facebook.
Friend A: Cool. Show me her profile photo.

(Alex shows his friend my profile photo.)

Friend A: Hmmm . . . I don't know . . . You call this cute?

(Alex checks my profile photo.)

Alex: I don't know . . . Maybe? Ah never mind.

(Alex puts away his phone. They go drinking and then the gig is on so they enjoy the music until very late in the evening. Afterwards, they go to a friend's apartment to smoke some hash. It is around five in the morning when everybody is stoned and Alex cries out.)

Alex: Shite! I think I just accidently added her!

Friend B: Who?

Alex: This Chinese girl I met.

Friend B: You were in China? China has good food.

Friend C: The moon is coming to get us!

Alex: Shit. Shit. I can't undo this now. What do I do?

Friend A: What are we gonna do? It's the moon man! Moon man is murdering the moon!

Friend B: Chill out. Watch me save your ass, loser!

(B takes out his phone and types.)

Friend B: Check your Facebook now, Alex.

(Alex takes his phone out and checks his Facebook. He laughs out loud hysterically.)

Friend A: What? Show us!

(A grabs Alex's phone and reads out: R.i.p. Alex. My heart was broken when I heard the news.)

Friend A: Epic! Wait!

(A takes out his phone and starts posting on Alex's wall. Then friends C D E F join in.)

The more I thought about it, the more it felt plausible. In this case, Alex would still be alive. He might be a dick but he would be alive.

Here is the fundamental question: if you meet a guy who you sort of like and he turns out to be a dick, would you like him to remain, unapologetically, a dick and pretend he is dead, or would you prefer he is actually dead, but possibly a good guy?

It was not entirely rootless speculation. For the start, Alex had 1,257 Facebook friends. And just for the last month, he checked in at Vicar Street twice (10 and 17 Feb), Grogan's three times (7, 8 and 20 Feb), The Lord Edward twice (5 and 22 Feb), The Long Hall three times (2, 14 and 25 Feb), and Bowes four times (I don't even bother to recheck the dates).

I understand you might say: But sure it's February, where can he go if not the pub? But still. Plus, how would you feel if I told you that among the fourteen visits to local pubs, Alex was feeling crazy for seven of them, excited on five of these occasions. There were only two times where he was tagged so I wouldn't be able to know how exactly he felt. But he certainly looked very well in the photos with his friends. And so did his friends.

So would it be actually possible that he was a philanderer who played a prank on me via Facebook, because I was, according to Friend A, not cute?

On the other hand, there were things that suggested a slightly different lifestyle. For instance, he had read 572 books on Goodreads, rated 493 of them (3.73 avg) and written 89 reviews. He volunteered for numerous (23) events at Insomnia Ireland, helping people who suffer from either coffee addiction or sleep deprivation. He was the guitarist of a band named

Imaginary Bananas on Bandcamp, on which they uploaded three songs ('How To Murder The Moon', 'Hippopotamus' and 'The Telly Is On'). He also hosted a tour on Airbnb, which was called *Phoenix Park Walk: learn about Irish trees and shrubs*. It charged 30 euro per person and had three five-star reviews.

And so on and so forth.

I slouched in front of my laptop, searching through all the online statistics of Alex Whelan. My roommate came over to knock on my door and she said: 'Would you stop watching Chinese soap operas? Work on your thesis.' 'Did my mother tell you to say this?' I asked her without turning back. 'No!' she exclaimed. 'She is only concerned about you, you know?'

'Relax. I am doing research for my thesis,' I said, scrolling down Alex's friends page.

'I can see from here that's Facebook!' she bellowed and left.

Never mind the thesis. For now, I needed to get to the bottom of this. I needed to know what kind of a person was Alex Whelan, was he really dead, and if so did he add me on Facebook right before the time of his death?

I looked into his 1,257 Facebook friends. There were 202 of them living in Dublin. So I clicked into the profiles of these 202 people and finally found a Micheál Hannigan who shared his timeline to the public.

It seemed there would be a *Black Books* night at the Bernard Shaw on Friday evening and Micheál was going. So I went and got a visual on him after a few minutes of scanning the crowd.

'Hi! Micheál!' I approached and tapped him on the shoulder.

He looked at me and was for a second visibly confused. 'Hi?' he said.

'I'm a friend of Alex,' I said. 'We met at Vicar Street a couple of weeks ago, remember?' He was at Vicar Street with Alex on 10 February.

'Oh!' he nodded. 'I remember now. Hello, how are you?'

I relaxed and poised myself. 'Good! I'm good, how are you?' I asked.

'Not bad. Not bad,' he said.

'So sorry about Alex. I couldn't believe it!' I sighed and shook my head.

'I know! I was just thinking. Jesus!' He rubbed his eyebrows.

I wanted to proceed but he asked: 'Sorry, can you remind me of your name again? I'm terrible with names.'

'I'm Claire,' I said.

'Oh,' he said. 'Claire?'

'Claire Collins,' I assured him.

He seemed satisfied. If it came with a surname it must be real.

And then we conversed. He'd had a very busy week programming, fixing a new application that was basically unfixable. 'The QA keep sending it back to me! I said send it to the engineers but nobody listened. It just keeps coming back to me.' My week wasn't great either. After three nights of toil I sent in my thesis before the deadline only to find out that the professor was on strike. 'Would it kill him to let us know the week before so I could save myself a full tin of coffee.' Another cold wave was coming from Russia. There was an amazing sauna place on South William Street. 'Speaking of which, isn't it incredible, the emerging culinary scene in Dublin?' From there we slid into the friction-free zone of food talk, where I went on autopilot for about fifteen minutes before I seized a window to terminate the conversation.

'It was so nice talking to you. But I really need to run now,' I said. 'And, if you don't mind me asking, how did Alex . . . you know? I heard it was an accident. How did it happen?'

'Oh, you didn't hear? Right, they probably don't want to advertise it . . . He killed himself. Cut his wrist in the bathroom. Can you believe it?' he added, shaking his head.

I went numb and I heard him asking: 'So are we friends on Facebook yet? Add me if we're not.'

I learnt this from my mother: if you want to ask something really important, leave it till the end. 'Don't just go in and ask. It's impolite,' she said. 'You have to talk to people. You have to listen to them. You have to warm them up and show them you care. And then ask what you really want at the end of it. Ask casually.'

My mother is the most capable woman I know. She is bright, hardworking and unbelievably adaptable. She raised me all by herself after my father passed away when I was small (eighteen months, she told me). In 2005, she met a divorcee on the internet and they soon fell in love. He came to China to visit her in the summer and proposed at the airport before he left. They got engaged and tied the knot in the spring of 2007. Afterwards, my mother sold our apartment and we moved to Ireland with her new husband, Eugene Collins.

Mr and Mrs Collins still live happily in the picturesque town of Cahir, Co. Tipperary. She renamed herself Amy and introduced me as Claire. 'Claire Collins.' She tried to sell the name to me. 'It sounds right, don't you think?'

'That is just not my name,' I told her.

'But it'll be easier for everybody! Come on, Xiaohan. It'd be good for you!' she said.

My mother has always known what is best for me. In the end, I embraced the name and learnt to take pleasure watching people's faces change when I said I was Claire Collins. 'Yes, that's me. It's a bit mixed up. Long story,' I'd say. Overall, it was a great conversation starter and a delightful pastime.

I didn't do this when I met Alex, though. For some reason, I told him my real name and coached him on the pronunciation.

'Sh-aw, H-ung,' I remembered him saying.

'That's perfect!' I laughed. I didn't let him know that I couldn't really remember the last time someone called me Xiaohan.

I took a taxi home after talking to Micheál Hannigan because I felt light-headed. My roommate and her boyfriend were watching TV in the sitting room. 'Hi, Claire, how's your evening so far?' the boyfriend waved at me upon my entry. My roommate said: 'Can you call Amy later? She said you haven't called for a week.'

'I'll call her,' I said, and closed my bedroom door.

Alex posted this on 8 November 2016:

Things we take for granted: A pint of Guinness. Packed and pre-washed spinach. Eight bananas from Costa Rica for one fifty. Sparkling water. Electric sockets. Toilet paper in public bathrooms. Short stories of Franz Kafka. Free streaming music. Google Maps. 4G data. Facebook friends. Being white. European Union. A Democratic president of the United States. Solidarity. Globalisation. Rationalism. Freedom. Life.

It got 210 likes and three comments.

Sitting on my bed, I read it about ten times, whispering the words through my lips, as if they were a spell.

I wanted to respond with something meaningful under the post. I tried and failed.

So I liked it.

211 likes.

I didn't think I'd have been moved by Alex's post if he hadn't been dead. Death was a titanic LOMO lens, through which every word and paragraph, every line of code and every algorithm looked solemn and prophetic.

In the early morning of 3 March, after watching the Japanese movie *An Autumn Afternoon* (without subtitles), after a few drinks at Vicar Street, and after accepting my friend request, Alexander Whelan sentenced himself to death.

What he left behind was this post, which was written right after the American presidential election, along with other posts about news he heard, books he read and music he enjoyed. There were also emojis, photos, video clips, events; in fact, his whole Facebook account, his Instagram, Twitter, Pinterest, Snapchat, Tumblr, PayPal . . . an entire world.

I believe I've made myself clear: this is a love story. This is a love story about boy meets girl. An Irish boy meets a Chinese girl in Dublin. They like each other instantly and decide to be friends on Facebook. It won't be long before they actually start seeing each other but the boy is dead. Except that in this case he leaves behind an enormous and self-proliferating online archive with which the Chinese girl will find no problem falling in love.

*

This is what our first date is going to look like:

We are meeting for Thursday lunch at Manning's Bakery and Cafe on Thomas Street. Before I go, I check on TripAdvisor and learn most customers recommend their carrot cake.

Me: I'll have a slice of carrot cake, then. And a latte.

The waitress: Good.

(She repeats and writes down our orders and leaves.)

Alex: So you're having cake for lunch.

Me: Why not? It's Thursday.

Alex: What's special about Thursday?

Me: Its lack of identity.

(Alex wheezes.)

Me: So what do you do?

Alex: I work at Maniac & Anarchist Co.

Me: That's not a real company.

Alex: This is what my Facebook says.

Me: And what do you say?

Alex: I say we should just trust my Facebook.

(I laugh. The waitress arrives with our orders. She lays out the cutlery, the cups and the plates, and leaves. Alex takes a sip of his coffee. I cut a corner of my carrot cake with the fork.)

Me: If I could just read and trust your online profiles, why would we need to meet in person? Is there anything you can tell me in the flesh that your Facebook can't?

(Alex thinks for a while.)

Alex: Here's the thing: how do you define knowing a person? If we have spent, say, a month together, we share the space, we eat, we drink, we watch TV and we have sex. But we don't talk – we talk about basic stuff but we don't have conversations. You don't know what kind of music I like and dislike, which college I went to, who my favourite writer is, etc. But we spend tons of time together. Under this circumstance, can you say you know me? Or, you've read my Facebook and other online archives, and we can trust all of them, okay? And you've learnt all about me. I like The Cure and I hate Maroon Five. I went to UCD. My favourite writer is Kafka. You know all my thoughts and understand comprehensively what kind of a person I am but you have never actually spent much time with me – like, we just met really briefly. Then, can you say you know me?

(I work on my carrot cake and finish it when Alex is talking. And I drink my coffee.)

Me: You are speaking hypothetically. But this is the reality: we are sitting here at your most visited cafe and I want to know something directly from you. Is that okay?

Alex: Shoot.

Me: Tell me, why did you kill yourself? And why did you add me right before you did it? If I had sent you a message there right away, would it have made a difference?

(Alex looks at me. And he smiles.)

Alex: What do you think?

Alex posted this a week before his death:

I'm thinking about moving to a foreign country. I'm not talking about Canada, New Zealand, the UAE or Spain. I'm talking about REAL FOREIGN. Not any version of little Ireland. No bacon and cabbage, fish and chips or any comfort food for that matter. No English. What I want is to extract myself entirely from this life and to land in a brand new one, in which I have no language, no clue of any cultural context and can find no trace of my own kind. People on Facebook, any recommendations?

Some suggested China. And one more cynical friend replied: *North Korea?*

I knew exactly what he was talking about. It was precisely how I felt the first year I came to Ireland and studied at the language school. And then the second year. And then the third. And the fourth the fifth the sixth.

'Claire,' my roommate said, knocking on the door. 'Stephen and I are going to Grogan's to meet friends. You want to come? It should be fun.'

So I went with them to Grogan's. And there were their friends, sitting around two tables pulled together: beautiful blonde women in their shining jewellery, tall men and their scented hair gel.

I was pointed to sit by a smallish guy with a friendly smile. 'Alan,' he introduced himself.

'I'm Claire,' I smiled back.

'So how do you know Laura and Stephen?' Alan asked me.

'Laura and my mother are friends,' I said.

'Oh?' He paused and took a look at Laura.

'I was joking. I'm her stepsister.'

'I thought so. I've heard about you before.' He laughed with relief.

Stephen brought me my beer. I took a deep gulp out of thirst.

'So you're from China,' our conversation continued.

'Yep,' I nodded.

'Tell me, what's China like? I've always wanted to go there.'

20

'I can't really say. It's been almost ten years since I left. It is probably very different now.' I drank another mouthful.

'Wow, ten years. Do you miss China?'

'Sometimes.'

'And how do you find Ireland?'

'Good. Beautiful country. Nice people,' I said, and finished my beer.

'You're drinking fast!' he finally noticed. 'Can I get you another one?'

'Nope.' I put down my glass and sat back. 'I'm good now. Let's talk.'

After taking on a moderate amount of alcohol I became interested in the conversation. We talked and laughed. And then we got up to go to the bar/toilet and switched seats subtly. New drink. New friend. Shake hand and smile. I'm Claire. I came from China. No, my English is not really good but thank you very much. Yes, I do like Ireland. Beautiful country. Nice people.

Later, in the cab home, Laura said: 'I'm glad you came. It looked like you were enjoying yourself.'

'Yes. I had a good time,' I said.

'So, how's Alan?' Stephen turned from the front seat and asked.

'How's Alan?' I asked back.

'What do you think? Any craic?' he pursued.

'I don't know. I only talked to him for, like, ten minutes.'

'So no craic?' Laura said.

'No craic,' I said firmly, making sure she'd include this in her report to my mother.

*

I put on repeat 'Hippopotamus', the song from Alex's band, and went on working on my thesis. It was a light song with subtle and intricate melodies, a sort of Scandinavian indie type.

> Once upon a time I was about to die
> Fired from my job and kicked out by my girlfriend
> She said go to hell you asshole
> She said don't come back unless you buy me the Ferragamo
>
> Once upon a time I was about to die
> I sat outside Heuston Station, begging for change
> I said I'm starved please I am starved
> I said I want to have a spring roll or I am gonna die
>
> Eventually my way walked a man from Sligo
> He said here you go, son, a ticket for Dublin Zoo
> He said trust me you just need to see the animals
> You need to see the animals and you will never die
>
> Once upon a time I almost died
> I went to Dublin Zoo to see the animals
> I saw giraffes, elephants and monkeys
> Sea lions, zebras and flamingos
> And I didn't even forget the hippopotamus
>
> Giraffes, elephants and monkeys
> Sea lions, zebras and flamingos
> And oh don't forget the hippopotamus
> Hippopotamus, hippopotamus, hippo, hippopotamus

*

It was not specified on the website but I believed it was Alex who wrote the lyrics. He seemed like that kind of a guy who would not forget to see the hippopotamus when visiting the zoo.

I found myself roaming on the internet again, tracing Alex's footsteps. It had been two weeks since he'd died. On his Facebook page, there used to be post after post of tributes, washing on to his wall like the most ferocious tide. And now his wall had gone quiet. Only once or twice a day, a casual *R.I.P.* would pop up, or a red candle emoji with praying hands.

Naturally, I decided to read all of these 203 posts, studying people's thoughts about Alex and their memories with him. He was described by lots of friends as *generous*. The word *passionate* came up fifty-two times. And then there were *adventurous* (thirty-one), *affectionate* (twenty-eight), *intuitive* (seventeen), *original* (fourteen), and *artistic* (ten). One said he missed his *whimsy*. Another called him *scintillating*. And a Susie Burns wrote he was *the most charismatic character in Dublin*.

We've lost the most charismatic character in Dublin. I don't know what you are gonna do People, but I'm getting PISSED tonight, she posted.

The most surprising post came in three days ago. It said: *So I quit my job, ended my lease and bought a ticket to Bangkok. You were right, my brother. Our life here has turned into a monster and it's time to run. Get out before it eats you alive.*

It was from Micheál Hannigan. I clicked into his page and there he was, already checked in at Brown Sugar, Bangkok, wearing a salmon-pink short-sleeve and a pair of sunglasses, holding a tropical-looking cocktail, grinning at the camera.

I laughed out loud. I laughed so hard until I started coughing.

Struggling, I pushed myself up from the desk and closed my laptop.

It was late in the afternoon and I hadn't eaten. I went to the kitchen, scavenging for food. There was a half-eaten cheesecake in the fridge and the expiration date was today.

As I sat by the kitchen table, saving the cheesecake from decay, I thought of the monster of life. I thought it might be hiding, actually, in my bathroom. It was dark. It was heavy. Its skin hairless. Its breath foul. Its eyes small and vicious. Its mouth enormous and greedy. It was this monster that had devoured Alex's life and it was now hiding in my bathroom, watching me.

'Claire!' Laura called behind my back. I shivered.

'What? You scared me!' I turned around.

'It's not me.' She passed me her phone. 'Amy is on the phone. She wants to talk to you.'

'Hello, Claire.' My mother had the voice of the English listening test.

'Hi, Mom,' I said.

'Where have you been? You didn't call me last week. I asked Laura to tell you to call me,' she said.

'Yes you did. And she told me,' I said. 'I was just busy.'

'Everybody is busy. We all have different things going on. But I call you. I call you because I think it's important. I prioritise,' she said, laying out the principles.

'A friend of mine died,' I said.

'Oh,' she exclaimed lightly. 'Well, I'm sorry to hear that.'

I didn't know what to say and she continued: 'You know what we say in Chinese, that *One who stays near vermilion gets stained red, and one who stays near ink gets stained black.* You should be careful about whom to be friends with. Dublin is a very mixed city.'

Knowing my mother, I really shouldn't have been surprised, but I was still stunned. I took a breath and said: 'It's not what you think. He was a good person.'

'I'm sure he was,' she agreed. 'Anyhow, I just heard from Laura that you didn't like her friend. She said you think he is not very interesting? Claire, I cannot believe I'm repeating this to you: before you make any decisions, can you evaluate yourself first? You are not a very attractive woman. You are a foreigner in this country. You are already twenty-seven and you're still in college, studying Journalism.' She stressed on *Journalism*. 'So don't be silly, daydreaming about some Prince Charming – that's not going to happen for you. Be realistic and efficient. We've wasted time already. When we came to Ireland, you had to go to the language school and then back to secondary school for two more years. So now you must act. Listen, there are reasons I arranged for you to live with Laura . . .'

She went on and on. My understanding was she probably had a bad day and she missed me. Since I moved to Dublin for college, she had turned more and more neurotic and then aggressive every time she called. Or it might just have been that Chinese, our native tongue, reduced us into the primitive form, made us insanely susceptible and vulnerable. I felt a burning sensation in my throat. It was just graphic.

The last time she'd called had been two weeks ago. It was the night of the FMNS meeting and I was running late but she wouldn't stop talking until after seven.

When I arrived at Eoin's I texted him and he came down to let me in. The movie had already started. There were six or seven people sitting in the room. Only silhouettes. On the big pull-down screen, a pale Japanese woman was staring blankly and uncannily. The buzzing sound of the projector rendered the space into an eerie stillness.

It wasn't long before I realised the movie was about a father and a daughter, a widowed father and an unmarried daughter, living together in their old and run-down house. They sat by a small table and ate together, in front of each a dish of vegetables and a bowl of rice. I started to cry. The movie was extremely quiet so I bit my lips and clenched my fists.

And that was when the strangest thing happened. There was this guy sitting beside me. I noticed his shoulder begin to tremble and his nose sniffing from time to time.

He was crying too. And tears were pouring out from my eyes. It was Alex and me, our silhouettes trembling, crying quietly while the Japanese father and daughter spoke, in a strange language, in black and white, without subtitles.

The Swimmers

Paul McVeigh

His da bought a van. A dirty yellow Transit. Old, but it was only intended for short distances, to take kids from the estate to the swimmers. Da loved going swimming. Loved kids. The younger ones who still liked to horseplay. Before they got hormones and all aware of themselves, Da said.

Giving something back to the community, his da was, sure, who could fault the man for that? And those kids adored him, looked at him like he was God. Still, all the same, even Wee John could see, when Da was around grown-ups, his smile tried too hard and his laughter came too quick. Maybe that was why Da wasn't liked by adults, though it didn't stop them sending their kids along. Parents were funny like that.

Way before then, before the van, when Wee John was *really* wee, Da used to make him go swimming even though he never wanted to. The thing was, Wee John couldn't swim. He more paddled. But that wasn't why he didn't want to go. It was because he hated being naked in front of people, ever since he could remember, especially because he was so skinny and small for his age and, well, underdeveloped.

Wee John envied how the other boys from school acted like

it was fun, changing together for sports, laughing and talking like they'd never given a thought to who saw their bare bodies. More, they'd go buck wild, like naked was how they were supposed to be, like they'd been set free. Wee John didn't know why he was so different. Why with each piece of clothing he removed he felt worse.

When Wee John finally told Da his secret, Da came up with a plan. They'd practise going swimming weekdays after school. When Wee John got home each day, he'd to go straight to his bedroom and wait for Da to come up. Da would tell Wee John to take off each bit of his uniform super-slowly, fold everything, like Da showed him, to be dead neat. Da would do the same and they'd talk, with no clothes on, and Da said Wee John could ask him anything he wanted. It was boys' time. Some days they'd go swimming for real, then, but sometimes they'd just sit.

Once, while they were naked together, Ma came in. Da explained they were getting changed before the swimmers, so they wouldn't have to do it there in front of everyone. He winked, like, I'll tell you later. Ma didn't look well. She said they were leaving it so late, they wouldn't be back in time for dinner. After that, Da stopped changing in the bedroom. Instead, he'd sit and watch Wee John undress. Sometimes, he would sit Wee John on his knee like he used to, and they would giggle. Da liked to say Wee John was his wee boy and wished he could stay that way forever.

Some days, they'd play-fight and wrestle, like big men from the TV. Others, Da tickled all over while Wee John squirmed and laughed. Wee John thought it was weird how he'd keep laughing even when Da tickled for too long and made his ribs sore.

It got so that they didn't go swimming at all, though they still called it that. Doesn't time fly? Da would say. Wee John didn't mind. He liked it better than actual swimming. That's why, one day, when Da stood at the bottom of the stairs, and called Wee John to *really* go swimming, Wee John was confused, and he panicked, though he hadn't meant to break his arm.

It was while Wee John's arm was in a cast Da bought the van. Drove home with it one day after work and not a word was said about it. That's how things were in their house when it came to Da. Sometimes, it felt like Wee John and Ma didn't exist until Da wanted them to. He conjured them into being when they were of use.

Wee John saw a poster in the local shop the next day, with Da's new mobile number hanging from little tabs you could rip off and keep.

SWIMMING AFTER SCHOOL
Boys Under 10 Only!
Call the number below

When Wee John's arm healed, Ma insisted he go swimming with Da and the rest. She wanted Wee John out from under her feet, she said, to give her head peace, after all those weeks of him moping around the TV after school. She was sick of him looking like the world had ended.

Finally Ma said, did he know how it looked that Da was taking strangers' kids swimming and not his own son? People round here didn't trust that sort of kindness.

Wee John couldn't do anything to please Da anymore but at least he could try to please Ma.

He followed Da's plan. Knew Da wasn't coming to watch him change so he got into his togs, before, all by himself.

The boys pretended to like Wee John when he got into the van but after Da drove off they ignored him. He was new and would have to fight for his place even if he was the *boss's* son. He spent the journey pulling at the swollen sponge bulging out of the tears on the old black leather seats. The van smelt oily, smoky and dirty, like the boys inside it.

At the swimmers, he went into the corner of the changing room. He was slow and silent and folded his clothes, ever so neatly, like Da taught him. Da wasn't watching, though, he was playing with the other boys, who pushed each other and filled the air with laughing and shouting. They made so much noise it took up all the space. As they fought their way to the pool, they left their clothes in messy piles on the floor, like shed skin. Da didn't seem to mind that these boys didn't change slowly, or fold their clothes the way he'd taught Wee John.

With them gone, Wee John made his own way there, hating the rough bubbled surface of the tiles on his feet. He crept past the toilets where rowdy stragglers were clogging a sink with toilet paper and tiptoed through the freezing-cold footbath with its slimy green floor.

The exit came out at the middle of the enormous pool, Olympic size, the sign said. The cold air caused goosebumps to rush up his arms. It wasn't just his mind that hated being naked, his body did too. Swimmers rinsed themselves in freezing-cold showers watering from the wall. They were not the same kind of human as he.

At the water's edge, he folded his arms and bent his right knee to rub his inner thighs together. He dipped his toe in.

Even though they said the pool was heated, it was never warm enough. He couldn't understand why everyone seemed so happy in the water, when it got in your eyes making them sting, in your ears making you deaf, up your nose making you choke and in your mouth making you gag. Who were these people? What was wrong with them?

He gripped his toes around the lip of the pool. People laughed, screamed and shouted, and the building seemed designed to echo and amplify their noise. To his left, he saw the boys with his father at the shallow end, some already in the water, some play-fighting up on the deck, trying to drag each other into the pool. He decided to wait until all were in the water before making his way down to join them.

An almighty force pushed him from behind. His neck cracked backwards while his chest kicked forward, arms jerking out. To the sound of laughter behind, he slammed into the water. It swallowed him and the screams from above became muffled. Bubbles of air from his mouth thundered against his nose and bashed at his eyes. His fists tried to grab but the water wouldn't be held. His legs thrashed and his toes blindly felt for the bottom.

When they finally touched the tiles, he bent his knees, pushed himself off and scissor-kicked to the surface. He bent his head back to keep his mouth as far from the water as possible. Kicking and paddling to stay afloat, he gulped air, like air was water and he was dying of thirst.

There was no one at the edge of the pool where he'd stood. He hadn't seen who the stragglers were in the changing room toilets, any of them from the bus might have pushed him.

There was no one there to help.

He tried not to panic, kicked and paddled towards the shallow end where he'd be able to stand and breathe and walk his way through the water to Da. He would tell, and Da would get mad and shout, punish them all by taking everyone home, right away. Da had been weird with him lately but this was serious.

Wee John took as deep a breath as he could and stopped kicking. It was a relief to rest his legs for a second, let himself sink to the bottom, where he used his feet to push himself up again.

At the surface, he looked to the changing room exit to see how far he'd travelled toward Da. It looked like he'd gone backwards! That couldn't be true. He kicked and grabbed at the water but was not moving forward. It was almost as if the water coming from the shallow end was a tide, pushing him away from Da and the other boys.

His newly mended arm hurt, so he had to rely on his legs and the other arm for paddling. He should call out but shouting *Help* was too embarrassing, he didn't want to look like an idiot. A swimmer appeared right next to him, head in the water, breaststroke, now head rising out to breathe.

Help! he coughed, and managed to touch the man, who dipped into the water again without stopping. Breathing fast and deep, head back, eyes to the ceiling, a wave came in the wake of the swimmer, sloshing water into his mouth and down his throat. He shook his head, kicked with all his might and choked the water out.

He sank again. He pulled his knees up to his chest this time, arms wrapped around them, then shot his legs to the floor and bounced up with as much force as he could, exploding out into the air, screaming *Help!* but everyone else was screaming too, having so much fun.

He kicked to stay afloat. No one was coming. He sank, knees up, bounced and exploded out again. *Help!* He came down as hard as he'd come out. And sank.

Da had tried to teach him to swim and Wee John wanted really hard to do what Da said but his body just wouldn't play along and it didn't matter how much he loved Da or how desperate he was to please him.

He was only wee sure, Da had said, towelling him dry one day in the changing room, don't be in such a hurry to grow up. It would all come together one day. But it didn't and then they started going swimming at home.

Wee John struggled, but the water was relentless. It reshaped itself so as to always be against him. He thought about giving up.

The last time Da had come to his bedroom, Wee John opened his jeans and lowered his pants to show Da his new hairs, they'd come at the weekend, out of nowhere. Da looked really embarrassed, like Wee John had done something he wasn't supposed to. Da left the room. Wee John didn't understand. He didn't put his togs on, waited for Da to come back up to watch. When Da called for him to go, *really* go swimming, Wee John came to the top of the stairs. He looked down at the open front door, the grey path outside cut short by the door frame.

Let's go, Da shouted from the street, in his angry voice.

Wee John's heart answered with a thud, hitting lower in his ribs than he'd felt before. He'd done something wrong. His body had. He'd always known he should hide it. Panic felt cold in his head. His heart dropped with each beat. A Da-shaped shadow jerked toward him on the path outside.

Da stopped in the hall, at the bottom of the stairs. Framed in the doorway, blocking the sunlight.

Don't have me going up there to get you, Da growled.

Catch me, Daddy, Wee John shouted, and jumped, arms wide open, like he used to when he was wee. But he was a big boy now.

Da didn't take him to the hospital. Children in pain were a mother's job, Da said.

Wee John bounced off the tiles again. Pain shot through his tired thighs and stabbed into his hips. He barely made it to the surface. When he opened his eyes they rolled up into their sockets. He felt tired, sleepy even. The world above the water seemed slowed down.

A small head came into view at the edge of the water, something for his eyes to focus on, to stop his vision spinning. A young girl holding on to the side. Her swimming cap was bright pink and strands of black hair clung to her face like liquorice twists. Hand over hand, she was pulling her way along the length of the pool towards the shallow end. She couldn't swim either.

A Partial List of the Saved
Danielle McLaughlin

The flight attendant who brought the beer was the same one who'd performed the safety demonstration an hour earlier as they'd taxied towards the runway at San Francisco. 'In the unlikely event of landing in water,' a disembodied voice had said as the woman popped a lifejacket over her head. 'Unlikely' hardly went far enough, Conor thought. He hated to be a pedant, but still. It was *unlikely* that he'd packed a European adapter, but one might yet materialise among the tangle of accessories he'd shoved in his suitcase as the cab waited by the kerb. It was *unlikely* that the man seated to his left would stop talking any time soon, but it was not inconceivable that some affliction of the throat might set in. It seemed wrong, somehow, that the possibility that they would all be plunged into the icy waters of the Atlantic to have their eyes eaten out by small fish should be placed on a par with these other, more mundane, eventualities. Surely, at a minimum, it was 'extremely unlikely'?

On the other side of him sat his ex-wife, Reece. They'd been married ten years when he discovered she was conducting an affair with one of her co-workers at the marine biology centre, a younger man called Dan. Or Quinoa Dan, as Conor privately thought of him, with his man-bun and his Converse and his vegan tray bakes. Conor had been to Dan's apartment once, in the days before the affair. He'd eaten flourless vegan cake for Dan's thirty-fifth birthday in a loft in an old bottling factory in Mission Bay, an open-plan rectangular space, with upcycled furniture and cork floors. When confronted about the affair, Reece said that she was sorry, but she didn't say that she would stop seeing Dan. Instead, she'd quietly packed a suitcase and left. That was in January.

———

'This might sound a little odd' was how he'd prefaced his request when he'd rung her on a Saturday evening in late April.

'Go on,' she said.

The affair with Dan had ended by then, and Reece was renting a studio apartment in Belmont. They were being civilised about the divorce, because what other way was there to be, Conor thought, at this hour of their lives, him fifty-two, Reece forty-seven. It wasn't as if they were high schoolers, maddened by young love's implosion.

'Remember how my father always adored you?' he said.

'Your father's a sweetheart. I'll always be very fond of him.'

'The thing is,' he said, 'Daddy hasn't been well lately.' He stopped. He'd thought long and hard about this call, but now he feared that he'd miscalculated. 'His lungs are bad, his heart is bad, his kidneys aren't too good either. It's his eightieth birthday on July tenth and Joanne wants us all to be there.'

'Us?'

'Yes, us. You. Me.'

'Oh,' she said. He heard a soft clunk on the other end of the line. He pictured her putting down the phone, winding her index finger round and round in her hair, as she'd always done when puzzled.

'Reece?' he said. 'Are you still there?' Was she in bed, he wondered? He imagined his voice travelling down the wires, revisiting his wife in her new bedroom.

'I didn't expect to be invited,' she said eventually. 'I was afraid your father might think badly of me. I worried he might blame me for the divorce.'

Well, who else would he be blaming? Conor thought. 'You mustn't mention anything about that,' he said. 'My father doesn't know.'

'That's the kind of thing a father should know, Conor. How could you not tell him?'

'It would kill him, Reece, it would break his heart. He always thought the sun shone out your ass.'

'Does Joanne know?' Joanne was Conor's sister.

'She thinks we're going through a rough patch.'

Reece was silent for a moment. 'Do they still ask after me?' she said.

'Of course,' he said. 'I tell them that you're very well.' He paused. 'It's a lot to ask, I know,' he said. 'I'll pay for everything, obviously.'

'I don't know, Conor. Isn't it a sort of . . . lie?'

'No,' he said. 'It's a kindness. My father won't last another birthday; he may not even last this one. I want to do this one small thing for him. I want him to die thinking we're happy.'

She said nothing to that. *Are you happy, Reece?* he wanted

37

to ask, but didn't. He wouldn't have minded if she was. After all the hurt, it would be a shame if neither of them was happy; it would be such a waste.

'Okay,' she said quietly, 'I'll go. I've always loved your father.'

———

The plane entered a pocket of turbulence and the Fasten Seat Belt sign came on. *Unlikely.* Conor gripped his beer more tightly. Next to him was a barrelly, red-faced man from Delaware who exuded heat like one of those bricks the Victorians used to warm their beds. Delaware Man worked for a company that installed panic rooms and he detailed the intricacies of these spaces, every strip-lit passageway, every *trompe l'œil*, in a wheezy patter halfway between sales pitch and sonnet. 'How the other half live, eh?' he said to Conor, and Conor was briefly offended at being so speedily, and accurately, consigned to a particular half. They were flying economy class, and the man's considerable frame overflowed the space allocated, his arm, leg, belly, the whole sweaty bulk of him committing one trespass after another. On the other side of Conor, Reece had carefully arranged her limbs so as not to touch him at all.

———

At Dublin Airport they hired a car and took the road north. The last time they'd travelled this road it had been summertime, not a dull day like this one, but a glorious day with the sun beating down, rugs stretched in front of bungalows, and bodies, eerily pale, prostrate on lawns like pieces of salt cod left to dry. Today the fields were shrouded in drizzle. The light was otherworldly, silver on the distant surface of the bog lakes. The previous autumn, Reece had gone to Lake Merritt for a training weekend with a group of conservation volunteers that included in their number Quinoa Dan. All lakes now held for Conor embedded images of Dan and Reece in a boat, Reece wearing shorts and a bikini, the sun browning her already brown shoulders as the boat carried them out to the eelgrass beds, or the nesting places of rare birds.

Reece fussed with the radio channels. She talked about eelgrass conservation, and about a new kind of solar panel they'd had fitted to the roof of the marine biology centre. Then she lapsed into silence. 'Don't you want to know anything about me, Conor?' she said eventually. 'Don't you want to know how I am? I acknowledge my part in how things ended, but ten years of marriage and in the past seven hours you haven't once asked how I am?'

'How are you?' he said.

Reece sighed, turned to look out the window. 'Never mind,' she said.

His father lived in Listrane, with Conor's sister Joanne. A mile before the town there was a monument, four busts carved in marble and set on a limestone base in memory of four local men captured by the Black and Tans during the War of Independence. He remembered as a child being told how they'd been taken to a shed, shot in both legs and the shed set alight. The window of the rental car was open and as they drove by, Conor thought he sensed the air grow denser, heavier.

'Is it possible, do you think,' Reece said, 'that something so terrible can inhabit the ether of a place?'

He had told her about the men, and the shooting, the first time he'd brought her here. 'You mean like a ghost?' he asked now.

'Maybe not a ghost, exactly,' she said. 'More like the way one photo can be superimposed on another.'

On previous visits they had always stayed with his family, but this time they could hardly share Conor's childhood room with its one bed. And he could hardly sleep on the sofa downstairs – Joanne was already asking too many questions. He'd told his sister they'd be staying at the hotel because Reece needed Wi-Fi for work.

'We have internet here,' Joanne said. 'I got one of those dangle things.'

'Reece needs a high-speed connection,' he'd said quickly. 'She's terribly busy at the moment.'

'I hope she's not going to miss Daddy's party,' Joanne said.

'She wouldn't dream of it,' he said. 'She's very fond of Daddy.'

The hotel, a small family-run affair, was the only one in town. To book separate rooms would have been to give themselves away, and so he'd agreed with Reece that he'd book a room with twin beds. But when he turned the key in the door, he saw that instead of two beds, there was one. Reece followed him inside, set down her suitcase. He stared at the neatly dressed bed with its scatter of cushions. He wondered if Reece would make him go down to the foyer and insist to the receptionist that they required separate beds. Perhaps he could persuade her to be pragmatic about it; after all, they had plenty of practice of lying next to one another in bed without having sex. It wasn't exactly outside their area of competence.

Things had not been unequivocally good in their marriage in the year preceding Quinoa Dan, a fact Conor had only recently conceded to himself. He might even make a joke of it. 'It'll be fine, Reece,' he might say. 'Just like old times.'

Reece sprang open the locks on her suitcase. 'It's fine,' she said. She unpacked a change of clothes, and her toiletries bag. 'I'm going to take a shower.'

He was surprised by her lack of fuss about the bed. Perhaps, he thought, it was a sign that she still had feelings for him. On the other hand, it could mean that sex was the last thing on her mind, and she was presuming that it was also the last thing on his.

The house where he'd grown up was in a cul-de-sac. It was pebble-dashed and had a garden to the front and a yard to the back, a respectable smattering of flowering shrubs, a square of gently aged tarmac where Joanne parked her car. When he rang the bell, the door wasn't answered immediately, but the curtains parted a fraction and an elderly woman Conor recognised as a neighbour, Mrs Dillon, peered out. The curtain dropped back into place and a moment later his father was at the door. 'Reece!' he said. 'Welcome, welcome. Come in.'

'Hello, Daddy,' Conor said, handing his father a bottle of whiskey.

Joanne came running out then, gripping Conor by the shoulders in greeting, kissing Reece, rolling her eyes in the direction of her father as they followed him down the hall. His father held the bottle of whiskey in front of him like a torch. He was wearing brown creased slacks in a style he'd adopted some twenty years previously and a grey Aran cardigan buttoned to the neck. His gait was slower than Conor remembered.

In the kitchen, his father waved a hand in the direction of Mrs Dillon. 'You know Agnes,' he said.

So that was Mrs Dillon's name. Conor couldn't recall ever hearing it before.

'Of course he knows me,' she said. 'Don't I remember him when he was in nappies!'

Conor gave a tight smile. 'Nice to see you again, Agnes,' he said. 'This is my wife, Reece.' It felt almost blasphemous, addressing Agnes by her first name. He couldn't remember ever calling her that as a child. Even to his mother, she had always been 'Mrs Dillon'.

Reece and Agnes shook hands. 'New tiles?' Reece said, tapping her foot on the kitchen floor.

'Yes,' his father said, pleased. 'Agnes thought they could do with replacing. And they've turned out very nice, I must say.'

Conor noticed the ease with which his father and Agnes navigated each other in the kitchen, his father's indulgent smile when Agnes knocked over the little porcelain salt dish. Joanne meanwhile was slamming plates of salad on to the table, cherry tomatoes rolling around like little red snooker balls. He kept expecting Agnes to leave, but it seemed that she was joining them.

'What's San Francisco like?' Agnes said. She'd taken a seat beside Conor, across the table from his father.

'Great,' Conor said. 'San Francisco's great.'

'Any Muslims?' his father said.

'There are Muslims, yes,' Conor said.

'We have them here now too,' his father said. 'In the full rig-out. Turbans, beards, the works.'

Conor cleared his throat, willed a suitable response to

present itself. He was saved by Mrs Dillon, who just then emitted a small hard cough, followed by a choking sound. Her eyes grew watery. She inserted a finger into her mouth and brought out something green and stringy, celery possibly, and placed it on the edge of her plate. She reddened as she stared down at it. Conor watched his father reach across and pat her hand. There was something troublingly intimate about the gesture, as if they'd engaged in some sexual act in front of him. He felt something else too, something he couldn't immediately identify, though after a moment it came to him. Jealousy. He was jealous of his eighty-year-old father and Agnes Dillon, Agnes who must be seventy-five, at least, and who was currently wiping saliva from her finger on to her plaid skirt.

'Daddy,' Joanne said, frowning, 'perhaps you could get Agnes a glass of water.' She turned to Reece. 'Any plans for tomorrow?' It was Friday, and his father's birthday wasn't until Sunday. Officially, they were on holiday.

'We're going to Belfast to visit the *Titanic* Museum,' Reece said. 'One of my ancestors sailed on the ship from Cobh. I'd invite you along, except I'm guessing you've seen it a million times.'

'I've never seen it,' Joanne said.

'Never?' Reece said. 'Then you must come with us!'

'I've never seen it either,' Agnes said. She looked across the table at Conor's father. 'Have you seen it, Dennis?' Dennis, it turned out, hadn't seen it.

'The more the merrier,' Reece said. 'There's plenty room in the car, isn't there, Conor?'

He rested his fork on the edge of his plate. A car trip with

Mrs Dillon. What fresh hell was this? The first he'd heard of the *Titanic* plan was when they were waiting for the clerk to fill out the paperwork at the car hire desk. 'Plenty of room,' he said, nodding.

Joanne stood up, began gathering plates, dropping them noisily into the sink. 'It's very kind of you, Reece,' she said, 'but I'm on the altar flower rota tomorrow. Anyway' – she looked pointedly at her father – 'I expect you and Conor would prefer to have the day to yourself.'

Agnes followed Joanne to the sink, began lifting out the plates again, stacking them neatly to one side. 'Never mind, Joanne,' she said. 'We'll bring you back a stick of rock.'

———

Lunch finished, his father and Agnes went to fetch groceries for Agnes's sister, and Conor, Reece and Joanne moved to the sitting room.

'What's going on there?' Conor asked, as lightly as he could manage.

'Love,' Reece said softly, 'that's what's going on.'

Joanne poured coffee, passed around cups and saucers and a plate of biscuits. She sat on the sofa beside Reece. 'I'm at my wits' end,' she said. 'The latest is that she has him on some new kind of tablets.' She put a hand into the pocket of her dress and produced two capsules, dented and squashed, one of them leaking fine silver granules. She held them out on her palm. 'What would they be, Conor?'

He'd tried, and failed, to explain to his sister that as a high school chemistry teacher he knew no more about pharmaceuticals than the average teenager; less, probably. 'I wouldn't know,' he said. 'I'd need to see the box.'

Joanne sighed, slipped the pills back into her pocket. 'I don't know where he keeps the box,' she said. 'He left these beside the telephone.'

'But it's sweet, isn't it?' Reece said. 'I think it's sweet.'

Joanne put down her cup and saucer. She blinked furiously, and for a second Conor feared that she might cry. When she spoke again, she addressed herself to Reece. 'You know what she has him doing now?' she said. 'Elder Yoga. I walked in on them the other evening. And now he's started talking about marrying her. It's galling, when I think of how she used to look down her nose at Mammy. At all of us. Wouldn't speak to us if she met us on the street. If it were anyone else it wouldn't be so bad. It wouldn't be ideal either, I'll grant you. But Agnes Dillon! She's after the house, of course, we all know that. And I haven't figured out how to tell Daddy that he can't marry her. Thank goodness you're here, Conor.'

'Me?' he said.

'Yes. I thought that you might have a word with him. He's always listened to you.'

For a second, he felt proud that she imagined him up to the task. And there were indeed plenty of warnings he could issue about marriage. How it had broken his heart, had left him a shell of a man who needed two different kinds of pills to get to sleep at night. But he couldn't say any of this to his father, who believed his son to be happily married.

Joanne was looking at him, expectantly.

'All right,' he said, 'but I'll need to wait for the right moment.' He excused himself then, and went outside, walked down the back lane that ran behind the houses and later joined the main road. He walked until he reached the monument to the dead patriots. He hadn't noticed before, but several of them were sporting expressions that could only be described as smug, though it was hard to see what they could have to be smug about. It was getting late now, the light seeping out of the day. He turned and began to walk back. He was no clearer about what he should do concerning his father and Agnes Dillon. A breeze rustled the trees that stretched green, luxuriant branches out into the lane, causing him to duck. It seemed to him that the evening possessed that exact combination of shadow and solitude that might reasonably be expected to deliver wisdom, or if not wisdom then at least a practical answer. But nothing presented itself.

———

That night in the hotel bedroom, they climbed into their one bed in the most matter-of-fact way possible. When the lights went off and there was only the soft illumination of the street lamps, Conor sneaked a look at his wife, if that's what she still was. She was lying on her back, staring at the ceiling. Her face looked calm, relaxed. It was impossible to guess what she might be thinking. Nobody gave herself away less than Reece; the apocalypse, or a crack in a Mason jar bought at a Goodwill sale: both of these happenings would cause the same quizzical but otherwise impenetrable expression to settle upon his wife's face.

'It's not for you to interfere in your dad's life,' Reece said. 'It's not for Joanne to interfere either.'

He felt as if she'd caught him staring. 'He's our father,' he said. 'If we don't interfere, who will?'

'He's an adult,' Reece said. 'He's free to marry who he likes. Anyway, I still don't see what the problem is.'

Earlier, when he'd arrived back from his walk, Joanne had spent a further half-hour attempting to explain the problem. She'd made what, in Conor's opinion, were several very good points. Reece had been unconvinced. 'Gold-digger?' she'd said, laughing. 'Oh, come on, Joanne, hardly!' and Conor had seen his sister's chin jut outwards, the way it did when she took offence.

'This might be the best thing that ever happened to Joanne,' Reece continued now. She was still staring at the ceiling. 'It might be the saving of her. She's in a rut here, looking after your father, has been for years. This isn't about your mother's memory, Conor. This is about Joanne not wanting to change, not wanting Agnes coming in on her patch.'

'Maybe Joanne is quite happy here on her patch?' he said. 'Have you thought about that?'

'Does Joanne seem happy to you?' Reece said.

Outside on the street, someone smashed a bottle against the footpath, and a dog took up a half-hearted wail. 'But where would she go?' he said eventually. 'What would she do, if she were to leave? A woman on her own, at this hour of her life?'

'I'm going to pretend I didn't hear that,' Reece said, turning on to her side to face the wall. She tugged the duvet closer around her shoulders. 'Promise me,' she said, with her back to him.

'What?'

'Promise me you won't say anything to your father.'

Who are you to talk about promises? Conor thought. 'I promise,' he said.

——

The *Titanic* Museum was appropriately huge, eight storeys high. From the outside it looked like an iceberg. Inside, the first thing that caught Reece's attention was a framed print from an old newspaper, an article headed 'A Partial List of the Saved'. Humankind had always pandered to hope, Conor thought, regardless of whether there was any basis for it. When did they publish A Definitive List of the Saved? To whom fell the task of deciding when hope had ended? He thought of the passengers bobbing about on that dark water, waiting to be rescued, and then he thought of the bodies that had settled on the sea floor and were no longer waiting for anything.

Reece's ancestor had drowned in the *Titanic*, but in the gift shop she bought a copy of the print anyway. 'Do you think your father would like one?' she said. He knew what his father would say about such things: a fool and his money are easily parted. But that was his old father. The new incarnation of his father was at this moment examining silk scarves with Agnes, taking one to the till in spite of her protestations, arranging it, lovingly, around her neck. They were like a honeymoon couple. Joanne was right, something would have to be said. Yes, his mother had been dead a long time; she had died the year he graduated college. But since his father had waited all this time and since he and Agnes hadn't experienced any crushing need for one another in the intervening years, was it unreasonable to ask why they should go upsetting the apple cart now, when it was hardly worth their while?

There was a ride on tracks where visitors were ferried through a reconstructed shipyard in brightly painted cars. Each car held two people. Agnes wanted to go on, but Conor's father was worried about his heart condition. 'Where's Reece?' his father said, looking around, but Reece was nowhere to be seen. 'Conor will go with you so,' his father said, and Agnes smiled and proffered her arm.

As she climbed into the car ahead of him, he noticed for the first time that she had a little bald patch on the top of her head, pink scalp surrounded by a white ring of hair, like a medieval monk. This close to her, he noticed that her elastic support stockings lent an orange hue to her legs. He remembered her scolding him for running on the street when he was a child, and her air of superiority when she spoke to his mother about Residents' Association business. *Now look at you*, he wanted to say, not so bloody superior now, are you? But he didn't. It wasn't kindness that restrained him, but fear of what she might say back. He was aware that he hadn't aged well; he was no Brad Pitt or George Clooney. He was no Quinoa Dan.

A staff member pulled the safety bar into position and the car trundled off. Was it possible, Conor wondered, that this might be an opportunity in disguise? A chance to have a little chat with Agnes while Reece was otherwise occupied? It would be a reasonable chat. He'd tell Agnes that she was a lovely woman, but that unfortunately – was 'unfortunately' the word? 'regrettably' perhaps – *regrettably*, she couldn't marry his father. He forbade it. But 'forbade' had a thwarted-lovers feel to it: Romeo and Juliet, Lancelot and Guinevere; it might only encourage her. He'd have to think of a better way of putting it.

'Is everything okay, Conor?' Agnes asked.

He became aware that he was drumming his fingers on the safety bar. 'My father is vulnerable,' he said. 'My father is old.'

'Aren't we all?' Agnes said.

He didn't like the way she used 'we', didn't like it one bit, but he was in no position to argue. He and this white-haired, slightly whiskered woman inhabited more or less the same space now. Being a high school teacher, he'd long ago come to understand that there were no meaningful degrees of old.

'I don't want anyone taking advantage,' he said.

'Anyone?' Agnes said.

'You,' he said. 'I don't want you taking advantage.' And then because she was looking at him strangely: 'I don't want you to marry my father.'

'Ah,' she said, in much the same way Reece sometimes did. She went quiet then, and looked away, seemingly absorbed by an original set of gates from the Harland and Wolff shipyard that the car had halted at. 'I won't pretend he hasn't asked,' she said.

Conor experienced the same feeling he got when he arrived at the metro just as the doors slid shut. 'What did you tell him?'

'I told him I'd have to think about it.'

He gripped the rail tighter as the car trundled on. What was there to think about, he wondered? 'My father is a good man,' he said.

Agnes nodded. 'A lovely man.'

'You'll break his heart.' It occurred to him that he was

supposed to be on the other side of the argument, but he knew that what he'd said was true.

'I'm going to live with my daughter in Canberra. She's been asking me for a while and I thought, why not, I'd like to see another part of the world before I die, and I'd like to see my grandchildren. I haven't told your father yet. Not until after his birthday. Maybe I won't have to tell him at all, he hasn't been all that well recently, and you know . . .' She trailed off.

The car had travelled up an incline past a replica of the *Titanic*'s rudder. Conor looked down, saw Reece waving. Reece's other hand rested on the shoulder of his father, who was beaming up happily. The car rounded a corner and when he looked down again, Reece had gone. His father was still standing there, his head tilted back, grinning like a child.

When the ride ended, he stumbled as he dismounted and his trousers snagged on the edge of a barrier. He recovered his balance in time, but now he had a loose flap of fabric on the front of his left thigh, a perfectly rectangular tear several centimetres wide. He frowned. His father rushed over to help Agnes out of the car, and she dismounted with the air of a 1920s starlet. Reece had arrived back and now she took Conor's arm, pulled him to one side.

'Did you do something terrible?' she said.

'No.'

'Did you say something to Agnes about her dating your father?' Nobody had ever been able to figure him out like Reece did. When he didn't answer, she sighed. 'I really hope you didn't say anything inappropriate, Conor.'

She took something out of her bag. It was another piece of merchandise, this time a postcard designed to mirror the Partial

List of the Saved, with a blank space added where, presumably, one wrote the name of the recipient. Conor thought it in bad taste. But Reece had bought a whole bunch of them, and now she offered him one. There was something ceremonial in the way she held it out to him, and he thought he detected a rare shyness as she watched him take it. He turned the card over, saw that she had written their names – Reece and Conor – just that, in the space provided. She had drawn a circle around the names. He looked closer. Possibly the circle was a heart.

In the car on the way home, he drove while Reece sat in the passenger seat and his father and Agnes sat in the back. He glanced in the rear-view mirror and saw that his father looked flushed, happy, as he talked nineteen to the dozen about what a great day it had been, what a good job had been made of the museum. 'Say what you like about the *Titanic*,' his father said, 'but it was some ship.' He paused to adjust Agnes's new scarf, which had slipped from her shoulder. Agnes was quieter than usual, gazing out the car window, and for a moment there was only the back-and-forth squeak of the windscreen wipers. It had started to rain as they left Belfast, a light drizzle that had gradually grown heavier.

Conor found himself hoping that at the birthday party on Sunday his father would strain so much to blow out his candles that the breath would become his last, and he would die happy in love and ignorance. It was unbearable: the thought of his father, once more, losing love; goodness knows, it wasn't as if the man had much time left for finding it again. He would persuade Joanne to light all eighty candles, he decided. He would not tell her why.

As if the thought had summoned her, a text from his sister

pinged into his phone. 'Still at the church. Chicken sandwiches in the fridge.' What would Joanne do, he wondered, now that the thing that was to save her was not, after all, going to happen?

And now they were nearing the war memorial again. They were almost home. He eased his foot off the accelerator, let the car slow, though he didn't stop. He desperately wanted to keep his father in the car as long as possible; to cocoon him in this space where nothing sad could be said as long as the drive had not yet ended. He would drive forever if he could, if it would save his father from anything. Reece reached across, put a hand on his leg, her fingers resting on the patch of bare skin where the fabric had torn. They were at the monument now, and this time he kept the car window closed. He had no desire to invite in those dead men with their bravery and their firm jaws. The wipers swept back and forth, sluicing water and, for all he knew, the invisible atoms of dead patriots off the windscreen. As they drove past, he nodded curtly to the four bronze heads, lucky men, Conor thought, who'd only ever been asked to prove themselves in war and insurrection, who'd never been asked to account for themselves in the more fearsome matter of love.

Legends

Louise O'Neill

Alannah woke with sweat at the back of her neck and a boy lying next to her. She rubbed the sleep from her eyes, trying to see who he was in the dim light. Hoping, just for one second, that it was—

'Morning, you.' He rolled over to face her. *Dylan*. The disappointment burned caustic in her throat as he pushed her hair away from her face, staring at her. He couldn't believe that she was real, actually there in his bed. That she had given in, allowed him to take what he wanted from her, after all this time. After . . . Well. She could hardly believe it herself.

'Hey,' she said.

His hands moved over her, tracing her ribs with his fingertips. Learning her by heart, every inch of her.

'Fuck, Alannah.' Dylan pulled a face as he knocked a knuckle off her right hip bone. 'You've gone so skinny.'

'No, I'm not,' she replied automatically, drawing the bed sheet up to cover her body. She always said this when anyone commented on her thinness, *no, no I'm not*, even though she knew her clothes were too loose, waistbands skimming empty spaces where flesh used to reside, the number on the weighing scales decreasing every day. But she didn't *feel* thinner. She wasn't sure how to explain that to Dylan, or if she even should. What would she tell him? That she stripped off her clothes and stood naked in front of the mirror, forcing herself to count each rising bone. *You are too thin*, she would whisper to herself but she knew she didn't mean it. Instead, she found that she was fascinated by how spare her body looked, how beautifully clean it had become. But as soon as she turned her back on the mirror, she forgot that image and in her forgetting it felt like she was still taking up too much space. People didn't understand Alannah, they never had, and they so quickly grew tired of trying. And so she decided to shrink herself and shrink herself in order to make sense to them.

'Okay.' Dylan leaned across her to the bedside locker, rifling through the drawer until he retrieved a lighter, packet of fags, Rizla, and a nodge of hash. She watched as he burned the hash, sprinkling crumbs into the rolling paper with some tobacco, licking the edges meticulously. 'Do you want some?' he asked, raising an eyebrow. 'The munchies might be good for you.' She shook her head, trying to pretend this was an entirely normal routine. Was it something he did every morning, his stash the first thing he reached for when he opened his eyes? *They're not like us*, her mother would say. That's what she said whenever Alannah mentioned any of the lads who had grown up in the council houses at the edge of town. *You've been raised a certain way, Lana. We've taught you to expect certain things. You need a man who will be able to provide those things for you.* Alannah always wanted to scream at her mother when she talked like that, speaking in absolutes about Alannah's future as if it was a fixed point that could never be moved, no matter what Alannah did or said. No matter what she wanted. It was 2018, she wanted to tell her mother, and she was only nineteen. She was at university; she was going to provide for herself, she didn't need a man to take care of her. But her mother would only laugh at her 'naivety' if she said that. *You'll feel differently when you're older and you have children.* Why, then, had her mother made Alannah work so diligently throughout school, why had she paid for extra grinds and revision courses and supervised study? Why put Alannah through all of that, reminding her daily of her 'potential' and 'ability', if her mother had expected her to give it all up when the time came to settle down? It couldn't be too early as that would be 'common', but apparently there was *something pathetic about these women in their forties deciding to become first-time mothers, don't you think, Lana? You don't want to be arriving to your children's graduation in a wheelchair, do you?* Her mother often asked her such things. Questions that were not really questions, but instructions hidden in plain sight. Alannah said she hadn't given it much thought, considering as she hadn't even had her own graduation yet. *Don't be smart*, her mother replied.

'Come on,' she said to Dylan as he picked a piece of tobacco out from between his teeth. She bent over to pick up her skirt from the floor. 'Let's go downstairs.'

Dylan and Aidan rented this house from Billy Waldron, a man who owned most of the village and was determined to claim the other half as his own in due course. It was said there was no property to buy anymore because Billy snapped it up as soon as it went on the market. Not that Dylan and Aidan could have afforded to buy, anyway. They worked in the local supermarket, also owned by the Waldrons, and lived pay cheque to pay cheque, using their wages for rent and weed and whatever pills they could get their hands on of a Saturday night. *Going nowhere fast, Lana, you mark my words.* Alannah reached down to hold Dylan's hand as he opened the living room door. She wasn't going to think about her mother right now.

The living room, like every other room in the house, was a study in squalor. A sofa with hard edges in pale pine. A lino flooring, her feet smacking off the sticky ground. Cheap yellow curtains half falling off the plastic rail, the sharp June sunlight needling into the room. There was a boy slumped at the dining table, his head resting on a placemat, and he kept raising his hand in the air in an attempt to swat the sun away from him, as if it were a particularly irritating fly. There were three men on the sofa smoking, a clatter of cans at their feet. And in the corner, in an armchair, was Aidan.

Cheers erupted when the men saw them, jolting the boy asleep on the dining table out of his stupor. 'Go on, my son,' Jimmy Ryan said, high-fiving Dylan.

'Ah, fuck off,' Dylan said, pretending to roll his eyes, but Alannah could see he was delighted by the reaction. His eyes snapped to Aidan. 'Alright, Aido?' he asked, pushing Alannah forward. She stumbled, grabbing the back of the armchair for balance. 'Sorry,' she said to Aidan. *Sorry that I'm here. Sorry that I'm with Dylan. I'm sorry, okay?* She wanted him to look at her in that way which made her know, bone-deep *know*, that he cared about her no matter what her friends said (*Alannah, come on! He's just using you, Jesus Christ, will you get a grip?*) or how slow he was to reply to her texts, oftentimes not even bothering to answer her at all. Aidan was just afraid, Alannah knew, afraid because he really cared about her and didn't know how to handle that.

'Sorry,' she said again, but Aidan wasn't looking at her. He was scrolling through his phone, ignoring Dylan and his ridiculously blatant attempts to parade Alannah in front of him. But, Alannah realised, he was also ignoring her. He was good at that, after all. He'd had plenty of practice.

'I should go,' she said quietly to Dylan. She didn't want to stay here. She wanted to be at home, under a scouring-hot shower, washing away the dried semen on her thigh, the regret. She would put on her pyjamas and crawl into bed, and she would try to sleep so that she wouldn't have to think about whatever happened last night. She wouldn't have to think about Aidan either. Aidan who was smirking at his phone, the way you only did when you got a text that was so utterly filthy, you couldn't wait to show your friends. She thought of the messages she had sent him, *cum on my tits, baby. I'm your dirty slut, amn't I? Fuck me, fuck me, fuck me*, and her stomach turned over. Who was he texting? Was it Roisin again? Roisin with her low-cut tops and bleached-blonde hair, the sort of girl that made Alannah's mother suck air through her teeth when she passed her on the main street (*she's just trashy, Alannah, I wouldn't let her outside the front door dressed like that if she was my daughter*) but whom every lad in town seemed to be obsessed with.

'Ah, don't go,' Dylan protested, taking her hand in his and holding it to his chest. He leaned against the back of the sofa and wrapped his other hand around Alannah's waist, pulling her in to him. She could see the metal fillings in his back teeth as he talked. 'Hang out here for the day,' he said, kissing her cheek as if she was his girlfriend. 'Stay,' he murmured, and she rested her chin on his shoulder, and her eyes met Aidan's. His phone was still in his hand but he was staring at her now, frowning. *Good*, Alannah thought. *Good*.

'So,' Jimmy Ryan said, reaching down to grab another can from the plastic bag at his feet. 'What's the story?' Jimmy was in his thirties, the same as the two men flanking him on the couch. Their hair was receding, their faces weathered by too many days on the hurling pitch (*suncream?* they would say, *do I look like a fuckin' homo to you, lad?*), their bodies running to fat once they had stopped training. The Lost Boys. Alannah was used to seeing them at parties such as this one, not that you could even call them parties. It was just the stragglers from the night before who refused to sleep; the ones who didn't want to accept the inevitability of the weekend being over and another Monday fast approaching. Those men were usually accompanied by a girl in her late teens, someone who giggled easily but who wasn't even that pretty. Not that it mattered. The girl was young, and men like Jimmy and his friends liked that. They liked girls who were young enough to be impressed by their tales of county finals won, and lost chances to play for Mayo because of nefarious 'inter-county board politics'. They liked girls who were too young to know better.

'Mayo are playing Galway at two,' Dylan said. He sank into the armchair next to Aidan's, drawing Alannah with him until she was sitting in his lap. She kept her feet on the ground, adjusting her body so that he could barely feel her. She wanted to give the impression that she didn't weigh anything at all. She was a wisp of a girl, insubstantial. She could float away easily if someone didn't hold her hand, hold her down. Dylan ran his fingers from her knee to her inner thigh, perilously close to her underwear. *Not here*, she wanted to say to him. *Not in front of all the lads. Not in front of*—

'We could go watch the match in Barrett's?' Dylan continued.

'Mayo had better win,' Alannah said, clearing her throat. She had to say something, she thought. 'Or I'll be shamed going back to college in September. Most of my friends there are from Galway.'

Jimmy smirked and Alannah felt her mouth go dry. They could be funny, these men, they had a cutting wit that had been honed from years of competing to see which of them could prove to be the most indispensable at a party, the gas man, the mad bastard, the *character*. Jimmy, in particular, seemed to have an unerring understanding of where another person's weakness lay, and how best to mercilessly exploit that weakness for comic effect. In the past, Alannah had been bent double with laughter as they teased each other, sly barbs that were so pointed, the recipient didn't realise he was bleeding until he was limping home, but she had been wary too. Everyone wanted to watch from the sidelines while Jimmy eviscerated someone else for kicks but everyone was afraid that they would be next, too.

'What are you talking about?' one of the men on the couch said, T-shirt straining against his soft belly.

'Oh, did you not hear?' Jimmy said, a cigarette between his lips as he grabbed a lighter off the coffee table. 'Ms O'Dowd here is at university in Galway. Studying law, no less.'

'Very impressive,' his friend said in a tone that suggested he had never been less impressed in his life.

'Did you not see the write-up in the *Leader*?' Jimmy inhaled deeply, smoke unfurling through his nostrils. 'Eight A1s, our little Alannah got. The pride of the town. Sure, we're not worthy to be in her company at all, at all.'

Alannah thought of her mother's face when she heard the local newspaper wanted to take photos of the family, Alannah holding her exam results certificate proudly. Monika, the Polish cleaner was told to come in for three hours that morning, while Alannah and her mother went to get their hair blow-dried. 'It's for the *Leader*,' her mother told them in Cutting Stylez salon. 'Alannah came first in her year with her Leaving Cert results, A1s in everything. The best results in Mayo, they told us.' All the women who worked in there gasped and told Alannah how brilliant she was, how smart, *not just a pretty face, are you?* And her mother seemed happy with her. 'We're proud of you, Alannah,' she said, and Alannah waited to feel better. She waited to feel whole, for once.

Jimmy looked her up and down. 'You were hotter in the photo, though. Are they not feeding you up in the big smoke?' His friends sniggered and Alannah's face burned. She tried to think of something clever to say in return, something that would shut him up. But she couldn't think of anything, so she smiled instead. No one liked a girl who makes a fuss.

'Will we play *FIFA*?' Dylan said, gently pushing Alannah off him as he stood. 'Me and you first, Aido?'

'Nah, I'm grand.'

'Afraid you might lose?' Dylan asked. He should have been joking, it was just a computer game, but his voice was undercut by something Alannah couldn't quite name.

'To you?' Aidan replied. 'Unlikely.'

'We get it, lads, you both have massive cocks,' Jimmy said.

'I'll play if Aido isn't up for it.' He and Dylan sat cross-legged on the floor in front of the television, controllers in hand, arguing half-heartedly over who got to be Ronaldo. Alannah curled into the armchair, letting her hair fall over her face. She closed her eyes, wishing that she was a child and she could make the world disappear just by doing so. When she opened them, she could see Aidan in her peripheral vision. That dishevelled blonde hair, his pale skin and freckled arms. Those arms that could lift her up while he fucked her against a wall, her legs wrapped around his waist, and he whispered in her ear how hot she was, how hard she was making him, how much he wanted to make her come. She never orgasmed, of course, but she got close to it with Aidan, closer than she had been with any other boy. Afterwards they would lie down together, naked limbs splayed, and Alannah wanted to fold herself into his side, to find a secret opening there that she could sneak into, nestle inside his heart and make a home for herself. But she knew he wouldn't like her to seem clingy so she stayed to her side of the bed and she acted like that was what she wanted too. *You're not like the other girls*, he would tell her, and Alannah thanked him, even though she secretly suspected that she was exactly like all the other girls. She didn't want him to see that part of her, the part that needed him so much that sometimes it felt as if she wouldn't be able to breathe until he told her he loved her and wanted her to be his girlfriend . . . Maybe, if he said that, she could believe she was good enough for him.

Alannah shifted in her seat. Should she just go home? *You're better than this*, her mother would tell her. Better than these men who would get older and older, but the video games would get newer, the weed would get stronger, the girls would get younger and more damaged. Alannah knew she wouldn't have been happy living in the village for the rest of her life. She had known that since she was a child, watching her classmates run around the schoolyard at break with a terrible sense of weariness, counting the days and the months and the years it would take her to grow up so she could leave. The exertion it would have taken Alannah to follow suit, to play House and Hide and Go Seek and Red Rover, to go to sleepovers and braid hair – she couldn't do it. So she stayed back, and she observed everyone around, learning from them how to act normal.

You can only go so far, if you want to stay here.

You can only achieve so much, if you want to be one of us.

She had wanted to leave the village, had filled in her CAO form with barely concealed glee, and yet she ached for it still. In sixth year, she would drive around the outskirts in her mother's car, telling herself that she could leave, that she could drive to the nearest village or even Galway if she really wanted, but somehow she felt inviolably bound to remain within the village's invisible limits. It wasn't until she was at university, surrounded by other young men and women who had been the best in their respective classes, who had probably had their photos taken for their local newspapers too, parents beaming beside them, Alannah knew that she had finally found her bearings. Then, she felt sorry for Dylan and Jimmy and even Aidan. In Galway, she could see that she was meant for more than that small village and an equally small life, and she could also see that everyone she left behind hated her for that; maybe they had always hated her for it. But as soon as she returned home, all she wanted was for them to accept her. For them to say that it didn't matter that she was smarter than they were or more ambitious or more driven. She was still one of them. Whenever something exciting happened in Galway, Alannah couldn't help imagining what these men might say. Her new friends, who had one-night stands and declared themselves feminists, who talked about Lindy West and Caitlin Moran and Roxane Gay and who asked Alannah to come to marches and protests with them, to join societies and to sign petitions. Her giddy experimentation with drugs that people in the village wouldn't have thought her capable of, coke snorted off a grimy cistern in a sweating nightclub, pills bitten in half and swallowed whole. That seemed different to Dylan's morning smoke, somehow, less pathetic because they were at college and he wasn't, because she was going places and he wasn't. Alannah felt as if she was changing, but much as she wanted people from home to be impressed by that, she feared they didn't even care. She was afraid they never thought about her at all.

'Where's Eoghan gone?' Jimmy asked one of the guys sitting behind him. The room hung heavy with smoke now, causing Alannah's eyes to water. 'He has the rest of the weed, doesn't he?'

'Probably gone back to Catriona's house,' Damien MacManus said.

'That fat bitch? He must be desperate.'

'Dude, he'll do anything for pussy,' Damien said. 'Remember that trip to Amsterdam? That hooker was fucking destroyed after him, she looked like she was going to start crying.'

They both laughed at this, but it was well worn, as if they had used this joke too many times before. It was just banter, Alannah told herself, trying not to think about what the college girls would say if they were here. She glanced at Aidan, wanting to see what his reaction was, but he was still on his phone. He had been on his phone constantly last night too. *Hey, Aidan,* she had said, walking past him on the way to the club bathroom. Wondering what he thought when he looked at her, whether he noticed her short skirt and her lips painted red, the way he liked them. Did she turn him on? (*I like it when you fuck me like that,* she would say to him, dripping hungry into his ear. *Do it harder, Aidan, do it faster.* He almost lost control, though, ramming into her, his face falling frenzied, and in those moments it was as if she didn't exist anymore. Alannah was gone and all that was left was her body. Maybe that's all he had ever wanted anyway.)

Lana! two friends from school squealed when they saw her. *Oh my god,* one of them said, unsteady on vertiginous heels. *You look, like, so skinny.* The other one nodded in agreement. *Too skinny, nearly,* she said, and Alannah knew she was jealous. *I've been so busy in Galway,* she said, *I keep forgetting to eat.* Later, when the nightclub finished, the overhead lights turned on and the girls instinctively rubbed beneath their eyes in case of smudged eyeliner, turning their heads so the boys couldn't see the smattering of acne beneath heavy foundation. Alannah followed Aidan outside, where queues were forming to get the bus back into the village. *Hey,* she said again, perching on a windowsill, her legs stretched out before her so he could admire them. She needed him to admire them, and her. She needed to feel beautiful tonight and she could only do that through his eyes. She reached out her hand to touch Aidan's but he stepped back. And then he was gone.

She unfurled herself now, and stood up. 'You're not leaving, are you?' Dylan's head snapped back to her, giving Jimmy enough time to score a goal, crowing with delight. *Why do you care, Dylan?* Alannah wanted to ask him. *Do you even want me here?* 'I'm fine,' she said instead. 'There's a bathroom under the stairs, isn't there?'

The bathroom was grim, a tiny tiled space with mould mushrooming in the grouting. The toilet seat was missing, there was no loo paper, the hand towel was damp and smelled of mildew. She hovered above the stained toilet as she peed, trying to breathe through her mouth.

There was a knock at the door. 'Two seconds,' Alannah said. She ran the cold tap, allowing the water to flow over her wrists before shaking them dry. 'Oh,' she said as she opened the door to find Aidan there, slouched against the radiator on the hall wall. 'Sorry, I didn't realise it was you.'

He didn't say anything.

'Aidan,' she tried, and she wished she didn't sound as if she was yearning, even if she was.

He didn't reply.

'Come on,' she said, beginning to get annoyed. 'What the fuck is your problem?'

'I don't have a problem.'

'Are you sure?' Alannah asked. 'Because it seems to me as if you do. You've been completely ignoring me for the last week.'

'I'm not ignoring you,' he said, standing up straight. 'How could I when you were traipsing around after me all night and then you come back to *my* house? How the hell am I supposed to ignore you if you're always fucking there, Lana?'

'Well,' Alannah said, stalling for time, warning herself not to cry. *Don't be weak.* 'Well, you're the one who followed me to the toilet.'

'I followed you, did I?'

'I was here firs—'

'I can't even take a piss in my own house now without being accused of stalking you?'

'That's not what I said, Aidan, I just—'

'Not everything is about you, Alannah. I know that might be a fucking shock to hear.'

'Alright, alright,' Alannah said, holding her hands up in protest. *Don't cry. Not in front of him.* 'I'm sorry. I shouldn't have said that.' He snorted, and made to walk past her into the toilet. 'Look,' she said, touching his elbow. He paused, tilting his head towards her. 'If you're upset about Dylan,' she continued, her voice dropping to a whisper, 'then I'm sorry. You know that it's you who I want to be with, don't you? Aidan, you know that. Come on.'

He pulled his arm away from her. 'Jesus Christ,' he said. 'Do you honestly think I'd touch you? Now? You fucked my best friend.'

'Can't be that great of friends, if you're hooking up with the same girls,' she retorted, as if his words weren't scraping against her brain, carving the letters deep inside her.

Do you honestly think I'd touch you now?

Do you think I'd touch you now?

Touch you now? Touch you now?

'And,' she said, swallowing hard, 'you think I didn't hear that you slept with Roisin last weekend? You're one to talk. At least I'm prepared to give you a second chance. Why can't you do the same, ha?'

'That's different.' He rolled his eyes. 'And you know it.'

'How is it different? Because I'm a girl? Don't be so sexist, Aidan.'

'Oh, fuck off with this feminazi bullshit. Is that what you're learning at college? Are you taking classes in how to be a slut?'

'That's not—'

'I'm surprised you gave it up to Dylan, of all people. Do you want to know what he sent to the lads' WhatsApp group last night? What he said about you? About your *performance*? There were marks out of ten. A pretty thorough fucking appraisal.' He reached out and touched her nipple, and she jerked back. 'To be fair,' he said, 'Dylan was right. Your tits did look better before.'

'Aidan,' she said, and she could hear her voice wobble. 'Aidan, please don't—'

But he slammed the toilet door behind him before she could finish.

'You okay?' Dylan asked as soon as she walked back into the living room. He was hovering by the door, two of the other men playing *FIFA* now. 'What were you and Aidan talking about?'

'What do you mean?'

'I saw Aidan go out after you,' Dylan said. 'Did he say something to you?'

'No,' Alannah lied. (*Do you honestly think I'd touch you now?*) 'He must have gone upstairs, I didn't see him.' (*You fucked my best friend.*) She reached down to grab her bag from the couch, checking to see if her phone was in there. 'Listen, I'm going to head home.'

'Aww,' he said as he walked her to the front door. He was slightly shorter than she was, Alannah realised. How hadn't she noticed that before? 'Are you sure you won't stay?'

'Yeah, my mam will be ready to kill me, I told her I was staying in Sarah's house but that I'd be home in time for breakfast,' she said. *Did you say those things about me, Dylan? And what's wrong with my tits?* She thought of the night before, how he had gasped when she had taken off her clothes, his eyes on fire. He had told her he wanted her then. They always said they wanted her until they had her.

She walked away from the house, one of a long terrace, all painted in colours of the rainbow when they were built during the Boom but run to ruin now. It was bright out, and Alannah wished she had sunglasses with her, anything to cover up her bloodshot eyes. Her skirt felt too tight, her heels too high, and she could feel the nausea begin to climb her limbs, cutting bile off her spleen, bit by bit, and forcing it piecemeal up her throat. A woman in her mid-thirties passed her, holding a little boy's hand. 'Mind the lady, Thomas,' she said, nudging her son out of the way. The child stared up at Alannah, fascinated. He would one day grow up to be a man, she thought, and he would have sex with women and tell them they were beautiful and special. He would hold a girl close one night, and then barely be able to look at her the next, as if the very act of putting his dick inside her had tainted her, *ruined* her. He would be just like the rest of them.

When she got to the main street, Alannah stopped at Barrett's pub. There was a blackboard hanging outside it, a small patch of vomit pooling beneath it that no one had bothered to clean up yet. 'All day breakfast!' someone had written in pink crayon in a swirling, childish hand. 'And a selection of paninis.'

I will have a salad, she told herself. That would be healthy.

It was important to be healthy. And, after all, she needed to eat, didn't she? Dylan had said she was too thin, and so had the girls last night. She should probably start eating properly. And a salad was fine. A salad was being good.

'What'll you have, love?' the waitress asked, handing her the laminated menu with the corners curling. She was in her fifties, dark roots in brassy hair, and she must have been new to the village because Alannah didn't know her and everyone knew each other here.

'I'll have the lasagne,' she said. (*But I won't eat all of it, I don't have to eat all of it. I can just have a quarter of it.*) 'And a side portion of chips.' (*I'll have one chip and I'll savour it and that will be it.*) She could feel the sickness rising in her, spreading its wings in her chest. She always felt like this after she slept with someone, as if she wanted to pare off all her skin, slice down until she got to the bones, fresh and bare. Why did she keep doing this to herself? But the start, when they would both take off their clothes, was always so promising. The flush of heat when the boys told her how much they wanted her, their hands on her body. Then they would tear at her clothes, a strange blankness in their eyes, and Alannah felt as if she could be anyone, that they didn't care who she was. She was just a hole waiting to be filled and they had staked their claim to be the one to do it. She knew that she couldn't change her mind, not at that stage, it wouldn't be fair. (*Cock-tease, fucking bitch, stupid whore.*) So she held her breath, and she waited for them to finish, waiting for them to give her body back to her. Whenever she left those rooms, she swore to herself that she would never do it again, and she hated the guy for not realising that she wasn't enjoying it, any of it. But she hated herself more. Always.

One bite of lasagne. A chip. *That should do you, Alannah. You are in control here.* Another chip. She thought of Dylan last night, her face shoved into the pillow as he fucked her from behind, telling her how hot she was, how wet her cunt was, how hard he was pounding it, and she said that she liked it, she said that she liked it. She said that she liked it.

'All done?' the waitress said as she came to pick up the plates. 'My, you made fast work of that. You must have been hungry!'

Alannah *was* hungry. She was always hungry. She just didn't know what she was hungry for.

She paid the bill, leaving the waitress a small tip. Then she went to the bathroom, tying her hair back off her face. She didn't want to make a mess, it was important to retain some dignity here, she felt. She leaned over the bowl in the cubicle, opening her mouth and relaxing her throat, chunks of half-digested food pulsating through her teeth. *Oh, Lana,* her mother would have said, *think of the dental bills, won't you? We're not made of money.* Alannah couldn't have explained to her mother that she loved this moment, that the relief was almost indescribable, and she was good at it, so good that she didn't even need to use her fingers anymore. She stayed there until she was finished. Until she felt empty.

Do you honestly think I'd touch you now?
Do you honestly think I'd touch you now?
Do you honestly think I'd touch you now?

She flushed the toilet, and went to wash her hands again, splashing water on her face. She looked at herself in the mirror, at her perfectly normal face.

She looked fine, she told herself.

Mikey Mulholland

Wendy Erskine

The train had just departed so Mikey got a coffee and sat looking out at the demolition of the old leisure centre. He'd been up from early. He woke in an apartment down at Clarendon Dock where he'd gone for a party. In the light of the dawn there was a great view of the lough. Some sleeping guy's hand rested on Mikey's dick as he watched from the sofa the Cairnryan ferry make its slow and steady progress. Now though Mikey needed to get a train out to Whiteabbey as a favour to his da. He was living back home with him for a few months or so. His da had downsized to an apartment that was similar to the one Mikey left in Manchester when Ian kicked him out. Ian bin-bagged up his stuff, only two sacks needed for all his worldly goods. But when Mikey looked, half the stuff that was in them he didn't really want anyway. There was also the cardboard box of records. He'd left that round a mate's house.

Back in Belfast he got a job easy enough in a hotel bar and before long he knew a whole new crowd. His da didn't set a date on staying or leaving. Just see how it goes, he said. His da was having a good time with a woman ten years younger than him. She was bubbly. They enjoyed city breaks and had visited

Prague, Edinburgh and Tallinn. She stayed over sometimes but mostly they went to her house. Mikey's ma, since the divorce, had moved back home to Castlerock where she spent her days walking a dog on the beach. She kept asking him to come to stay.

Will do, yeah, he said. When the good weather comes.

No parties Mikey, his da warned him. Nobody back. Do what you want to do, live your life, I've no problem with it, seriously I don't, but I'm not wanting to be coming home to a scene from a Frankie Goes to Hollywood video. You know what I mean?

Mikey knew what he meant, more or less.

Today he had to see Hugh, his da's uncle. That old fella had been on the phone to say he was going to be a guest on a local radio show. It was a programme featuring celebrities or people who had achieved something significant in life. They talked about their experiences and selected a few meaningful records. But the difficulty was that Hugh had no interest in music.

Why go on a show to play music if you've no interest in music?

Because you've been asked, his da said. I said you'd go out there and pick a few tunes for him, come up with a few ideas.

What they even want him on for anyway, old fella like that?

Second World War veteran.

That gets you on the radio to talk about music?

There's not many of those old geezers left you know. To talk about life. The music's just there to lighten it up.

You go. Jesus, I'm not trekking the whole way out there, Mikey said. He was looking at his phone to see if he had any missed calls. He was half expecting he might have. His da had his woman back the other night because there was something wrong with her central heating. They went to bed early except they didn't go to bed. They just sat in there talking. Mikey heard them. His da said something and then she laughed and because she found it funny he said it again to make her laugh more. Jesus. Mikey put on some tunes, turned them up loud. Later he phoned Ian's number. He didn't know what he should say: hiya? how's it going? missing me? But it went to voicemail and instead of leaving a message Mikey just recorded five seconds or so of silence. But Ian would know that he had rung though.

Mikey, his da said, you're here rent-free, know what I mean, you're not asked for anything. Nothing. Know what I mean?

I'll go as a favour but you owe me big time, Mikey said.

He was still watching the demolition of the leisure centre when he realised that the train he'd been waiting for had in fact gone. In the other station they called the trains, a guard shouted Larne line! so everyone knew it was time to board, but here no one did anything to alert you. He could have left to get a bus but he was happy enough spending another half an hour there. No big urgency. That place that was selling the muffins, baguettes and coffees was actually also a bar. They were running a discount drinks promotion: a premix vodka and tropical energy drink. That was why they were playing reggae. Mikey saw three women at the next table drinking it. He'd get one himself, why not. Down below, between the remains of the leisure centre and the station, was the car park. Mikey watched a man get out of his car, look round, then slip into an adjacent one. He couldn't see her face but there was definitely a woman in the driver's seat. Not a bad place for a hook-up. More out of the way than a city centre car park, but not so obscure that you

74

were conspicuous in trying to get there. Maybe they would climb in the back seats, take off the laminated passes. When the next train came, unheralded by a shout, Mikey quickly got another premix to take on the journey. He felt in his pockets for his headphones when he sat down but he must have left them back in the house when he went home to get changed. Couldn't find where he'd put the ticket either, but sure the fella had already punched it, so it didn't really matter.

All those new buildings, and the dregs of old ones. As the train snaked out of the town and across the bridge he could see the dome of the shopping centre, the roof of the hotel where he worked, its air-conditioning units, that high-rise bar (always freezing), and lines of monitors in the offices, the backs of people's heads. Folks all dreaming of the weekend for sure, but a long time to go, still only Tuesday. He knew. He'd worked in those sorts of places. He'd met Ian somewhere like that, Ian with the glasses, bit tubby to be honest, not a lot to say for himself. But at the end of a work night out for someone who was leaving they ended up together. Mikey was surprised. Ian brought him a slice of toast and a cup of tea in the morning. Toast and a cup of tea, Christ almighty. Even his ma never did that. Mikey said, Look mate just to say this is a one-off. Know what I mean? I'm not really into anything too permanent. No offence like.

Hugh's house was up a road Mikey half-remembered. Behave at Hugh and Elsie's house, he got told if they ever went there on a Sunday. They're not used to kids. That train journey had only taken ten minutes but Mikey could have happily sat there indefinitely. Must have been good when you could smoke on the train, smoke and chill and watch everything roll by, although maybe not so fantastic if your destination was only ever going to be Larne Harbour.

It was Elsie who opened the door. Look who it is, she said. It's Michael.

It's me, he said as he stepped into the hall.

Michael, you're all kitted out in the leathers.

It was true that he was wearing a leather jacket. Let me take that for you, she said, although he hadn't made an attempt to remove it. So, you've made it all the way out to us.

Looks like it, he said.

There was a barometer in the hall above a stand for umbrellas. Its hand pointed to 'fair', just as it had done for centuries. Their kitchen hadn't changed much either; there were the same plastic table and chairs, the beige lino and nicotine-coloured units. The cooker was a relic. Mikey knew a bit about kitchens. His longest-ever job had been at an interiors place, where he had been required to sketch for a variety of punters a rough A4 design of what a new kitchen might look like. Mikey had done a year and a half at art college before jacking it in after a series of failed assignments so that's why the interiors bosses gave him that particular task. He managed to make things look pretty convincing, although it was mostly all bullshit: the wood-burning oven over in the corner was never going to happen. All fantasy land. People actually intending to take it further were passed on to the next level for a more realistic 3-D design. There was a couple, good-looking pair, interested in a sleek birch job and Mikey immediately clocked the guy as somebody he had fucked some months previously. His girl had straight little eyebrows that went diagonal when she frowned at the prices. The guy's eyes didn't move from her face as she gave the rough dimensions of their kitchen space. When she moved away to check the price of a sink unit Mikey drew a large dick on the A4 sketch and handed it to the bloke. He left it on the table and walked off to join his girlfriend.

Elsie slowly led Mikey to a room so flooded in light that at first he couldn't see the small figure sitting in the armchair. Besides the sun coming through the big window, there was an overhead light and two table lamps, full beam.

Michael, Hugh said.

Hiya Hugh, how's it going?

You're late.

Well, Mikey said, I'm here now.

So it would seem.

Mikey took a seat on the sofa.

You're not just late. You are in fact extremely late. We were led to believe by your father that you'd be here by mid-morning and I would judge this time of the day to be well past that. Hugh looked at his watch. *Well* past that.

I wasn't sure of the trains.

They no longer provide timetables?

Hugh was wearing a heavy beige zip-up fleece, and on top of that a blue padded body warmer. Under the fleece there was a check shirt, and a tie precisely knotted. He had a rug over his knees and resting on the arm of the chair a paper was folded so that it presented the crossword. Hugh was still holding a pen.

Well you're here now, as you say.

A fumble at the door and Elsie came in carrying a tray of tea things which clinked as her hands shook.

Now, she said. Here we are.

Hugh indicated with his pen the best place to put the tray.

She was making those sandwiches at half past nine, said Hugh.

Adele gave me a hand, Elsie said. She's our person who calls in.

Making the sandwiches at half past nine. So I'm hoping they've kept alright until this time of day.

Michael, what can I pass you? Elsie said.

The talk turned to the divorce halfway down the teacup.

We were sorry to hear about it, Elsie said.

I remember their wedding, Hugh said. It was a very cold day. Raining very heavily when we came out of church.

Was it, Hugh? Elsie said.

Yes. I hear your father's got himself a fancy woman now.

Michael, would you like more tea? she asked.

No I'm fine.

So what is it you're doing with yourself these days? Hugh asked.

Was in Manchester for a while but back home for a bit. Just seeing what turns up. Got a job in a bar at present.

A bar! Elsie said.

There's always going to be jobs in bars, Hugh said. For people who want to work in bars.

Michael studied something, didn't you Michael? Elsie said.

Art and design.

Oh, so that's what you did, Hugh said. Art. He returned to his crossword. Without looking up he said, No word of you getting married?

Hugh, Elsie said. Nowadays they've no intention of getting married until they're much older.

I was just asking a question. A question that requires a simple yes or no answer.

No, Mikey said. Not married. Sure who would have me?

Hugh raised his head and looked at Mikey in a way that suggested who indeed.

Yes well who indeed. It ended up becoming a regular occurrence, finding himself back at Ian's. When Mikey's lease ended and Ian asked him if he wanted to move in, he thought, no harm in it. Temporarily like, but why not? Ian had his ways though, programmes he wanted to watch at certain times, meals on certain days. You couldn't have a takeaway on a Wednesday night, it had to be a Friday or a Saturday. Have a beer, sure, but not until after six. Don't leave those trainers lying there. Rinse the fucking sink! Ian never wanted to go out even though if he did he always had a good time. He sat at home watching films where nothing happened. Mikey you think it's slow if there's not a rape and murder in the first three minutes, he said. Ian always wanted to have sex the same way. Mikey didn't. He didn't even want to have sex with the same person. Mikey stayed out all night on occasion, turning his key slowly and tiptoeing in on return. Ian never asked too many questions. But then he came back early one time and found Mikey with a guy he met in a bar. But I hardly even know him, Mikey said. Jesus it was nothing. Look you know what I'm like. Christ sake, I'm a desperado, I know that, but come on, wise up. But Ian said, Give me back your key. Because that's it. I've had enough. What you getting on like that for, crying and everything? Mikey said. Didn't I say I was sorry?

So, Hugh said, let's get on with what you're here for. I seemed to remember, and your father confirmed it on the phone the other day, that you have an interest in music. Elsie, show him the letter would you?

She went to the sideboard and lifted it from a silver, tiered tray. The BBC logo was in red on the envelope. Dear Mr Mulholland, it said, and then on the next line, The Music of My Memories. Kind thanks for your proposed participation . . . prior to the recording a session with a researcher and the presenter . . . very helpful if you could bring a list of records you want to play . . . maximum of three hours . . . light lunch provided . . . transport by arrangement.

Wonderful to have been asked, Elsie said.

Listened to it on occasion, Hugh said. Preferred it when it was presented by the man.

Yes but he died last year, Elsie said.

I know he died. What has that to do with the fact that I preferred him? Hugh put down the paper. So, you've brought the music with you? He looked around as though there should be a bag of it somewhere.

No, said Mikey. I didn't bring anything. You not got anything here?

Elsie pointed in the direction of a wooden cabinet. A clock in a glass dome rested on top of it.

Be careful when you're lifting that clock, Hugh said to Mikey. It wasn't cheap.

The clock on the floor, Mikey lifted the lid of the cabinet and inside there was an old record player, grey with dust. There was a slide button to indicate the 33 or 45. He crouched down to examine the stylus, a ball of fluff caught on the needle. Mikey realised that both the vase and the crystal bowl to his left were sitting on big dusty speakers.

Find anything? Hugh asked. Anything of use?

That's our gramophone, Elsie said.

There was a space for records in the cabinet, grooved slots for singles and albums. Mikey pulled out a couple of thin paper sleeves that once enclosed singles and a piece of plastic that allowed records to fit on the spindle of the turntable. Beyond these finds there was only one record, *Little Donkey* by Nina & Frederik. On the sleeve a young couple in identical yellow tops stood beside a kind of Middle Eastern-looking window. There was the silhouette of a distant donkey. The record player wasn't plugged in and Mikey was surprised that when it was, a small red light came on and that, when the arm was lifted, the turntable rotated.

What came through the scratches and fissle when the needle went on the record were the harmonies of Nina & Frederik as they sang a song about a donkey making its dutiful way to Bethlehem. The trumpet solo in the middle went on for a while and at that point Hugh returned again to his crossword.

When the record was over, Mikey asked Hugh if he had enjoyed it. Would it be a contender for the show maybe?

Not particularly, he said. So no.

Elsie wondered where it had come from.

You must have bought it, Hugh said. Who else would have bothered with something like that?

That it? Hugh asked. Nothing else there?

Mikey looked again but there were no others. The only sound in the room was the syncopated ticking of two clocks.

Well, concluded Hugh. We've reached a state of impasse.

Very unfortunate, Elsie said, biting her lip.

You've no CDs? Mikey asked.

No, said Hugh. They used to come with the newspaper but they got put in the bin.

Have you got CDs Michael? Elsie asked.

No. I got records. Somewhere. When Ian made him give back the key he said, What about my stuff? Come back and get it tomorrow, Ian said. He kipped the night on a pal's floor and was back the next morning at Ian's. He pressed the buzzer but there was no answer. He pressed it again, held his finger on it. He banged on the door. Ian! He gave up buzzing and sat down, his back against the brick. At about nine the door opened. Ian looked terrible. He handed Mikey the two bin bags without saying a word. And then the box of records, without saying a word.

Obvious. The phone was what he should be using here. A few searches would get the job done and get him out. But when Mikey looked the charge was at 6%.

I don't suppose you guys happen to have an iPhone charger? he asked.

Indeed we don't, said Hugh.

Well we can use this phone to listen to some stuff. Maybe not for long though.

Give Elsie back that letter would you? Hugh said. He got to his feet, slowly. The fleece and body warmer bulked his body out, but his legs were skeletal. He was looking around for something, his stick, and Elsie passed it to him.

We'll go to the other room, he said. We're getting nothing done in here. And there are various things that I need to show you in the other room.

They proceeded down the hall to a sombre little room with a desk and two chairs. There were photos on the walls in neat configurations: landscapes, Hugh and Elsie on a grassy bank, Hugh and Elsie at a grey slab of a monument somewhere, Hugh and Elsie on a train. There was a military insignia mounted on wood and a gold-coloured trophy in the shape of a man holding a racquet in the air. Mikey saw a stack of consumer magazines. Car insurance on trial, home insulation on trial.

You ever listened to this programme that we're here trying to get things sorted for? Hugh asked.

Nope.

The records people choose, they don't even play them until the end. They just play the start.

Is there anything you like the start of?

Although the fleece and body warmer didn't move, Hugh shrugged.

You never thought any time, now what's that they're playing? That's good.

Not really. I have other things to think about.

The heat in the house was tropical. Mikey could see the air warping above the radiator.

They usually start with schooldays on the programme, Hugh said.

So give us a rough idea of when you were there.

The schoolhouse was always cold. The walls always felt damp. Whitewashed walls. Damp when you touched them.

Jesus Christ he was going to be there all day.

1927, Hugh said. 1927.

Mikey looked up music popular in 1927. The first thing that came up was 'Stardust' by Hoagy Carmichael.

Could be something you like, Hugh.

They strained to hear it because the sound was low to conserve the battery. There was no visual so Hugh had to look at a photo of Hoagy Carmichael at the piano.

So what do you think of it? Mikey asked after twenty seconds or so.

Not much. It was just somebody playing the piano. I've heard the piano before. It's just one of those things. The piano.

You don't want it then?

No.

What about folk music or classical or country?

What about it?

Maybe try country. Give me a year.

I retired from work in 1988, Hugh said.

That turned up Dwight Yoakam and Buck Owens, 'The Streets of Bakersfield'. In the video a woman put a dime in a jukebox and two men in Stetsons started to sing.

Well, Hugh said.

Possibility?

Not really.

Pick another year, Mikey said.

1963.

That a special year?

No. You just said pick a year Michael.

A search for 1963 top hits produced 'Be My Baby' by The Ronettes. For fifteen seconds there was a visual of The Ronettes performing a dance at the Moulin Rouge Club in Los Angeles before the phone conked out.

Well Hugh, that would seem to be it.

I could hear nor see very little on that thing of yours anyway, Hugh stated.

The screen on Mikey's phone was very cracked. He'd dropped it more than once. He'd stuck one of the plastic covers on it, but a lot of the glass had turned white so it looked frozen in places. He'd got used to it though.

So, that last one from 1963. Not bad?

It was for women, Hugh said. I'm sure women would like it.

Hugh reached down to a box that was under the desk. He struggled to pull something out. This, he said, is what I'll be bringing with me.

It was a photograph album. It said Photograph Album on the front in looping gold. The prospect of work this evening was starting to seem appealing, even though the time would drag because it was one of the slowest nights of the week. Hugh's hands gripped either side of the book, the networks of veins raised and blue.

When the book was opened there was a row of kids in front of brick, their faces no bigger than match heads. The paper was yellow and spotted, dirty-looking. Hugh glanced at it briefly and then turned the page to another similar photo, but with kids in a different configuration.

Long time ago that, Mikey said. Did the trains run every half-hour or every three-quarters of an hour?

There were triangular mounts on the corner of each picture. It wasn't like somebody had just Pritt-Sticked in all of the stuff.

This was our old house, Hugh said, looking at the next page. This might well have been the day when we got the keys. We'd just got married.

Elsie was in the photo in a tight jumper, her hand shading her eyes from the sunlight. When Ian saw his number, missed call, heard the silence, what had he thought? It wasn't impossible that Ian could lighten up a bit, you know, wise the fuck up. And fair's fair, it wasn't impossible that Mikey could also wise the fuck up too, come into line a bit.

We went to the same church, Hugh said. She sat there – he pointed to an imaginary pew – and I would have been sitting – there. I only went in the morning but Elsie went in the evening too.

Well if you went in for the church big time, why don't you pick a few hymns?

Hugh turned the page.

Sit down and go through the hymn book with Elsie. Pick out a few faves.

Possibly, he said. I suppose I could do that.

Hugh, Mikey said, got to be honest, I need to be heading on here. The next train is pretty soon. Anyway, those BBC people will be able to sort you out with whatever it is you need. Those guys'll have a full-on collection of stuff.

I'll probably think about the hymns, Hugh said. Plenty of them to choose from anyway.

He turned to a new page and a photo of fields and hedges and tents.

Transit camp, he said.

Next there was a grainy shot of a mountain and in the foreground thick foliage.

Now don't be telling me that's your old house as well, Mikey said. Garden was in some state when you moved in.

It's Burma, Hugh said.

I was only joking Hugh.

Burma. I was a sniper. I used a Lee-Enfield No. 4 Mark I.

Hugh turned another page. So don't let me keep you Michael, if you need to go on. And the train's on its way. You'll not want to miss it again.

A few photos had come loose from their mounts and were

stuck in the crease. Hugh lifted one of them and held it nearer to his eyes. It was faded like all the rest, and yellow, dirtied. This one was of a young man, top off, fag hanging from his mouth, shovelling something. Mikey leaned in to see it too. The fella was glancing sideways, maybe at somebody out of shot, giving a sarcastic look to somebody who'd maybe just said something dumb-ass. He was fucking gorgeous. That face, all planes and angles. That look. But more, that body. So hot. The hours, the sheer effort you would have to put in to get that shredded. Mikey had tried going to the gym, off and on. There was a place where he had gone in Levenshulme. It was mainly boxing training. Most of the guys were straight. It was on the first floor and as he went up the stairs even the smell of the place was a turn-on.

Who's that guy? Mikey asked.

It's me. Who do you think?

There was the fella at that boxing club. He and Mikey ended up in a derelict house. They climbed in through a window round the back. A muscle kept jumping in the guy's jaw. He didn't speak a word. Mikey thought for a moment that the guy might murder him but when Mikey knelt down and the guy's hands were gentle on the back of his head he knew he wouldn't. Hugh closed the book. He had to hold on to the desk to pull himself to his feet. He sighed. You'll need to get the train, he said. Elsie! he called. Michael's going.

When he got to the station he only had to wait fifteen minutes. His carriage was already full of young girls going to see a boy band. He vaguely recalled seeing posters for it. Some wore T-shirts with the most popular member's handsome face across their chests. When they tumbled out at Belfast Central, the girls raced up the steps two at a time.

You certainly do owe me one for that trip, that's for sure, he wanted to say when he got into the house but his da wasn't even there. Out no doubt for a jaunt with his woman, his fancy woman. Mikey plugged his phone in to the charger and went upstairs to have a shower, although he doubted there was a lot of point when his work clothes were stinking from that party anyway. When he came down wrapped in a leopard-skin towel that the woman must have left on some occasion, he thought there was probably time enough for a beer. A quick check of his phone and he saw that Ian had rung. In fact, he'd rung twice. No message though. The beer was cold from the fridge and Mikey sat looking out at the woman across the road unloading bags of shopping from the boot of her car. She brought two in, came out, lifted another two. Then her fella came to lift the bags of fire logs. Mikey closed his eyes and took a last drink of beer. The guy in the derelict house became some guy from the bar, became the picture of Hugh. He didn't feel like ringing Ian. He'd need to go and get dressed. That duty manager had had a word with him a few times now about timekeeping.

Mikey didn't hear the programme but his da said that Hugh had spoken well. He picked some hymns and a thing about a donkey.

Stretch Marks

Elske Rahill

A slit of rose light parts the curtains. Donna's husband is sitting on the side of the bed in his suit trousers, a foot pulled up on a knee. He is topless and his belly – looser now, a cleft bulge either side of his navel, sudden copse of hair beneath – folds over the waistband as he bends to ease a sock on to the foot. His arms are casually muscled, his chest firmly contoured, but it's his hands that she loves best. The square fingertips, thick fan of bones, the dark skim of hair on their backs. She wants to kiss his hands. She wants to put her face into his palms.

'Morning, baby.' The nausea wrenches her eyes shut. Even talking is too much. Even looking.

He twists around to face her, rubs her foot. 'Morning. How are you feeling?'

'Sick. Can you pass me the sick bowl.'

'I brought you toast.'

'Are the boys okay?'

'They're fine. They're gone to school. I can't find a shirt, do you know where a shirt is?'

'Pass me the bowl.'

'Here. Do you know where any of my shirts are?'

'Sorry, baby, I think they're all dirty. In the laundry. Sorry. I feel so sick.'

'I'll find something.' He strokes her thigh firmly, pats her hip. Donna thinks of horses' flanks. 'Don't worry,' he says, 'just sleep. Sleep, Donna.'

'I feel just so sick.'

When she wakes the day has swollen to full noon heat beyond the curtains. It's a Wednesday – a half day – and she hasn't got the lunch on; hasn't even thought of what to make.

There's a dry glass on the bedside table, and two dry slices of toast. She sucks at her lips – the thick, crackling bottom lip, then the top – catching with her incisors and scraping back a fine layer of desiccated skin. She stinks – of course she does, meaty drifts rising from under her floral-print pyjama set, grime caked to the soles of her feet. Under the duvet, she itches the ball of one foot with the toes of another, and the dirt rolls up under her nails.

The boys will be home soon and there's nothing on the stove.

She hoists herself on to her bum, settling her breath before swinging her legs off the side of the bed. She's hardly made it into her robe before the bile burns up into her mouth and she's grabbing for her sick bowl, holding it under her face while she lurches to the bathroom, pulls down her pyjamas, lands on the open loo just in time. With each heave and retch a spurt of piss hits the toilet bowl.

Afterwards she sits there panting, the air rough on her acid-stripped throat, cotton-wool-shrill on her back teeth, watching the puke settle to a lurid pool in the bowl on her lap. It's a metal bowl with a non-stick bottom. She has used it for bread dough and pastry dough; pasta dough and muffin mix and beating egg whites into fluffy peaks. The thought of that makes a guilty little turn in her gut, as though by some perversion she's just polluted all the cakes and spaghetti she's ever fed her family.

Donna brushes her hair before going to the mirror. She looks a fright: eyes sunken, livid lips, puffed sinus cavities remoulding her face, and over her cheeks a pink stain spreading to the shape of a splayed butterfly. The midwife wrote the name of it down for her – *chloasma*. She said to try washing her face with vinegar.

She is four months on – the sickness should have passed by now. Turns out her grandmother was right: 'Girls are the worst.'

Her other pregnancies were carried through with dignified wellness – she glowed and exercised and rubbed her belly proudly and nothing was a bother to her – but this is different. This time she is needy, she is weak and she is useless. She knew it was a risk, another child at her age – a kind of hubris in it, an ingratitude, perhaps, for her four healthy boys.

She has been avoiding her eyes but now she looks. Even her irises seem to have faded – a tired grey where once they were striking blue – but it's the way the skin creases around them that stings. Her mother's eyes! That's what it is – her mother looking at her, gloating. Who does Donna think she is?

Lunch. She is not the kind of mother who forgets to make lunch. There are potatoes, aren't there? In beside the washing machine, she's sure of it. And did she ever use that pork roast she took out of the freezer?

She washes her face violently, rinses one foot under the bath tap, then the other, bending painfully to rub the sandy grains from between her toes, stands wiping them on the floor towel like a dog covering its dirt.

She searches the wardrobe for something suitably mute, something dowdy, but all she can find is a nice striped maternity dress, navy and hot pink. She heads down to the kitchen without checking the mirror. The dress must make her look even worse, the juxtaposition of pretty neatness and the mess of her face. Oh well. First she will get the lunch started, then she will fill the dishwasher, wipe the table – she might even manage to run the hoover around.

At the foot of the stairs she becomes aware of a low, manic hum, growing louder as she nears the kitchen, and she realises she's been hearing it all morning like something breaking through a dream – an engine of excited insects.

There are glossy bluebottles clattering at the seams of the plastic bin, walking sleepily on the floor, circling the air and clocking themselves repeatedly against the swing lid. The chicken bones – that's what it is, Monday night's chicken remains at the bottom of the black sack. She walks past the bin. Frills of maggot eggs are dotted along the rim. She can't face it yet. She lets the tap run hot into the sink, adding a generous squeeze of green-scented dish soap. She'll wash the pot for the potatoes as planned and start the water boiling. Then she'll find the rubber gloves and take out the bin. Bleach. She'll get the bleach at it.

*

A wriggle. Something full and moist; something juicy turning and whirring there under the bend of her big toe.

Rubbing the pot with a felted sponge, she is so determined to steel herself against disgust that she almost ignores it. For a moment she scolds her imagination, a thing like that wouldn't happen, but it is, she can feel it – the rotation of its tiny balloon body, the shiver of its wings. And it isn't afraid of her, only disgruntled when she lifts her foot and sees it amble away. It's very dark, purplish, an elderly bluebottle – could it even be furry? Spiky fur like a thistle bud. She vomits, neon bile shattering the lather. Lucky she was at the sink.

For the rest of the pregnancy that sensation will keep coming back to her – on the toilet, in the bath, peeling potatoes – the wings trilling on her just-washed skin and the petrol gleam of its body as it hobbled off, vibrating with ignominy.

———

The day is caustic white, breaking in between the drawn curtains. There's a heatwave promised. The baby shifts under her skin, hooking a piece of itself into her rib – a hand or a foot. It must be mid-afternoon at least. Thursday afternoon. Beside the bed, two slices of toast have cooled and warped.

Donna is wondering where her phone is, wondering what time it is, and planning the laundry – first a ninety-degree pale wash, then a quick-wash-forty for the rugby gear – when she hears the electronic ding of the doorbell, then the front door squawking open.

She pushes her face into the pillow. She won't vomit. She is so tired of vomiting.

'Donna? Yoo-hoo? Hello?'

The bottom step gives a little groan – someone's on the stairs.

'Hellewooo? Donna?'

'Yes!' Donna hasn't spoken since yesterday, and her voice is tiny – it strains, creaks, afraid of itself. She tries again – 'Just a minute! Wait!'

She scans the room for her robe; the tea-stained mugs, the spilling laundry – she is a failure. She lifts a pair of big tracksuit bottoms from the bedroom floor and pulls them on under her too-short maternity nightdress.

A small, hamster-shaped old lady with spindly arms – her neighbour Esme – is standing at the top of the stairs, a hand on the banister and her chin lifted like a town crier calling 'Dooonnaaaa' in two long sing-song syllables.

'Hi, sorry,' says Donna. 'Hi. Sorry, Esme. I wasn't well this morning.'

Esme has a small, oblong head, neat as a bird's, and cheeks spongy with healthy old age. Instead of the traditional blue perm, she dyes her hair rusty black and has it chopped tight to her skull. She falls silent for a moment while she takes in the sight of Donna. The maternity nightdress is a ribbons-and-satin thing, ambitiously sexy. It sits all wrong on her anyway, but the big tracksuit bottoms make it puff out around her hips as though she's floating in a rubber ring.

'Sorry to disturb you, chicken . . .' Esme is wearing a triangular woollen coat with a houndstooth pattern. It makes Donna feel too hot. 'The door was on the latch. I thought I should check that you hadn't passed out somewhere.'

'No, no. Just. I've just woken up. I'm not feeling too bad . . .' Esme raises her eyebrows and Donna notices, for the first time, that they are tinted blue-black, too harsh against the fragile hatches of her skin. '. . . I mean compared to yesterday. Would you like a cup of tea, Esme?'

'Well . . .' Esme checks her watch. 'Maybe a quick coffee,' she says. 'Why not?' Donna makes for the stairs, but the old woman pinches her gently on the elbow. 'I have time for you to get dressed. Get dressed, Donna, it'll make you feel better. I'll wait in the kitchen. I brought some tea for your boys – I know you haven't been up to much.'

Back in the farty frowse of her bedroom, Donna untangles herself from the nightdress and kicks off the tracksuit bottoms. Too late for the toilet, she vomits on her feet and a shot of hot urine streaks down her leg. She uses a sock from the laundry basket, sliding it up from ankle to butter-soft thigh. The smell of dirty laundry makes her retch again. She steps out of panties translucent with piss – one foot, then the other – and all at once she can see and smell and hear her grandmother. The last days of her; her stern humiliation as her notions all dissolved; the great white knickers she still wore and the way she frowned that time as Donna cleaned her shins with baby wipes; 'Oh Donna,' she said, 'wouldn't you be ashamed?'

The striped dress again – it's all she can find. She combs her hair quickly. The baby's hiccups judder her pelvis. She rubs her belly in circles, trying to soothe them. Esme has made dinner for Donna's children. Donna is useless.

Esme's coat is arranged over the shoulders of a wooden chair. The kitchen isn't too bad. There are just four bowls and spoons on the table, crusted with this morning's porridge, which

Esme is stacking grimly. She is wearing a lemon seersucker blouse and crudely stonewashed jeans that reach high on her thick waist, like the jeans worn by 1980s pop stars. Her nose wrinkles a little as she takes the bowls over to the sink.

'Oh no,' says Donna. 'Leave them, Esme.'

Esme sets them on the draining board, raises her hands in surrender. 'I won't touch another thing.'

She starts to unpack a large wicker basket, naming each item as she lays it on the table.

'Blackcurrant jam,' she says, 'for your darling husband . . .'

Something about the way Esme says *darling* – half sarcastic, half affectionate – makes Donna feel both foolish for loving her husband and unworthy of him. The toast he left her this morning – did she even thank him?

'. . . he likes it, doesn't he? He can have it on his bread in the morning, or as a snack when he comes in from work . . . Do you never make jam?'

'No. I tried a few times. Never works out . . . My grandma used to make apple jelly . . .'

She used a huge pot, and a muslin bag hanging from a hook in the utility room.

'I'll tell you next time I'm making it. I'll take you through it . . . You can't learn that sort of thing from Google. Now what have I here . . . Ginger tea for your nausea – the girl in the health shop recommended it—'

'Thank you, Esme, that's very—'

'This is for supper.'

A baking tray covered generously in tinfoil. Donna notices the hammock of curdled skin on Esme's upper arm as she peels back a corner of the foil. A sweat of onions and some other smell Donna can't quite name.

'Just put it under the grill for a few minutes,' says Esme, smiling proudly at her creation – flaky pastry topped with ham, onions, flecks of green and rounds of rheumy white cheese.

'You shouldn't have, Esme.'

'Well, we can't have all your big men going hungry.'

Donna smiles but she's afraid she looks insincere, more sickened than grateful. It's the smell – onions and garlic and browning butter, the talciness of aged skin and what is the flowery scent? A perfume maybe – Grandma's perfume. Her kitchen. Her work-thickened palms, the way her cheeks trembled that time – 'Wouldn't you be ashamed?' – the spare, mannish calves.

Esme pulls out the chair next to her coat, sits. 'So you're still not well?'

'Really not well,' says Donna, shaking her head. 'Unbelievably not well . . .'

'Well, isn't it strange? Usually it's just the first three months. What are you now? Seven?'

Donna nods, tamping coffee into the portafilter. 'I think it's in my family. I think my grandma was the same on girls . . .'

'I didn't get sick once,' says Esme, using her hand to scoop breadcrumbs and scraps of onion skin into a little hill on the table. 'I suppose I didn't have time to be sick. I had to work.'

'My grandma was sick on girls, but not boys . . .'

'Do you have a wet sponge, Donna? Pass me a wet sponge. That'll do . . . There's chocolate or something dried into the table here. Ice cream . . .'

'I told you about my grandma before, didn't I? She raised

me, or sort of. She was eighteen when she got pregnant with her first child – did I tell you that? Her mother knew before she did, tried to give her a yellow soup for it. Grandpa had only been courting her a few months . . .'

'You need a new sponge, Donna. This one is old.'

'They got married quickly but she was so sick that she had to live with her mother until the baby came. But it died. The baby died when it was a few days old.'

'Very sad.'

'At the funeral my grandma's mother-in-law said the baby's death was God's punishment.'

Esme blinks at her, nods. 'People can be very cruel, I know that well. When I moved here I told people I was a widow. There was shame in being an abandoned wife. People were suspicious. Word got around I was the one that left and they wouldn't serve me in the newsagent's, now that's the truth.'

'Will you have cream in your coffee, Esme? Or milk?'

'I wasn't a very good mother to Maggie. She could be difficult. I had to work and I was lonely – ostracised – and I don't think I was a very good mother to her—'

'Well, you make up for it now,' Donna says.

A tight smile twists Esme's lips. 'You know, when I was eight months pregnant, I could still wear my own clothes – can you believe that?'

'Gosh,' says Donna, holding up a carton of cream. 'Esme, would you like cream or milk in your—'

'Eight months pregnant walking along O'Connell Street, and some fellas behind whistle at me – fellas whistled at me a lot in those days. I dressed classy. Well, don't I turn around, the belly on me, and "Oh sorry," they said, "sorry, love" . . . I was delighted with myself . . . I never had any belly scars neither.'

'Stretch marks? Me neither. Well, so far. This time, though . . . who knows?'

Donna is afraid of stretch marks the same way she is afraid of her mother's eyes in her face and the wings shadowing her cheeks like a portent.

'Stretch marks,' says Esme, 'yes. Not one.'

One evening, near the end, Donna's grandmother asked for a bath. Donna thought her navel surprisingly high. There were pale, fretted lines radiating from it like an iris. She wondered who had cut the cord that made it, and whether they had bandaged cotton wool and a coin over it, the way Grandma did with Donna's children.

The next day, her grandma was taken into hospital and she didn't speak again after that. She was hooked up to machines that made her breath bubbly, and for days the only sounds she made were the same turkey gobble and drowning spew of a newborn – the great effort simply of being – and it was hard to tell if she was trying to stay, or fighting for release, forced back by the drip and her body's insistent breath.

Donna puts a drop of cream in Esme's cup before pressing the button on the machine. She places the coffee in front of Esme, and sits opposite with a mug of the ginger tea.

'Sorry about the filth,' she says.

Esme nods: 'You see that corner there?'

The slated blind over the back window is bunched up at one side. It got stuck like that some months ago.

'I have decent lace curtains that would fit that window,' says Esme, 'if you want them . . .'

'Thank you.'

'One day when you have an hour, just take that blind down, clean the whole area with suds . . .'

'Thanks.'

'I'll drop them over tomorrow.'

'Oh, I think it will be a while before—'

'How was it made, the yellow soup?'

'For a miscarriage? I don't know. Turmeric maybe? Could you get turmeric in Ireland back then?'

'I heard of it, but I never knew how it was made . . .'

'My grandma came downstairs one morning after getting sick and her mother had the soup waiting. She was sick the whole pregnancy and it was a girl, the one who died. And then she had lots of boys no problem and she was sick again on the last one – my mother. So I think it's cause it's a girl. I think it must be.'

'Well, this vote.'

'The referendum? Do you know it's on this baby's due date?'

'Well, day and night it's on the radio – ugly stories; ugly things. It's all they talk about.'

'I went over for an abortion when I was nineteen.' Donna has said it. Why has she said it? 'I told my grandma I was going for the shops and she was thrilled with that – she gave me extra money and all – but then I forgot to buy anything. She was so disappointed when I came back with nothing.'

After her grandma died, Donna started telling everyone – the hairdresser, the dentist, that friendly woman on the train. It always left her feeling embarrassed and bewildered by herself. Why does she want Esme to know? And she wants to say more. She wants to tell her what it was like to wake up, groggy from the sedation, and know from the lightness in her guts that her future had been wiped blank. It's only recently that she's started thinking about the relief in her chest, the way the nausea lifted away, and the revolt down in her body – the great mournful cramping that spread out through her limbs and up her neck, the shocking black clots that came out of her all night. Her friend Deirdre was living in London. They hadn't even been that close in school, but Deirdre took the day off work and waited for her in the clinic. Donna remembers feeling painfully conspicuous in that huge pad as they rode the tube back to Deirdre's flat.

'I was really sick that time too, so, I don't know, but maybe it would have been a girl.'

Esme's hands are spread flat on the table. There's a ripping pain in Donna's throat and she's not sure if it's her confession making her feel like that, or the way that Esme's nails are shaped into pointed petals and painted candy pink. Donna can't look at Esme's face so she looks at her hands – the fine spray of bones and the dewy scrunch of skin, the brown splotches. Esme draws her hands back so that they are perched on the edge of the table now, her eight fingernails aligned. She taps one nail – clock clock – on the table.

She raises her coffee to her lips and puts it down again without drinking. 'I had a cousin, you know. My younger cousin Gerty. Gerty was only fourteen and so plain it was hard to imagine how she got that way. She wouldn't tell me how it happened, but she asked me to help her. She wanted me to tell her how to do it – me being older, she thought I'd know. I didn't know. I had heard about coat hangers and yellow soup and all that but I really didn't know anything. I was shocked, you know. And it is a sin. Murder. I told my mam. Gerty disappeared then shortly after. Went into the laundries and never came out.'

'You think I'm terrible, Esme.'

'To each to their own.' It takes Donna a moment to understand what Esme said, because she speaks so quickly that it sounds like the chirrup of a bird – *tweetchtwoo*. Then Esme taps the table again. 'Yes.' She turns her head and looks at the back window, taking in the pawed walls and splintered slats, exhales wetly. 'I never went to see Gerty. I went years without so much as thinking about her.'

'That's very sad,' says Donna.

'It's all this on the radio has me thinking about her. I never knew much about the yellow soup, you see. Where would you learn a thing like that? Well, I have a hairdresser's appointment. Thank you for the coffee, Donna.'

As Esme stands, she tosses the sponge across the table. 'Throw this out. It's not hygienic. I have a three-pack of sponges in my house. I'll drop one in the letter box.'

When Esme has left Donna remembers her tea, cold now, tatters of grease patching the surface like a torn membrane. The blind is crooked on the back window, and there in the upper corner of the enclave – oh, did Esme see it? – swaddled in a dusty spider's web, the crisp carcass of a fly.

———

There are no windows in the labour ward.

Afterwards, Donna will think there is something in the fact that the baby came on her due date. She will think it significant that only the night before the first stretch marks had opened under her skin, vague as watermarks, pink, and so fragile they are almost beautiful. She will think it means something that in the delivery room she is still wondering what this must have been like in the laundries – were they forced to stay on their backs? Did they understand what was happening when the contractions began, when the waters came gushing out of them? Did they give birth silently, too frightened to scream, were they chastised for crying out in the final thrust? She will wonder if it is narcissism or its opposite to think like that, linking herself to other selves. She will wonder if this way of remembering – as though every moment is a dot that can be joined – is a kind of madness or the only way back to herself.

'Please pop up on the bed for me,' says the midwife. Donna shakes her head, 'Just a minute', rocking on her heels, rocking herself open, pulling her back long to make way for the great tremor of this labour coming on. The midwife is younger than Donna. She looks at her sidelong, a little wary, a little cross at her disobedience. She seems tense, and Donna does not trust her to keep away from the white drawers-on-wheels, labelled with codes representing modes of cutting – 'caesarean', 'episiotomy' – things she has so far avoided.

'This is my fifth,' says Donna, 'trust me', before another contraction shudders down through her and she sways into it, letting a great, low call resonate out of her like the sound of a whale.

'Shhh,' says the midwife. 'Breathe in – and out.'

Her grandmother gave birth in her childhood bedroom with her mother tending her. She was proud of making no noise to frighten her little sisters outside the door. And the cousin? Was she guided by kind hands, or bitter-bellied virgins, or was she left to feel her way alone?

The water breaks in one great crash over the speckled grey floor. It is ice-clear with blooms of blood through it.

In the delivery room, things move quickly. The contractions shift from long, tugging shudders to huge fast quakes. She had forgotten again the force of it, the great waves of sensation, the way it takes her with it, the way she can only trust it, and then she is hunkering down and a great howl is sounding up through her, stretching to a shriek and she can hear rage in it, and irreverence and dissent and something darker and older than her body.

'Shhh,' says the midwife, 'breathe. Get up and I'll measure.'

'I think it's now,' says Donna. 'I think she's coming.'

In a roar the head opens out of her, the shoulders muscle through, and she can feel the slide of belly to feet and then there is silence.

Later, Donna will understand that the grey sheath draped over the baby like a shawl is the caul. She will remember how large the baby seems as the midwife holds her up, the way the bald pod of her eye slivers slowly open, the way she is somehow too far when Donna reaches for her, and she will remember how slowly the midwife uncoils the cord from her neck and how it is still silent now while the midwife struggles to cut it. The blades just squeak off it and she grimaces and tries again and it is already cut when Donna says, 'Shouldn't it be my husband . . . Leave the cord. Please wait a while . . .'

'No. It's an emergency. Baby needs to breathe.'

She is gone then, the baby in her arms.

Afterwards, Donna will remember looking at the clock again and again, but being unable to read the time. She will remember saying, 'But' and, 'Oh no. Oh. Oh no.'

Her husband holds her head against his. 'It's okay.'

'I think she moved,' says Donna. 'Did you see her move? I saw her move.'

'Will I go and find out what's happening?'

'I don't know.'

Neither of them can say anything else: But. Oh no. It's okay. But.

Her husband's brow is very wet and he presses it to her temple.

And she says, 'Our baby' and, 'Oh no.'

'It's okay, baby, you did well. You did so well. We'll stay here. They'll come and tell us.'

Her husband loves her and that seems to her a kind of miracle, a sacred kind of thing.

But oh no.

She looks down at her body: the pink-streaked belly running over the wonky swell of her womb, her legs still splayed, the thick of cord coming out of her. There is a kind of horror in the painlessness of herself. She has never really looked at an umbilicus before – the magnificent colours of it, purple and grey and putty blue, and the toughness of the clear skein on it. She lifts the severed cord, tugs, and is surprised that her body doesn't register her touch.

There are no words that come. No feelings. This happens. That's all Donna knows, this happens. Whatever it is, it has already happened. If not to her, then to someone.

What was it like for those girls? Did they touch their babies? Feed them? Before they were taken away. For her grandmother, to lose the little girl who had sealed her fate? There is no wisdom in this, none at all. All Donna knows now is the terrible particularity of everything.

A nurse she hasn't seen before enters the room.

'Our baby,' says her husband, 'our baby . . .'

'I don't know. They've taken it for oxygen. I was asked to come and deal with the placenta. It's dangerous to let it stay in any longer.'

'No,' says Donna. She will remember with shame that she wants to keep it in: proof of her daughter and a provision for her own death.

The young midwife enters. She does not look at them, but crosses and writes something on a file at the other end of the room. Then she turns and says, 'Your baby . . .' and the moment opens. Whatever it is, it has already happened.

Transactions

Sheila Purdy

Early on the first Saturday in January, Rose Kathleen Philomena Kelly got up from the hard chair. The front room had gone cold but she couldn't go to bed. Instead, she moved the blind, saw how dark it was and felt something at the window.

'Can you hear me, Rose?' The letter box rattled. 'It's Mary. Open up.'

At the mirror, Rose tied her hair in a velvet scrunchy, then cleared some things off the hall table and opened the front door. Paddy's next-door neighbour, in anorak, pink woolly scarf and hat, was standing there.

'Mary?' she said. 'What's the matter?'

'I didn't want to frighten you, Rose, so I said I'd come over. Poor Paddy is in the ambulance on his way to Vincent's.'

'In the ambulance—'

'He collapsed, took some kind of turn.'

'At home?' Rose pictured the ambulance outside Paddy's, the stretcher and the doors closing.

'In the kitchen. I went in with the paper. Then he didn't answer – and then there he was.' Mary took hold of her elbow, pressed.

'God. You must have got an awful fright,' Rose said. 'Could he talk?'

'Tell you the truth, I couldn't get much sense out of him.'

'What happened, do you think, Mary?'

'I don't know. The cat's dish was on the counter, and when the ambulance went, I found the fork, but no cat food. Would it be his heart?'

'The little white tablet,' said Rose. 'I bet he forgot to take it.' She looked at Mary in the new scarf. 'Did you have to walk here in this cold?'

Mary touched the tassels.

'Getting you out at this time . . .'

As next of kin, Rose would have to get dressed, sit on the bus for the hour to Elm Park, then wait.

'By the time you're there, they'll have him settled. Go and get dressed.'

Rose didn't say any more.

'Hurry on – you'll not forget to ring me later? I'll light a candle.'

'Thanks, Mary.'

Rose climbed the stairs and changed into her skirt and jumper. She laced her ankle boots, got ready for the cold.

Thinking ahead, in the kitchen, she scraped butter on what was left of the batch loaf, wrapped it in waxed paper, and put it in the tote along with her purse and a few other things. She buckled her coat belt, turned off the light and shut the front door behind her, knowing the wait at the hospital would be long.

The stop was at the far side of the roundabout – and if the driver hadn't seen her and waited, she would have missed the bus.

'Well,' he said, 'that's a cold one.'

Inside, she took the seat behind the empty disabled bay, saw only reflections in the dark windows. The bus travelled slowly on gritted roads, juddering all the way. When the time came, she pressed the bell for her stop, gripped the bar and stood up, realising as she did so that her hand was shaking.

At the bus shelter outside St Vincent's, the air smelled of the sea. She ran her finger down the timetable, noted the time of the last bus, then went to the main gates, where the concrete building faced her. The path through the grounds sparkled with ice, and when she was close to A&E she paused beside a thorny hedge, tried to heed where she was. When an ambulance pulled in, and a patient on a trolley was pushed with a rattle through the double doors, she could smell the insides, the blast of antiseptic.

She used the pedestrian entrance, went in passing a hazard warning, *Slippery Floors*. Such a dull place: plain grey walls, the noticeboard heavy with warnings. Beside a cold drinks machine, a Christmas tree with silver baubles glinted. People waited, talking quietly – some on chairs, others left standing. She rubbed sanitiser on her hands until it evaporated, and then went to the man behind the glass.

'I'm here for Paddy Kelly. He was brought by ambulance.'

'Patrick Kelly. Are you next of kin?' The name on his badge was *Jay*.

'I'm his sister.'

'I've two Patrick Kellys here.'

'It's his heart. He was in before.' She rested her tote on the counter.

Jay's desk was tidy. He had a stapler, a dry-ink marker.

He looked up. 'You wouldn't know his admission key?'

'His admission – I wouldn't, no.'

'Have you his date of birth?'

'He's sixty-three, October twentieth.' Her twin, but she didn't say.

'Would you have his PPS?'

Rose paused, felt herself redden, called it out.

'Right. I think I have him now.'

She confirmed her address and phone while he tapped the keyboard.

'Take a seat, the nurse will call you.'

'Is he bad, do you know?'

A phone on the desk buzzed.

'They took him straight for evaluation.' Jay answered the phone, hand on the receiver, and mouthed, 'Vending zone is over there, cafe opens at nine on Saturdays.'

In the waiting area, she chose a chair near the back where she wouldn't have to talk to anybody. A boy put a coin in the Pepsi machine and it fell through, came out the metal hatch. He pushed it back, watched it fall then slid it through a few more times until someone told him to stop. From time to time the door opened, another name was called and somebody else went in.

Rose went over, took a cup of water from the cooler and sat back down. She looked in her bag at the bread for later, felt her purse with the debit card inside. Now might be the time to put it back in Paddy's – before he noticed it gone. If the worry was going to keep her up at night, like it had last night, the thing wasn't worth having. In her mind, she could see his name, the stand-out capital letters, the short expiry date – and tried to remember her last transaction, where it had been used and for how much, and what for?

When all the chairs around her were occupied, and she'd read a *Herald* someone had left behind, and when she'd almost given up, a door opened, a nurse came out, and called her name.

Rose went over.

'The doctor wants a word, Rose.'

She was led along a corridor through doors that opened on to a work area with emergency medical rooms along one side and the waft of ammonia, iodine, fresh Elastoplast. She followed, keeping out of the way of staff, doctors and complicated-looking things.

'Patrick's down the end. It isn't far.'

Rose kept her eyes down, braced herself going past the curtained rooms until they reached the last.

'I'll tell Dr Sullivan you're here,' the nurse said, going in.

Rose looked past the curtain, to where staff, wearing scrubs, were busy at a workbench. Paddy was lying on a raised trolley bed, half-covered with a cotton blanket, a back-to-front hospital gown around his shoulders. There were tubes coming from his nose, electric pads suctioned to his chest – red, white, yellow wires connected to a machine to keep him running. The side of his face was bruised, one arm punctured with a plastic tube. The place was well equipped, technical-looking, much like the inside of Paddy's garage before he threw in the towel: overalls, coloured wires, jump leads, batteries, shining oilcans, Swarfega – all kinds of things, each in its own place, down to the paper-towel dispenser on the wall.

Paddy, when he saw her, sighed and lifted his hand. 'Rosie.' His voice broke a little. 'She's here,' he said to the person tidying back the drip.

'Are they looking after you, Paddy?'

'I'm a bit caught, would you loosen that blanket?'

Rose pulled, upsetting the wires.

'The doctor needs to talk to you, Rose,' Paddy said.

A man in scrubs with a neat beard came over.

'Ms Kelly? I'm Dr Quincey Sullivan.' He shook her hand. 'Could we have a quick word, would that be all right?'

He directed her into a sectioned-off area the size of the vaccination room in McKenna's pharmacy. Light came from computer screens, and through a window she could see Paddy in the bright bay beyond.

'As you know, Paddy was brought here by ambulance, he's in a bit of bother.'

'Is it bad, Doctor?'

'It's the heart we're concerned about. He's being monitored – that's the bleeping you hear.' He pointed to a screen with coloured graphs, changing numbers. 'We've given him an anti-arrhythmic to revert his heart to normal, but it isn't working as we'd hoped.'

Rose tried to remember, nodded.

'The rate came down but it's back in the one-sixties.' He touched the screen. 'It's unsustainable the way it is. We're running tests for possible causes.' He reached for a chart. 'To get the numbers down our only option is an electric shock to the heart,' he said. 'It's not without risk. Paddy knows.'

It was worse this time: if the treatment went wrong he could die. Next of kin, she thought, and in her mind she saw Paddy as a child, the two of them with towels, walking to the sea baths bare-legged in their flip-flops, him carrying an inflated car tube for a float.

The doctor was waiting, expecting an answer.

'If there's nothing else, Doctor,' she said, 'I suppose it has to be done.'

'Good girl,' he said, and patted her shoulder.

Someone brought a form. She signed in a wide rectangle on the red-looking document.

'We'll get on with it now, give him some sleepy stuff. And as soon as we can, we'll update you.'

Rose moved back over to the trolley bed.

'Did you sign for it, Rose?'

'I suppose I did, Paddy.'

'That's it decided so.'

'What happened to you?'

'I dunno,' he said.

'You have a bruise.'

'I want you to look in at home – put something out for Puddin'. It's well past her dinnertime now. Don't forget, Rose.'

'All right,' she said.

'She's not a mouser, can't fend for herself.' He seemed to get sleepy, his eyes tried to stay open.

'Are you asleep, Paddy?' She touched him, pinched a little.

'We'll talk when it's over,' he said.

A nurse came with a file, said she needed some information. She took Rose to a relatives' area, seated her near the fire doors, and sat beside her.

'Are you Paddy's only living relative?'

'I'm the only one, I suppose.'

'There's just a few questions, then we'll organise a cup of tea.'

She asked about Paddy's meds, diet, circumstances, and put marks in the boxes. Rose told her about the blood pressure, the Lisinopril tablet – if she was saying that right – the aspirin, the little white tablet for the heart. Some of the answers she had to make up, but she got through them all and while the nurse wrote notes, Rose looked around, two teenage boys sitting nearby who looked like they'd been crying. When the nurse stood up to go, Rose reminded her about the tea then sat waiting. People came and went, the entrance to the relatives' area opened and closed and a draught let the antiseptic blow in her direction until the nurse came back.

'Tea, wasn't it?'

Rose nodded.

'There we are. Any concerns before I go?'

'No. I'll have this now.'

When the nurse left, Rose unwrapped the bread. It didn't taste too bad, considering. The tea in the foam cup was still hot, and she sipped as she ate. They would expect her to stay, and she wondered how long it would take. What would the result of the electric shock be? Maybe the jump-start would make his heart go back to normal and he'd be allowed home. She ate the bread slowly until it was all gone and the tea was finished. Then she folded the paper, put it in a bin with the cup, and made up her mind to go to the Ladies. There was one nearby but an old lady had gone in so she wandered farther along looking for another, followed the corridor past an area with patients in dressing gowns and slippers, some with walking aids, a child with a white balloon. She went right or left following overhead arrows until the corridor turned empty and quiet.

When it grew colder, she felt herself near the mortuary and tried to turn back another way but medical equipment, left idle, made it difficult to get past. So she kept on until she found the toilets.

The assisted disabled stall she chose doubled as the baby-changing area with a table that opened downwards. For some reason, maybe just to pass time, she turned out the contents of her tote bag. A jar of lip balm rolled out among the scratch cards, her purse, a folded umbrella and a small cone-shaped bottle with a gold cap. The balm was cold, apricot-flavoured, difficult to spread. She found a pair of long blue earrings, put them on. There was nowhere to see herself so she turned her head from side to side to feel them and imagined what she'd look like, then she took them off. Using the little bottle, she misted some scent behind her ears. She tried the mouth freshener which sprayed aniseed, it said, but tasted of liquorice. When she had looked through everything, she put it all back in the tote.

Later in the afternoon, sitting near the fire doors, when her feet had turned cold as stones, Rose stood and walked around to pass the time. She came to a silent TV showing overweight men throwing darts at a board and an on-screen clock which calculated the score. In school Paddy had won the final-year shield – easily doing the subtractions himself in his head. She was still there watching when Jay came to say Paddy was out, and if she wanted she could go in and see him.

Paddy looked upset, his hair messy, he didn't seem to want to talk – or maybe he wasn't up to it. His half-closed eyes were swollen underneath with fluid, and his face blotched yellow and purple. There wasn't much she could do but nudge to see if he was awake.

'It's me, Paddy, are you any better?'

'They say I'm still ticking over,' he said.

'That's good you got through that bit, anyway.'

She was whispering, and his voice too seemed odd.

'They've more tests to do.'

'They want to know what's the cause,' she said, 'what's wrong with you.'

He went quiet as though he was thinking, not looking at her.

'Ask them will they let me home,' he said.

'I can't ask them that.'

After a while he turned towards her. 'I suppose I don't mind, Rose.' He sighed, struggled a bit with himself.

'Don't mind what, Paddy?'

'It was only money,' he said. 'And you know there's more there, Rose, if you need it.'

He looked at her as though he couldn't or didn't want to see her, and it made her pull back.

'You must think little of me, Paddy.'

'It's not that – it's just that I don't understand.'

She wanted to leave.

'You'll not go off now, Rose – you'll stay around till they move me.'

'All right, Paddy.'

'Get yourself a cup of tea.'

Rose nodded.

'Where's my coat,' he said, 'there's change in the pocket.'

Rose didn't move.

'And get yourself a custard bun.'

She moved off into the corridor, back to where she'd been. She thought about what the treatment had done, what was on his mind, and she distracted herself watching a different young man trying to get his coin inside the broken Pepsi machine.

Around 8 p.m., Dr Sullivan came along, looking clean-faced,

wearing a dress shirt and tux, scent, and glossy long-toed shoes. He was holding his phone and car keys.

Rose stood up.

'I'm afraid your brother's showing no improvement,' he said.

'So he's worse?'

'A short while ago, the Cardiac Specialist Registrar on duty reviewed his results and ordered his transfer to Coronary Care, for specialist treatment.'

Rose nodded.

'So we'll be moving him shortly.'

'Moving him,' she said, and got out of the way.

A nurse came over, a chrome upside-down watch pinned to her pocket.

'Will you bring his things, tomorrow, when you're coming?' She gave Rose a piece of paper with a list:

Slippers/pyjamas/dressing gown
Underwear/socks/stockings
Toothbrush/toothpaste
Comb/hairbrush
Razor/shaving foam
Sanitary towels
Health aids, i.e., reading glasses, hearing aid, etc.
Please do not bring valuables or large amounts of money to the Hospital. The Hospital cannot take responsibility for personal belongings and valuables.

She touched Rose's arm. 'Don't worry.'

'Will he be all right?'

'We'll do our best.'

There was a delay waiting for the porter but he came and wheeled the bed, the drip and equipment attached. Paddy's face seemed a better colour, with his eyes shut, the monitor bleeping. Rose stayed all the way, and followed them into Coronary Care. At the nurses' station, they admitted him. By then it was nearly a quarter past nine at night. The bed was steered into a space between a locker and a chair, a brake was lifted – and someone drew the pink, limp curtains.

When Rose left the hospital, it was well dark, and icier. She caught a late bus and got off a stop before home. The wind had strengthened and she crossed the car park, went into the supermarket. Swirling pieces of litter blew in the door with her. She tightened the velvet scrunchy and passed a sign, *Tonight's Lotto Jackpot 8 million euro.* Her ticket, she searched her purse – hoped she hadn't lost it messing around with her things in the hospital. She checked to see if she had enough for what she needed.

Walking through the bread aisle with its half-empty shelves, she wondered what he'd meant.

'It's only money,' she said out loud.

A young fella buying a Big Toast pan looked over.

'Only money,' she said, and he went on with his bread while she stood looking at the pittas and wraps. She didn't think she was a greedy person; it was just that she couldn't make the Carer's Allowance stretch to the small things, the things she wanted. One day, in the newsagent's, she'd seen rows of scratch cards for sale, backlit, behind plastic glass, all different colours, shining. She'd imagined scraping the silver paint, seeing the matching icons, symbols and letters and getting free goes. That day she hadn't enough on her, so she went to his house and took the debit card – she'd guessed he kept it in the drawer along with the PIN – meaning to put it back. The scratch cards weren't winners, but they were colourful and pretty, pleasant to scratch. The next day she'd bought more, and after that, every now and again, some little things, for herself.

In the next aisle, on her way past Fresh Produce, she tore off a plastic bag. She must remember to buy milk and toothpaste. With just the smallest share of the 8 million euro, just four numbers, she could pay Paddy back, maybe even buy that warm hat-and-scarf set from Dunnes, just for herself. Then she remembered if she used the in-store machine between Hardware and Magazines, she could get some money right now. She changed direction, crossed through the Pampers aisle, took the debit card out and was heading to get the cash when she was stopped by a man standing at Magazines, looking at the paperbacks.

'I heard about Paddy. Is he home?'

'He's asking to get home but they're keeping him in. I'm just getting a few things for him now.'

'Are visitors allowed?'

'I don't know. I'm going in early tomorrow.'

'Why don't I give you a lift home?'

She paused.

'C'mon, Rose, gather up whatever you need here. I'll drop you.'

'Thanks very much but I think I'll walk. I've been stuck inside all day.'

As Rose moved away she saw things she should have bought for Paddy the first time he was in hospital. Thinking back, she recalled how someone on the ward had lent him *The Van*, and how Paddy had given her the names of two other books, and his debit card and PIN to get cash from the machine in the hospital. That afternoon, she'd gone and spent the withdrawal, but, for some reason, never bought any books. After a few days had passed, she'd gone back to see him but if Paddy had remembered, he'd said nothing.

Scent from potted chrysanthemums and buckets of tired lilies, reduced, brought Rose back to the real world. She put the debit card back in the tote, went in search of toothpaste.

At the Cosmetics shelves, she stopped. Rows of lipsticks, eyeshadows and rouge glinted, and narrow display mirrors reflected her face as if to say they'd seen her before. It was hard looking at herself, her skin leathery and lined, and she stepped away – only to find tiny bottles of nail polish sparkling with flecks of silver and gold. She must think where she'd put the ticket. Opening the tote, she searched right down to the bottom.

At the self-checkout, she scanned the milk and toothpaste, broke the fiver to pay, and when the machine told her, she took her items and change.

Outside, the wind carried a cold feel of winter and in its strength she weighed the little plastic bag with the milk and toothpaste in one hand against the tote bag in the other. Out of the dark, a man in a bright jacket came forward and stopped her.

'Excuse me. Have you paid for all your purchases?'

She looked but couldn't really see his face.

'I have to ask, madam. Is there anything you haven't paid for?'

She held up the plastic bag so he could see. 'Milk and toothpaste.' She handed him the receipt. 'It's paid,' she said.

Another man came along. 'We've got it on camera, go ahead,' he said.

'We have to ask you to come back in the store with us.'

When she turned back, she saw her neighbour coming out carrying his messages. Rose straightened her windblown coat, loosened the belt and, escorted by the two security men, made it back inside.

The men took her to a small area past toilets and a storeroom then opened a door. She looked back, saw the neighbour watching, distant, as she was led into the manager's office.

The room, lit by a fluorescent strip, was stuffy with Sure deodorant and she sat where she was told by a man standing behind the desk turning a pen in his hand. A female employee came in and stood, arms folded.

Rose couldn't look at anyone.

'Do you know why you're here?' the manager said.

Rose shook her head.

'Watch this, please.'

On a screen, Rose Kathleen Philomena Kelly, a woman of undeclared means, and whose feet had been cold all day, featured in black and white. An overhead camera showed pictures of her coming into the supermarket, then standing in the Cosmetics aisle. She saw herself stretching for something, a small thing, or maybe two things. They seemed to get lost in her sleeve – then she was reaching into her bag, then she walked off-camera. The screen flicked to a different angle, then another, showing the same thing from different points of view. There was even a close-up of when she'd looked in the narrow mirrors.

The man in the bright jacket didn't take his eyes off Rose; the female assistant, her nails lacquered red, looked everywhere.

'Do you want to show us what's in your bag?' said the manager.

'It's just my little bits and pieces.'

'Right so, the guards will search it when they get here.'

She didn't move to open the bag. She didn't think they'd call the guards.

'The guards are on the way.' He sat down. 'They have the power to search. It's all part of the process.'

She put the bag on the desk and let them have the gold nail varnish and silvery eyeshadow. A security man stood the varnish upright, put the eyeshadow beside it. Then the manager slid out the lip balm with his pen, saw it was used, put it back.

'Why weren't these cosmetics paid for?' he wanted to know. 'They're not on the receipt.'

As best she could, she explained that it was a mistake.

'Are you sure?' he said. Then he replayed the video.

He asked the man in the jacket to scan the price of the items, pressed the printout in front of her on the desk.

'Fifteen euro and thirty-four cent.'

She focused on a wallchart, some tinsel that was moving in the draft.

'We have powers to hold you accountable. It's our policy to prosecute,' he said. 'It's a pity it's come to this.' He put his pen down, and left the room.

Confined, cold and being watched, Rose sat waiting for a long time, rubbing her hands.

When the manager came back he brought two guards wearing luminous jackets with 'Garda' reflector tape on the sleeves. The young guard took her details then the grey-haired guard stepped forward.

'Rose Kelly, you are being arrested under the Criminal Justice (Theft and Fraud Offences) Act 2001, Section 8. You are not obliged to say anything unless you wish to do so, but whatever you say will be taken down in writing . . .'

Rose stopped listening, but she could hear the guard's voice, knew he was reciting a warning for the courthouse.

When the guard finished, Rose saw a chance. 'Can I go home now?' she said. 'I need to go home.'

'You can't ask that,' the young guard said, writing it down.

He brought her to the door.

Both guards led her out the back in the dark to the patrol car; the store was closed, lights out, shutters locked. Then she was taken down the road, to the station.

They walked her along a path, into the front hall, through a passage and into an office – it was by then 01.15 on the big digital clock. They handed her over to a guard working at a keyboard, beside him a cap with brown felt antlers, a sprig of holly. He told her to wait, pointed to a hard chair in the corner.

After a while a female guard came in with a young man in handcuffs, no laces in his trainers.

'Howya, ma'am,' he said to Rose when he was passing.

Rose couldn't think; and he was led away.

At about ten to two, the guard stood and emptied the tote on to the counter. The scratch cards slid out with the other things – flakes of tobacco and old cigarette papers mixed in. He recorded the items:

Umbrella
Purse with coins (€0.98)
Visa debit card

pencil stub

used bus ticket, dated 06 January

All Cash Lottery cards (€20 x 17, used)

Perfume bottle, Marc Jacobs Honey (vaporiser, gold cap,
Sample Only: not for sale)

lip balm

breath freshener

Blue clip-on earrings, 1 pair, 3.95 IMPULSE

Rose watched to see if he noticed anything.

'Is this property yours?'

'Yes.'

He picked up the debit card, turned it over.

'Who is Patrick Kelly?'

'He's my brother.'

'Your brother?'

'Yes. My twin – he's in the hospital, at Vincent's.'

The female guard came in, asked did Rose have laces, was she wearing a belt, and told her to take her coat off. She found a lottery ticket in the pocket. 'Tonight's draw,' she said. 'Do you want fingerprints?'

'Not this time,' he said, without looking up.

A printer started and he lifted the page, looked at his watch, and wrote something. Then he handed it to Rose.

She read what he'd written: *The store is proceeding to prosecute. Will appoint and instruct on Monday January 8.*

She signed on the broken line.

Then he put the lottery ticket in front of her. She paused, and signed it too.

'See yourself as a winner, do you, love?' he said. 'We're

detaining you pending charges and you'll be brought for interview with detectives in due course. You have the right to a phone call.'

He sat back at his desk, folded his arms.

She looked at him, the goldy buttons down the front of his tunic.

'A phone call,' she said.

Maybe the phone call was to reach a solicitor. She could ring Mary, but then everyone would know. Maybe if she got the number she could ring the hospital, ask for Jay. She pictured the badge with his name. By rights, she should tell Paddy, but it was too late for that now.

On the way to the cells, the female guard stopped at a tea machine, held a cup in place, pressed a button for hot water. She spoke quietly with two workmates in plain clothes who were drinking coffee. Both gave Rose a good once-over. In her head, she tried to go through what they would make of her transactions on Paddy's card and how they would call it theft, what they would have her say. When the machine stopped, the cup was lifted and Rose was taken down to a holding cell.

Inside, the smell of sick and Jeyes Fluid was hard to take. A bench for sleeping stretched along the wall, its legs bolted to the concrete. When the female guard noticed her velvet scrunchy she took that too, then went out the door and locked it.

Rose stared for a minute, looking at where she was, puzzling over what she'd done to end up here. She found the cardboard cup but didn't lift it, a cup half-filled with grey tea. In the time it took for the tea to go cold, thoughts and worries of the life she'd had up to now seemed to go away, and in their place the trouble she was in became clearer: *caught shoplifting, held pending charges* – serious trouble she'd brought on herself. Slowly she put it all together. The more she figured, the more she couldn't bear to think that Paddy had known all along, and had said nothing. If she could pull through until the morning, she'd go back in and see him. She wished for one more day, supposed she'd have one. She went over, lay down, and stretched out flat on the bench.

BrownLady12345

Melatu Uche Okorie

The room was full of children – lots of them. Hunched over computers in groups of fours and fives. Joseph stopped hesitantly by the door, for the only other adult in sight was Mohammed, the Eritrean man employed by the hostel manager to look after the computer room.

'It's Saturday,' Mohammed said, and shrugged, looking amused, as if Joseph had asked him why there were so many children. He motioned for Joseph to follow him, then led him to a computer with an Out of Order sticker on it. He stood beside Joseph, cracking his fingers, as they waited for the computer to boot.

'I'm looking for a new house, my friend,' Mohammed said after a while. 'My place now is no good at all.'

Joseph pulled out the chair by the computer and sat down. Mohammed was a man prone to exaggeration. He used to live here in the direct provision hostel with Joseph, before he got his refugee status two years ago.

'Oil heating, my man,' Mohammed continued, in no way put off by Joseph's silence. 'No good for children, you know. And it fucking is hard now to get house for Blanchardstown, noooo house at all for even any place for this fucking Dublin . . .'

Mohammed paused long enough for Joseph to ask him why, but Joseph continued to sit quietly, staring at the now-blue screen of the monitor. Mohammed leaned forward and moved the computer cursor around to show Joseph that the computer was ready for use. But Joseph remained motionless.

'Everywhere for this joint,' Mohammed carried on, his voice rising, 'everybody is fucking complain! People fucking losin—'

When he unexpectedly stopped talking, Joseph lifted his head. A little boy was tugging on Mohammed's shirt. The child was about five years old. He did not say a word to Mohammed, only pulled at his shirt. After a few seconds of this, Mohammed sighed resignedly.

'One minute, my friend,' he said, raising his index finger at Joseph. He took the little boy's hand and led him towards a computer.

As soon as he was alone, Joseph quickly typed 'dating in Ireland' into the computer. His hands trembled on the keyboard as he waited for the search results. Soon, the monitor filled up with dating site options.

Dating for the Overs – Are you a mature, free and single over-thirty looking for love? Then look no further. Simply complete the form below and get instant, free access to thousands of members near you. Joseph scribbled down in his notebook: Dating for Overs – free. Next was *Dating for Professionals – Clients will be interviewed and required to pay a certain fee.* Joseph wrote this down also. He lingered his cursor over it. There is a bit of safety around this one, he thought, but for the fee and the profession. What would he say was his profession?

He continued down the links – *Sunshine Dating, Star Dating, Meeting Singles, Eco Partnerships*. No one in the pictures on the dating sites looked like him. They were either too young or too old, too happy or too fat. An ad for African and Asian women looking for love popped up. Joseph clicked on it. Instantly, images of naked women filled the screen in front of him. Joseph closed the page immediately, his heart pounding. He glanced over his shoulder and was relieved to find that none of the children was looking his way and that Mohammed was fiddling with some wires at the back of a computer.

The next page he opened was a Christian dating site. The pictures this time were of men and women in wedding clothes. Joseph's eyes brightened and he settled into his chair to read the testimonials. But soon, the cheerful words and happy pictures began to irritate him and he felt suddenly tired.

For far too long, he had tormented and taunted himself with questions about what he came here to do. They say it is not good for a man to be alone, and Joseph agreed; but he had also enjoyed the peace after Eucharia left. If truth be told, he had been grateful for it. For in every man's heart, there is a certain relief when the woman leaves, even the best of them, for then you can choose to wash or not wash; or choose to sleep in the morning and stay awake all night. But it is only temporary, you see; for even a bad woman becomes The One if that was who you were left with. In no mood to carry on browsing, Joseph logged off the computer.

Joseph found Mohammed using another computer with an Out of Order sticker on it.

'I'm going now,' Joseph said. 'I'll come back tomorrow to

finish what I was doing.' He folded and refolded the notebook in his hand.

'We don't open Sunday, my friend,' Mohammed replied, looking up. 'And Monday is my off-day.'

'Oh,' Joseph said, looking over at the computer he had been using. 'I did not know that.' Three teenage boys were now standing over a seated fourth boy as they waited for the computer to reboot.

'Come back Tuesday,' Mohammed said, watching Joseph closely. 'And morning is better.' Leaning back on his chair, he smiled slightly. 'More private then.'

Joseph stiffened. Nodding awkwardly, he quickly exited the computer room. He would have loved to go and sit on a bench in the nearby park and quieten his mind, but it was now April. He didn't like it when the days were long. The darkness brought him a special kind of comfort.

'But I shall get to like it one day,' he promised himself softly.

Joseph could not bring himself to go back to the computer room on Tuesday, or any of the days in the following weeks and months. He shivered to think of other eyes looking over and seeing what he was doing. But at Christmas, Joseph unexpectedly got a laptop. It was a second-hand one given to him by a man he had befriended at the church. As soon as he checked to see that everything was working well, Joseph went and bought an internet broadband stick. The first time he was alone in the room he shared with two other men, Joseph went back online in search of the date sites he had browsed at the accommodation centre computer room.

It had been a few months since that day at the computer

room and so only some of the websites came up. He scrolled through them, not opening any, his chest expanding and decreasing, his hands trembling as he searched for something else this time. He found it and stopped, his body heating up. The home page had two options: a man looking for a man and a woman looking for a woman. He ticked man looking for a man, and for what kind of man he was, lady or butch, he ticked lady, and for skin colour he ticked brown. He picked the username BrownLady12345 from the options they gave him, and filled in other details as well, that he lived in Dublin and would like to meet like-minded individuals who lived in Dublin, and that he was slender, had brown eyes, was kind and considerate and loved reading. When he was done, Joseph closed his laptop with heavy hands. All that was left to do was wait. His heart skipped and jumped in a body so stiff he had to will any part of it to move. Surely, he would not be rejected here, he kept thinking to himself. An hour turned into hours, and the day turned into days, and Joseph continued to check his inbox. It remained empty except for a welcoming email from the dating site.

Joseph told himself he must get over his disappointment. To feel more frustration at this point of his life would be difficult. After all, this could be God's way of telling him something. He decided to go back to the websites he had been looking at in the computer room. He chose one for his local area and registered. Not long after he completed his profile, choosing Simply-Joseph as his username this time, messages started coming in.

The first to send Joseph a picture and phone number was someone called Deirdre. Her profile said she was forty-five and a make-up artist. Minutes after he sent her his mobile number and picture, which he'd had his roommate take of him for that very purpose, she sent him a text.

> hi hney hw abt metin up
> tday if ur free.deirdre.

He read the text several times before he could understand it.

> Yes, that will be very
> nice. Thank you, Joseph.

he replied. Her next text suggested they meet up for coffee, and she named a place and a time that Joseph gladly agreed to. With €20 in his wallet, Joseph walked into town. He prayed the money would be enough to buy her coffee and snacks at least – if she was the type who would let him pay for her. He hoped she was. He was dressed in his best suit. It was becoming harder for him to tell if he was looking older than his forty-seven years on earth. The coffee shop she had chosen was easy to find. He checked the time on his mobile phone before going in. He was twenty-five minutes early.

Inside, a young couple sat with a buggy next to their table. The girl looked up at his entrance and whispered something to the young man, whose head was hidden behind a magazine with a picture of a well-muscled man on the cover. The young man raised his head slightly to glance at Joseph, before lowering it back behind the magazine. Joseph faltered. He wondered, as he chose the table farthest from the couple, what it was about the sight of him that had interested the young woman in the first place.

The smell of fried food lingered in the air, making him hungry. A man Joseph took to be the proprietor entered the room from another door. He stood behind the counter and Joseph looked away, quickly. He could not afford to order until Deirdre arrived, and so he kept his eyes pinned to the door.

The time he and Deirdre had agreed came and went. He sent her a text, asking if she was on her way, but there was no reply. Two middle-aged women stopped in front of the coffee shop window, and Joseph's heart leaped, but they only looked at the stencilled menu, their fingers running up and down the list as they consulted one another before finally walking away. When the young couple got up to leave, Joseph got to his feet, too.

The next day, as soon as he was alone in the room, Joseph was back on his laptop. The emotion that had lodged in his heart the night before was finally dissolving. He busied himself deleting requests from the dating site to upgrade his membership. He did not feel like going into the chat room. A message alert came up and, hoping it was from Deirdre, Joseph opened it. The message was from a woman called BECCA1980 which said:

Hi, I saw your profile and
I'm interested in getting to know you more.

Joseph hesitated, even though his heart was beginning to jump and skip again. But on second thought, he wrote back:

Hi, I am Joseph. Please,
what is your name?

A blinking yellow envelope appeared almost immediately.

Becky. Where are you from?

Joseph replied again:

Ghana. What about you?

Donegal. I've been to Mali before.

Joseph's eyes softened. It was of no importance that he did not know anyone from Mali and he had never been to the place himself. The fact was, she had been to Africa and that made her a kindred spirit. Joseph replied:

Oh, that is good. Did you
like it?

I loved it!

Accompanying the message was a picture of a woman – dark hair, curvy, beautiful. It must have been a picture from when she was in Mali, because she was sitting under the shade of a palm tree in a red sundress, an unpainted school building behind her. Joseph sent her his one picture of himself.

Lovely, xxx.

she wrote in reply.

*

There was another mail from her the next morning. It said she would like to meet if he was up to it and that she would drive down to him. She didn't ask if he had a car or not. He texted her his address, agonising over whether or not she'd recognise it, what she'd think of it, and him. He became filled with so much trepidation he started to wonder why he had agreed for her to come at all.

When he went out to meet her at the accommodation centre's reception office, her face lit up, and that pleased him, as well as her long flowing skirt and long hair. Suddenly, he felt taller. He observed her closely as she wrote down her name on the visitors' logbook and as she listened solemnly to the girl behind the reception desk telling her that all visitors must leave the centre by 6 p.m. And his smile widened as he led her up the stairs to his room, listening to her chatter. When he had told his roommates that he was expecting a visitor and would require some privacy, they had stared at him as if he had grown ten heads, and Joseph's eyes had slid self-consciously to the floor.

The room was big but low-ceilinged. Opposite, on the left-hand wall, there was another door, always shut, which led to an adjoining room; even now, muted voices could be heard coming from there. The whole room had almost no furniture in it apart from the beds and a wardrobe with three partitions. He pointed out his bed of the three in the room and she sat on it. He sat slowly down on the one that was opposite her. She smiled at him as she reached for her bag. Placing it on her knees, she took out a bottle of red wine.

'Oh, but I bought a drink for you,' Joseph said, jumping up. He had forgotten to take out the six-pack of Coke he had purchased from Centra earlier that day.

'Ah, don't worry.' She waved him back down with one hand as she brandished the bottle. 'We can start with this.'

He sank back into the bed, but shot up again when she asked for cups, thankful for something to do. She was standing when he turned to present her with two plastic cups and then they both sat down again, smiling.

She started talking about her trip to Mali as she opened and poured the bottle of wine. 'It was just lovely, I must tell you! Lovely! Just lovely!' she kept repeating. He nodded vigorously. He could tell she was one of those people who thought the best of everything.

She told him about her three children, how her oldest liked football, and how unalike her twins were, as one was into athletics while the other enjoyed drama and music. She dissolved into a hearty laugh when something in her narrative amused her, and he envied the easy way she talked about her life, relieved that she didn't comment on the fact that he didn't have much to say, as had been said of him on many occasions.

Then she did something that startled Joseph: she put her cup on the floor and came over to his bed, smiling broadly, then she took his hand in hers, leaned forward and kissed him. When she pulled back, her smile was brighter.

'I have to tell you about Eucharia,' Joseph stuttered. He could not suppress the burning need to do so. He pulled back from her and began moving his lips. 'Things just did not work out,' he said, shaking his head, as if warring with something inside of him. 'After just eighteen months.'

She sat beside him, nodding for him to keep going.

'Then she met another man,' he said, barely audibly. Something was trembling on his lips and any moment now, it would jump out. Any moment now . . .

She closed the gap between them and kissed him again.

'She said I'm not a proper man,' Joseph whispered when she lifted her head.

'Yeeaah . . .' she said, drawing out the word, waiting for him to dismiss what Eucharia had said as the foolish talk of a bitter woman, but when nothing of that nature happened, her hands dropped from his shoulders.

He looked up. She had finally guessed it, he thought, that he was a man who had given up.

'It's okay,' she said instead. Her smile was strained and there was now a slowness to her words.

Something about her breathing made him take her hand. Her eyes were downcast, and he imagined her on the inside, struggling and failing to conjure up the cheerfulness she had come in with. He wondered if he was the first person who had ever succeeded in deflating her like this. Either way, the thought saddened him.

'I have to go,' she said, standing up. 'I need to pick up the kids.'

He nodded and got up, still holding his cup. She walked quickly to the door and opened it.

'So, I'll see you, then.' She turned and smiled brightly at him, avoiding his eyes at the same time.

'Yes . . . OK . . .' he murmured in acquiescence.

Behind the closed door, he listened until her light footsteps receded, his chest unclasping slowly.

Pillars

Jan Carson

Louise is forty-seven when her pillar arrives. She has not ordered one. She doesn't have the sort of money required to maintain a subscription. Even a moderately sized, short loan number would be beyond her means and yet this is a deluxe model, almost three foot tall and equipped with both day and night functionality. She doesn't know where the pillar has come from – how to make it go away.

On Monday she simply wakes to find the pillar floating at the end of her bed. It is still dark. The pillar is in night mode: a child-sized block of flames, hovering just below the ceiling. It hasn't scorched the roof. It isn't even real fire, though the similarity to flame is uncanny. Louise doesn't know how long it's been there. Minutes. Hours. Days. These days she's not the most observant. Important things slip past her: friends' birthdays and dental appointments, gas bills, tax returns and parent-teacher interviews. People are quick to make an exception for her. 'You're not yourself at the minute,' they say, trying not to look perturbed when she arrives two hours late for dinner. Louise is a muddle since Martin left. She can't seem to get the line of herself straight.

She tries to remember Sunday night clearly. Was there a pillar of fire hanging over her bed or not? She recalls the evening as a series of snapshots only vaguely linked, like cells sandwiched together in a comic-book strip. She remembers a third glass of wine and a voicemail from Martin. 'Please, do not call here again. Goodbye.' Another glass of wine. Then, a valiant attempt to mark Year 9's *Animal Farm* essays. Tears in front of the television. Rising to mute the volume, because the remote couldn't be found and the sound of canned laughter was making her feel anxious. Falling over the coffee table. Spilling the wine. Crying some more, then losing the energy for it, because what was the point in sobbing when there wasn't anyone around to sympathise? Finally, crawling into an unmade bed. Not sleeping. Sleeping. Not sleeping again. No sign of a flaming pillar. No sign of anything untoward. But had she looked up? Had she, hell.

Louise has not looked up in over a month.

When she wakes the whole room is flaming around her: curtains flicker, tongued shadows dance against the wallpaper, the wardrobe mirror pitches each warm lick back at her, and shimmers. At first she wonders what this fiery thing is and why the smoke alarm hasn't gone off. It takes her a moment to realise it's a pillar. She's never been this close to one before. It looks different from the pictures she's seen on the internet. Taller. Brighter. Less threatening. There's something captivating about the way it is neither moving nor standing completely still. A line of Yeats comes to mind, *nobleness made simple as a fire*, quickly followed by the shudder of remembering what it feels like to teach this poem to Year 11, rows of faces curdling with boredom. There is no heat off the pillar. No noise either. But it is beautiful. Louise cannot take her eyes off it. Consequently, she is late for work.

Later that evening, emboldened, she will run her hand through the pillar's flaming core and find it is not even warm to the touch. The sensation will be similar to holding a hand beneath a garden sprinkler: soothing, liquid, vaguely reassuring. It will tickle.

By the time she finally leaves for school it is light out and the pillar has transitioned into daytime mode. Now, it is a three-foot block of soft, vaporous cloud. Like a long winter breath streaming in front of her. It precedes her journey, guiding her out the front door, into the car and all the way along the dual carriageway. It hangs just above the end of the Fiesta's bonnet, high enough to ensure it doesn't form an obstruction, low enough to remain visible. At school she doesn't mention the pillar though it's painfully apparent, the only one in the staff room. Her colleagues are too well mannered to say anything. They look round the side of the pillar – which is easier to do when it's in cloud mode – and ask if she's had a nice weekend. It's been misery from start to finish.

'Lovely, thanks,' says Louise.

In class the children stare. Some of them have their own pillars; smaller models, decorated with baubles and bright stickers. Every term another handful of students acquire a pillar of their own. The Head has called it an epidemic and proposed a series of special assemblies on more traditional solutions. He favours medication, therapy and extra rounds of detention. In response the Deputy Head has said that 'epidemic' is a very reactionary word. These children aren't troubled, she's said. They are suffering from mental health issues and should be treated with all due care. And isn't it wonderful, she's added, that there's help out there for young people nowadays, even if it is a little unorthodox?

The Deputy Head listens to a lot of Radio 4. She is very popular with those students who are struggling to cope. Sometimes they follow their pillars to her office at lunchtime and eat their Müller Fruit Corners sitting around her desk. The Deputy Head has even helped some students receive pillar referrals from their GPs. She has not yet encountered a colleague with a pillar. In the staff room at break time she makes a point of looking directly at Louise and smiling, as if to say, 'I see you there, with your pillar. What a brave woman you are. What a role model for us all.' Louise smiles back. She doesn't want to join the lunchtime picnic in the Deputy Head's office. She feels it would be unprofessional. Still, if her pillar thinks it's for the best then she won't have much choice in the matter.

The pillar, Louise realises, constantly pre-empts her next move. 'Don't eat the chocolate,' it suggests, and sleeks across the kitchen ceiling, drawing attention to the fruit bowl sitting on the bench. 'Don't phone Martin again tonight,' it whispers, and coerces her away from the telephone, out into the back garden, where she finds herself weeding flower beds. Don't do this potentially disastrous thing. Do this sensible thing instead.

It isn't rocket science. Anyone with a functional thought-life could make these sorts of decisions for themselves. But Louise is not functional at the minute.

She begins to rely upon the pillar. The pillar is one step ahead of her, guiding her eye to the student who requires a little extra attention, pointing out the shortest checkout line at Tesco's, dragging her off the road to the petrol station when she's just about to run out and hasn't noticed yet. It doesn't take Louise long to accept that the pillar knows better than her. She is happier and more efficient when she isn't making decisions by herself.

She loses weight. She joins a walking club. She manages to mark all of Year 9's *Jane Eyre* essays without resorting to wine or sarcastic scribbles in the margins. After a few weeks she even builds a profile on a dating website. She includes an upbeat blurb, likes and dislikes, and a flattering photo taken in Alicante last summer: early-evening sunshine, tanned shoulders, Martin cropped out, so you can barely see the ghost of his arm creeping into shot. She hasn't let her profile go live yet. But she knows she will. Very soon.

Louise wonders how she ever managed without a pillar.

———

But the pillar brings its own problem. Everyone who sees it knows Louise needs help. She might as well write 'NOT COPING' across her forehead in permanent marker. It's that obvious. She frequently clocks people trying not to stare, which only makes their staring more pronounced. She hears the things they're not saying. 'Look at the sketch of that one. Can't even catch the bus without a bloody cloud to guide her.'

Louise's sisters are the sort of people who mock pillar owners. They'd never say anything to a person's face, but in private, on the phone, after a drink or two, they can be absolute bitches. Louise isn't naive. She knows that she's exactly the kind of person they'd be laying into if she wasn't their sister. Her clothes don't sit right. Her lipstick gets on her teeth. She talks over other people in conversation. 'A disaster waiting to happen,' her late father would say. So far she's managed to avoid her sisters but there is a niece's birthday party at the weekend and, shortly afterwards, Christmas. She can't hide the pillar from them forever.

She tries telling her mother on the phone. 'Mum,' she says, 'what do you think about pillars?' Her mother starts into a long story about Jean-next-door who has a son, who has a girlfriend, who got a pillar last November, just to help her through Christmas. How at first it helped and later didn't, so she wound up trying to kill herself by drinking toilet cleaner and managed to get the dosage wrong, and in the end didn't die but ruined her speaking voice altogether. Afterwards, they wouldn't give her a refund on the pillar. This seems to be the main point of the story. 'Oh,' says Louise, when her mother finally pauses for breath. She isn't sure how to segue into discussing her own pillar. She asks her mother about the garden instead.

Her mother is never any help. Louise calls hoping for sympathy, or at the very least a listening ear. She wants someone to say,

'Yes, it is shit that Martin left you for a girl who is twenty-five years younger and still able to get away with pigtails. But you are brave and you are strong. You will get through this terrible time. Cry. Drink wine in moderation. Don't be so hard on yourself.' Instead her mother is resolutely chipper. 'Look on the bright side, Lou,' she says, 'at least there's no children involved. Divorce is wild hard on children.'

Louise thinks that she would have liked a child. It might have helped to stave the loneliness off. It's too late for children now. There are so many parts of her life which feel like they are suddenly over. She can make herself cry just thinking about the things which will probably never happen to her: children, grandchildren, wearing a bikini, changing career, going to Thailand or Vietnam on the sort of holiday that isn't a package deal. She tries not to admit any of this to herself. Instead, she sticks motivational quotes to the fridge with magnets. 'Be your best self.' 'Yes, you can!' 'You are fearfully and wonderfully made.' This is a bit from the Bible that one of the classroom assistants once wrote down after finding her crying in the book cupboard. It was nice at the time and she'd wondered about the possibility of becoming friends with this woman, whose name was Melanie. Later, Melanie tried to coerce Louise into joining an Alpha group at her church and all the niceness evaporated out of the situation. She felt then like one of those people targeted by double-glazing salesmen on the phone, and immediately stopped bringing extra KitKats to share with Melanie during coffee break.

Still, she's kept the Post-It. She likes the idea of being fearful and wonderful. It makes her feel like Kate Bush, and also a little unhinged. Sometimes she dances round the kitchen singing 'Wuthering Heights' in her dressing gown, making the sleeves flap like wings. Before the pillar this was a large part of her coping mechanism. Also, reading the sort of books which would attempt to take her messed-up life and turn it sideways so she wasn't lonely, she was actually free.

At first she borrowed these books from the library. Then she began to suspect the librarians were mocking her reading habits. So she tried to mix it up, slipping a few romance novels into the pile, dabbling in the travel section. Eventually she ran out of energy for subterfuge and began ordering her self-help books off Amazon. Now she has the pillar, Louise can't possibly go back to the library. She doesn't want the librarians to see they were right about her all along. She cannot bear the soft way they'll look at her as they pass her books across the counter. She is accumulating fines. She doesn't even care.

———

Louise is determined to be shot of her pillar before the end of term. She looks the process up online. There are only two ways to *terminate your relationship* with a pillar. You can cancel your subscription or you can become functional enough to negate the need for a *bespoke life guide*. It is impossible to cancel a subscription you haven't set up so she decides to focus instead upon becoming functional.

She files for divorce. This is hard, and requires some wine, but she gets through it, phoning Miranda – who teaches history and is currently on her third (or is it fourth?) husband – for advice when the paperwork starts to overwhelm her. She feels significantly better once the divorce is in progress. She cleans out the garage, donating Martin's ski gear to Barnardo's. Then, she purges the mantelpiece of photographs and knick-knacks, until there is nothing left of her ex-husband, not a single mug or sports sock. The pillar hangs over all her good work, cloud by day, fire by night. Sometimes Louise thinks it is twinkling with pleasure. But this could well be a trick of the light.

Her colleagues have become accustomed to the pillar now. She notices them not noticing it. Occasionally they pass right through its cloudy edges en route to the toaster or microwave. They don't even flinch. She is reasonably popular these days, more than she's been in years. People can see her new-found confidence. They compliment her outfits. They include her in discussions about films and politics, assuming she'll have something insightful to contribute. They draw her aside by the photocopier to ask her advice on unruly students, new haircuts and where to go for half-term break. Louise carries herself differently when walking. Head high. Shoulders back. Belly sucked and tucked like a much younger woman.

She changes her dating profile from dormant to active. The pillar doesn't exactly tell her to do this, but it does hang over her laptop throughout. Three men contact her within a matter of hours. One lives in Alaska. This is hardly practical. One sends her a picture of his penis. He is only twenty-one. It is not a bad-looking penis. She doesn't reply, but keeps the picture just in case she might require cheering up at some point. The third man is called Nigel. He seems reasonably normal. He has an approachable look, like a kindly greengrocer. His interests are reading, conversation and his pet tortoise. Because her eye is now drawn to such things, Louise notices the shadow of a pillar, clouding just behind his ear. In some strange way this reassures her. She writes back. 'What's your favourite book?' 'What's your tortoise called?' 'Do you fancy getting a coffee sometime?' Her own pillar undulates above the laptop, rising and falling gently as if it is breathing. This is the closest it's ever come to exhibiting emotion.

Louise goes on three dates with Nigel: coffee, dinner, cinema. They don't talk about pillars, or the circumstances which have led them to acquire one. On the first date, Louise says, 'Sorry, I didn't mention it before. I hope it's okay . . .' And Nigel says, 'I have one too . . .' and shrugs. Then they both glance up and smile. They don't say the word out loud. Not yet. Not before they've even got started. After the third date they kiss clumsily up against Louise's Fiesta, which is parked behind the shopping centre. Whilst embracing, their pillars combine to make an enormous, flaming beacon. It flares up into the night sky, eight feet above their heads. Louise hasn't expected this. It is quite romantic. Thankfully it's late at night and she's parked in a quiet street. Neither of them are the sort of people who appreciate an audience.

For the fourth date Louise invites Nigel round for dinner. She makes risotto and shaves her legs. She hopes he will stay over, then wonders if this is a dreadfully bold thing to hope for. She asks Miranda if sex is considered appropriate on a fourth date, at her age, with the divorce not even properly through. Miranda says, 'If it was me I wouldn't even have made it to the second.' She makes a mental note not to ask Miranda for relationship advice again.

Nigel arrives five minutes early with a bunch of chrys-anthemums. He has made the effort to dress up. He is wearing a freshly pressed pair of slacks and a burgundy pullover which perfectly complements his pillar. Louise leaves him in the living room with a glass of wine while she goes to find a vase. They call backwards and forwards to each other across the hall. 'How was your day?' 'Is the traffic bad out there?' The normalcy of this is tremendously reassuring. She can imagine the two of them years from now, in the same room, or someplace similar, having the same conversation. The pillar does its deep-breathing thing. She thinks it must be happy and wonders if this means that she is happy too.

She is trimming the flowers' stems at a diagonal angle – because this means you'll get a few days' extra bloom out of them – when the office phone rings. 'Excuse me,' Louise calls out, 'I'll just get that.' She leaves the flowers sprawled across the kitchen table. It will be her mother. No one else calls at this time of the night, no one but her mother and Nigel, and he is already here, making himself comfortable on the sofa. It isn't her mother. It is a person in a call centre somewhere in England. She thinks it is a huskily voiced woman, but it could just as easily be a man.

'Mrs McClean?' asks the voice.

'Yes,' Louise says. 'I'm in the middle of something. It's not convenient to talk.'

'This will only take a minute.'

'I don't have a minute.'

'I think you'll want to hear this. There's been a mix-up. I'm calling from Pillars.com. You own one of our bespoke life guides, don't you? A deluxe model with day and night functionality?'

Louise doesn't speak.

'Mrs McClean?'

'A pillar?' Louise manages. 'Yes. Although I never ordered one.'

'Exactly. As I said, there's been a mix-up. The pillar wasn't intended for you. It was ordered by a Mr Martin McClean.'

'My ex-husband,' Louise says, very quietly, for it's like being punched, just hearing his name out loud.

'Ah,' says the voice, 'that makes sense. There was a mix-up with the addresses. His credit card's listed to this house but I'm guessing he doesn't live here anymore.'

'No,' says Louise, 'he doesn't bloody well live here anymore.'

She puts the phone down quickly before the voice can say her pillar is going. She looks up into its dark, flickering eye and stares. She doesn't know how to function without it now. How to stand, and walk into the living room, and lead Nigel by the hand, up the stairs, into her bedroom. How to talk, and sit, and seem like a normal person in his presence. She doesn't even know how to get the risotto from pot to plate without burning the arse out of it like usual. Even the smallest action suddenly seems impossible without a pillar to guide her.

She keeps staring, eyeballing the pillar until the memory of it is implanted on her retina. She thinks about Martin, with his high-flying job and his pigtailed lover. Martin, sitting in front of his computer, ordering a pillar to lead him through the mess of his own sadness. She pictures him crying. This is easy enough to imagine for he's the sort of man who weeps at the drop of a hat and it's been a particularly emotional year. It is a mean little comfort to realise that Martin is weak too, weak and struggling. 'Maybe,' thinks Louise, 'we're all just holding it together for show.' What a strangely liberating thought.

When the light goes out of her pillar – the snuff of it lingering as a thin twist of birthday-candle smoke – Louise doesn't feel hopeless. Neither does she feel lost. For there's only one door out of this room and it opens into the room where Nigel is sitting on her sofa, nursing a lukewarm glass of Merlot. She will walk into the room and join him. This much is obvious to her. She has no idea how the rest of the evening will play out. Perhaps she'll know, without being told, how to move easily and confidently from one moment to the next. Perhaps she'll require leading. But, isn't this how it is for most people, almost every living day?

Echo

Stuart Neville

I'm lucky. I have two birthdays. The ninth of March and the second of September. Two cakes and two presents. On Christmas Morning, there are two piles in the living room. I don't know if I get more things than other kids. Maybe I just get the normal number of presents split in two. One pile is always girls' things, but that's okay.

Today is my twelfth birthday. The second one. The real one.

There are bottles on the coffee table in the living room when I come downstairs. The lino on the kitchen floor is cold on my bare soles, so I walk on tippy-toes. Angus looks up from his bed in the corner, blinking. He sighs and huffs, buries his nose between his paws, and goes back to sleep.

The Crunchy Nut Corn Flakes are kept in the top cupboard, out of my reach. I bring a chair from the table, careful not to scrape it across the floor, and place it beneath my target. I climb up, open the cupboard, and grab the box.

Later, I'll have Weetabix without sugar, and I won't complain. Mum will be happy, and Dad will wonder how he gets through the Crunchy Nut so quickly.

I wash the bowl and spoon, dry them, and put them back.

Not a word.

Back in bed, the sheets are cool. Dry, thank God. The first time in weeks. I burrow in, like a worm through soil. I flex my toes between the cotton.

Clanking bottles wake me up. Mum sings to herself downstairs, 'She's a waterfall.'

The Stone Roses, I think. She only plays them when she's had some wine. On LP, spinning on the old turntable that Dad bought at a vintage fair.

I like the crackle and hiss, but you can only hear them when you're up close. Close enough to see your reflection wavering in the black vinyl.

For the second time, I get out of bed and go downstairs.

I do lots of things twice.

'Morning, sweetheart.'

Mum takes a bowl from the cupboard, drops two Weetabix in, and a splash of milk.

I eat at the table, in the same seat as earlier.

'Do you think the postman will have anything for you?'

I shrug.

She strokes my back.

'Bet he will.'

I look up at her. Her face is dry and lost. Her eyes are red.

Today will not be a good day.

'Where's Dad?' I ask.

'He's having a lie-in,' she says, and clears the last of the bottles into the recycling bag. 'Are you looking forward to your party?'

'Yeah,' I say, but I'm not.

Two hours of forced smiles and thank-yous. No school

friends will come because I don't go to school. Mum teaches me. She used to be a primary school teacher. There's a blackboard in the front room, but it's rarely used. Mostly, I read books. People from the education authority come round sometimes. Mum smiles for them. So do I. They go away happy.

The only guests at my birthday party will be my parents, Aunt Laura and her latest new boyfriend, and Granny Carol.

Granny Carol will get weepy. Aunt Laura will put an arm around her. Mum will start clearing up while they're still eating. Dad will wait for them to leave, then he'll excuse himself and go back to his office upstairs in the attic.

That's the easy part. Before that, it'll be the photo album. I wonder how long she'll go before she gets it out. Maybe an hour or two, if I'm lucky.

'Can I walk Angus?' I ask.

'Your dad walks the dog,' she says, sitting down opposite.

'He could walk him again,' I say. 'Later on. Angus wouldn't mind.'

'No, sweetheart. It's too dangerous. Those roads. And you can't go into the Folly on your own.'

'You said I could walk him when I was old enough.'

'Twelve isn't old enough. What if you fell in the river?'

I realise my mistake.

'I couldn't lose you again,' she says.

'Mum,' I say, trying to undo what I've done.

Too late. She's gone.

She stands, goes to the bookcase against the far wall. I watch as she finds the darkest spine on the shelf, lifts it out, brings it back to the table. She tightens her dressing gown around herself, sits down, opens the photo album to the first page.

A baby, pink and blind, in a clear plastic crib, white bands on its ankles. Its head lies to the side, a puff of dark hair on its scalp.

'Eight pounds,' she says. 'You were a good weight. Healthy. You came out at two in the morning. Like a purple mole, you were. But, Christ, you screamed the place down. Me and your dad in floods.'

She touches the photograph.

'No medication at all. I took the pain, every bastard bit of it.'

More pictures. Dad holding the baby. Aunt Laura and some other boyfriend, Granny Carol with tears in her eyes. Stronger and bigger before the cancer broke her.

The baby grows, gets longer in the limbs, fatter. The eyes open, first blue, then deep green. A helpless thing, held in someone's arms, then sitting up and smiling, pink gums. Then one tooth. Then the single photograph of the child clinging to the edge of an armchair, standing, turned to the camera, grinning with that one tooth.

Then still and pale in a box, a white gown, flowers all around. Mum weeps.

I want to leave the table. I can't. Not now. Her tears smack the plastic that covers the photograph.

Finally, she sniffs. Exhales. She reaches across and squeezes my arm.

'Thank God you came back,' she says.

They sing 'Happy Birthday' in the front room. The school things, the blackboard and the desk, have been cleared away. Mum sets the cake in front of me. I blow. Twelve flames die.

'What did you wish for?' Granny Carol asks.

'Can't tell you,' I say.

Can't. Won't.

Mum would slap me around the ear if I said the wish out loud. Then she would go to her bedroom and wail loud enough for me to hear through the burn and the sting.

The cake is from Sainsbury's. It's not bad. The use-by date was yesterday, but it isn't dry.

Granny Carol has a sherry. She asks to see the photo album. Mum says not now, maybe later. Granny Carol goes quiet and faraway.

Aunt Laura's new boyfriend is called Trevor. He is very polite, always apologising and stepping out of people's way. Always offering to carry things, or tidy things away, or give up his seat.

I think he wants everyone to know how polite he is, which means he's not really polite at all.

The talk has gone on for an hour, and I am half asleep, when Trevor says, 'I was sorry to hear about your first child . . .'

His words trail off like someone falling. I look up, a sudden hollowness in my middle.

Everyone is quiet for a moment, then Mum says, 'Thank you. We don't talk about it much.'

Aunt Laura's face is pale, her mouth a perfectly straight line.

Trevor shifts in the hard chair. 'Sorry, I didn't mean to . . .'

His apology dies in his mouth.

Granny Carol clears her throat and says, 'I'd like to see the photo album, please.'

Mum nods. She stands, goes to the kitchen and the bookcase there, and returns with the leather-bound album in her hands. She places it in Granny Carol's lap.

Granny Carol takes a breath, then opens the album. She stares at the first photograph, her lips rubbing against each other.

'Such a wee dote,' she says. 'So content. Most content child I ever saw in my life. She hardly cried at all.'

She touches the picture, just like Mum did earlier.

She turns the stiff pages, one picture after another. She cries.

Mum watches me.

I say nothing.

Aunt Laura hugs me before she leaves. She hugs me hard, like she means it. I go upstairs. Angus follows, nuzzling my heels.

Mum and Dad argue. I hear them barking at each other from below.

I lie on my bed, grab Dad's iPod from the bedside locker. He hasn't noticed it's missing yet. It usually takes him a week or two before he comes looking for it. I push the earbuds in as far as they'll go. I choose a Led Zeppelin album.

They're from the olden days, but I like them. The singer has a squeaky voice. The song is called 'Black Dog'. Angus is black, apart from the white patch on his chest. He curls up at my feet.

Melody sits on the end of the bed.

I ignore her.

I sing to myself, a hoarse whisper about big-legged women and their lost souls.

Melody stares. And stares.

'Piss off,' I say.

She does not.

I kick her lower back. Angus hops off the bed. She stares harder.

I groan and pull the earbuds out.

'What?'

She smiles. 'Happy birthday.'

I turn over on my side, face the wall. But I still feel her there.

'What do you want?'

She lies down beside me, her back against mine. Her bare toes seek the gaps between my jeans and my socks. They tickle, but I don't tell her to stop.

'Just to say happy birthday. No need to be a pishmire about it.'

I think about getting up and leaving the room. Maybe see if Dad will let me use his computer. Instead I say, 'You'd be fourteen by now.'

'Thirteen and a half,' Melody says. 'You can't count.'

'Mum doesn't really do sums.'

'It's called maths.'

'Whatever. We just do reading.'

Melody asks, 'Do you wish you could go to proper school?'

'Sometimes,' I say. 'The other kids would pick on me, though.'

'They might not.'

'They would. Definitely.'

I had a friend once. Just for a few days, summer before last. His name was Dale. He used to walk past our house when I was playing in the front garden. One time he stopped and asked what I was doing.

'Building a fort,' I said.

Four chairs from the kitchen arranged in a square, and a tablecloth over the top.

'Can I come in?' he asked.

We played all day until Mum realised I'd taken the chairs. She would've slapped me if Dale hadn't been there. She asked his name. She asked who his parents were.

'Yes, I know them,' she said, like it mattered.

Dale came back the next day. I took him up to my bedroom. He said, 'Wow' when he saw the toys. There were dozens of little men, a couple of women, and some robots. And a big spaceship. They had been my dad's. He found them in the attic when Granda Tom died and Granny Carol wanted somewhere smaller. The attic that he made an office when we took the house. I don't remember very well, I was small. But he gave me the toys.

I explained all this to Dale. He picked up two almost identical figures.

'You've got two Boba Fetts,' he said.

'Two what?'

'Boba Fett,' he said. 'The bounty hunter. He was in *Episode Five: The Empire Strikes Back*.'

'The what?'

'*Star Wars*,' he said, laughing like I'd said something crazy. 'The films. You know, the movies?'

I shook my head. Fear crept up inside me, fear that I had failed some test, that he would walk out thinking me a fool for not knowing what he was talking about.

'You've not seen them?' he asked. 'Seriously?'

I shook my head again, felt my eyes go warm, something thick in my throat.

Do. Not. Cry.

He smiled. 'Look. This is Luke Skywalker.' He picked up one figure after another, showed them to me. They looked very small in his thick fingers. 'He's a goodie. He's a Jedi Knight. But not yet, not in this outfit. And this is Darth Vader. He's the main baddie. But he's kind of a goodie as well. And this is Han Solo, and Chewbacca, and these are stormtroopers, they fight for Darth Vader. And you know what this is?'

He pointed to the spaceship. I shook my head.

'It's the *Millennium Falcon*.'

We played for three hours. Space battles. Dale was good at the noises. Pew-pew-pew! Vvvooommm! Grraarrr!

He said I could come round to his tomorrow to watch *Star Wars*. *Episode Four*, he said, the best one.

I told Mum at dinner that night. I told her Dale's house was just around the corner, number twenty-three. I asked please, could I go, please? Dad watched Mum across the table while she sat there quiet. After a while, he put his hand on hers.

'It's just around the corner,' he said.

I wanted to get up from my chair and hug him.

'You can walk him round,' Dad said. 'The film's, what, two hours? Walk him round then go back and get him.'

I wanted to say I could go by myself, but I knew to keep my mouth shut.

Eventually, she nodded once and said, 'All right. Two hours.'

Dad smiled at me. Mum's hands shook.

I woke up early the next morning, my tummy full of scratchy things. I couldn't hold a thought in my head other than *Star Wars*. Dale had said it was brilliant, told me the entire story, but I didn't care if I knew how it ended. I wanted to see it anyway. I went to the toilet so many times, Mum asked me if I was ill. She picked out my clothes for me. She took a long time about it, crying when she couldn't find the socks she wanted me to wear.

I told her it didn't matter about the socks.

'Of course it fucking matters,' she said, her voice high and cracking.

We found them at the bottom of the laundry basket half an hour later.

At five minutes to two, the socks still warm and damp from sitting over the radiator, Mum closed the front gate behind us. We didn't speak as we walked to the end of our road, and turned into the next street.

Number twenty-three stood at the far end. It looked like a nice house. A nice garden. Flowers and all. The gate didn't have any rust on it, didn't squeak when Mum opened it.

The doorbell worked. I heard it chime inside. I saw the shape of a woman through the frosted glass, and Dale beside her. I saw their hands moving. I heard them whispering hard. Then Dale walking away.

The door opened. Dale's mum was pretty, like in television adverts. She looked at my mum, then at me.

'Hello,' she said. Her smile looked like it didn't belong on her face.

Mum nudged me.

'Is Dale in?' I asked, even though I'd seen him through the glass. 'He asked me to come round. To watch *Star Wars*.'

Her smile looked like it hurt. 'I'm sorry, love, Dale's not well today. Bit of a cold. Sorry.'

Mum took my hand in hers. 'It was just for a couple of hours,' she said.

'I know,' Dale's mum said. 'But honestly, he's got an awful dose. I wouldn't want your lad to catch anything.'

Mum's hand squeezed mine tight, squishing my fingers together.

'He was so excited,' she said.

'I'm sorry,' Dale's mum said, easing the door over. 'Honestly.'

My mum said, 'You bitch.'

Dale's mum stopped the door a few inches from its frame, her pretty face suspended between. 'Excuse me?'

'You fucking bitch.'

I started to walk away, but she kept hold of my hand.

Dale's mum said, 'Look, there's no call for that kind of language. Not on my doorstep.'

'He's not good enough to play with your lad. I know. He's got a nutjob for a mother, and a failure for a father. You don't want the likes of him around your boy. That's it, isn't it?'

'Listen, Mrs Chaise, I know you've had some problems, and I do sympathise, but that doesn't give you an excuse to go around abusing people in their own homes. Now, I'd like you to leave.'

I tried to pull my mum away. She stood firm.

'You're a fucking stuck-up cunt,' she said.

Dale's mum stayed quiet for a moment, her mouth open, before she said, 'Get out of here now or I'll call the police.'

She slammed the door.

Mum let go of my hand.

'Please, Mum,' I said. 'Let's go. Please.'

Mum stood there, breathing hard. Then she looked around the garden until she saw a big green ceramic flowerpot. She picked it up, grunting at the weight of it.

'Please, Mum, don't.'

She threw the pot at the door. Bang. Compost and green ceramic fragments scattered. A crack in the glass.

Mum grabbed my hand, hauled me back home.

The police came half an hour later. A man and a woman. The woman did the talking. Small voices. Kind voices.

No charges. Just stay away. You and the boy.

Mum stayed drunk for a month. Dad did the cooking.

The next time I saw Dale, he called me a fucking weirdo, said my mum was a mental hippy, and hit me so hard in the stomach that my pee was red for a whole day.

Melody stayed away for ages. Because I was angry, she told me later. She doesn't like me when I'm angry.

I don't know if she really likes me the rest of the time. She says she does, but I'm not sure. Sometimes she calls me the Walrus. Not because I'm fat. I'm not. Because of the song by the Beatles.

I am the Walrus.

I am he as you are me, or something like that.

It's on Dad's iPod. My back to hers, I take one earbud out and hand it over. She pushes it into her ear.

We listen to olden-days music together until it gets dark and I get hungry. By then, she's gone, but she'll be back tomorrow.

Mum says she's too tired to do school stuff today. I can go and play in my room if I want. She sleeps on the couch. Dad stays up in his office.

He says he's working, but I don't hear the clatter of his keyboard when I listen at the bottom of the narrow stairs that lead up to the attic. I'm not allowed to disturb him when he's up there. That's the worst thing I could do. It would break his concentration.

Dad hasn't written a book in years. He's started lots, but not finished any. He used to talk to Mum about it. Now he just stays in his office.

I go to Mum and Dad's bedroom.

The curtains are closed, and the bed isn't made. Clothes on the floor. The room smells like sweat and warm earth. I turn on a bedside lamp, the one on Dad's side, with all his notebooks and the scribbles I can't read.

I cross to the big chest of drawers. The second drawer down is open a little bit, clothes spilling out over its lip. I open the bottom drawer and smell something like old damp towels.

There are clothes in here that haven't been worn in years. And broken things, a hairdryer without a lead to plug it in, a razor with no batteries. An old passport. It's Dad's. I've looked at it before. It has stamps from America and Australia and other places. He used to travel a lot for his books. Now the passport's out of date.

What I'm looking for is at the bottom. A folder made of orange card.

Inside there are pages from newspapers. Some of them proper famous papers, like the *Sun* and the *Mirror*, but most of them are local papers like the *Belfast Telegraph* and the *News Letter* and the *Ulster Gazette*. The pages have turned yellow. They all have that same photograph from Mum's album, the baby holding on to the chair, smiling. That one tooth.

Toddler Swept Away by River.

Swollen River Claims Little Melody.

Local Child Drowned, Family Devastated.

I read one of the stories.

An Armagh family is in shock today as it comes to terms with the drowning of toddler Melody Chaise. The mother had removed the child from her buggy to walk along the bank of the Folly Glen River, known locally as the Folly, which had swollen due to recent heavy rainfall, when Mrs Glenda Chaise reportedly slipped and fell, losing her grip on the child's hand.

I read another.

The grandmother of local toddler Melody Chaise has spoken of her family's utter devastation at the child's tragic drowning. Carol Mawhinney said the little girl, an only child, will be desperately missed by all who knew her. Mrs Mawhinney said, 'I don't know how we'll get over this. I'm so worried for her mummy and daddy. How can they survive it?'

And another. This one has a photograph of the funeral. Dad carrying the white coffin, his face all crumpled up. Mum looking like a ghost.

The Coroners Service for Northern Ireland has ruled that the recent drowning of a fourteen-month-old girl was a tragic accident. The coroner stated that weather conditions in the days previous to the incident contributed not only to deeper and faster-moving water at the Folly Glen River, but also to poor footing along the path that runs alongside.

I know the river. I've been there lots of times.

Once, Mum took me. She walked me along the path to the fence made of wire and wood with the steep drop on the other side. Mum said the fence didn't use to be there. She stood beside me, holding my hand tight, looking at the water. It moved slow and lazy.

She asked me if I remembered. I said no, I didn't.

I've gone back other times. Sometimes if Mum has a nap, and Dad's upstairs working, I go to the river. It's only a few minutes away from our house. Some days I go to that spot, where the fence wasn't before, and other times I don't. I like the trees and the quiet. In the autumn, the squirrels run and hop through the leaves on the ground. I wish I could bring Angus so he could chase them.

I think he could catch one. I would watch him eat it, his teeth red. The guts spilling out.

I'm kneeling by the chest of drawers, the newspaper pages on the floor in front of me, picturing the dog eating the raw meat. The tiny bones breaking. It gives me a feeling that I think I shouldn't like.

A movement in the corner of my eye. I spin around, fall on to my arse.

Melody sitting on the edge of Mum and Dad's bed.

'You were touching yourself again,' she says.

'Piss off,' I say. 'I wasn't.'

'Yes you were. Pervert.'

I stand up. I cross the few feet of floor to the bed. I open my hand and slap her cheek. Her head rocks back. She closes her eyes for a few seconds. I feel the burn on my own face, and the heat on my palm.

When she opens her eyes again, she asks, 'Do you want to bite me?'

She reaches out her bare forearm. I take her skin between my teeth, close them until I can't stand the pain anymore. Tears roll down her cheeks, and she wipes them away. I see the twin red crescents on her forearm, exactly the shape and colour of the ones that have appeared on mine.

She looks down. I know what she's looking at. I want to hit her again, but instead I walk towards the door.

'Hey, Walrus.'

I stop. My insides are hot with anger. 'What?'

'You're forgetting something.'

I turn and see her pointing to the newspaper pages on the floor. 'Shit,' I say. I go back and gather them up, put them in the folder, return the folder to the drawer, arrange the old clothes and broken things as they were before I disturbed them.

Melody asks, 'Why don't you ask Mum if you can look at the papers? She'd probably let you.'

'I don't want her to know I'm looking at them,' I say.

'Why?'

Her cheek has a red handprint on it. I can still feel the sting of it on my own skin. The anger that burns my insides turns to something else, something heavier.

'Because she'd look at them with me, and then she'd start crying again.'

Melody shrugs. 'Why do you want to look at them anyway?'

'Dunno.' I sit on the bed beside her. 'To see if I remember.'

'Remember what?'

'Falling in,' I say. 'Drowning. What it felt like.'

She takes my hand in hers. 'But you didn't fall in. I did.'

'But I am he—'

'—as you are me. I know.'

We sit quiet for a while. Her fingers aren't warm or cold on mine. They're just there. I ask, 'Do you remember what it felt like? When you fell in. When you drowned.'

'No,' she says.

'You'd think you'd remember something like that.'

'Well, I don't,' she says.

'Why not?'

'Because I am he—'

'—as you are me—'

'—and we are always together.'

Those aren't the real words, but it doesn't matter. They're still true.

Quiet again. Then I say, 'Sorry for hitting you.'

'S'all right,' she says. She leans close to me. 'Do you want to go to the river now?'

'Yeah,' I say.

I peek into the living room. Mum is lying on the couch, her breath raspy in her throat. A bottle of red wine is open on the table, a mostly empty glass beside it. I leave her there and close the front door as quietly as I can. The garden gate squeaks. Inside the house, Angus barks like he does at the postman. I know if he wakes Mum, she'll just shout at him to shut up before she rolls over and goes back to sleep.

I go to the end of our road, turn back into the Crescent, then into the Ballynahone estate. The houses here are smaller than ours, newer, and uglier. I've been beaten up here a couple of times. Today it's all right, though, because most of the kids are at school. Except the ones who mitch off, but they aren't around either.

There's a playground down some concrete steps. Mum used to take me here when I was younger. She says I'm too old for swings and slides now.

The Folly is on the other side of the playground. You have to open the gate and go through. A path leads down into the trees. Soon, you can't see the houses, only the brown and grey trunks, and the leaves, still green. Conkers, hidden in their shells, lie on the ground. I kick at them as I walk. Some of them I stamp on. Like little skulls crushed under my feet.

The river cuts through our side of town. It used to be bigger. It carved a bowl out of the earth, Dad told me, and that's where the trees grew. The ground slopes down towards the water until you reach the gravel path at its bank. Today, there isn't much here. Just a stream. It smells of chemicals, and suds clump on the surface, foaming around the stones that poke up out of the water. Dad told me there used to be fish here. Tiny ones called sticklebacks, he used to catch them in buckets when he was a kid, but they're all gone now.

Melody walks behind me.

'Are you going to that place?' she asks.

'Maybe,' I say.

I walk towards the bridge. Halfway across, I stop and look over the railing. I see a wheel off a bike gathering mud and weeds. Rusty beer cans and plastic bags. Next big rainfall, when it turns from a dirty stream back into a proper river, the rubbish will be washed away. Like old memories.

'Come on,' Melody says.

I follow her across the bridge to the gravel path on the other side. She stays ahead of me. The ground dips up and down. We pass the picnic area with its benches and burnt patch in the grass. Where the path cuts closest to the river, there are fences of wood and wire. Melody stops at one.

I put my hands on the fence. Look over. There's a drop on the other side, straight down into the water. Even if there wasn't enough water to drown in, you'd break your head on the stones. I lean a little further.

I imagine my head hitting the stones, going blind from the pain and the shock of it, warm things spilling out.

Dad says imagination is a curse. Picturing the worst horrors you can think of, then writing them down. Maybe that's why he doesn't want to write anything anymore.

The water moves like a fat snake.

'It was summertime when you fell in,' I say.

'Was it?'

I imagine what it felt like. Slipping, falling away. A hand holding my hand, then not, then down into the water.

'I think it must have been cold,' I say. 'Even if it was summer.'

And how fast the water. Swept away, just like that. They found the little body half a mile downstream, snagged on fallen branches.

'Why don't we remember?' I ask.

'Maybe we were too young,' Melody says. 'Or maybe we don't want to remember.'

'Maybe,' I say.

I know Melody isn't real. Not real in the way Mum and Dad are, or even Angus. I know she lives in my head. I know the real Melody I talk to has never been, never grew up like that, never learned to talk and run and hit and bite and all the things she does.

But still, there she is. And she is we and we are all together.

Melody stands close. 'I think what Mum says isn't true.'

'What?' I ask.

'About you and me.'

'What about you and me?' I ask.

'About you being me.'

I don't answer. I look at the water, the fat snake.

'What if you're not me?' she asks. 'What if I'm not you?'

'Shut up,' I say.

'What if you're just you and nobody else?'

'Fucking shut up,' I say. Loud enough so my voice comes back to me through the trees.

'I think she didn't slip,' Melody says. 'I think I didn't fall.'

'Stop it,' I say.

'I think she carried me down the bank,' Melody says. 'I think she brought me down there, and she put me in the water.'

'Stop,' I say.

'I think it was cold,' Melody says. 'So cold. Right to the bones of me. I think she held me under. I was scared. I looked up and I could see her face through the water. Her hands were hard on my shoulders. I think I could hear her screaming. I tried to cry but I was too cold inside and it hurt.'

'Shut your fucking mouth,' I say.

I turn to look at her, to slap and bite her, but she isn't there. Instead, along the path, Mum stands staring back at me. Slippers on her feet. Her coat buttoned tight. Her eyes wide. Her mouth turned down, her lip shaking.

I try to think of something to say. Some reason I can give her.

Mum marches towards me, her open hands cutting through the air. I open my mouth. She raises her fist. It hits me below my eye, a hard slam against my cheekbone. I fall down, my head light.

'What are you doing?' Her voice is high and shaky.

I scramble back. The gravel is wet and stinging on my palms. The heat beneath my eye grows hotter and heavier.

She follows me. 'What are you doing here?'

I try to speak, but I can't find the breath.

'You're not allowed to come here on your own.'

'I'm sorry,' I say. It comes out as a whisper.

'You're sorry?' She shakes her head. 'You're fucking sorry? You little . . . you . . .'

She falls on me.

I bring my forearms up, try to keep her hands away, but it's no good. The nails and the knuckles, the ring she wears on her left hand.

I wish someone would come, pull her away, make her stop. But no one does.

Hot, hot pain above my eyes, and they fill with blood. I am blind. I cover my face with my hands. Her weight shifts on me as she leans back.

'Oh my God, sweetheart, I didn't . . . I didn't . . .'

I hear her voice. Know her position. I take my hands away from my face, blink, see light and shade. Push myself upright.

Her voice wavers as she touches my cheek.

'Sweetheart, I—'

I put my shoulders and my neck into it. My head snaps forward. I feel her nose crushed against my brow. She rocks backwards and I feel the heat of her blood on my chest. I roll sideways, and she topples over.

She cries out. I wipe at my eyes, regain something of my vision. She falls back against the fencing, nothing more than sticks and wire. It cannot hold her weight. The sticks and wire give way, and she tumbles back.

I wipe at my eyes again, watch her fall, taking the fence with her. As she slides down the bank, her foot catches in the wire, whips her body back and down.

The sound of her head meeting rock echoes through the trees like a gunshot.

I stand, wiping more blood from my eyes, blinking it away. At the edge, at the torn-away fence, I look down. Her eyes are open wide. Her mouth is working, like she's trying to tell me something. The shallow water around her head swirls with red.

Melody stands beside her, looking.

Mum's eyes turn to where Melody stands. Wide and wild. Melody says nothing, only watches as Mum becomes very still. Then she climbs the bank, up to where I wait. I follow her home.

I go to the bathroom, undress, and clean myself up. The cut on my forehead isn't as bad as I thought. I hold a wet facecloth against it, and the bleeding slows.

When I go downstairs, still in my underwear, Melody sits beside me on the couch. We watch cartoons on the television. Old ones and new ones. Most of them I'm not allowed to watch, but I don't care, I watch them anyway. Melody holds my hand, the one that isn't holding the facecloth against the cut.

We know this time is precious. We know it will end soon and we will have to talk to the police and think of lies to tell.

But for now, there are cartoons.

May the Best Man Win
Kit de Waal

Patti looked up. He was a white. In those days, in that corner of Birmingham, everyone that drank in The Carpenter's Arms used the side entrance; only strangers made use of the front doors, slabs of carved black teak, ornate brass and stained glass, one side boarded up. So when those doors swung open at nine thirty on a damp Saturday night in December 1981 everyone knew it would be a stranger, someone from out of town. But no one expected the somebody to be white. The man walked right in, pushing both doors wide, holding them open for those that followed.

Twenty-year-old Patti Rooney, mid-shift behind the bar, counted four of them, all men. The only other white people in the pub were herself and Stella Hickey, who had been living so long with Delroy Barratt that she was a black woman in all but hue.

Patti stopped wiping the dull counter and looked from the
. strangers to the four black bus drivers gambling a week's pay in the ripped leatherette booths; the rheumy-eyed West Indians in trilbies and overcoats huddled over their chipped ivory dominoes. Then to the three urban warriors, louche and

unripe, scratching the paint off the starving jukebox. Nothing had stopped, exactly, but everything was half-speed and it had all become very quiet. Patti's boyfriend Fitz was the only one still making a noise but that was because he was propped up on a high stool at the bar singing into his empty glass, too drunk to notice that walking right past him was a white man in a blue leather trench coat carrying thick black gloves with the sure-footed swagger of a king. Behind him, looking ill at ease, were three men. The last two carried between them a huge television set.

The King stopped right next to Fitz, who looked up, jolted backwards and had to clutch the man's coat to stop himself falling off his stool.

'Hey, man! You! You can't just come in here!' he shouted. 'Hey, man! You! What you doing in here?'

Fitz poked the King in his chest and shoved his face up close. Patti held her breath. If there was another fight she would lose her job and if she lost her job she would lose her little flat and if she lost her little flat she would never speak to Fitz again. The King's followers looked around. One of them took him by the arm.

'Eddie, mate. Come on. Let's go.'

But the white man sidestepped Fitz and shrugged off the cautious hand. He moved the empty glass aside and slapped the counter twice. He was smiling.

'Perfect, this is! Bloody perfect. You can stop struggling, lads. Put the box here.'

It took all the King's men to lodge the television safely on its stubby legs and manoeuvre its huge grey face towards its audience. Only then did the King deign to notice Fitz.

'What you drinking, mate?' asked the King.

'Me?! You asking me what I'm drinking? You come in here, move my things and ask me what I am drinking?!'

'That's right, chief. Shall we say rum? Looks like rum to me. Smells like it and all.'

Without waiting for a reply, the King turned to Patti and winked. Patti almost laughed. His eyes were bright, and the same blue as his coat. They lit up the room.

'If I'm right, and I think I am, love, fill him up, there's a girl. A double. Quick as you can. And when you've done that, set me up with a Jameson's and the same for my boys. We've just carried that bugger five hundred yards or more.'

He turned around and pointed at his men.

'Don't just bloody stand there, you lot. Get it working. The fight's about to start!'

He pulled from behind the television a long grey lead and held the plug up to Patti.

'You got a socket anywhere behind you, love?'

She looked up above her where there was a small grey television hissing on a narrow shelf, jagged white lines sprayed all over the screen. She looked back at the King and shook her head.

'I can't get it to work.'

'Unplug it, love. It ain't worth the electricity. Stick this in instead and then stick another rum in his glass when he's finished that one. Keep him topped up.' He nudged Fitz. 'Alright, mate? Don't want to disturb no one. Just want to watch the boxing. Got halfway down the bloody M6 and there's nothing moving. Didn't budge an inch for two hours. Never gonna make it home in time for the fight. Even bought myself a new telly for the occasion. So I says to myself, Eddie, I says, find yourself a plug, find yourself a bottle of the finest John Jameson Irish and find yourself a bit of company that know a blind punch from a swipe. Went to a right dodgy place up the road but they didn't look pleased to see me, if you know what I mean. Walks in here and, well, I feel welcome.'

He said the last bit loud enough for everyone to hear but the pub was still unnaturally quiet. One of the King's men began fiddling with a button on the front of the television and another with the aerial behind, and as Patti put their drinks on the bar the King caught her eye and gave her another wink. He looked at her as though they had a secret together. As if they had met somewhere before a long, long time ago and he was reminding her of what they did and what they knew.

'That's my girl,' he said.

And then he turned, addressing everyone and no one in particular in a loud clear voice.

'Hope you don't mind! Hope I'm not intruding, friends!' he shouted. 'Only I want to see the greatest boxer in the world! Anyone with me?'

The pub was full. Every black face turned to look at him. The King's followers took a step back, pressing themselves together against the bar, but the King still smiled, not taking his sparkly eyes from the television. He turned a big dial on the front and suddenly the noise of cheering and clapping filled the room. A voice said in feverish tones, 'Three-times heavyweight champion of the world Muhammad Ali has entered the ring!'

The King alone cheered.

'Go on, mate! Go on!'

Fitz brought his drink up to his lips and muttered something under his breath. The white man caught it.

'You're joking, aren't you, chief? Losing it? Did you say losing it? He ain't losing it! Got a bit older, that's all. Look at him! Look at him! He, that man there, he is the greatest boxer this world has ever seen or ever will see. Look at him! He's fucking beautiful!'

The King blew a kiss to the beautiful man in his white robe and red gloves. Someone laughed. The bus drivers got up from the tables and walked slowly towards the bar, towards the screen. One of the King's men caught Patti's attention and asked for more drinks, three pints of lager and some peanuts. The leather jackets hovered near the edge of the television and the trilbies with the dominoes told them to move aside, they were blocking the view.

Ali began sparring around the ring, throwing punches at imaginary foes, prancing and skipping to the adulation of the crowd. And then another black man entered the ring. The noise was deafening. People were chanting 'Ali! Ali!' but the second black man whirred around holding his arms aloft, throwing punches and, as far as Patti could tell, pretending that they were shouting for him.

'Get out of it!' shouted the King.

One man stood away from the rest. Everyone called him Reds. He had been watching the white men since they walked in. He wore a suit with a tuft of crimson silk in the pocket and his dreadlocks lay like skeins of rope over his chest.

'Hey, you there.'

But the King took no notice.

Reds took a step closer to the television. 'I said, you there,' he repeated.

The King turned and Reds spoke to him, slow and clear.

'I don't want Ali to win. Berbick is from my parish, mister. My countryman, that.'

'Is he?' the white man responded. 'Kingston man, ain't he? Jamaican. Yeah, he's good, big geezer, got some weight and he's tidy but have you seen who he's up against tonight?' He let the question hang. 'What you drinking, anyway, chief?'

Without waiting for a reply, the King nodded to Patti and she quickly pulled the top off a bottle of beer and placed it in front of the Rastaman.

The King walked round the bar with his hand held out. 'Eddie Lovett, mate.'

Patti watched. Everyone watched. The Rasta paused and then took the hand and they shook. The white man held him long and close.

'You've got a great countryman there, my friend. A great fighter. But as far as champions go, I've got to go with Ali. May the best man win.'

The King released him and went back to his friends and the crowd from the tables. Drinks were ordered thick and fast and Patti was soon rushed off her feet. Men were shouting at one another about weight and statistics. Patti didn't understand a word but from time to time she would look up and see the blue eyes of the King on her. The King's smile reminded her of Mr Cunningham who gave her an 'A' for Irish Composition. 'A lovely story and a neat hand,' he wrote in red at the bottom of the page. She showed her father, who gave her two shillings, and ever after her mother would hire Patti out to write wedding invitations and thank-you notes for family and neighbours. Patti earned enough to buy a new fountain pen. She still had both, the composition and the pen, in a painted wooden chest at home in her little flat overlooking the canal, down the hill from The Carpenter's Arms.

Every time the King smiled, she smiled back and tucked her white-blonde hair behind her ears. And somehow, she kept up with the orders and clearing the tables and wiping down the bar. She hoped the beer would last.

The boxing match had started in earnest now. The noise in the ring and the noise in the pub was deafening. It was like a party. People were taking sides and there were good-natured arguments, pushing and shoving and a lot of swearing, more than usual.

The King kept his smile throughout the fight and even his men seemed to have forgotten where they were. Every time a round ended there was a loud discussion of tactics and replaying of significant punches. The King was in the thick of it, fan, tutor, jester, star, and then there was Fitz, now so drunk he had slid off his stool and someone had propped him up in one corner of a booth. He was singing into his glass again and Patti wondered how she was ever going to get him home.

Patti realised the match was coming to an end and Ali was going to lose. The commentator said so and everyone but the King agreed. The King's man was tired and had begun to stumble. The King had his arms up, doing the work for him, fists clenched, throwing them forward, up and under. One two! One two!

'Go on! Go on!' he bawled. 'Get off the fucking ropes! Hit him!'

The commentator said there was a minute to go.

'Knock him out!' screamed the King.

The crowd was alive. Drinks were being spilled all over the floor and the counter. Patti could only glimpse a corner of the screen at a sharp angle but she could see the King and while everyone else had their eyes on the telly she could look at him properly without anyone noticing. He had long hair, light brown with streaks painted here and there of grey and blonde. A lovely face, strong like a man's should be. A dimple on each cheek and dark eyelashes curled, up and out, a frame for the eyes. Sapphire, she thought. He was tall, broad-shouldered, upright, solid. She noticed then that his shirt was blue as well as his coat and his eyes, and she wondered if everything else that Eddie Lovett wore would turn out to be blue. His socks, his vest, his underpants. She'd never seen anyone like him.

The commentator said the fight was over.

'Who's won?' she asked. Nobody answered. The King held his hands up and the room went gradually quiet until only the commentator could be heard.

'This has been a tremendous fight. Ali, in much better shape than many people anticipated, has done all he could. But is it enough? He's been slow tonight, slow and—'

'Fuck off!' the King shouted. 'Slow my arse!'

Someone laughed and slapped him on the back.

'. . . and as we wait for a decision now, it's anyone's guess . . .'

The King was swearing again and banging his fist on the bar. Patti couldn't stand it any longer. She ran round to the front of the bar, scooped up some dirty glasses, shoved in and got to see a corner of the screen. A short man with a bow tie entered the ring and began shouting numbers into a microphone. There wasn't a sound in the pub. Some glasses stayed halfway to the mouth, some were lowered in slow motion on to the bar. Suddenly the King put his hands up to his face and shook his head.

'Out-fucking-rageous! No way! I don't believe it!'

He turned to the crowd in the pub.

'Are they joking? Are they fucking joking!'

Patti ran back round behind the counter as everyone began to commiserate with the King, even those who had been cheering for the other man. Bits of the fight were replayed on the telly and the conversation turned to the beautiful man's future and whether or not he would ever box again. The King beckoned Patti towards him and put a fiver on the counter.

'That's for you, love. You've been diamond tonight. Diamond.'

She blushed. 'I can't take that. I've just done my job.'

'Go on. Get yourself something nice. Been on your feet all night in this din. Hard job, bar work.'

'I know, but . . .'

'But nothing. Unplug that lead and pass it here. And look.'

He slid a piece of paper towards her under the money and on it was a telephone number.

'If you ever need a job in London, look me up.'

As she went to take the paper, he held on to it for just another second.

'In fact, if you don't need a job look me up. Or ring me on this number. Tomorrow maybe.'

Patti wondered if anyone had overheard but no one seemed to be listening. So she took the number and the five-pound note, gave him the plug and he went back to the fight's post-mortem. By eleven thirty the pub was almost empty. Only the King, his friends and a few stragglers were left, with Fitz drunk in his corner.

'How you getting home, love?' he asked her.

Patti felt ashamed but she had no choice. She looked over at Fitz and decided to say it all at once.

'I live with him and we have a child together, Damian, and he's six.'

The King didn't miss a beat.

'Good-looking, I bet.'

He didn't raise an eyebrow. He didn't look her up and down or make quick calculations about her age, poor judgement and easy virtue. He didn't wonder whether her mother had thrown her out for being a slut that had brought disgrace on her family and Catholics all over the world. He just looked at her with their secret between them. And his eyes the colour of summer skies and tropical waters.

And just like that he told his men to pick up the telly. The King turned and left, his blue leather coat disappearing like a cat's tail through the polished brass of the strangers' door.

Patti cleaned up, tidied and chivvied the last man out. Bar towels in her bag for the wash. Coat on. Took the keys from the hook. She slipped the money and the phone number in her pocket. Lights off.

'Fitz,' she said, once and then louder.

The drunk stirred and opened an eye. 'Who won?'

'I did,' she said.

The Eclipse

Darran Anderson

She lay there, quite serene, and informed us in an offhand way that all the houses in the cul-de-sac were burning to the ground. None of us looked at her, or each other. I noticed her dinner congealing next to her, on the bedside cabinet. Her food always went untouched. She looked forward to it coming, religiously, and when it arrived she began again to look forward to it coming again. The tumour that nestled under her skull was benign, a curious term for something that would, in all likelihood, end her life. It was weighing against her brain, distorting its functions, warping in effect an entire universe, *her* universe. She could still talk, still see. On a good day, she could still shuffle herself to the bathroom. What it wreaked havoc upon was time itself. I thought of those old phrenologist skulls with different qualities mapped out in rooms: Inhabitiveness, Veneration, Secretiveness.

Her decline was charted on the internet, in comments and timestamps. She began to leave cryptic messages, inappropriate replies. She'd 'like' intimate messages between virtual strangers sixty years her junior. Someone in the family noticed and mentioned it in passing and soon everyone began to witness the small personal collapse of a human unfold in her own unassuming words. Having spent a lifetime in the medical profession, she must have suspected something was wrong. They found recently acquired and abandoned books on stress and mindfulness in her house. Perhaps it was easier for everyone, including her, to ignore the issue rather than confront it. It was a routine appointment that finally brought matters to a head. She had awoken one day, dressed in her Sunday best, left her house, careful to double-lock the door behind her, and walked to the tube to catch a train to her doctor's surgery, one stop along the line, for a check-up. Crossing the road, she was perplexed to find the station gates locked. The streets were deserted except for the occasional drunk staggering home and cars gliding over the rain-slick streets. By chance a transport worker was hanging around after his shift and approached her. She had, it turned out, lost all ability to tell night from day.

My aunt and uncle were dispatched from Ireland, driving over by ferry, to bring her home, even though the capital had been her real home for over fifty years. She had watched over them when her sister, their mother, had died tragically young of cancer and old debts were duly repaid. When they arrived, they found her house in immaculate condition. Pristine beds, plush cushions, polished silverware, and all the food rotting in the fridge.

To pay for her care and to make sure no one broke in, an uncle moved into her house, sending rent back. Adrift after something resembling a breakdown, I joined him. He was a nurse too, a pain specialist. I barely saw him, except on the evenings when we'd go to the local pub, suspended sometime in the 1970s, to watch the football together. The place was full of Irish navvies, who worked and drank hard and sat for hours in silence. I used to wonder what they must be thinking but maybe that was the point – to escape thought for a while. I too sat there in silence.

Her street lay between two tube lines, out in Metroland. You'd be reminded occasionally by the horns of passing trains. The canals were a stone's throw away. A pub here and there – The Rising Sun, The Black Horse, The Red Lion. For an hour after sunset, the concrete of derelict factories would glow. Birds filled their rooms. One morning, I saw a falcon soaring above a motorway. It was a strange hinterland. Not quite city, not quite country. In those days, I walked the heels off my boots. Sometimes, I'd sit in the garden watching the neighbour's cat crawling over the sheds and garages. There were vapour trails in the sky. The sun barely rose above the rooftops.

The nights were filled with sirens and fireworks and yells. Alarms like children's toys. I'd keep the curtains open, with the light off, watching the neighbours appear and disappear at their windows, rectangles of light in different colours and different sequences against the darkness. I watched a woman standing in her doorway, smoking and staring up at the sky. No stars were visible, only the red lights of sleeping cranes. As the night hours passed, the sounds of the city became less distinct, until they were absorbed in almost a hum, like the song of the sea or a distant storm. My sleep was plagued with ceaseless restless dreams.

As she lay elsewhere, in a strange house, watching trees outside melt like wax or discovering staircases under her pillow, I was continually reminded of my great-aunt. She had kept countless photographs of family members on the walls of almost every room. Coasters of places she'd been. Kitsch religious iconography. The Virgin Mary in porcelain. St Michael's Mount in watercolour. Books with pages folded at the edges as if interrupted mid-reading and then never returned to. Postcards stuck to the fridge with magnets. Sitges. Kötschach-Mauthen, Kelly Hill Caves and the Three Sisters, Katoomba, Gatehouse of Fleet. Smiling pictures of her late husband, a handsome kindly Kerryman who'd drunk himself to death in the very same pubs I sat in. I asked the patrons if they remembered but they couldn't place him. 'I'm sure I'd know him to see.'

The mirrors of the house were all empty and had recorded nothing. The walls were thin. You'd hear the neighbours as if someone was treading on the floorboards upstairs and you'd have to remind yourself that it is people and not places that are haunted. It was like staying inside the memories of someone else. An invasive presence. I dared not move a thing. It was impossible to move in, psychologically. A house or a life in suspended animation.

Almost every day, I found myself in deserted tube stations. Leaning my head against tiles spelling 'NO EXIT', watching the minutes count down in yellow dots. Feeling the warm subterranean breeze from the tunnels. Occasionally seeing mice dart over the tracks and on to the platform. Waiting for the last train; often the only person in the carriage. I'd sit and close my eyes and feel, with sudden clarity, the train hurtling downwards; imagine the buildings, even the river, high above me and passing fast. I began to think of all those tunnels and stations and staircases and lift shafts as the valves and arteries of some vast mechanical creature, below the city, asleep for the time being. I'd awake each time, just before my stop.

As winter took hold, I began to get ill but ploughed on, buying time and an imitation of energy with codeine, coffee and whiskey. It was around then that the rains began, rains that seemed inexhaustible.

Despite the signs of forthcoming apocalypse, life continued almost as normal. At first, attempting to walk off the fever that plagued me, I almost appreciated the downpours. Gradually, however, as my health waned, a sense of alarm began to rise in my chest. I followed the water cascading down the steps and took shelter on the underground, remaining on trains for hours, to destinations I knew nothing of, getting off simply according to the mystery of their names and finding, at every station opening, impenetrable walls of water. I returned to the trains and tried again, taking my place among commuters, mastering the ungazing gaze, the fear of the evil eye. I'd flick through discarded newspapers on the seats. A seed vault designed for eternity in an Arctic mountain had flooded. Workers at Alaskan rubbish dumps were having to chase away starving polar bears with flares and gunshots. Concrete buildings were cracking in Siberia as the permafrost began to melt. An interstellar asteroid, christened 'Oumuamua', was detected for the first time, tumbling through our solar system. It had already passed the earth and was fading into black by the time they gave it a name.

An automated message, posh and female, instructed passengers not to give money to beggars. It was difficult to tell if a human had recorded it or if it was just a series of computer-generated sounds. A German family, oblivious to the warning signs, walked through the train, at full thunderous speed. No one stopped them. I settled into a daze and only became aware we'd gone from underground to overground with the buzz of a text. She had taken a turn for the worse. Could I start boxing up her possessions? I traipsed through the rain to the house. A light was on but the place was empty. I went through the drawers, sifting through papers, setting aside the ones that might be needed. There were stacks of videotapes with pencil scrawls but no video player. I thought of a home movie an ex-girlfriend had shown me. It was holiday footage, the kind only cared about by the people filming it, except it was set in Windows on the World, at the top of the World Trade Center. Every single shot, every person in the background, every fitting in the surroundings became suddenly unique, suddenly interesting, given it was footage from empty cubes of sky.

Buttoning my coat and fixing my scarf, I had absent-mindedly grabbed and pocketed a book from the shelf. An old hardback novel. I made the train doors just before they closed. Standing room only. I clung to the rail as the train shuddered into motion. A few stops in and the crowd thinned out and I took a seat. I gazed up at the linear maps, looking at where the route separated.

I leaned forward and reached into my pocket. The book was old enough, 1958, but it wasn't a novel at all. A ninth edition of *Baillière's Pocket Book of Ward Information*. A little nursing manual. Full of scales and equations. Latin abbreviations. The classification of drugs. Maintaining respiration. Fluid and electrolyte balance. Blood transfusion. It occurred to me that my great-aunt had been a nurse for over half a century. I looked around the carriage at the faces. Far from an amorphous mass, each was startlingly different. She'd have made an impact on innumerable people down the years. No object left behind could come close.

I got off at my stop. The train pulled away, off towards the end of the line. The lights of moving rooms disappearing into the night, showers of sparks under the carriage, magnesium-bright. The rain had stopped. The world was not ending, not collectively at least, though it was always in the process of ending for someone. The eclipse was revealed individually and you only saw it once. Few got to speak of it. I watched the train disappear and turned for the steps. Across the sea, under a sky indistinguishable from night to day, a cul-de-sac was silently burning.

Privacy

Belinda McKeon

Behind, so behind, on the baby journal.

Hi darling, today you—

Today your mother couldn't be bothered, again, to pick up the pen.

Today you are two weeks old. Today you are four months old. Today you are—

Eight months, three days and just under twelve hours. When I looked at the clock that night in the operating theatre it was ten to two. Hands on the steering wheel. In the photographs my freckles look like a splash of dirty water. They held her up over the sheet – the tarp – but I was too late to see all of her; I only saw her feet, for a second, her feet and her ankles, bloody and soaring. Mornings, when we lie in bed, she sometimes traces her pointer finger along my scar.

'You came out of there,' I say to her, and she looks at me with all the incredulity that statement deserves.

Privacy

Hi darling. Today you are—

Yesterday I put a naked photo of her on Instagram. She is sitting upright, grinning, her eyes huge and blue, and her pointer finger is out again, aimed this time at Amal Clooney on the cover of *Vogue*. I gave it the caption *Hey look! It's Alexander and Ella's ma!* because Amal Clooney has twins around her age, and everyone is so careful never to refer to Amal Clooney as George Clooney's wife, and that, along with a tiny baby holding this month's *Vogue*, was the joke. But the post only got fifty-seven likes. Usually the baby would be up in the hundreds. It's her nakedness, I know; people disapprove. Even my friends – I should say, my online friends. Do I not understand the internet, I imagine them thinking. Do I want to put my baby in danger? To have some pervert use her image for a sneaky wank?

I think, as long as they don't actually get their hands on her, it doesn't really affect her, or me, and maybe it saves a real baby? And anyway, the controversial bits are covered by the magazine, and maybe the image of Amal Clooney, Middle Easterner and feminist, will put the perverts off their wank?

I am so glad, a lot of the time, that I have so few people to whom to say things out loud.

Hi darling. Today you—

Today is the day we are busy being in the middle of. Running with it, our things scattered around us, as though suitcases

191

have burst out of an overhead locker. There is no time to find
the book and write its aspects down.

———

She is up from her first nap when we spot the excavators. We
are at the window, saying good morning to the street. Good
morning, trees! Good morning, cars! Good morning, Mr
Dawson's house! Good morning, B&B! Good morning, No
Parking 8 a.m.–3 p.m. Thursday sign! Good morning, weeds!
We can get a good three minutes out of this game in the
mornings, the baby's neck craned to see as much as she can,
the nosiness of her entire gene pool kicking in. In my arms,
she is so warm, so solid. Plush, like a little velveteen couch
I have to carry around with me. The bulk of her, the way it
has doubled and tripled on itself in the months gone by, still
shocks me; I feel as if someone has been taking one child from
me and handing me back another one, over and over. When
she wants something, she points, a tiny, rigid E.T. finger that
makes people smile. What I don't tell them is that I think she
picked that gesture up from watching my husband and I prod
and stare at our phones. That she already thinks the world is
hers to tap and scroll. Well, babies are meant to think that,
aren't they. Just maybe not quite in that way.

(This is not something I put on my Instagram.)

The excavators are five young guys, in their twenties and
thirties. I knew they were going to turn up this week sometime.
Joe next door has a plumbing problem, a downstairs toilet

that belches its contents back up when it rains. When he talks about it he closes his eyes, his face creased with exquisite pain. Joe's house and our house are attached, are actually a single house, almost two hundred years old, which is truly ancient in this kindergarten country, and the plumbing systems are ancient as well: a clay pipe that runs from his garden across our garden and from there onward to who knows where. The city was magnificent once: thousands of Federal and Victorian mansions, a tramline through the cobbled streets, a train station designed by the architects who did Grand Central, a park by Olmsted and Vaux. Then the sixties came, urban renewal and white flight, and they demolished everything from here down to the river – the beautiful old streets, the brownstones and the storefronts; got rid of the train line and let all the green spaces run wild. Within twenty years it was the murder capital of New York State, which meant real estate so cheap for the first wave of gentrifiers that it was practically free, and they don't like to be called gentrifiers, that first wave, but by now we are very definitely in gentrification territory, on the fourth wave, with Brooklynites fleeing Brooklyn and restoring what's left of the historic district, and here we are, in a former inn from the 1820s, with our toilet waste disappearing off into the underworld of a city that itself long ago disappeared.

The baby and I are on the doorstep now, me in my bedroom slippers and she in her milk-stained onesie. The excavators are ignoring me, although they are wandering the street right in front of me, clearly looking for something, clearly needing some question answered; it is as though by standing out here like this I have made myself impossible to be seen. I suspect it is some kind of class signifier here, to come out like this for a gawk; to stand at the threshold and keep an eye on the comings and goings. In Ireland, it is just what you do, but here, I don't know. Here, it is not *done*, I think. Not unless you are poor, and maybe not unless you are poor and black. And with a baby on your hip, all the worse, probably. But this is getting ridiculous. There are five of them, tripping over each other.

'Can I help?' I say.

They stop, but not one of them responds; they all look at each other, like a team on a television game show. The baby looks up at me, squinting with concern.

'It's alright,' I tell her. 'Mommy's just talking to the men.'

'Um,' one of the men finally says, and he is clearly reluctant as he moves towards me, stepping between our car and Joe's, already shaking his head, his shoulders hunched. I'm going to be useless, he's thinking. I'm going to be worse than useless: I'm going to be difficult, and awkward, and a big job to get around. Joe isn't here, and not only do they have to dig up his shit, they have to explain things to the woman next door, and Jesus Fuck, once in a while, could things not be—

'It's fine,' I say brightly, and I smile. 'I know what's going on.'

The guy stops. He's not the tallest of them. Stocky and sunburned. His T-shirt bears the company name; they're all wearing the T-shirt, I notice. 'You do?' he says doubtfully.

I nod. 'Joe's dropping his wife off to work, but I can help you.' I jiggle the baby. '*We* can help you,' I say, and every one of them smiles on cue.

I know what I'm up to. I revolt myself, I really do, but this behaviour kicks in before I get a chance to catch a hold of myself, and anyway, invariably, the second that chance presents itself

I simply avert my eyes. I'm having too much fun. Adrenaline is rushing through me, chasing coffee laced with Zoloft. I'm being one of the boys, and at the same time gerrymandering the boys into thinking that I'm cute, even – these days – for an old one, and I'm being incredibly sound, and incredibly easy-going, and incredibly good craic, really, if these American boys knew what craic was – and so laid back for a mother! The baby is on my left hip now, bobbing and swaying, showing them her rosebud lips and her wonderstruck eyes, and I think, how good for them, these young guys, to see that a woman doesn't just fade into boringness when she has a baby. You know? That motherhood doesn't mean you disappear into supermarket aisles and laundry piles and breastfeeding forums—

I'm no longer breastfeeding, which is a pity right now for my breasts, but I think they still look good; my top is baggy, but the baby has pulled it tight against me, and if I clench my stomach muscles, what's left of them, and if I walk ahead—

'So Joe's due back soon?' says the guy right beside me, the one who dragged himself to the doorstep. 'You said he was just dropping his wife off?'

'Oh yeah,' I say. I'd forgotten about that. I'd forgotten about dropping that little detail, and it complicates, now, the film – frankly, the porno – I seem to be showing on the projector screen of my mind. Because I know why I mentioned that, why I made it sound the way I did. As though Martha, who has a PhD in Social Justice and works for a think tank at Columbia, needs to be chaperoned to and from her job. She takes the train because she can get work done during the commute, and Joe drops her to the station because they have one car, and they have one car because two cars is toxic and expensive and unnecessary: but it seems I don't want the excavation boys to know that. They are white men, blue-collar, and although I didn't see any bumper stickers, up here, an hour north of the city, it's becoming safer to just assume. The pickup breathing down your neck on the highway, and charging past you, a flag rippling from the empty truck bed, then swerving back into your lane so that you have to be quick with the brakes. Oh, they just care about the economy, but they would also quite happily see you strung up for being un-American. Or, they're not crazy about him, but you can't pretend he's not Better Than Her. Or, they just feel it was high time for a change around here. And he's a businessman! He knows how to negotiate! They don't want the man to be their pastor. They don't want the man to be a saint. They don't need him to be a suitable prom date for their daughter, but to tell you the truth, they wouldn't say no if he wanted that. And to tell you another thing, neither would she.

So you say things like this to them just in case. Just in case they look at you and hate you, you with your old house bought on the cheap in a town they consider a slum; you with your shabby car, ordinary and unperformative; you with your short hair and your ironic fluffy slippers and your cute baby that you had at almost forty years old. You self-absorbed cunt.

'Ma'am?' Doorstep Guy is saying, and the baby is pointing at him, and cackling, but he is oblivious to her zany little sweetness, because he is waiting for something from me. In the porno, this would be a glass of ice water, for which he'd have to follow me into the house. The baby would go – somewhere – deposited into the laundry basket, maybe, as I led him through the basement and up to the ground floor, and the sign she and

I carried on the gun-control march after Parkland would have
to be gotten out of the way quickly, and I'd have to get to the
radio before he could make out that it was playing *Morning
Edition*, and Doorstep Guy isn't even the attractive one out
of the five of them, that's probably the redhead, and shit!
They're all brothers! How did I not clock that before now? The
name on the T-shirts, an Italian American surname, *& Sons*.
Five sons, every one of them gone into the family business
– the father must be unbearable. Bragging about *the boys,
the boys* at every summer barbecue, at every Thursday-night
poker table, in the church car park every Sunday: *the boys, the
boys, the boys*. My poor father-bullied young excavators, their
futures decided for them, their T-shirts printed and handed
out to them, probably, the day they turned sixteen. One of
them looks around that, actually; his skin still with the teenage
bloom, his hair still with the sleepy, thick tangle. He sits on
a garden chair while the others are poking around the yard,
marking it out as though getting ready for a game of five-a-
side. He smiles at the baby. I try to get the baby to smile back
at him, but she's whining. It's a pity. She really does have an
irresistible smile.

'I was saying, we were told there's a dead cat a couple of feet
under,' says Doorstep Guy.

Ah. The cat. Light of our lives, furry hot-water bottle on our
loins, possessor of the imagined cranky-asshole voice before
the baby came along to share it, then claim it, and slowly
dying of cancer the last couple of years, it turned out, though
we conspired to pretend he was just getting a little bit lazier,
and a little bit skinnier, and a little bit more needy of a spot on

either of our laps, where we might – we realised afterwards – get warm.

I do not like to think about the morning I got up to hear a noise that could only mean, if the cat was making this noise, if I was not imagining it, that he was dying. It was the kind of noise that only a dying animal makes: low and long and terrified.

I was not imagining it. And I could not find him, staggering around in the vicinity of the noise as though I was the one who had, overnight, gone blind (as he had, along with other things); I shouted for my husband, and shouted that it was not about the baby, in case I worried him, but of course this was something to worry over too—

This was something over which to feel our hearts break.

Twelve years he had been with us, a mischievous, beautiful pal. Whenever we argued, he would run around the room, protesting; when we watched TV, he would sit between us, scowling at the screen; when I was in early labour, he lay against me, knowing about the pain.

He had ten nicknames.

The vets were kind, and the baby smiled at the cat as he slipped away, and stroked his head, gently, the way she had already learned to do.

The eyes into which we had stared so often rolled back until they were not really eyes anymore, and there was something crusted on his nose, and his fur was soft but already so dead and cold.

We wrote his chief nickname on the little cardboard box, and in the hole with it we laid his toy mice and lobsters, like an emperor's terracotta army, and we covered him over, and we cried.

*

And six weeks later, Joe sent us a text to say that the digging would have to go through our garden as well, taking in the exact spot where the cat had gone down, and he was sorry for the inconvenience, and to let him know if there was any issue.

Let him know? He probably heard me through the wall. Crying and swearing and – well – caterwauling, and having to be calmed down by my husband with a sequence of drinks containing plenty of gin.

But, 'Oh, yeah,' I say now, breezily, as though the fact of the cat, of our poor little meepkins, is something I have only just recalled. 'He's there,' I say, and I point to the miniature dolmen my husband built for him, two butty megaliths and a capstone made from broken pieces of the city's old blue paving. There are dead flowers on top of it; I have been leaving him flowers from elsewhere in the garden every couple of days. I have been scattering crumbs near the dolmen, too, so that birds will come and perch on it, and I imagine him saying, 'Fuck you, Mom', in his asshole voice, but secretly enjoying the company as they flutter around his tomb.

'Got it,' says Doorstep Guy, and then he must see something in my face, because he adds, 'We'll be careful.'

'Oh yeah,' I say, attempting a shrug, and I turn it into a jiggling of the baby, who responds with a tired whine, and so I take the baby back into the house, where it is still, infuriatingly, only 8.15 a.m.

——

There's a lot in here, Mark writes back after I've sent him my story, *but it's not seeming like a story to me yet. I think, sit with it. I think, the shape will come to you, if you sit with it, for another while? Sit on it? You know?*

Mark and I have been sending each other our drafts since our first year in college, when I told him that his novel pages about a student's unrequited love for his philosophy lecturer's daughter were 'in the tradition of Austin Clarke', and he told me that my short story based on my father's angina was 'electric, Electra-ic even!', and in spite of this we still kept talking to each other and sending to each other. His new novel is about saints, he says; saints of the future, and every day it hasn't arrived in my inbox is another day I don't have to face it, and face the conversation with him afterwards. But he is right: my story has no shape.

It's just, you don't just dump things on to paper like that, Mark replies, when I text him to say I got his email.

But, he texts again fifteen minutes later, when I haven't written back because the baby is awake and I don't want her to see me using my phone, *I know how it is. You know?*

I sit down to it during the baby's second nap and add a paragraph about the tree across the street; how it is russet, how it is laden, how the car beneath it is at once dust-laden and glistening in the morning sun. Maybe it would be possible to put a character into that car. Maybe into that tree.

I need: new glasses, better skin, the willpower to drink less alcohol and more water, the willpower to go back to exercise, the willpower to write things again and to finish things, the willpower not to go on Poshmark all the time and sell my old dresses for ten dollars when they cost seven dollars to mail.

*

The baby needs: to crawl, by this stage, probably. It is our fault, I think, that she has not worked out that there exists the ability to crawl. She hated tummy time, so we didn't see the point of putting her through it, and we worry now that she is never going to make the move from sitting up and laughing at us all day long to rolling over on her front and dragging herself around the floor. I find myself thinking that maybe I should model it for her, a couple of times a day, to insert the idea of it, the possibility of it, into her head: that I should pull myself along, or scoot, for the first while, and then graduate to using my feet to push myself forward, and that then, after a week or so, I should press my knees to the ground, and put my arse in the air, and clomp around the downstairs rooms, calling out to her. I imagine her careful, appraising stare. I imagine the moment when she would look away, her attention claimed by some mote of dust or outside noise. Here, the birds are cacophonous in the mornings. The finches have built their nest over the front door again, in the space between the porch light and the glass, and the family, red-splashed, dance about in the transom like hipsters at a rooftop party.

Hi darling. Today you—

————

A hard knock on the door comes around one. When I answer it to see Joe standing there, I curse him silently, because the baby could have been sleeping. But the baby is in my arms now and he pays no heed to her, so I quickly come up to speed; this is not a baby-admiring moment, not a baby-considering moment, and I should act, too, as though she is not even there. Joe and I have a tense and rapid conversation about sewerage; his problem may just have become my problem, he tells me, because our sewage flows into the same common pipe, and the common pipe has been found to have rotted away.

'Which means that everything' – and he pauses so that I will definitely get his meaning – '*everything* from both our houses has been going, for who knows how long, into the ground.'

Isn't that just a septic tank, then, I want to say, but Joe's tone suggests that septic tanks are another of the things that you don't do here. Standing on your own doorstep, hanging your clothes to dry in the garden, letting your shit seep into the soil. Besides, there's the Tampon Panic to attend to. The Tampon Panic is familiar, I imagine, to every person who menstruates and who has, at some stage, to call a plumber, or to ask their landlord to call a plumber for them; the Tampon Panic is the dawning horror that it's all going to be revealed to be your fault, and that you're going to have to face them, the shameful, faded shoal of them, lodged in a pipe bend, billing by the minute, and that the plumber, or your landlord, or your neighbour, or your husband, will be standing beside you as you face them, holding his breath in distaste.

That this nightmare vision has never actually been made manifest doesn't loosen its hold on me as I follow Joe around to where the crew are at work, the baby on my hip again, her pale-blonde crown exposed to the midday sun. She is gnawing at her fingers, talking into them fervently. The sound of her voice constantly astonishes me. That the baby would have her *own* voice, and not just some generic baby voice, is something I had not understood. Her own timbre, her own cadence, her own swoop from soft gabbling to despotic shrieking. *Gach,* she is chanting now, *gach gach gach,* and I don't tell her that it is an Irish word, because it is not.

There are no tampons. There is no anything solid, at least not in the hole they have dug, which is at least six feet wide; there is no pipe, because Joe was right, it has entirely rotted away, having been made of clay, having been cast when Roosevelt was still ranching cattle. There is a thick gurgle of brown slime down there in the dirt, from which we all avert our eyes, and up here there are several shovels stuck into the turf, the blades caked, and a large mechanical excavator, to which I do not remember having given permission to enter, but then I am easy-going that way, standing barefoot as I am over the watery grave of my own shit, and my neighbour's shit, teetering with my baby daughter on its edge; easy-going enough to joke with the workers; easy-going enough to pretend to be fascinated, as they are, by the clunking and shuddering of the machine; too easy-going, even, to even feel that bothered when Joe tells me that this is going to cost us thousands, maybe tens of thousands, that we are going to have to pay to have the gardens of the entire block torn up, that the city is going to do nothing to help us, that the city thinks we're idiots for buying these old houses in the first place.

'It'll be okay,' I tell him as he heads, agitated, back to his own house, and the look he gives me might be enough to puncture my weird little high, if I weren't enjoying myself so much, enjoying the fuss of all of this so much – it is like a barn raising, all of these people in my back garden, even if instead of raising the barn they are destroying the ground. It feels like community. It feels like—

Where the fuck is my cat?

I only see it now, as I call out another reassurance to the departing Joe. The flattened dolmen, its three parts stacked on the grass, the two smaller slabs on top of the larger one. The hole over which I am standing, I see, has a tributary extending right across our garden and into next door's, a narrow channel that they must have dug by hand, which travels like a motorway through the spot where the cat was laid. My throat thickens, and my arms feel useless; I step back from the opening in case I let the baby go. Nobody notices my sudden shakiness.

'Where's the cat?' I say, but I am too quiet to be heard over the noise of the excavator, which is dangling its bucket over another patch of ground, advancing and retreating; the crew's eyes are fixed on its surprisingly tentative dance.

'Where's the cat?' I shout, and now they do look, two of them, or three of them, and they immediately look to each other, and one of them, the red-haired one, repeats my question. There is a shrug, a distracted shake of the head, and their attention is immediately on the machine again; they are like boys on a school tour, riveted. But I can tell that the red-haired one is watching me in his peripherals, a tiny dark darting at the side of his gaze, and he is blushing, too, I see now, his pale complexion betraying him.

'Hey,' I call to him. 'The cat, I asked you. Where is my cat?' My voice climbs an octave on the second *cat*, and the baby grunts and kicks back into my hipbone, as though she is disappointed in me for losing my cool in this way, but I have looked more closely at the channel now, and I can see that it is deeper than we buried the cat, and that therefore he is definitely up here, somewhere, with us again, and I find myself terrified that I am going to see him, or smell him. I feel that he is haunting me, that they have forced him to haunt me, and that this is something that, off his own bat, he would never have been inclined or frankly bothered to do.

The red-haired guy scans the garden, frowning, and begins to say something, but I cut him off.

'Don't fucking *show* me where he is! I don't want – I don't want to!'

I sound hysterical – now they all turn to look at me – and I am furious about this. This was not how I came out here to sound, barefoot and in ninety-dollar running capris from three years ago, and in an oversized blue cotton shirt, so informal and breezy, and with a ridiculously cute baby in my arms. I came out here to sound unflappable. I came out here to be refreshingly relaxed and light-hearted and so fucking likeable, even as they dug a ten-thousand-dollar hole in my garden, and even as that hole gurgled with my shit, and my husband's shit, and our neighbour's shit, and his wife's shit, and even as the Code Compliance guy (how did he get here?) looked right through me and the City Engineer turned up and walked on my fucking begonias – through all of this I grinned, and raised a wry eyebrow, and cracked jokes, and jiggled the baby, and now they have reduced me to a sputtering wench, and the baby has crapped her nappy, I realise, which obviously doesn't matter to anybody, except to her.

'Ma-am,' one of the others says, and he seems to understand his mistake immediately, and lets his gaze slide back to the excavator, and apparently decides to pretend that he has said nothing at all.

'You said you'd tell me if you were going to take him up.' I direct this to Red, although I am not at all sure that it was him I spoke to this morning; it could have been Doorstep, and I can't remember which of them is Doorstep. But Red is nodding.

'I'm sorry, ma'am.'

'Would you stop fucking saying that?'

He looks confused. 'I'm sorry, but – I am sorry. It's chaos out here. We'd intended to' – he searches for the word – 'inform you—'

'It's not a fucking fallen soldier!' I say, which probably insults them, because they probably have another brother in the military, the only one who could get away with not going into the family business, and come to think of it, it also insults the cat, because he *is* a fallen soldier to me, scrappy little dude—

The excavator breaks ground, its teeth savaging the lawn, and there's a murmur of appreciation from the boys. The baby, too, is now riveted; she cranes her neck so that her head is hanging sideways in that way that always makes us laugh.

But I'm not laughing.

'Where is my cat?'

He casts about again, looking to every corner.

'Don't *show* me!'

He grimaces in exasperation. 'I'm not going to show you.'

'Because you don't know where he is.'

He spins around toward the house. 'BRODIE!' he roars.

'Who's Brodie?'

'My brother,' he says, and he shouts the name again.

'Just how many of you are there?'

But Brodie – it's the kid – is coming around the side of the house, trying to get his phone back into his pocket before his older brother can see that he's been dicking around on it instead of doing whatever he's supposed to be doing.

'The cat,' Red shouts at him. 'What did you do with the cat?'

'You gave my cat to this child?'

'The box?' Brodie says.

'The coffin,' I say, completing my retrogression in the eyes of Giordano & Sons.

'It's in the van.'

Throaty groans from the brothers who are pretending not to listen. 'Fuck,' says Red.

'What?'

'You put it in the van? It's ninety degrees out!'

'You told me to put it somewhere safe!' whines the boy.

'It's been dead a month!'

'Please stop,' I finally say. It's actually been two months, but I don't feel like sharing.

Brodie is sulking. He's staring to the side, his pretty mouth in a twist, like he can't believe the shit he has to put up with from these people. The baby points, wanting to be brought over to him, to touch him, probably; his skin is radiant. How old is he? Seventeen?

'Shouldn't you be at school?' I say.

He gives me daggers. 'I'm twenty-one,' he says.

'Oh.' I try to laugh in Red's direction. 'I can't even tell anymore.'

'Get the cat, Brodie.'

'No, man.'

'We have to ride back in that van afterwards. Get the fucking cat.'

'I'm not going in there,' Brodie says. 'You didn't tell me it had been a month.'

From behind us I hear a sob of laughter. The excavator bucket rams into another patch of ground. Joe is over in the unmolested section of his garden, studying his tomatoes. Code Compliance and Engineering are enjoying their billable minutes, leaning against the fence. The baby rubs her eyes.

'I'll do it,' I say, and I hand her to Red. She is delighted. He has still not caught up sufficiently even to react. Brodie sits heavily down on a garden chair and takes out his phone.

'Van's open,' he says without looking up.

'It's *what?*' Red says, and the baby gives him an adoring smile. 'Ma'am,' he says, a moment later, but I am already gone.

I will say three things about my reunification with the cat. His weight is different. When we took him home from the animal hospital that day, I held the box on my lap, and it made me smile, that the weight of it felt so exactly like him.

Now I can tell that something is shifting slightly inside the box when I lift it, and as it shifts, so does the smell.

The third thing I will say is about the smell, and that is that I hope a trace of it stays in their Ford Transit for the rest of time, and with that in mind, after I vomit Zoloft and coffee on to the kerb, I use my free hand to slam the rear doors shut, loud enough for Giordano Senior to hear.

Back in the yard, one of the retiree women from the condos on the other side has shown up, and she has the baby now. Red is standing over one of the holes with his brothers, and Brodie has slunk off again. The woman stares at my feet.

'Are you alright, Linda?' she says.

'My name's not Linda,' I say, marching past her towards

the back door, but I don't think she hears me, because I say it without opening my mouth.

'I think the baby needs changing,' she calls after me.

I manage to hold my breath until I get to the basement fridge. Then I fumble the door, and almost drop the box, and get a lungful, and a disconsolate howl escapes me, and then he is deposited, in between the extra almond milk and the probiotics we never use, and before I go into the garden again, I put on my shoes.

It is May. There are barges on the river. What smells have been released into our garden now mingle with the smell of the wisteria on Joe's side of the fence, tumbling over on to ours. There are men in my garden, strangers, with their backs to me, digging holes and looking in holes and standing around holes, clocking up their fees, hour by muscle-bound hour. I am a woman with a baby in her arms. The baby points, her little index finger going out so insistently that it bends slightly upward. I look to see what she is pointing at. I don't know. The sky, the air, a bird, a leaf, an idea. A person, high up, watching her, watching us, from a tree.

The Adminicle Exists

Eimear McBride

I saw you. I saw you. I got you by the shirt. I stopped you
walking into the road.

Blue skies.

Greyish High Road   WIDE
                    Children playing on bikes.
I held tight on. And onto you tight. You didn't know the stops
anymore.
Roaring at the driver you calamatised the bus. I pressed you
to the pole. My foot entrapped your foot. There was no choice
but stay.

WAR MEMORIAL   TFC   CHEAP FLIGHTS TO ANTIGUA
SEND MONEY CHEAP HERE   TESCO   TESCO
      TESCO   LONDON UNDERGROUND
                           STOP
The state of that – cigarette burning on a pile of sick.

I pulled you by the shirt. You did not object. Down into the
intestines. The escalator descended. You stood notably upright
like demonstrating sane, but I kept your cuff between my

finger and thumb. I watched you on the platform. I watched you by the train. I let you get onto it first. Indignantly you eschewed a seat. I did not press. The doors juddered shut and the windows soon went black.

I have you. I have you. Across bumps and irregular speed.

You stumbled with momentum, despite anticipating stops. You grabbed onto me. I tried to talk you down from the shouts, but you only half-heeded my plea.

I hate how you scream like a child. My palms itch red to slap you quiet. I should not do that though and, at least, know not to do.

But all the Londoners made out not to see, for which I blessed their maligned courtesy and restraint. Even more as I pushed you – at Highbury and Islington – away. You need though, you need it. No don't, I say, I don't want to kiss you now. Here. Ever again. I NEED TO. I NEED TO. YOU KNOW IT CALMS ME DOWN. Stop shouting. Please stop shouting. Alright. Anything to

Slither. Your fucking tongue. Getting itself right into my mouth so you will feel better and I will feel? I will be? But this is happening to you, not me. My body the locator of your self-discipline, it seems. Even so though – enough!

EVERYTHING STOPS. And that is the tube, not me. Get off now. This is our stop. It takes all my ingenuity to catch and drag you off while you, like a UFO, boggle at the platform then test the ground beneath your feet.

Up the stairs, the many stairs. We went to the outside once more.

Lively, all this life around. Consumers' pretty things. If we
had any money, if we had anything, we'd live like this too.
Ha ha ha, you shout.
                    Shoppers! What wonders you possess!
                    What credit cards! What overdrafts!
I see what you see, and my pockets are as light, but the
salvage remains on me.
So
Never mind all this.   Listen.   No listen.   I mean it.
Follow me. Follow me.
I didn't even know which road I went to. But I know it now.

        Let me in.   Let me in.   Let me in.   Let us in.
Pleasepleasepleasepleaseplease.

And there is respite. Someone opens the door. She says Can I
help? I say I have nowhere else to go and she says Yes. Come
in. Come on in. If he'd like to take a seat just there.
                    Sit down.
                    Sit.
                    Please just sit.
                    Please just sit while I explain what's
                    happened.
                    Just sit.
                    No sit.
                    Please just fucking sit.
                    I won't be a minute, okay?

I gave it up. You up to them. All the details. I had no shame.
Your lost articulation. Your lost rag. I was sympathetic.
Enlightening. I was not angry. I was a benevolent master of
your domain and, even when they pressed for everything,
never said I feared you'd kill me in my sleep.

So they said, with smiles, why don't you come through?

She'll wait here, they said You'll wait for him, won't you?

I'll be right here, I said, I'll wait. Go with them. I'll see you
later. Everything will be fine.

My own lies twist but they can't listen. Jesus Christ lock him away.

You agreed then, drawing to your height. Showing your
dignity, as you imagined it. You would provide information,
even seek their advice. And they took you out.

                THANK GOD – But also, not. And also
                not very far.

The vigil then. I am well behaved. I smile when smiled at. I
draw no attention to myself. I just wait here now, as expected.
I am a very good citizen. I am cognisant of what they're doing
for you so, by extension, me. I make no attempt to shirk. I
shoulder all responsibility. And I don't just want to run.

White crossed light.   Your voice somewhere
Magazines to be read.   Other side of the wall
Red squares and grey squares. Paper thin.

In my seat.   Is that you screaming?
Tea?   I hear
Thanks very much   Maddening,
                                                maddening in your
                                                distress.
I dream of smoking.   Help me HELP ME.
                                                Help me Help me.
My kingdom for a cigarette.   But
                          The door opens.
                          The door closes.
                          And then there are more.

Rats in traps.   Fish in nets.   Heads in hands.   Hands on
faces. Irises dilated.   Leading or lead.
                                                Tell me your name. Over and
                                                again.
                                                Tell me your name.
                                                Tell me your name.
              I REALLY NEED A NAME FOR YOU . . . PLEASE.

And I am concealed behind their distress. I take pride in
keeping my own to myself. My face wears pity even if feeling
disgust. Pull yourselves together, I almost shout. But I do not.
Of course, I don't do that.
                          And
                          The door opens
                          The door closes
                          And then there are more
The angry.
The incapacitated.

The full of shit.
The too many drugs.
The too much drink.
The fatally confused.
The terminally entitled.
The poor.
The lonely.
The hungry.
The sad.
The fucked up on the street.
The fucked up in the head.
The hopeless.
The helpless.
The feckless.
Myself.
I am here as well.
Then
An inner door opens. A man walks through. Your voice
screaming somewhere, other side of the wall. I listen with
care. I separate your words out.
AM I CRAZY? AM I CRAZY? ARE YOU GOING TO LOCK
ME UP?

But when he smiles at me, I
smile back. You may expect
me to smile. I will also be
good-mannered. I will not
shout or show distress. I'll
be pleasant for hours. I
am built for this. I possess
the stamina for taking

shit. For a woman, I am
very sturdily constituted –
which is really just as well
as this could happen again
and again and again. To
you. And me.

The door opens.
The door closes
And then there are more.

A woman slaps her daughter.
A man curses at his wife.
A girl vomits on the floor.
A girl wipes it up.
A boy throws a magazine.
A man slams his fist.
A pile of people pile on him.
I hardly jump. It's only violence after all.

And I hear you scream the other
side of the wall.
I hear you not scream the other
side of the wall.
I am very sick of your problems.
I hope they will lock you up.
I insist I hope they will let you out.
Really, I hope they will let me out.
I don't know what to do.

I'd like some different magazines.

A sharp blow to the head.

Some fucking family around to offer me a hand.

> I would like to be wasted.
>
> I would
>
> like
>
> I
>
> would like

Who fucking cares what you'd like? You stupid FUCKING CHILD.

> A door opens
>
> A door closes.
>
> And then there are more.

I don't want to look at these people. I can't believe I'm here. I
don't want to be one of them.

Hey you! Hey you! Stop fucking watching me!

> Hey yourself! What the fuck does it matter what
> I see? Just get back to whichever useless fuck-up
> you brought in and leave me alone OKAY?

Okay, sorry, I didn't mean anything by it.

> Fuck you.

> There now.
>
> Don't there me.
>
> Just sit back down. How long
> have you been here?
>
> Since the early morning.
>
> Have you been told to wait?

It's expected I will.
What have they said?
They haven't said anything.
I've been told nothing at all.

I'm sorry about that. I'll see what I can do.

He's doing much better.
He's calmed down a lot.
We're just getting him tidied
back up.
Tidied up, why?
Stuff he did to his clothes . . .
stuff he did to his head.
And now?
He's fine.
Will he stay that way?
We're hopeful but . . . we can't
promise anything.
No   of course not
He's lucky to have you.
He is.

The door opens.
The door closes
And then there is you.

Less wild-eyed, saying I'm alright. Saying I'm much better.
Saying everything will be fine.
And they tell me You'll need a lot of rest. They ask me to be

responsible for ensuring you get it.

Now, you'll make sure he gets that, won't you?

I'll handle everything.

We smile at each other.

They offer you to me.

Hi, I say How're you doing?

You say Sorry about earlier. Sorry for everything.

I am very glad to see you calm but I wonder if you'll kill me tonight?

And

We take each other's hands.

I say Thank you very much.

I sign the forms.

I smile at the receptionist.

I make apologetic eyes to the person I cursed at.

Then I find our way out onto Marshall Street.

I ask how you feel and you say you are exhausted.

Well, I suggest, I've about three quid left, do you want to get something to eat?

Wings

David Hayden

A man is thrashing against a wall, fists hitting the brick, hips pushing into the dark. The girl underneath him inclines her face and slowly searches the street for witnesses, for what happens next. She looks up and sees a face staring down at her. The man shakes her off and straightens himself while she pulls down her skirt.

The boy turns back into the room. His brother is twisted in a rope of sheets, knees pulled up, arm bent across his face. The boy picks up his blanket and places it over the cold, still form and returns to bed. Television noise rises up the stairs: the steady, pushing tones of the news being told. A plate and cups chink and grind. His father is having a supper of two crackers, a sardine, perhaps a small piece of cheese, and tea with sugar. His mother is there too somewhere.

There's a coal fire downstairs but the heat doesn't reach the bedrooms. In a few weeks' time the window sweat will turn hard, hoary white and the streets will echo with cheap explosives. A few rows of houses and a concrete wall are all that are needed to silence the sea, but the boy knows that it is out there.

Wings

He falls asleep and wakes suddenly in the paused and silent air. He swings his feet to the floor, walks to the landing and stops. The stairs descend into the middle of the living room. The night is thicker below but there are no teeth in the darkness like in his dreams. He catches himself holding a breath, his heart trips about, returns to normal. His sisters' door is closed. Yesterday he was in their room playing with shapes cut out from a cereal packet. The younger sister came in and didn't ask him to leave but put on her cassette. He gathered his figures and left.

Across the landing and into the toilet the boy fumbles about for what he needs. He takes himself in hand and aims carefully at the side of the bowl, as if his little stream might wake the world when the cold and lonely dogs of the neighbourhood have failed to. He wants to wash his hands but turning on the tap makes the pipes sing and shudder, so he wipes his fingers on a piece of tissue paper.

At the head of the stairs he stands still then starts to walk down, placing his feet carefully to avoid creaks and warps. Instead of air the room is filled with a grey-blue haze of cigarette smoke. A single point of orange light comes from an ashtray sitting on the mantelpiece next to a postcard from home.

———

That morning his father woke the family early. He was taking them out for a ride, for a treat, then he wasn't, they could all go to hell, then he was, but everyone had to get ready immediately. His mother pulled together the rough panels of his coat but left, distracted by banging and shouting upstairs. His brother had fallen or jumped out of the window and into the garden.

A grey balaclava wrapped around his head made his cheeks itch. The boy tried to thread the wooden triangles into their loops to close the coat but his gloves made this difficult. The last one was joined when his brother came barrelling out of the kitchen and battered him hard in the back. The boy tripped forward, lifted into the air and cracked through the rippled glass of the dividing door. His mother came downstairs shouting. She picked him up, shook the glass off him and checked his face for red lines.

'Martin. Would you look at it? Not a scratch on you.'

'Saved by the balaclava,' said his sister.

The others stood aside as his father appeared. Martin's back warped, his shoulders pulled down, as he tried to lose some of his little height. The smell of tobacco and sandalwood surrounded him. His father bunched a good fist, pulled his arm back making a whisper in the air, and paused before swinging hard. Martin took the blow on his head but kept his footing.

'Sit down there and don't move an inch.'

His sister swept up the glass and everyone departed, leaving Martin alone.

The room seemed suddenly cold. Martin imagined building a fire: newspaper screwed into tight balls, dry, white slices of wood, a few pieces of coal balanced on top. Tears washed down his face. He wiped them away with first one glove and then another. Standing up, there was a sharp crack under his shoe.

In a shoebox under his bed was an old coin, some marbles, an incomplete set of cards that illustrated the race for space. There were three magazines full of stories of things that looked like they could not have happened, but apparently they had (except they hadn't). There was a grubby paperback about mythical creatures that Martin had found in the street and a storybook about Vikings.

Martin went downstairs, opened the front door, walked up the street past one, two, three houses, lifted the lid of a bin and placed the box inside.

There was a Monday test to prepare for on the Norman invasion. Martin looked at his homework but did not do any.

In the kitchen a small table carried six sticky dishes, six teacups and one plate dotted with crumbs. Martin filled the bowl and washed up.

He sat down and looked out into the garden. A row of lupines bloomed mauvely near the window, at the far side of the path a sycamore tree stood shrugging in the salty breeze. The coal shed door was slightly ajar.

Martin took a tea towel, dried and put the delph away. He thought about making himself something to eat but could not be sure what he was allowed to use. In the fridge there was enough milk to last the weekend. In the bread bin there were two quarters of soda bread. He carefully loosened a cracker from the packet and poured a cup of water.

Martin clunked on the big brown switch of the radio and a slow spread of yellow light appeared behind the panel, illuminating unvisited places marked in gold letters: Hilversum, Luxemburg, Frankfurt. The dial spun easily in his fingers and stopped. A high, cheerful voice sounded out.

Martin lay on the sofa listening to songs; problems that he has to solve. The words come from a bright world of longing where time always begins again with the next song.

Martin fell asleep and woke thinking of another cracker,

then slept again. He woke to a key scrabbling in a lock. Startled and rose, switched off the radio, ran the cup into the kitchen, returned to the foot of the stairs. The fumbling continued. He looked down, brushed the cracker crumbs from his jumper then ran upstairs.

Martin sat straight-backed on the edge of his bed, his hands on his knees, squeezing on and off. There was no knowing. Everything was quiet. He heard a dense flitter of birds by the window. The front door opened. There was thumping on the stairs. Martin's big sister dipped in, her plaits swinging.

'Daddy's on the warpath.'

The front door boomed shut.

For a long time there was no sound. Silence made his bones ache. A white ball of choke stuck at the bottom of his throat. His tongue would not sit right in his mouth. Hunger became an impossible notion. Martin thought of the Normans. He no longer knew anything about the Normans. He managed to swallow but couldn't push away the slight, hovering hope that what would come next would be nothing, followed by nothing and nothing.

A cup exploded in the kitchen. It was bound to be a cup. His cup. There was yelling and pleading, then loud steps up the stairs. Martin balled himself on the floor, his father red-faced, stamping, missing, furious, stamping, stamping, then kicking. Never anywhere that would show. The rage working on before running out.

His father went downstairs for his tea.

Martin stayed on the floor in a curl, holding on to the carpet, trying not to pee, attending to the throb in his back. The room

darkened. He rolled over and rose on his knees and saw his
brother sitting on the bed staring at him. He looked sorry but
didn't say anything.

'It's not your fault, Michael.'

Michael looked quickly away to the door and back again.
Martin hadn't heard a sound. The door opened and their big
sister stood there in her nightie.

'Martin. You can go downstairs now.'

Two men with dark-rimmed glasses and identical suits
stared out of the screen, everyone laughed except for those in
the room. His father, rigid and still in the armchair, looked into
the air somewhere above the television.

In the kitchen was a bowl of soup and an end of bread.

'You're all right,' said his mother.

Martin nodded.

'No harm done.'

He nodded again.

The soup went down in an instant and she handed him a fig
roll, looking over her shoulder to the door as she folded the red
packet down and fitted it in a tin.

'Tea?'

'No, thank you.'

'Are you sure?'

'Yes, thanks.'

Martin walked out from the kitchen and turned to the stairs.

'Nothing to say to your old man then?'

'Goodnight. Goodnight, Daddy.'

———

Martin has never been downstairs at night on his own and in the quiet his compacted thoughts lift up and away. The yellow rind of his soles buckles on the cold linoleum floor of the kitchen. All the surfaces are clean and dry.

He looks around. For the first time he notices that there are no pictures on the walls, no ornaments on the shelves or the mantelpiece.

Martin brings down the biscuit tin, tears open the packet and takes two, three fig rolls, packs the first two into his mouth and begins to chew. The light winks on in the fridge as he grabs a bottle. He makes a deep mark in the silver top with his thumb, peels it off and lets it fall to the floor. Martin takes a long, cold drink before eating the last biscuit.

At the garden door he rests his palm on the handle and looks through the glass into the night. There is a slight gritty squeak as the door opens. Loose folds of purple cloud billow across the sky. The concrete step and path are cold and dry. A pair of eyes shine yellow as they turn towards the house. Martin looks down at his white, bony feet pointing out from under the frayed stripes of his pyjamas. At the coal shed the wind catches the door and he steps inside. Martin sees, in the quarter-light of the moon, a cordial bottle and takes it by the neck into the house.

Black footprints track from the kitchen to the living room. Martin remembers about the Normans, that they were Vikings and architects, builders of castles, conquerors. He opens the bottle, pours the greasy yellow liquid in a circle around him, tipping the remainder on to his head. In the ashtray, within reach, a cigarette smoulders. Martin turns to the creak and the shifting air behind him, and sees his mother at the foot of the stairs. Martin's mouth moves soundlessly. Loud as day she speaks.

'Maybe . . . Maybe you could get some wings.'

Lambeth

Jill Crawford

There is a Grain of Sand in Lambeth that Satan cannot find
Nor can his Watch Fiends find it: tis translucent & has many Angles

William Blake, Jerusalem

On her way out of the Sainsbury's Local, Joanie gives the bearded man a bottle of Highland Spring, a baguette, a packet of grated cheddar, a punnet of cherry tomatoes, a bag of Pink Lady apples, an egg-and-cress sandwich, and a KitKat. The man is a vegetarian; she checked on the way in. When she hands him the food in a plastic bag, he says –

Thanks. It would've been easier to give me the money.

Perhaps. But she wants to spend her change at the flower stand on the ragged cornflowers or the still, clenched lilies. She doesn't want to give him money, even if he wants money. Who is she to give him money?

She goes to the Continental Deli, where she buys two kinds of olives, fresh chillies and bright herbs for the green salad for supper. She chooses a bottle of Petit Chablis in M&S, and heads back along Brixton High Street for home. Approaching Iceland, she remembers she has forgotten root ginger and frozen fruits of the forest. She gets those, a veda loaf, salted Irish butter – Dromona Spreadeasy since it's made in Antrim – fizzy cola bottles and three lemons. The supermarket is cold.

She walks to the tills via the cereal aisle: corn, rice, wheat, oats, barley, and the sugary kinds that her family never did. When she first came to London, she ate Shredded Wheat and warm milk with half a banana for every dinner; they had that before bed when she was little.

Last year, her university friend Nadège made a TV documentary about Iceland: they are meant to be the happiest workers in the country. The young woman at the counter looks cheerful. Joanie gives no indication that she has noticed the scar in a clean diagonal from forehead to jaw, as if someone wished to cross out her face but was interrupted midway. The young woman looks as though she may be of South Asian origin. Can she say that? Should she not have noticed? Anyway, the young woman is undoubtedly local.

Joanie emerges, now bearing three shopping bags – one canvas, one from M&S, one from Iceland – and proceeds. Ahead of her, five young girls walk, side by side, bloating across the wide pavement, traversing the rim of Electric Avenue. The one in the middle tosses a Coke can over her shoulder. Joanie gives a soft yelp as it rebounds off her chest. She is wearing her pale-pink tweed coat with the cream knitted collar and the mother-of-pearl buttons, which is dry-clean only, and which her ex-boyfriend bought her; fortunately, the can is empty. Without looking back, the girls walk on. She sets down and picks up her bags.

At Boots, she overtakes the girls. She rarely goes in there, due to the achingly slow queue and astonishing number of prescription-seekers in disquieted or altered states. Her dad was a pharmacist.

Having passed, she angles her face back to eye the girls

from the front. Taking care to erase any irritable edge from her voice, she speaks to the middle one –

You know, there's a bin over there.

She doesn't think she would have spoken if the swaggering thrower had not been white and the ringleader. That's somehow clear. All of the other girls are black. It doesn't matter. She had simply noticed it. They are about twelve years old, and of varying sizes. The thrower spits on the ground and says –

Fuck off.

Joanie remains extremely calm. Mild as yoghurt, she gestures to the bin a second time –

Look, it's right there. See?

She knows as she speaks that she is pushing. She is aware of choosing to press. She doesn't know why she wants to press but feels alive for having done so. She walks on, past the entrance to the Reliance Arcade with its pleasing scent of popcorn, past the H&M and Barclays Bank, up to the curve that was once the grand Victorian pub of the Prince of Wales Hotel and is now occupied by KFC, from which she only eats when she comes home on the night bus, unsober. Their chicken makes her wheeze.

When the blow comes to the lower-left portion of her skull, behind the ear, she is thinking about whether to put pomegranate seeds or toasted pine nuts in the green salad. Her head rings at the thump of the clenched bones. Whirling round, she finds the smallest of the five girls, who looks about ten. She is puny, hopping from one foot to the other, fists raised to box. The girl looks over at the others, to the middle girl in particular, and turns back, ready. Joanie says –

I'm not going to fight you.

The girl bounces in a semicircle around her. She pants –

Do I care? I'll mess you right here.

Joanie looks around. They are surrounded by people. It's rush hour on Brixton High Street, home time. A man in his thirties, in a sky-blue shirt, walks straight past without faltering. He saw the whole thing. He doesn't even hesitate, doesn't ask if she is okay. Fuck him. Fuck this dude, who has recently moved to Brixton but doesn't *live* here. He just sleeps here in his newly renovated flat, bought with a generous down payment. Had she witnessed this, she would never have walked by. She looks at the boxing girl. Her ears ring. Her cheeks bloom. She is acutely conscious of her pink tweed coat. Again, she says –

My god, I'm not going to fight you.

The other girls pass, snickering. They cross the road. The small girl remains, fists up, poised on the balls of her feet in exactly the same stance Joanie's mum taught her to take when playing tennis, to be ready for any way in which the ball might come flying.

The girls drift past the front of the Ritzy and through Windrush Square, which her friend Tommy, who worked for Ken Livingstone yet voted for Boris Johnson, helped redesign. It takes in the cinema, the library, and the Black Cultural Archives. The girls split around the great patient tree at the centre of the square that faces the entrance to Lambeth Town Hall, where Acre Lane meets Brixton Hill. There are flags dispersed through the branches of the tree: thick bands of green, white, black, and a red triangle balanced on one point. The girls merge again, heading for Effra Road. Cars and buses edge forward, and then flood in opposite directions.

Drawing a tight breath, Joanie angles her face up, attempting to focus on the ghost sign on a gable at the end of Rushcroft Road: *Bovril*. Above, a plane scrapes the blue ether. It softens into a fine white blur. A few clouds flock behind the sand-toned bell tower of St Matthew's. Two seagulls glide on the wind, parallel. She wants to say to this girl –

I know what I may look like, but I am not one of *them*. I've been here a decade. I have no money. I live on credit. I rent a room from my flatmate. It only accommodates a queen-size bed, a wardrobe, and a side cabinet that doubles as a wash basket. The walls are thin.

She wants to say to this girl –

This is not my fault.

She says –

Why did you do that?

The girl stares at her, an edge of lip caught under the white teeth, warm hard eyes, resolution dug into her forehead. Joanie remembers the ringleader back in her own school and the girls who vied to please her, committing mean acts, betraying self and others to ingratiate. She would go home to her mum each evening and complain –

All I want is a real friend. They're so mean, and you can't ever get away.

She turns from the girl and strides down Coldharbour Lane. The light is ebbing. Her chest thrums. She listens for footsteps coming behind. There are none. She glances back. The girl is gone. Joanie is going to the police station to tell them what this violent young girl did. Her head ripples. She walks fast. That wee girl punched her in the head for nothing. Who does that? And how could a ten-year-old body strike with such force?

Her pace drops as she crosses Electric Lane, passes the Book Mongers and the big old building she sees from her bedroom window – the final squat to be cleared at the behest of the mayor. There's a sign outside: *Premium Apartments for Sale.* They have given it a fresh name. They are building, building everywhere, every day, even on a Sunday. Of late, Brixton has become a nightmare. She doesn't belong. This place belongs to the young girl. The wine bottle clanks in the M&S bag, clanks in her skull. She has forgotten to get flowers. She should go back and get the flowers. No, she'll text Vanessa and ask her to pick some up from the station. The air is glowing.

She makes a chicken-and-apricot tagine with jewelled couscous for dinner, puts the pomegranate and pine nuts in the couscous, and keeps the salad green. Over dessert, a homemade ice cream bombe drizzled with sweetened fruits of the forest, she tells her friends about the girl. They laugh at how she bobbed like a boxer. Joanie is careful to seem magnanimous.

Bea says –

That's an actual assault. You should have gone to the police.

Joanie replies –

I almost did. What would happen to her?

When she wakes next morning, her head pounds. While playing Giant Jenga and smoking double apple shisha, they had polished off the whole bottle of white port that Noel brought from Lisbon for her thirtieth birthday gift. She is no longer angry with the young girl. Joanie wonders where she lives. Up Brixton Hill in some estate, she supposes. What the girl did is beginning to gather sense. The place on Joanie's head, behind the left ear, is tender, spongy. If she shaved off her hair, there would be a lump and a mark in some unnatural colour of flint, sickly yellow, dark dark red. She is still furious with the shit in the sky-blue shirt who walked past, pretending he hadn't seen. She remembers him distinctly. He had a bland peach face and neat hair the shade of glasspaper. He was carrying a briefcase. Who does that? Was he afraid they would beat his skull in?

She looks for the guy on the walk to the tube station on her way into work. She looks for him in the Starbucks queue, on the train platform, in the carriage. She looks for him while walking home after work. She looks for him on Guardian Soulmates, on Tinder. She feels strongly that it was his fault. It was not his fault. Also, it is.

She admires the young girl, the lambent grain in her eye and her raised fists with their angular knuckles. It is distressing, she thinks, that the ringleader was white.

All of the people in Joanie's building are white, with the exception of the girlfriend of the annoying Welsh lawyer, the one who screams *Cuuuuuunnnnt* at the television when his rugby team loses. Joanie hasn't seen her around in a while. At least four people in the building went to Oxford University. Its stamp is on the envelopes that come through the slit into the cage; they sort their own mail. The guy next door is in tech. He's a pillhead. The couple below are doctors of some sort. The two ground-floor flats are occupied by transient renters. They have been broken into three times.

Not long ago, on the evening before the last squatters were evicted from the last squat, there was a noisy party. The residents gathered on the roof to barbecue, smoke, dance, yell.

She watched them from her bedroom that looks towards the covered market. Their music pumped deep into the night. The pane rattled to the thudding bass. Open paint tins were hurled from the roof, crashing, rolling back and forth. Her ears throbbed. It was impossible to sleep.

In the morning, paint dashed the walls and the ground of the courtyard. The entrance to the residence was barred by a close line of policemen. The mayor showed up briefly for photos. By evening, all of the people who had lived there were gone. Outside, their spirits draped the streets – a roaring quiet.

Someone keeps breaking into Joanie's hallway to take drugs. They mustn't like to do it out in the open. She discovers a crack pipe, slid under the hall carpet on the last flight up to the top floor, where she lives.

One night, she comes home to find the two adolescent foxes sniffing around the base of the skip. They pause, and she halts, and they gaze at each other. As she goes into her building, she then sees two young men at the base of the stairs, by the door of one of the flats. She says –

Hi.

As she passes, one of them drops something, a credit card, and she stoops to retrieve it –

Oh, here you are.

It is oddly bent. She smiles and he smiles as she hands it over. He says –

Fanks.

She climbs. It doesn't occur to her what they might be doing until she reaches the third floor. She keeps climbing and when she arrives at the top, she enters quickly, double-locks the door, and texts the Welsh lawyer, who in turn rings the police. She loves it here. She loves it. One end of their street is so well preserved that the facade is used in Edwardian TV dramas. They have an independent wine parlour.

When her flatmate gets back from a festival, Joanie tells her what happened. Cam says –

I don't know why you texted *him*.

Joanie replies –

I don't either. I just did it without thinking. I'm mortified.

While searching the internet for the provenance of the ghost sign on the gable that edges the road, she finds a blog called Faded London, in which it is claimed that Bovril partly takes its name from a substance that appears in a novel first published anonymously in the late nineteenth century. *The Coming Race* depicts a highly evolved subterranean utopian society, endowed with a potent and enigmatic energy source called Vril, an all-penetrating fluid mastered by a people called the Vril-ya, who exploit it to heal, destroy. So ingenious is this energy form that a few young and gifted Vril-ya might use it to erase entire cities at will.

Jack's Return Home

Adrian McKinty

'The rain rained.'
Ted Lewis, *Jack's Return Home* (1970)

I woke from a night of heavy sedation to find myself in the flat in Cumbernauld. To be here at all was baffling but to still be here after nearly eight months was nothing short of amazing. Sylvie, next door, said that we lived on the worst floor, in the worst building, in the worst estate, in the worst town in Scotland. I was only somewhat sceptical. Cumbernauld was the only town in Scotland that I knew, so there could possibly have been shittier places, although you'd be hard pressed to think of anywhere outside of an actual war zone where the people looked so beaten and stupefied. The Carbrain Estate was indeed grim: a Le Corbusier machine for living which had become a decaying concrete machine for escaping life through solvents, Bucky and heroin. But Sylvie was wrong about the seventh floor of the Rennie Building. The gangs of neds, dogs and feral children seldom came up here and we were in the sweet spot between the flooding and the rats.

Naariya had turned the flat into a home and it felt safe. Relatively safe. I had, admittedly, made a few mistakes in my tradecraft. I had used my actual first name and you could imagine a scenario whereby Uncle Andy decided to lay down a few grand on a private detective. It maybe wouldn't be so difficult to find a skinny wee mucker called Jack with an Irish accent in central Scotland. And if Uncle Andy *was* looking for me it wouldn't be to give me a stern talking-to; no, it would be the full *Lion King* treatment. You know the drill, or perhaps you don't, and if you're in the latter category consider yourself fortunate.

I switched on the phone and half a dozen different Facebook, news and Google alerts told me that my father was dead.

He'd been in a coma for a week and according to the BBC Joanna had 'reluctantly agreed' to take him off life support.

I'd been rehearsing getting this news since the shooting itself and I'd imagined me bursting into tears and weeping over the iPhone. That didn't happen. I just sat there in the dark looking at Joanna's platinum hairdo which she'd clearly gotten yesterday in anticipation of being on the telly.

We'd drifted apart, of course, Dad and me, although the numbness wasn't because of that. And it wasn't Joanna's fault either. Joanna didn't like me and the feeling was reciprocated but I didn't blame Dad for hooking up with someone who was only five years older than myself. No, what I felt was more like relief than anything else. What the BBC and the papers didn't know was that his cancer had come back with a vengeance. All those Facebook posts he'd made in the last two months attacking the racketeers and drug dealers had been a form of assisted suicide.

The Belfast method.

I woke Naariya. 'He's dead,' I said.

She put her arms around me. 'I'm so sorry,' she murmured. 'You must be so upset.'

'Must I?'

'Of course. In all those pictures you were always your daddy's little girl.'

And maybe it was the way she said it or maybe it was that choice of words, but then I did begin to cry. And once the waterworks began they didn't stop for a long time.

Curtains, coffee, a stab at breakfast.

The rain was drumming against the glass and pouring out of the gutters into the storm drains seven floors beneath us. It was loud but if you strained your ears you could hear the bloody Fates weaving their threads into a new pattern. Scotland was evidently too dull for the bastards.

Naariya didn't believe in the Fates weaving new patterns. She said that after conception Allah sends an angel to put a soul into a person and this soul has a Secret Text written upon it with that person's lifespan and all their future deeds, good and ill. None of it can be changed. She believed all that shite.

'Of course you're going back for the funeral,' Naariya announced. It was not a question.

'I doubt it. I'll have to wait and see,' I replied.

'You have to go. It's your father.'

I looked into her coal-black eyes. 'Honey. Maybe I haven't explained it very well.'

She shook her head. 'You think Belfast is more complicated than Peshawar? Bitch, please. I get it. Maybe better than you do. If your uncle Andy barred you from the funeral it would make him look weak. He's not going to be made to look weak by a five-foot-two spiky-haired lesbian. In public at least he'll hug you and say all the right things and when it's over he'll warn you to fuck off again.'

'What's the point of me going back?'

'So you can see your father put in the ground? Saying goodbye, closure, all that good stuff.'

'They don't allow women graveside in the Presbyterian tradition. Women stand at the gates and it's the men who put him in the ground. It'll be closure for Uncle Andy. Throwing dirt in Dad's face. I might as well stay here.'

'I could go with you if you like. Moral support.'

'Since when did you get so sentimental?'

'Since my own family kicked me out of the house, maybe? Your dad was always super-nice to me on the phone.'

'I don't think he knew what was going on between us, sweetie.'

'Your dad was sharper than you give him credit for.'

I looked out the window at grey, rain-soaked Cumbernauld. It was July so it was no doubt bucketing down over Belfast too. July was the wettest month of the year, for it was well known that God hated the Orangemen and their marches.

I briefly considered last night's chess game on the table by the window seat. I was in deep trouble. Naariya was always several moves ahead. Me da would have given her a run for her money but not me.

'It's your move,' Naariya said.

'Forget it. I resign.'

'That's you all over, girl.'

Naariya made me tea and biscuits and when she went out to work I sipped the tea and waited for the phone to ring. I'd called my cousin Ginger earlier to get the lie of the land and she'd promised to call me back. Finally it rang. My Secret Text was about to become manifest.

'It's me,' Ginger said. 'Listen, I talked to your uncle and he says you can come back for the funeral. A special dispensation. You can be in Belfast for seventy-two hours. Ok?'

'I'll be safe?'

'He guarantees it.'

'I'd like to hear that from the horse's mouth.'

'No chance. But this is absolutely his word. Cast-iron guarantee. You're his niece. He's not going to harm you.'

'What about my dad?'

'We don't know who did that.'

'Of course we do.'

'Look, are you coming or what?'

'I'll have to see,' I said.

Ginger lowered her voice. 'There's many here who'd like to see you, Jack, have a wee word, like.'

'Goodbye, Ginger.'

That night, when I told her about the free pass, Naariya insisted on coming too, but I wouldn't let her. It wasn't about who she was. You'd think that a bass-playing lesbian Muslim from Manchester would be obvious trouble-bait in Loyalist North Belfast but actually Naariya charmed everybody she ever met. She'd meet Big Scotchy, my dad's former right-hand man, and approve of his beard and ask if he'd ever managed to get any extra work in *Game of Thrones*, which of course he had. She'd say that Ginger's wee dog was adorable and compliment her long copper hair, she'd tell Uncle Harry that she loved his moustache. She'd mean all those things too. She was a people person. Everybody liked her. Except her immediate family, of course, who wanted to murder her. No, the reason I didn't want her coming with me was the boring old safety issue. Just in case this free pass wasn't as free as Ginger made out I didn't want her to be collateral damage in my shitty wee regional theatre production of *Hamlet*.

I flew to Belfast the next afternoon and got picked up by Ginger at George Best. It was raining too hard to do anything so I spent the night playing Scrabble with Ginger and my auntie Agnes. Agnes was a past master and got 'coxswain' on a triple word score.

The funeral was the next morning.

The church service was in Carrick Presbyterian. It was very Presbyterian. The coffin was left outside in the rain while a stern-faced Elder read from the Old Testament.

UTV and the BBC were outside too with their cameras but no one had any comment for the reporters. Joanna hugged me when it was over and we cried together. Uncle Andy was up in the balcony watching everything. In the opposite balcony there were a couple of police detectives observing the proceedings and making notes. Unfortunately no one yelled out: 'Oi, you dozy peelers, there's your murderer right there!'

The Elder gave us a stern talking-to and a bit of Ecclesiastes: all is vanity, death is coming, better a handful of quietness than two hands full of toil . . .

Aye.

Polo mint smell, coughing, psalmody, the Minister being *very* careful what he said in the eulogy.

Window wipers on max as we drove the short distance out to Victoria Cemetery and waited at the gates while the men put him in the ground. The rain was hard and cold and cathartic and everyone was steaming afterwards at the wake in Ownies Bar.

I sat in the corner with a pint of cider. No one talked to me cos Uncle Andy was here. No one could be seen talking to me.

After a few pints Uncle Andy cleared the froth from his goatee and got up to make a speech. Boilerplate. Da's early days in the shipyard and how he had defended his people against terrorism in the eighties and nineties before the cancer had riddled his body and clouded his mind. Then Andy looked my way with those drink-sodden, pitiless green eyes. 'And it's great to see wee Jackie here today. A lot of you don't know that it was me who called her and told her to come. Couldn't have her missing her dad's funeral, could we?'

There were murmurs and a few nods from Andy's table but I noticed nothing but stone faces from most of the others. Uncle Harry and Scotchy however were looking at me with an intensity I didn't like at all. They were cooking something up, something that apparently involved me.

'Wee Jacqueline, aye, it's great to see her even if it's only a flying visit; she's away tomorrow back over the water, to a place called Cumbernauld if I'm not mistaken,' Andy said, and grinned.

Bollocks. How long had he known where I was living? And what would he do with this information? A chill went through me. Not for me. For her. For Naariya.

That would be the way of it, wouldn't it? Nice and ironic – just the way the Fates or the Secret Text liked it. She's running from her crazy da, ends up in a Scottish arse end of nowhere and gets topped by a hood looking for me.

Andy concluded his remarks with an unlikely tale of my dad and him on a stag do in Spain. Nobody believed a word of it but Andy could have you kneecapped or worse so everybody laughed at the end.

Back to Ginger's house, soaked, spooked, scared.

No Scrabble today.

Just me up in the spare room messaging Naariya: 'Mistake to come here. On the noon plane tomorrow. Stay safe.'

I looked out the window at the grim surrounds of Castlemara Estate. Rubbish everywhere, upturned shopping trolleys and baby buggies, a wet donkey tied to a concrete breeze block, intimidating UVF murals promising 'death to touts and informers'.

A knock at the door.

Voices.

'They want you, Jack,' Agnes said. She couldn't meet my eye.

I walked downstairs expecting a hood for my head and a gun pointed at my chest but instead it was Scotchy, Ginger, Uncle Harry.

'Jack, we were wondering if we could have a word?'

Over to the living room. Tea, digestive biscuits, Auntie Agnes making herself scarce. I sat in the replica Finn Juhl chair Dad and I had made together for her back in his joiner days.

'Well?'

Uncle Harry cleared his throat. 'Your dad should never have been killed. It was a sin. Andy knew he only had weeks to live . . .'

'It was probably that last Facebook post that tipped him over the edge,' Scotchy continued.

My dad's last Facebook post had been a direct attack on the Loyalist paramilitary network of East Antrim and North Belfast. He had called them nothing more than glorified racketeers, pimps and drug dealers. He had said the leadership was corrupt and morally bankrupt. Coming from my dad, a former commander of the East Antrim Brigade, this kind of talk meant something.

'He wasn't saying anything that was news to anyone, was he?' I said.

Harry glared at me. 'We all knew that you didn't go around saying stuff like that, no matter how true it might possibly be. That sort of talk is very dangerous.'

'Me da wasn't afraid of anyone.'

'No,' Scotchy agreed sadly.

'Here's the thing, Jack,' Harry said, clearing his throat. 'Since you've been away it's gotten worse. It's about Andy. They used to call him Mad Dog back in the day. Did you know that? And now your father's out of the picture he's promising a "night of the long knives" to clear out the dead wood. That's a direct quote.'

'Andy does not know how to keep a low profile. You seen his Rolex?' Scotchy asked.

'Tell her about the car,' Ginger muttered.

'He bought himself a bloody Bentley. New. Canary yellow. He's driving around Carrick and Belfast in a yellow Bentley,' Scotchy said.

I sat through five more minutes of complaints about Andy's ineptness, cruelty and vulgarity. I said nothing. Silence descended upon the room. The kind of ominous quiet where the real work of the conversation is done.

Uh-oh.

'So, what exactly is the purpose of this wee talk?' I asked.

Ginger and the two men looked at the floor.

'What can *I* do? Have a wee chat with him? Yeah, right.'

As always in Belfast it was better to say less.

First Ginger looked up. Then Harry. Then Scotchy.

Scotchy cleared his throat. 'You were always the apple of your father's eye. He trusted you. He relied on you. If you were a boy . . .'

Oh shite. *This* is what they want? They're too afeared to do it themselves so I'm supposed to bloody do it for them?

'But I'm not a boy, am I? And Andy was not worried about telling me to leave town even when my dad was alive,' I said.

'Your dad was a shadow of himself. If it hadn't been for the cancer, a man like Andy would never have had the chance to waltz back in from *his* exile,' Harry said.

'I'm a daughter but you're a brother, Harry,' I said. 'You're the natural successor.'

Harry shook his head quickly. 'Brother-in-law. Different thing completely. And I'm not the type. As you know, Jack, I'm good-living, I couldn't possibly . . .'

'I don't think you folks have thought this through. I'm gay. I have a girlfriend who's a Muslim,' I said.

'None of that matters,' Scotchy interrupted. 'You're your father's daughter. That's what counts.'

'The apple didn't fall far from the tree,' Harry added, helpfully.

I shook my head. 'This is a ridiculous conversation.'

Another long silence. An exchange of looks between Ginger and the two men.

Then born-again Christian Uncle Harry produced a crumpled brown paper bag from his overcoat and set it in the middle of the coffee table.

I shook my head.

'Czech CZ 75 and a suppressor. Never been used. Came

from one of the shipments Gaddafi sent over in the 1980s,' Scotchy said.

'Are you familiar with the CZ 75, Jack?' Ginger asked.

I looked at her.

'It's just a standard 9mm pistol,' Scotchy explained redundantly.

'He goes to the shed to smoke his cigarettes and read the papers every morning. Margaret won't have him smoking in the house. Shed is right at the bottom of the garden. Near the back gate,' Harry said.

'No foot traffic down there,' Ginger went on.

'And he's regular as clockwork, so he is,' Scotchy added.

'You could set your watch by him,' Harry agreed.

'Seven o'clock,' Ginger said. 'Seven fifteen to be on the safe side.'

I sighed heavily and put my hands over my eyes. 'Forget it. This entire conversation is madness.'

Harry got to his feet and looked through the window. 'It's not going to stop, is it? Should have brought my golf umbrella.'

Scotchy stared at me. 'We can't go until we get our answer,' he said.

'Why?' I asked. 'Why would I do it?'

'You know you'll never be safe unless he's gone. If he's bold enough to hit your da . . .' Scotchy said. 'Has to be you, Jack. You're the one we've been waiting for,' he added, with the hint of mysticism he was known for.

'If anyone else does it, it'll be a war,' Ginger said more pragmatically.

'Whereas with me it's what?'

'A wee family dispute. That's all. People will say that Andy had it coming.'

Scotchy stood up and put on his coat. 'Well?' he asked.

I shook my head slowly.

Just because we were in bloody Belfast it didn't always have to be melodrama. The city had changed. It had grown up. Belfast was a place of Michelin-starred restaurants and new hotels and women over from Liverpool on hen nights. Belfast was *Game of Thrones* and *The Fall* and endless craic on a Friday night, rain or shine. This kind of talk from these pasty-faced people in their slacks and cardigans and Clarks shoes was twentieth-century business.

No one thought like this anymore. It was a cliché, it was dull, it was immature. It was an atavistic brooding Ulster death cult that I had broken free of by slipping across the sheugh.

Ginger, who had lived in London, should know better. And these men with their guns. Grown men. Uncles, dads. So-called born-again Christians. Was their imagination so palsied that they could only think of solutions that involved shooting someone in the back of the head? Those were the old ways. This was the world of memes and iPhones and Instagram feeds.

This world was #2019. That world was #1690.

Nope. I wasn't going to fall for it. It wasn't going to be *my* narrative no matter what the bloody Secret Text said.

I shook my head again. 'I just came for a funeral,' I said. 'And that seems to have been a mistake.'

'We need you, Jack. It has to be you,' Scotchy insisted.

'You should take your bag with you,' I said. 'I'll be heading out in the morning.'

'To go where? Do you think there's anywhere you'll be safe from him? He's not going to stop.'

'I'll be safe enough. Take your bag.'

'We're leaving the bag,' Uncle Harry said.

'Take it with you.'

'We're leaving it.'

I sighed again and shook my head. 'Whatever. You'll find it here when I head out tomorrow.'

Scotchy and Harry walked to the door and buttoned their raincoats. Scotchy put his umbrella up inside and got a disapproving look from Ginger.

'That's bad luck, so it is,' Ginger said.

'Bad luck on the house, not on me,' Scotchy replied selfishly.

I stayed in the bedroom and didn't come down for dinner.

It grew dark. The rain continued. I heard the front door about ten.

Voices.

Footsteps on stairs.

A knock.

'Come in.'

It wasn't a complete surprise to see her.

She said nothing.

I said nothing.

Another one of those conversations.

We got into the tiny bed together. It was cold now. It was July and it was freezing.

She held me tight.

'Good flight?' I said at last.

'I had to come. Your cousin Ginger told me everything,' Naariya explained.

'Everything what?'

'The plan.'

'What plan?'

'*The* plan. I think it's a good idea. If you don't mind doing it.'

Mind? Well, yes. There was that, wasn't there? You could say that Uncle Andy had it coming but there were so many people in this town that had it coming. Who had fashioned me into the tip of the spear? Biology was not destiny. I was my father's daughter but this was not the path I had wanted to carve out for myself.

'I wanted to go to art school,' I said.

'Your drawings are good. You could still go,' she replied.

'And in this plan of theirs what's supposed to happen afterwards?' I asked.

'You do it and then all your father's friends, comrades and retainers will come by one by one to kiss the ring.'

'They won't.'

'They will.'

'Kissing the ring is a Catholic thing.'

'You are completely unable to think in metaphors.'

'Maybe it's the foetal alcohol syndrome.'

She laced her fingers between my fingers and smiled and kissed me.

Rain on the roof at midnight.

Rain overflowing the gutters in the predawn light.

I put on my anorak and went out for a walk.

Huge miscalculation.

A Jag pulled up next to me. A door opened.

'Get in the car, Jack.'

'Or what? You'll shoot me right here in the street?'

'We'll shoot you right here in the street,' the hood said.

I got in the car.

It was a classic. Me falling for a classic. Dad would not be pleased. They drove me to Woodburn Forest. Two in the front. Two in the back.

The grave had been pre-dug and was already filling with water. This burial I would get to see.

'Andy sends his regards,' the voice said.

The grave was suspiciously deep and Andy's goons were notoriously work-shy.

'Wait a minute, is this a drea—'

I woke in the chilly spare bedroom of Ginger's house. Naariya was next to me. I went to the window and looked out. There was no idling car. No men waiting for me.

In New Belfast there would never be a car waiting for me.

In Old Belfast there would be.

'I told you, I reject this storyline,' I whispered into the dark.

I tiptoed downstairs.

There was a pair of surgical gloves in the paper bag. I put them on. I put the anorak on. I put a scarf over my mouth and went out into the apocalyptic downpour.

The rain was cold and vertical. The sea spray was cold and horizontal.

Half an hour later I was back.

I started the immersion heater so I could have a bath.

When there was finally enough hot water I filled it up, closed the blinds, killed the lights, lit one of Naariya's vanilla travel candles and sank beneath the surface for a while.

Dad had showed me how to walk with a firearm, two-handed, looking down the sight, not the way the movie-imitating hoods round here carried their pistols – sideways, arms bent.

Foolishly, Uncle Andy had left the shed door open to ventilate his pipe smoke. Andy had been sitting at that enormous workbench my joiner father had built for him.

Andy had seen and heard nothing. He had made the journey from existence to non-existence between heartbeats.

When I came up out of the water Naariya was sitting on the edge of the bath looking at me.

'It's over,' she said. Another statement.

'Is it?'

'Yeah. Are you ok?'

'I don't know how this even happened. I came over here for a funeral.'

She smiled and slowly shook her head. 'You came over here so that you and I could be together.'

'What do you mean?'

'My dad and my brother and my uncle would have hunted us down over there, but they're not going to be able to get me here.'

'We're staying here? In Belfast?'

'I think we have to.'

'You won't like it.'

'I like it already. Listen, Jack, when I saw you were gone this morning I Skyped with Sylvie. She'll say that she was video-chatting with both of us the whole time. In case anybody asks if you have an alibi.'

'No one will ask,' I said to the ceiling. I looked at her. 'How long have you been thinking that we might move to Belfast?'

'A while.'

'Did you tell anybody that?'

'I might have mentioned it to your dad.'

'Oh.'

'He approved.'

'Did he?'

'Yes.'

Now I understood everything. As in our chess games Naariya was always several moves ahead.

'So now what happens?' I asked.

'I suppose we'll see, won't we?'

They began telephoning that very morning.

Ginger and Auntie Agnes gave us the front room.

Naariya curled herself on the sofa and I sat in Dad's chair and as the rain turned to drizzle and the sun considered a cameo appearance, cars began pulling up outside, and they all trooped in, one by one, to kiss the ring.

Feather

Nicole Flattery

Leaving, I was allowed to choose from a line-up of six. The
wardens said the partnership initiative catered for people
who could be made uncomfortable by my presence on the
outside. To see me walking the streets with another – possibly
holding hands with another, possibly snuggling with another,
possibly going to bed early and getting the full eight hours
with another – would make them feel relaxed. Relaxation was
essential to a productive life and could be achieved by coupling
up, listening to low, sensual music and lighting scented candles.
After everything, did I want people to be relaxed? Did *I* want
to be relaxed? Yes, I said.

The figures behind the glass were of differing heights and
appearances, familiar to me in a way, as if I might have passed
them fleetingly in elevators. Moving up, moving down. One
or two carried briefcases that intimated business transactions.
I pointed to a not-unattractive face. I raised a single finger in
an easy, life-defining gesture. The wardens exchanged a look
but they didn't comment on my choice. They knew from
previous interactions, the way I sometimes howled in anger

254

and collapsed, slamming my face hard on the meeting room floor, that I was a headstrong woman.

In the meeting room, my new partner – whom I gifted the pleasingly average name of Simon – stomped the floor, staring with his bright eyes, bumping into furniture, being antisocial. He could do nothing to conceal his essentially ugly nature. He was like me in that way. In the future I could imagine him screaming, 'Where is the money? Pay the bills' and so forth, but conversation hadn't developed between us yet. Good conversation was hard to find. Not everybody was cut out for it. Simon knocked over my water glass, leaving a long, clear puddle. What would Simon be able to do for me? Would he paint my toenails electric colours? Would I sit in the passenger seat of his car as it kicked up dust? The place smelled like Wednesday's food, plastic meat and yellow vegetables, because it was Wednesday. I took a last look at the meeting room where my parents liked to take turns crying. When one finished, the other would start. It was so perfectly synchronised. It was likely they practised it at home. In the meeting room, every week, sat in the same chair, looking at the same carpet, producing the same standard noises of incomprehension, my life happened without me.

'You're about to be returned to a world in which you've never once felt at home,' a warden explained. 'To assist you we've put your things in this plastic bag.' He held up the bag.

'That's very kind,' I said. I took my stuff and clutched at Simon. It was time to go.

On the pulsing bus we passed through my hometown, that infinite white line. Passengers watched me and Simon carefully, as if we were exhibits under glass. I looked ahead at the line, scanning its slight and familiar curves, as the catseyes carried us home. My whole life was this straight road leading to that one moment. I used to want to be an electrician so I could drill under the surface, figure out how it all fitted together, pull the wires on the whole place. When I worked in the tall building, I would press buttons in the lift, moving swiftly up and down, always thinking that when the doors opened I would be greeted by the gravel road of my hometown. I often stayed in the lift, eyes shut, as the doors opened and closed. Now I touched my fingers, ran them over Simon's soft body. I thought, 'These are my fingers. I've had them for twenty-five years. It's not too late for them.'

I remembered, as Simon and I walked through the halls of my family home, that we always had a lot of items we didn't need, and nothing had changed. That was a detail they used in the papers – the size of my house, the furnishings, the shiny machines that squealed for a few days and then were sequestered as if they suddenly disgusted us. All of it painted an unfavourable picture of me. It made me look spoiled, which was just one of a number of accusations thrown in my direction. This house gave me a headache. I was an only child and, as a young girl, demanded to be farmed out to draughty halls, where I learned to move with other girls, dance, my fingers moulded to my hipbones, my neck tilted, staring at an open sky. This house ate me alive. When I was eight, I took my best friend's hand, Laura then – no, someone else; they changed, the girls, the hands. I exhausted people from an early age. We jumped off a wall before a ballet recital, our white tutus flying up like a hundred feathers. It was just scratches, nothing more. Why did we do it? Boredom, maybe. To escape the exam. To see what would happen. But fear wasn't the reason, and boredom wasn't the reason either. And maybe it was then everything was decided.

I did the introductions. My parents looked like replacements, after-school-special parents with one single, shared expression between them. My mother eyeballed Simon's body. It was unlike her to be so perverted. I realised I didn't have a clue who she was anymore. She said she was glad I had met somebody. It was not easy to meet somebody in my circumstances. She was trying and her attempts made me feel like my heart was being ripped out of my body. My father, silent and unmodern, who disagreed with all romance, just stared at Simon – arms flapping, tongue frozen. I don't think they found him all that attractive or interesting. They never liked anyone I brought home. I never got it quite right. We all sat. We said prayers. It had been five years since I held real cutlery. It was colder than I remembered. I spent a long time examining my hands. Simon put his whole head on the plate and ate that way. A strange noise came from my throat. I was laughing. I was the only one.

My bedroom was unrecognisable. They had binned photos of my friends, smoothed down rough edges, cling-filmed my bed headboard, removed everything I could use to hurt myself or other people. It had been a long time since I had undressed in front of anyone but the wardens, so I left my bra and underwear on. Simon and I both lay down, his stick legs over mine, like electric wires stretching over the sky-blue of the duvet. It was nice to have something solid beside me because I don't think I had ever felt so alone. I was lying there wondering what he was thinking and I knew he was lying there wondering what I was thinking. Through the wall I could hear my parents discussing us, expressing their disapproval in their double bed. They said that I wasn't right, I wasn't behaving right. That was hardly a new and personal discovery. They said something about an abattoir, about putting Simon in an abattoir. They didn't want that huge, disgusting animal in their house. Or maybe the huge, disgusting animal was me. I wrapped my arms tight around Simon, buried my face in his. I wondered if we were already in love, had fallen in love in an afternoon, like two people forced to share an umbrella in a thunderstorm. I thought of other couples I knew, like my mother and father, in an abattoir, grinning on as carcasses moved around them. I saw blood streaming down a face. My mind felt like it had been mauled, as if essential parts had been clawed out. It was the darkest country road. It was porous, a chain-link fence with some daylight moving through it. I fell into a fitful sleep beside Simon's living, warm body.

In the morning there were vicious scratches down my back. I washed hair down the bathroom drain. It felt good to be clean. My mouth tasted feral so I spat and watched that blob disappear too. We had to go to the office where they handed out jobs, where I would have to fill in a form that told them everything about myself. I filled in a form with a pencil near its nub, fading on the first line. A woman said it was going to be hard to place me, and I said fair enough. I had a history of getting in fights, being physically intimidating and rude. I had previous for smirking and walking away from things I didn't like and not coming back. Very accurate, I confirmed. Both are indeed accurate. There was my time in prison. There's that, I agreed. It was going to be difficult to place me and many things I wanted I wouldn't be able to have. She sincerely hoped I would do well in my endeavours but she couldn't help me.

'Well, thank you anyway,' I said. 'Thank you for that.'

But, since I was here, since I was sitting down, I wanted to know what other departments were in this building. Was there a department where you could get back what you loved most? Was there a department for loneliness? Was there a department for redemption and forgiveness? I tried to tell her that I had once worked in an office, not exactly like this one, in a taller building, but similar, similar ceiling fan. I hadn't been to college, but I had done my best. I'd ordered office-casual clothes online. I had *clients*, for fuck's sake. And I was back and it was sort of like being back from the dead hahaha because nobody would tell you how anything worked. But now, what was of utmost importance was getting on so my partner – he couldn't hold employment – and I could have car insurance, and maybe house insurance and, after that, a house.

'You have to have a house before you can get house insurance.'

'Whatever you think is best,' I said.

'That's crucial,' the woman repeated, 'the house first.'

Post job office, Simon was waiting for me, looking lazy, unconcerned, stamping one patch of ground in the car park. I guess he expected me to take care of him. I had my own bad habits to kick so I didn't want to nag yet. I was famously easy-going and often let people take my food from the communal office fridge, and had weekends that lasted for five or six days. My town was unchanged, abandoned but for one shop, three or four non-judgemental bars, the car park we stood in. I knew this place by heart, like the back of my hands, people said, though the backs of my own hands were becoming increasingly unfamiliar to me. Leaves swirled around us in complicated gusts, as if being propelled by an unseen wind machine. Daylight poured through the gaps of the chain-link fence I had once stood against in second-hand seductive poses, thinking freedom was having sex in the back of cars. I had lost my virginity in this car park. It was to a man much older than me. There were always men much older than me wherever I went. Take a seat, untie your shoes without hitting the leather, lose the school uniform. It wasn't an extravagant time.

'I lost my virginity here,' I said to Simon. 'Who did you lose your virginity to?'

He didn't respond, just continued clawing the ground.

'She sounds lovely.'

I was always showing my solidarity to women in small ways like this.

'In a car though,' I confirmed. 'I'm not a savage.'

As we stood there, round pebbles began to hit Simon's body. White feathers flew through the air. The little pebbles made no noise as they landed. Simon didn't fight back, just reared mournfully back on his scrawny legs. He seemed like someone who had experienced a lot of abuse and now just accepted abuse. 'Oh,' his soft pose said, 'more abuse? Fine.' I wonder where he had been kept before we met. He was full of surprises. I didn't know what it was like as a man to be in a situation where stones were being thrown at you. He handled it well. There were two neighbourhood boys doing the throwing, screaming, making 'Bucka!' noises. A full spectacle. They were tiny, but their laughs were huge. They were crazy. They fired another round of pebbles. There were always crazy people in my town. I could see that madness very clearly now.

'Let's go.'

Simon looked at me as if to say: 'Where?'

'Somewhere where something is going on.'

The bar was old, hardwood floors, containing years of humiliation and regret. It was familiar as if it held fifty versions of myself, everyone I could have been. The jukebox kicked up a song I didn't know. Someone had left someone else. The man couldn't get over it. It was sad, although I didn't know the people involved. I had a vague feeling that I wasn't supposed to be drinking, that drinking was something I was never encouraged to do. I might even have had classes in how not to do it. Voices murmured. Not a single word of endearment was called out. The barman turned away. I used to be scared of strange men and now strange men were scared of me. Simon waddled, neck first, over to the torn couch and threw himself on it. I had been here with friends, I knew that much. I had one friend who was clever, one friend who was beautiful, one friend who was funny. I had all the types of friends and we caused a lot of carnage when we went out together. Skimpy clothes on the bedroom floor, spilling fruity scents all over each other, getting shitfaced, all that. They would look at the men I gathered – driving me home drunk, calling me garbage, answering calls from their pretty, uptight wives – wave their fingers in my face and tell me they weren't good enough for me. I had a taste for things that weren't good for me. Not one visited. We went through every emotion together – all the rotten, the ugly, the periods of anorexia which we rotated between us, the insecurity, the bouts of self-delusion in the name of love. I survived being a child with them, I survived being a teenager with them, it was only when I became an adult that the air went all wrong, that I made people worried.

Not one visited. I had no claim on them, I just wondered if they hated me before or after. I sort of didn't want to dwell on that topic.

'No animals in this establishment,' the barman said.

I gestured to a man sitting on a high stool, a half-empty sickly black mixture in his sight, a dog sitting attentively beside him. I ordered two of something, it didn't matter what. The barman put down napkins. It was a rust-coloured dog with long, feminine eyelashes and a bowed gaze that I associated with servitude, the kitchen. The man, his steroid arms rippling out from under his T-shirt, a bulging scar on his forehead that reminded me of a trip in the back of an ambulance, glanced at Simon. Through the window, the afternoon was turning into evening. The day was lost already.

'Nice chicken,' he said. 'Big. They must have grown him specially for the lady.'

I nodded. The stench of him and his animal was awful.

'They gave me a useless dog.'

I nodded politely at the dog. I thought I might throw up.

'It's a good idea. Something to stand between you and the world.'

The bar was suddenly quiet. It was a silence that lasted.

'What were you inside for?' he asked.

'Excuse me,' I said, 'I've no idea what you're talking about.'

The barman slammed my drinks down. 'Fucking bitch.' He practically spat at me.

I brought the drinks over, two dark glasses of red, and placed them on the table. I shook a packet of crisps but didn't open them. I didn't want to stay here but I didn't want to go back to that house, to the room that was cleansed of myself. There was a view from the bar window, a straight line leading to hills where I had once stood and screamed my own name. Right now, someone in the town was laughing, someone was closing the only shop, someone was making a decision that would determine the course of their whole life. My hands were shaking as I held my glass, my hands were disappearing and reappearing as if it was natural. I closed my eyes and pretended Simon and I were on a country break to test our compatibility. We were crossing brooks, rivers and streams, in total silence. We were falling asleep, angry, after too much fresh air. I couldn't even get my fantasies right.

'It was an accident,' I said.

Simon's slow eyes remained fixed on mine. His body heaved as if containing sobs.

I pushed the crisps towards him. 'Do you dance at all?'

He didn't answer me.

I talked then for a long time. I had to tell him that eye contact was hard, that daylight was hard, that I often got nervous when I spoke, that friendships couldn't be maintained, that people on the street might hate me with every fibre of their being and might feel the need to tell me this, that there had been an awful lot of blood on that woman's face, an awful lot. Simon looked embarrassed, like I was disclosing too much about myself. He looked away but I wasn't finished. I wasn't anywhere near finished. I didn't want there to be secrets between us. I was still here, still in one piece, still wanting things. I swallowed my drink. I was thirsty. I wanted everything to be normal, I wanted to feel alright. And we could be together. If he wanted, I could still wait at home all day, looking forward to him coming home from work? If he wanted, I could check my watch in anticipation? If he wanted, I could set a timer on the oven for five minutes before he walked in the door and wait for it to tick-tick-tick? It was fully dark by the time I completed my list. I needed another drink. I told him there was a history of extreme love in my family. I knew he had been instructed to stay with me and I didn't want to put him under pressure. But there was something promising happening between us. He could leave anytime. But I would prefer if he didn't because I didn't have anyone else. I didn't have anyone else. We were a good match. I really needed another drink.

What happened next was unexpected.

The man, with his cute dog locked under his shoulder, asked if I wanted to come with him. He was a real man going for a drive, out of town. I thought there was going to be a fight and it made me quiver with excitement. Simon pushed himself off his chair. If he had sleeves he would have rolled them to his elbows; it looked like he was about to wrap something up in a big way. I guess I still wanted a man to hurt himself for me. I never learned a single lesson.

'I'm taken.'

'He's a chicken, love,' the man said, giggling. The light in the bar made everything terrible.

Feather

I leaned forward to Simon's body and licked it from the top to the bottom. Feathers got caught in my teeth. A soft pile of feathers fell from my mouth to the table. I spat.

'That's the most disgusting thing I've ever seen.'

I slung my arm around Simon. 'It's insane,' I said. Even the dog turned away.

Night moved in further. The street lamps were lit. The other people in the bar mostly ignored us except for the odd remark. I had a few more drinks. I grew more expressive. I made plans for us. I explained that, although we were unconventional, there was no reason we couldn't have what other people had. Although I had lied to all the others, I would never lie to him. I asked Simon if he wanted to dance. I still had rhythm; I was still young. I had my whole life ahead of me. As a girl, I used to dance. I put on a slow song. Someone had left someone else. I outstretched my hand. I held Simon's huge body against mine, propped him up and tried to make him move. His body was so open and vulnerable. His body. Feathers fell to the floor as if a pillow had exploded, spilling its contents. We swayed. I was having trouble breathing because the moment was beautiful. I held him close. On my shoulder, where Simon's face rested, I could feel fat teardrops fall. He was crying. I wanted to understand why he was crying. I wanted to understand everything. We could love each other. We could know each other. We had a lot of time.

Colour and Light

Sally Rooney

The first time he sees her she's getting into his brother's car.
He's sitting in the back seat and she gets into the front, closing
the passenger door behind her. Then she notices him. She
cranes around, eyebrows raised, and then turns back to Declan
and says: Who's this?

That's Aidan, Declan says. My brother.

I didn't know you had a brother, she says mildly.

She turns around again, as if accepting the inevitability of
having to speak to him. Older or younger? she asks.

Me? says Aidan. Younger.

The interior of the car is dark, and she narrows her eyes
before concluding: You look it.

He's only a year younger, adds Declan.

The woman has turned away now to roll down her window.
She has to wind it down using the small lever on the door. Your
parents were busy, she remarks. How many others are there?

Only us, says Declan.

They got it all out of the way quickly then, she says. Sensible.

Declan is pulling out of the parking space back on to the
main road. Cool night air floods through the open window. The

woman is lighting a cigarette. Aidan can only see the back of her head and her left arm, elbow angled.

I'll drop this lad home and then we'll go for a spin, says Declan.

Sounds divine, says the woman.

On their right, a row of houses and shops, which taper off as they reach the end of town. Then the caravan park, the golf links. Does the woman already know where Aidan lives? She doesn't seem curious about how long it will take to get there. She exhales smoke out the window. The surface of the golf course glitters darkly.

What do you do, Aidan? she asks after a minute or two.

I work in the hotel.

Oh? How long have you been there?

Few years, he says.

Do you like it?

It's alright.

She flicks the stub of her cigarette out the window and starts to roll it up. The car is much quieter then and things seem to hang unspoken. Declan says nothing. Aidan bites gently at the rough side of his left thumbnail. Should he ask her what she does for a living? But he doesn't even know her name. As if apprehending this very problem, Declan says: Pauline is a writer.

Oh, Aidan says. What kind of things do you write?

Films, she says.

For some reason Aidan does not wish to seem surprised by this knowledge, though he doesn't think he's ever been in a car with a screenwriter before. He just makes a noise like: Huh. As if to say: Well, there you are. The woman, whose name appears to be Pauline, swivels unexpectedly around to look at him. Her hair, he notices, is pulled back from her forehead by a wide velveteen band. She has a strange smile on her face.

What? she says. You don't believe me.

He is alarmed, feeling he has offended her, and that Declan will be angry with him later. Of course I believe you, he says. Why wouldn't I?

For a few seconds she says nothing, but in the darkness and silence of the car she looks at him. In fact she's staring at him, right into his eyes, for two or three seconds without speaking, maybe even four full seconds, a very long time. Why is she looking at him like this? Her face is expressionless. She has a pale forehead and pale lips, so her mouth appears as one delicate line. Is she looking at him just to show him her face, the face of a screenwriter? When she speaks her voice sounds totally different. She simply says: Okay. And she stops looking at him and turns around again.

She doesn't speak to him again for the rest of the journey. She and Declan start talking between themselves instead, talking about people and events that have nothing to do with Aidan. He listens to them as if they're performing a play and he is the only audience member. Declan asks her when she's heading off to Paris and she tells him. She takes out her phone and starts trying to find a photograph to show him. He says someone called Michael never got back to him about something and Pauline says: Oh, Michael will be there, don't worry. Outside the windows, darkness is punctuated only by passing headlights and, far up in the hills, the flickering lights of houses, hidden and revealed through the leaves of trees. Aidan has a feeling of some kind, like an emotion, but he doesn't know what the emotion is. Is he annoyed? Why should he be?

Declan indicates left for the estate. The street lights grow brighter as they approach, and then the outside world is populated again, with semi-detached houses and wheelie bins and parked cars. Declan pulls up outside Aidan's house.

Thanks for the lift, Aidan says. Have a good night.

Pauline doesn't look up from her phone.

———

He sees her again a few weeks later, in the hotel. She comes in one night for dinner, with a group of people Aidan has never seen before. She's not wearing a hairband this time – her hair is fixed quite high on her head with a clasp – but it's definitely the same woman. Aidan brings a carafe of water to the table. Pauline is talking and everyone else is listening to her, including the men, some of whom are older and wearing suits. They all seem very fascinated by her – and how unusual, Aidan thinks, to see grown men hanging on the words of a girl in that way. He wonders if she is famous, or somehow important. When he fills her glass she looks up and says thank you. Then she frowns. Do I know you? she says. Everyone at the table turns to stare at Aidan. He feels flustered. I think you know my brother, he says. Declan. She laughs, as if he has said something very charming. Oh, you're Declan Kearney's brother, she says. Then turning to her friends she adds: I told you I knew all the locals. They laugh appreciatively. She doesn't look at Aidan again. He finishes filling the glasses and goes back to the bar.

At the end of the night he helps Pauline's party to get

their coats from the cloakroom. It's after midnight. They all seem a little drunk. Aidan still can't tell if they're friends or colleagues or what they are to one another – family? The men are watching Pauline, and the other women are talking and laughing amongst themselves. Pauline asks him to call some taxis for them. He goes behind the desk and picks up the phone. She places a hand delicately on the counter, near the bell.

We're going to have a drink at my house, she says. Would you like to join us?

Oh, Aidan says. No, I can't.

She smiles pleasantly and turns back to her friends. Aidan dials the taxi number, gripping the phone hard against his skull so the ringtone shrieks in his ear. He should have said thanks at least. Why didn't he? He was preoccupied wondering where her house was. She can't live in town, or he would know her. Maybe she's just moved to town, maybe she's working on a new film. If she even really writes films. He should have paused for a second to think about her question, and then he would have remembered to thank her. On the phone he orders two taxis and then hangs up.

They'll be here shortly, he says.

Pauline nods without looking back at him. He has made her dislike him.

I didn't know you lived around here, he says.

Again she just nods. He has the same view of her now as he did in the car the other week: the back of her head, and her neck and shoulders. When the taxis arrive outside, she says without turning to him: Give Declan my best. Then they all leave. Later the waiter who cleared their table tells Aidan they left a huge tip.

A few days later he's working the front desk in the afternoon, and a queue has formed while he's been on the phone. When he hangs up, he apologises for the wait, checks the guests out of their rooms, wipes their keycards, and then sits down on the wheelie chair. Guests really don't have to do that – wait to be checked out. They can just leave their keycards on the desk and walk off, out of the hotel, without the formal goodbye. But Aidan supposes they want to get the official go-ahead, or for their departure to be acknowledged in some way. Or maybe they just don't know they're allowed, and assume they're not without being told they are not, because after all, at heart, human beings are so extremely submissive. He taps his fingers on the desk in a little rhythm, distracted.

Declan and Aidan are in the process of selling their mother's house. Declan has a house of his own already, a smaller one, closer to town, with a twenty-year mortgage, so it doesn't make sense for him to move in there. People thought Aidan would move in, seeing as he's renting somewhere outside town and has to share with housemates, but he doesn't want to. He just wants to get rid of the place. Their mother was sick for a long time, though she wasn't old, and he loved her very much, so it's painful to think of her now. And in fact he tries not to think of her. The thought creates a feeling – the thought might not in itself be a feeling, it might be only an abstract idea or memory, but the feeling follows on from it helplessly. He would like to be able to think of her again, because she was the person on earth who loved him most, but the time hasn't come yet when it's possible to do so without pain – maybe there never will be a time. And, in any case, it's not as if the pain goes away when he doesn't think of her. A pain in your throat might get worse when you swallow, might be almost unbearably painful when you swallow, but that doesn't mean the pain is gone when you're not swallowing. Yes, life is full of suffering and there's no way to be free of it. Anyway, they're selling the house, and Aidan will come into a little money, though not a lot.

That night Declan comes to pick him up from work, very late, after two in the morning, and Pauline is in the car, lying in the back of the car, apparently drunk. Ignore her, Declan says.

Don't ignore me, Pauline says. How dare you?

How was work? says Declan.

Aidan closes the door and puts his bag down at his feet. Okay, he says. The car smells of alcohol. Aidan still feels he doesn't really know who this woman is, this woman lying on the back seat. She's coming up fairly often in his life at this point, but who is she? At first he thought she was Declan's girlfriend, or at least a candidate for that role, but then in the hotel the other night she seemed different – glamorous in a way, with all those men looking at her – and of course Declan wasn't there, and she even invited Aidan for a drink afterwards. He could ask his brother: How do you know this girl? I mean, are you riding her, or what? But Declan's sensibilities would be, let's say, offended by that kind of thing.

How would you get home if you didn't have a lift? says Pauline.

Walk, Aidan says.

How long would it take?

About an hour.

Is it dangerous?

What? says Aidan. No, it's not dangerous. Dangerous in what way?

Ignore her, Declan repeats.

Aidan is my good friend, says Pauline. He won't ignore me. I left him a very generous tip in his restaurant, didn't I?

I heard about that, he says. That was nice of you.

And I invited him to my house, she continues. Only to be cruelly rebuffed.

What do you mean, you invited him to your house? Declan asks. When was this?

After dinner at the hotel, she says. He rebuffed me, cruelly.

Aidan's face is hot. Well, I'm sorry you felt that way, he says. I can't walk out of work because someone invites me to their house.

I didn't get an invite, Declan says.

You were busy, says Pauline. And so was your brother, obviously. Can I ask you something about your job, Aidan?

What? he says.

Have you ever slept with any of the hotel guests?

For fuck's sake, Pauline, says Declan.

They are driving past the caravan park again now, where the smooth curved roofs of the caravans glow serenely with reflected moonlight, white like fingernails. Beyond that, Aidan knows, there is an ocean, but he can't see or smell or even hear it now, sealed up inside the car with Pauline laughing and the air smelling of alcohol and perfume. Doesn't she know that Declan doesn't enjoy that kind of banter? Or maybe she does know, and she's aggravating him on purpose for some reason Aidan doesn't understand.

Don't listen to her, says Declan.

Another car flashes past and disappears. Aidan turns around to look at her. From this angle her face is sideways. It's actually quite long, like an oval, like the shape of a headache pill.

You can tell me, she says. You can whisper.

You're flirting with him, says Declan. You're flirting with my brother right in front of me. In my car! He reaches out and punches Aidan on the arm. Stop looking at her, he says. Turn around now. You're messing and I don't like it.

Who were all those people in the hotel the other night? says Aidan. Were they your friends?

Just people I know.

They all seemed like big fans of yours.

People only act like that when they want something from you, she says.

She lets him continue staring at her. She lies there passively absorbing his look, even smiling vaguely, allowing it to go on. Declan punches him again. Aidan turns around. The windshield is blank like a powered-off computer screen.

We're not allowed to sleep with the guests, he says.

No, of course not. But I bet you've had offers.

Yeah, well. Mostly from men.

Declan appears startled. Really? he says. Aidan just shrugs. Declan has never worked in a hotel, or a bar or restaurant. He's an office manager with a Business degree.

Are you ever tempted? says Pauline.

Not usually.

Aidan touches the window handle on the car door, not winding it up or down, just toying with it.

We did have a writer in the other night who invited me back to her house, he says.

Was she beautiful?

Pauline! says Declan. You're pissing me off now. Just drop it, okay? Jesus. This is the last time I do you a favour.

Aidan can't tell if Declan is still speaking to Pauline now, or to him. It sounded like he meant Pauline, but Aidan is the one receiving the favour of a lift home, not her, unless there's another favour running concurrently to this one. Everyone falls silent. Aidan thinks about the linen room at work, where all the clean sheets are stored, folded up tight in the wooden slats, bluish-white, smelling of powder and soap.

When they pull up outside his house he thanks his brother for the lift. Declan makes a dismissive gesture in the air with his hand. Don't worry about it, he says. Pauline's face is visible through the back window, a pale oval, but is she looking at him or not, he can't tell.

———

Two weeks later, the arts festival is on in town and the hotel is busy. Jackie has to call Aidan in for an extra shift on Friday because one of the girls has laryngitis. He finishes work at ten on Saturday night and goes down to the seafront for the closing ceremony of the festival. It's the same every year, a fireworks display at the bottom of the pier. He's seen the display ten or twelve times now, or however long the festival has been going. The first time he was just a teenager, still in school. He thought his life was just about to start happening then. He thought that he was poised tantalisingly on the brink of life, and that any day – or even any minute – the waiting would end and life itself, the real thing, would permanently begin.

Down on the beach he zips his jacket up to the chin. It's crowded already and the street lights on the promenade cast a spooky grey glow over the sand and sea, like a ghost light. Families pick their way down the beach with prams and buggies, bickering or laughing, and boats clink in the marina, a noise like handbells ringing, but random and disconnected. Teenagers drink cans on the steps and laugh at videos. People from the festival hold walkie-talkies to their ears and stride around importantly. Aidan looks at his phone, wondering if Declan is around, or Richie, or any of the gang from work, but no one's put anything in the group chat. It's cold again this year. He puts his phone away and rubs his hands.

Pauline is already walking toward him by the time he sees her, meaning she has seen him first. She's wearing a big oversized fleece that drops down almost to her knees. Her hair is pushed back from her forehead by a hairband again.

So you do have days off, she says.

I actually just finished, he says. But I'm off tomorrow.

Can I watch the fireworks with you or are you with someone?

He immediately likes this question. Turning the question over in his mind only seems to reveal additional angles from which it can be admired.

No, I'm on my own, he says. We can watch together, yeah.

She stands beside him and rubs her arms in a pantomime of being cold. He looks at her, wondering if the pantomime demands some kind of response from him.

I'm sorry I was such a mess the other night, she says. When was that? Last week, or whenever. I think Declan was annoyed afterwards.

Was he?

Did he say anything to you about it?

Me, no, says Aidan. We don't really talk about things.

The lights overhead go down and the beach is in darkness. Around them people are moving, huddling, saying things, taking out their phones and shining torches, and then at the end of the pier the fireworks begin. A line of golden sparks shoots upward into the sky and ends in a coloured point: first pink, then blue, then pink again, casting its brief hypnotic colour on the sand and water. Then a whistling noise, low as a breath, and above them in the sky, exploding outward, blooms like flowers, red and yellow and then green, leaving soft glimmering fronds of gold light behind. A dark sky afterward, and smoke. Cheering and applause from the people around them. Fragments of conversation. Phone screens lit in the darkness. Then it begins again. When the fireworks burst, it's silent colour and light at first, and seconds later the noise: a loud crack like something breaking, or a deep low booming noise that goes into the chest. Aidan can see the tiny missiles flying upward hissing into the sky from the pier, tiny and dark, almost invisible, and then shattering outward into fragments of light, glittering like pixels, bright white fading to yellow and then gold to darker gold and then black. It's the darker gold, just before black, which he finds most beautiful: a low ember colour, darker than a glowing coal, and fading. Finally, so high above they have to crane their necks to see the whole shape, three dazzling yellow fireworks, consuming the sky, eating the whole darkness, the size of the world. Then it's over. The street lights come back up.

Beside him Pauline is rubbing her face and nose with her hands. Cold again. Aidan realises, obscurely, that a lot depends now on Pauline having enjoyed the fireworks – that if she didn't enjoy them, if she thought they were boring, not only will he no longer like her, but he will no longer have enjoyed them either, in retrospect, and something good will be dead. He says nothing. Along with everyone else they turn back and leave the beach. It's only possible to walk at one speed, the speed of the crowd, which seems like the slowest and least comfortable speed at which it's possible for humans to move. Even at this pace Aidan keeps bumping into people, small children keep running out unexpectedly in front of him, and prams need to move past and people in wheelchairs. Pauline stays close by him still, and at the top of the promenade she asks if he'll walk her home. He says sure.

She's staying in one of the houses on the seafront. He knows the street, it's where all the holiday homes are, with glass walls facing the ocean. As they walk, the rest of the crowd begins to fall away behind them. When they reach her street it's just the two of them alone in silence. There's so much he doesn't know about Pauline – so much, it strikes him with a different and slightly surprising emphasis, that he would like to know – that it's impossible to begin asking questions. He doesn't know her surname, or where she's from, what she does all day, who her family are. He doesn't know what age she is. Or how she came to know Declan, or how well she knows him.

You know, as to what you were saying the other night, says Aidan, I actually did sleep with a guest at the hotel once. I wouldn't go telling Declan about that because he doesn't approve of that kind of thing.

Pauline's eyes flash up at him. Who was the guest? she says.

I don't know, a woman staying on her own. She was a little bit older, maybe in her thirties.

And was it a good experience? Or bad?

It wasn't great, says Aidan. Not that the sex was bad but more that I felt bad about it, like it was the wrong thing to do.

But the sex was good.

It was okay. I mean, I'm sure it was fine, I don't even remember it now. Something at the time made me think maybe she was married. But I don't know for a fact, I just thought it at the time.

Why did you do it? says Pauline.

He goes quiet for a few seconds. I don't know, he says. I was hoping you wouldn't ask that.

What do you mean?

You just seem like someone who understands these things. But when you ask that it makes me feel like I did something weird.

She stops walking and puts her hand on a gatepost, which must be hers. He stops walking too. Behind them is a large house with big windows, set back from the street by a garden, and all the lights are switched off.

I don't think it's weird, she says. I used to have a boyfriend who was married. And I knew his wife – not well or anything but I did know her. I'm not asking why you did it because I think it's sick you would sleep with someone who was married. I suppose I just wonder, why do we do things that we don't really want to do? And I thought you might have an answer, but it's okay if you don't. I don't either.

Right. Well, that makes me feel better. Not that I'm happy you were in a bad situation, but I feel better that I'm not the only one.

Are you in a bad situation now?

No, he says. Now I would say, I am in no situation at all. I feel like my life basically isn't happening. I think if I dropped dead the only people who would care are the people who would have to cover my shifts. And they wouldn't even be sad, they'd just be annoyed.

Pauline frowns. She rubs the gatepost under her hand like she's thinking.

Well, I don't have that problem, she says. I think in my case there's too much happening. Everyone always wants things from me. At this point everyone I've ever met seems to want something or another. I feel like if I dropped dead they'd probably cut my body up into pieces and sell it at an auction.

You mean like those people you were with, at the hotel.

She shrugs. She rubs her arms again. She asks him if he wants to come inside and he says yes.

The house is large and, though furnished, appears curiously empty. The ceilings are high up and far away. Pauline leaves the keys on the hall table and walks through the house switching lights on in a seemingly random fashion. They reach the living room and she sits down on a gigantic green corner sofa, with a flat surface so large it resembles a bed, but with sofa cushions at the back. There is no television and the bookshelves are bare. He sits down on the couch but not right beside her.

Do you live here on your own? he says.

She looks around vaguely, as if she doesn't know what he means by 'here'.

Oh, she says. Well, only for now.

How long is now?

Everyone always asks questions like that. Don't you start.

Everyone wants to know what I'm doing and how long I'm doing it for. I'd like to be really alone for a while and for no one to know where I was or when I was coming back. And maybe I wouldn't come back at all.

She stands up from the sofa and asks if he would like a drink. Unnerved by her previous speech, about going somewhere alone and never returning, which seems in a way like a metaphor, he just shrugs.

I have a bottle of whiskey, she says. But I don't want you to think I have a drinking problem. Someone gave it to me as a present, I didn't buy it myself. Would you have even a small half-glass and I'll have one? But if you don't want one I won't have one either.

I'll have a glass, yeah, he says.

She walks out of the room, not through a door but an open archway. The house is large and confusingly laid out, so he can't tell where she's gone or how far away.

If you want to be alone, he says aloud, I can go.

She reappears in the archway almost instantly. What? she says.

If you want to be alone like you were saying, he repeats. I don't want to intrude on you.

Oh, I only meant that— philosophically, she says. Were you listening to me? That's your first mistake. Everything I say is nonsense. Your brother knows how to deal with me, he never listens. I'll be back in a second.

She goes away again. He wipes his hands down on his jeans. What does it mean that Declan 'knows how to deal with' Pauline? Should Aidan ask? Maybe this is his opening to ask. She returns with two half-full tumblers, hands him one, and then settles down on the sofa beside him, slightly closer alongside him than where she had been sitting previously, though still not touching. They sip the whiskey. It's not something Aidan would ever drink of his own volition, but it tastes fine.

I'm sorry about your mother, says Pauline. Declan told me she passed away.

Yeah. Thanks.

They pause. Aidan takes another, larger sip of whiskey.

You're seeing a lot of Declan, are you? he says.

He's sort of my car friend. I mean he's my only friend who has a car. He's very nice, he's always driving me places. And he usually just ignores me when I say silly things. I think he thinks I'm a terrible woman. He wasn't impressed with me the other night when I asked you those vulgar questions. But you're his baby brother, he thinks you're very innocent.

Aidan pays special attention to the fact that she has used the word 'friend' more than once in connection with Declan. He feels it can only have one meaning – a thought that makes him feel good. Does he? he replies. I don't know what he thinks of me.

He said he didn't know if you were gay or straight, says Pauline.

Ah, well. As I said, I don't talk about things with him.

You've never brought a girlfriend home.

You've got the advantage of me here, Aidan says. He's telling you all about me and I don't know anything about you.

She smiles. Her teeth are extremely white and perfect, unrealistic-looking, almost blue.

What do you want to know? she says.

Well, I'm curious what brings you to live here. I don't think you're from here.

That's what you're curious about? Good grief. I'm starting to think you really are innocent.

That's not very nice, says Aidan.

She looks wounded for a moment, looks into her glass, and says sadly: What made you think I was nice?

He doesn't think he can answer this question. In truth he doesn't think of her as particularly nice, he just thinks of niceness as a general standard to which everyone accepts they can be held.

She puts her empty glass down on the coffee table and sits back on the couch. Your life isn't as bad as you think it is, she says.

Well, neither is yours, he replies.

How should you know?

Everyone wants your attention all the time, so what? says Aidan. If you hated it so much you could fuck off on your own somewhere, what's to stop you?

She tilts her head to one side, places a hand lightly under her chin. Move to a remote seaside town, you mean? she says. Live the quiet life – maybe settle down with a nice country boy who works hard for a living. Is that what you had in mind?

Oh, fuck off.

She gives a light, irritatingly musical laugh.

I don't want anything from you, he says.

Then what are you doing here?

He puts his glass down. You asked me to come in, he says. You asked if we could watch the fireworks together, remember? And then you asked me to walk home with you, and then you asked me inside. And I'm the one who's inserting myself into your life, am I? I never wanted anything from you.

She seems to consider this, looking grave. Finally she says: I thought you liked me.

What does that mean? So if I liked you that means something bad about me?

Irrelevantly she replies: I liked you.

He now feels utterly confused as to why they seem to be arguing, confused to the point of abrupt despair. Right, he says. Look, I'm going to go.

By all means.

He experiences this parting with her – this parting he himself announced spontaneously and called into existence – as an excruciating ordeal, almost a physical pain. He can't quite believe he's going through with it, actually standing upright from the sofa and turning away toward the door they entered through. Why is everything so strange now? At what point did his relations with Pauline begin to violate the ordinary rules of social contact? It started normally enough. Or did it? He still doesn't even know if she's his brother's girlfriend.

She doesn't rise from the couch to see him out. He has to make his way through the half-lit, cavernous house alone, fumbling through dark hallways and at one point a dazzlingly bright dining room toward the front door. He can't remember how far they walked into the house together. Why did she say that, about settling down with a 'nice country boy'? She was just trying to provoke him. But why? She knows nothing about his life. Why does he even think about her then? At this moment, reaching the front door of Pauline's house, with its glazed glass reflecting back at him an unrecognisable image which he knows to be his own face, this strikes Aidan as the question without an answer.

———

Several weeks later he's in the back room trying to find a continental power adapter for a guest upstairs, when Lydia comes in saying someone at reception wants him. Wants what? he says. Wants you, Lydia says. They're asking for you. Aidan closes the drawer containing the hotel's selection of adapters and, as if in a dream now or in a video game, his actions under the control of some higher intelligence, he stands up and follows Lydia out of the back room, toward the front desk. He already knows, before he sees or hears Pauline, that she will be there waiting for him. And she is. She's wearing a dress made from what looks like very soft, fine cloth. An older man is standing beside her with his arm around her waist. Aidan just notices all this.

Alright, Aidan says. How can I help?

We're looking for a room, says the man.

Pauline touches her nose with her fingertips. The man swats her arm and says: You're making it worse. Look. It's going to start bleeding again.

It is bleeding, she says.

She sounds drunk. Aidan can see her fingers are bloodied when she draws them away from her face. He bends over the computer at the desk but does not immediately open the room reservations interface. He swallows and pretends to click something else, actually just clicking nothing. Is Lydia watching him? She's at the desk, just a little way to his right, but he can't tell if she's looking.

For how many nights? Aidan says.

One, says the man. Tonight.

They're not going to have anything at such short notice, says Pauline.

Well, let's see, says the man.

If you'd told me you were coming, I could have arranged something, she says.

Relax, says the man.

Aidan swallows again. He's conscious of a kind of throbbing sensation inside his head, like the flicking of a light, on and off. He moves the mouse around the screen in a show of efficiency and then, impulsively, pretends to type something although there is no keyboard input open on screen. He's certain Lydia must be watching him. Finally he straightens up from the computer and looks at the man.

No, I'm sorry, he says. We don't have any rooms available tonight.

The man stares at him. Lydia's looking over at him too.

You don't have any rooms? the man says. Every room in the hotel is taken? In the middle of April?

I told you, Pauline says.

Sorry, says Aidan. We can get you something next week, if you'd like.

The man moves his mouth like he's laughing, but no laugh comes out. He removes his hand from Pauline's waist, lifts it up in the air and lets it drop against his own body. Aidan is careful not to look at Pauline or Lydia at all.

No rooms, the man repeats. All booked out. This hotel.

I'm sorry I can't help, Aidan says.

The man looks at Pauline.

Well, what do you want me to do? she says.

In response the man lifts his arm up again to point at Aidan.

Is this your boyfriend? the man says.

Oh, don't be absurd, says Pauline. Are you going to develop paranoia now on top of everything else?

You know him, the man says. You asked for him.

Pauline shakes her head, dabs delicately at her nose, and flashes a kind of apologetic smile at Aidan and Lydia across the desk. I'm sorry, she says. We'll get out of your way. Can I ask you to call a couple of taxis? I'd really appreciate it.

Oh, we can't share a taxi? the man says.

Coldly now, Pauline replies: We're going in opposite directions.

Under his breath, with a kind of frozen grin on his face, the man says audibly: I don't believe it. I don't believe it. Then he turns around and walks toward the large double doors of the hotel entrance. Lydia picks up the phone to call the taxi company. Pauline, without any interruption to her demeanour, lifts the hotel pen from the desk, takes the pad of paper, writes something down and then tears the sheet from the pad. She takes out some money, encloses it in the note and pushes it across the desk toward Aidan. Looking only at Lydia she smiles and says: Thanks so much. Then she exits, following the man through the double doors.

When the doors swing shut, Lydia is still on the phone. Aidan sits down and stares into space. He hears Lydia saying goodbye, then he hears the faint click of the receiver replaced in its cradle. He just sits there. Lydia finds the note on the desk and nudges it in Aidan's direction with the end of a pen, like she doesn't want to touch it.

She left this for you, says Lydia.

I don't want it.

Lydia uses the pen to flick open the note.

There's a hundred euro in here, she says.

That's okay, he says. You take it.

For a few seconds Lydia says nothing. Aidan just sits staring blankly straight ahead. Presently, as if making up her mind, Lydia says: I'll put it with the tips. She wrote you a note as well, do you not want that? I think it just says thank you.

You can leave it, he says. Or, actually, give it to me.

Lydia gives it to him. Without looking at it, he places it in his pocket. Then he rises from the chair to return to the back room, where he has to find the power adapter for the guest upstairs. He won't see Pauline again before she leaves town. She'll be gone in just a few days' time.

The Lexicon of Babies

Sinéad Gleeson

The Palimpsest Council was outraged. There was spluttering and shouting and much stamping of feet, because they knew, of course, that they might be the last generation to have actual feet. There was no mistaking that this was an incendiary turn of events. The council had only been in existence for two years but had attempted to preside fairly over all the changes in this new world. Everything had been so singular up until then, but now every birth was like buying a pack of football stickers and tearing open the wrapper. Still, each set of parents was coochy-cooed in the bliss of their own progeny, whatever it turned out to be. From the eel-slick birth to the big reveal, they were heart-skip happy. Mostly, anyway.

No one knows how it started. How the country's howling babes, all soft folds and blue eyes, were replaced by letters. Actual L-E-T-T-E-R-S-letters. Fonts instead of fontanelles. What were once pudgy, obstreperous infants now came into the world as life-sized letters. Instead of having a boy, girl, or non-binary infant, women were giving birth to the alphabet, or Lexicon Babies as the Palimpsest Council called them. The first case was reported in Cloughjordan, Tipperary; then Inistioge,

Skeheenarinky, Ballinafad, Ringaskiddy, and a cluster of births in the Burren. One woman had twins close to the Irish border, and was in all the papers because one of the babies was a U, causing a resurgence in headline puns and sectarian tension. There was conflict about the Irish-language alphabet, which has fewer letters than its English counterpart. Gaeilgeoirs up in arms as the shadow of colonialism rose up like a famine ghost.

Some of the mothers bragged about the number of stitches they had.

– Well, mine was W, so you can *imagine* . . .

– D was huge. Tore me to pieces, but you know, *it was worth it.*

Their partners stayed quiet, and remembered how much they were shouted at in the delivery ward. The robust physiognomy of the new letter-babies meant that they could eat from birth and did not require milk. Breastfeeding became a thing of the past, an old ritual like burning sage or using a payphone. There was a monument to cabbage leaves in the old part of the town. Breast pumps dumped at the doors of museums. On school tours, in later years, children passed them in glass cases and assumed that they were once used as torture devices in wars.

Everyone wanted X, Q and Z babies. Their size, their complicated shape, was a physical declaration that the mothers had suffered. A demonstrative martyrdom. Vowel babies were not so in demand. There were more of them, and they were considered common. Coupled with the ease of their births, they become a source of derision for the mothers of consonants.

Some things, of course, stayed the same. The women competed in that way new mothers often do, in the desperation of their virtuousness and the projected high achievements of their offspring. M babies, all angular hairpin lines, were excellent dancers and were duly enrolled in ballet and experimental tap classes. L babies were naturally suited to yoga. The babies at the latter end of the alphabet were more cerebral – no one knew why – and were often found in the library, munching on the corners of large-print books. The Y babies had a talent for music, thanks to their forked limbs. Some played instruments, though drums were particularly popular, necessitating the purchase of expensive ear protectors. The babies also had a penchant for hip-hop: Kurtis Blow, Wu-Tang Clan, Missy Elliott.

Here are some more things about the babies.

They could walk from birth, standing up like jelly-legged antelopes in the hospital. They tired easily though, and still required lordly transportation in buggies. Some of the babies had top-of-the-range prams. Souped-up fancy models in titanium and neon shades that were only slightly smaller than motorbikes. Most people could not justify the expense, but parents of M and W – wide babies – had no choice. I and A parents, aware of the stigma around vowels, of how they were looked down on for their ordinariness and frequency, knew that their offspring would have a harder time. Vowel parents deemed college attendance essential if they were to have any kind of life. They carted their babies around in boxes from supermarkets, saving on pram expenses that they could put towards the fees. That was on the assumption that college fees, or indeed college, would still exist when the babies were of an age to go. The less favoured letters simply had to work harder in a world that preferred their elite alphabetical peers. The discrimination was meted out in small, icy moments;

in garden centres and coffee shop queues. Everything was changing, but the unspoken consensus among adults was that it was important to carry on as before.

The babies had no pronouns. Not in the spirit of modernity or fluidity, mind, but because the English alphabet had no gender, and the council was glad of small mercies amid the crisis. There was no reason to dress babies in pink or blue now, but these tiny dervishes were inveterate consumers, their mothers attuned to sartorial trends. This season's colour was taupe, so all the babies looked naked from a distance. Or as if they were wearing some weird extra layer of baby skin. Of course the babies still had hearts and lungs. Each one still shat like a cannon, cried from hunger or tiredness, or when bulbs of tiny teeth sprouted in its mouth.

On the day it happened, the Palimpsest Council had disbanded for the summer recess. Two months of coastal trips and cloudless skies, the motorways centipeded with cars, beaches buzzing with mothers slathering suncream on little B and Y. It was when the city was mostly drained of its population that the mothers of the Z babies (*Zed*, not *Zee*) decided that *they* deserved their own section of the park. The mothers felt that there was something about the last letter of the alphabet that imbued it with both a spiritual and a political significance. They had, after all, pored over Greek history and civilisation, and knew well that Omega meant 'great'. These babies were gods. Destined for greatness. Who could argue with what history and etymology had determined? The Z mothers set their plan in motion by cordoning off a slab of green for their precious offspring. A little grass suite, with an ostentatious slide, a specially adapted roundabout, and an odd little boat for the Z babies to lie down in when they needed a nap. These babies considered prams beneath them and each was carried around in a sedan.

It was at this point – later known as 'Parkgate' – that the full extent of what lay ahead became clear.

The Z mothers decided that vowels should not be allowed to mix with consonants.

They waved around certificates in Greek history bought online, muttering about vowel babies being the equivalent of Alpha, the lowest-value letter. The segregation was subtle at first, but there was resistance, and Z husbands were coerced into forming a militia of fathers to enforce it. The babies collectively thumb-sucked while the parents schemed. It took just days before congregations of Es and As constituted an act of assembly. The consonant mothers felt some unease, which they swatted away, guiltily glad that *their* babies were not the subject of persecution. But marrow-deep they knew this was wrong, and before long antipathy was replaced by molten fury. They'd had years of inequality themselves, and here was the chance to claw something back, to reach out to their vowel brothers and sisters. To shout loudly in the street. The babies' neurons were also expanding. Each hippocampus was growing, and the babies – upon realising how little power their singularity had – began to seek out other letters. The formerly downtrodden vowels were suddenly treated with respect, as comrades-in-arms. Who were the Z babies to think that *they* were better than everyone else? Injustice rattled in their bellies like coins in a jar. The newly united non-Z offspring leapt into action. Large demonstrations were organised. Gangs of ostracised babies began to assemble on the streets. The city centre was awash with the jagged corners of M and K and E. The mothers walked respectfully alongside them, laden down with changing bags and GoPros: in case of arrest, they'd at least have their own version of events on record. The babies were nothing if not enthusiastic about civil disobedience. Some of the older toddlers looted the pram shops; others were dressed in black, wearing berets. One or two had sunglasses and covered their faces with scarves.

Meanwhile, the Z mothers began to dress their babies in custom uniforms with gold epaulettes. En masse, they resembled an army of tiny Francos. They hired a composer to write a new national anthem, combining elements of Wagner and the Amen break. On the once-immaculate streets, the non-Z babies began to mobilise and arrange themselves. They swapped positions and – with some spelling advice from their mothers and the handful of fathers who showed up – began to spell out their disaffection.

W-E   P-R-O-T-E-S-T
W-E   P-R-O-T-E-S-T
W-E   P-R-O-T-E-S-T

Line after line marched by:

O-V-E-R-C-O-M-E

T-O-G-E-T-H-E-R

N-O   H-A-T-E

The past froideur between vowels and consonants was replaced by a solidarity, aware as they keenly were that it was not possible to spell 'Freedom', 'Protest' or 'Shame' without using A and O and E. The babies' shared hatred of the Z babies' hierarchy united them. There had been recent rumours that mothers, upon discovering that they were carrying vowels, were aborting them. This was denounced as nonsense propaganda by the more hardcore among the Z camp, but still the rumours persisted.

A woman called Jane (not her real name) became the de facto leader of the Z mothers, and had a swish office over at their HQ. She had two Z babies and spoke very loudly all the time. She was fond of saying things like: We will never let their inferiority get in the way of our right to protest! Jane-not-her-real-name spent lots of money on posters and flyers and roped in her computer friends to help with online ads and algorithms. Certain TV news programmes started showing only Z-baby news. One small independent channel, operating out of an old shipping container, aired documentaries about the reality of life for non-Z babies, until Jane-not-her-real-name shut it down. She talked of war and threatened to separate mothers and babies; to send dissenters to former holiday camps and old convents. On a quiet morning, a group of vowel and consonant mothers and babies were pepper-sprayed and put in cages after a peaceful protest outside Z baby HQ.

The city felt cyclonic. A frenzy of discrimination had been whipped up, and all the usual bastions of good behaviour – kindness, compassion, consideration – spiralled around, lost in its dark funnel. People stopped going to work. Food rations began. Electricity was shut down at 10 p.m. every night. Helicopters hovered, blades chop-chop-chopping until the small hours. Searchlights swept the streets as if desperately seeking out stricken sailors. But the world was watching, on propagandist channels, and footage smuggled out; on old digital cameras, and out-of-date smartphones.

Something was changing. Not just because summer arrived early, bringing with it the smell of heat-soaked garbage. The Z babies grew hot in their uniforms, the pomp now replaced by sweat and chafing. They had time to think, in the shade of their sedans, full-nappied and parboiled. With their newly accelerated sentience, they could sense the injustice. The badness of it all. They were still wobbly as little drunks, gurgling and spit-bubbled about the mouth. But they knew that they were being propelled towards a movement where everyone else was making the decisions. It was as though their mothers had rouged up their cheeks, dressed them as cowgirls and entered them into a talent competition against their will.

On the kind of Tuesday that usually wouldn't warrant an entry in the Palimpsest Council log, something finally *did* happen. A mother-called-Aoife came forward with a revelation. She talked her way past security at the Z baby HQ and made her way to the eighth floor, where the big brass mommas were, the ones who knew the president and politicians; the ones who had started everything that day in the park. In the lift, the mother-called-Aoife had second thoughts. She peered into her buggy and the coils of her gut turned, as though she'd been fired, or told *it's not good news*. But the baby was curled up, blissful and oblivious. The floors flashed by in red pixels, 6 . . . 7 . . . 8 . . .

PING

The lift opened its jaws. Head held high, she forced her shoulders into an iron line, adding a swagger to her hips. Barely five steps in, the Z mothers began to rise from their desks exchanging looks, their bodies turning in unison, an involuntary act of curiosity. The mother-called-Aoife knew that Jane-not-her-real-name was short and protuberant. A sort of spud of a woman with an awkward side-parting that was, in an unfortunate act of mirroring, a little on the Hitler side. She manoeuvred the 360-degree wheels between the desks. The mothers encircled her as she scooped up her baby and strapped it in a practised manoeuvre across her breasts, which were now, she noticed, leaking like tears.

The mothers stared at her. The infant itself was ignorant of the eyeballs arrowing up and down its small shape: a means of assessment. It was almost a C, except the lower part looked as though it had been straightened out on a smith's forge. Domino-dot eyes moved over the baby, not computing. Was this some sort of misshapen O? Had there been some negligence at birth? A foetal anomaly?

Jane-not-her-real-name pointed at something and all the women stared. It looked like a piece of shoelace, or perhaps part of the elaborate sling the woman had buttressed across her body. But the string appeared to be a solid object, in and of itself. *I have a purpose*, it declared. The string-type object was attached to something that was separate from the baby. Round in shape, a mini-globe. Skin the same colour – a baby shade – made of tissue or mucus. But its purpose was undeniably umbilical, joining the two parts of the strange baby together.

The mother-called-Aoife smiled a little, a mix of pride and fear.

– It's the first one.

The mothers covened around.

– Unique, the doctors said.

Jane-not-her-real-name shuffled through her memory, pulling files from boxes. She knew this type of symbol. What was it again?

The mother-called-Aoife's smile froze. The corners of her mouth slipped. There were quiet tears, soon replaced by choking sobs and snotty rivulets.

– I don't know what to do. Who'll even want it? It's not a Z, and it's not a letter. It's not even a fucking vowel.

At this point, she began to wail. A sort of tribal sound. A rainforest lament. The mothers looked at one another. The feeling in the room was hard to gauge. The Z mothers could not tell if this stranger was friend or foe. The other mothers would either embrace or shun her and her baby.

Or they would see an opportunity.

– See, I thought if I came to you, we could figure something out, y'know?

She hiccupped in a crying-too-hard way.

– Any time it joins in a protest people will assume that it's being rhetorical, or undermining the message. When there's no baby like this one it's . . . well . . .

The baby emitted a soft gurgle, its new-baby smell all nappy and talc. Someone handed the mother-called-Aoife a glass of water, and her ululations finally subsided, a reverse flood. She clutched the hook and dot of her infant protectively. The light was changing and there was a finality to everything, not just the day. Weeks had gone by. It was exhausting to feel that superior all the time. The world was complex. A last train rumbled on the viaduct outside, and the Z mothers, in one collective thought, began to realise that they could choose hope or exploit the situation, and that their Z babies were – for all their supremacy, their zigzag angles – only letters. Heck, they were a less complicated version of W turned on its side, if one thought about it. They were just babies. Tiny noise machines that compacted food and defecated. Loud compost bins with limbs. Was this really worth it, all this strife? Some of the mothers realised they felt uneasy. And tired.

In the days that followed the coup, Question Mark baby, now known as Supreme Majesty QM, Chancellor Question Mark, or simply The Sovereign, took to the throne (though it was more of a gilded highchair with wipeable surfaces) with the blessing of the Palimpsest Council. Instead of a crown, there was a jewelled sunhat with matching bib, bearing all the letters of the alphabet. The Z hierarchy was abolished, and the mothers of Z babies imprisoned and forcibly sterilised. The vowels were now treated fairly in almost all walks of life. Lexical nepotism was gone. Rumours that the Q and M babies were given favourable treatment because of their shared alphabetical heritage with the sovereign were hushed up. No more Question Mark babies were born, but a marriage was arranged for The Sovereign upon reaching adulthood, with the only Ampersand born to date. The mothers learned to know their place, to understand that their incubatory role was a divine gift bestowed on them. That they should be grateful and silent, revelling in bountiful joy if they were lucky enough to get pregnant again. The babies got along well enough, without all the forced hegemony. They swapped toys, caused a run on avocados, and knew in the tiny bird hearts beating in their alphabetical chests that they were the centre of everything.

Alienation

Arja Kajermo

It was still dark and something had woken me up. I put out my hand for my mobile. It was 3.17. Too early to get up. I would have to stay in bed at least till five. I tried my old trick: *Just lie with your eyes closed until sleep comes.* Sometimes it works. Even when you wake between three and four, which is the Hour of the Wolf when everything seems impossible and anxiety takes a hold of you. It is when you are at your lowest, the hour when people whose lives are ebbing die. I know, we are all of us dying, every living moment. I closed my eyes. No wolves in Ireland. I just lay there dozing until the gulls started screaming down the chimney at dawn and it was safe to get up.

The house is unnaturally quiet in the mornings now that the children are grown up and have left home. They both chose to go to university as far away from Dublin as possible. It's good that they are independent but I miss them. When they were around I had a title. I was Mother. It's the only official title I have. I am *Mother*, I reside in the *Family Home*. There was much legal wrangle to get to live in the family home with the kids. Now, with them gone, I don't have a title, I am 'Yer Wan in the Corner House', and that's a description, not a title.

The dog was curled at the foot of the stairs with her nose up her bum. She opened one eye then shut it again. As I stepped over her I noticed an envelope on the hall carpet. Bit early for post. When I picked it up, I saw it was grubby and had no stamp. Must have been delivered by hand last night. I tore it open and there was a handwritten note in pencil. It read:

We know you are the person or persons who illeagally dumped bags of rubbish in the garden of 86, Brian Boru Avenue we just want you to know that we have reported you to the Gardai and Dublin City Council Litter Warden. Identify yourself immidiatly and take your rubbish back before this matter escalates or we will Prosecute. The Residents.

The anger flooded up in me. But . . . poor spelling? Faulty logic? Should I ignore these unfortunates? No, this was outrageous. Besides, I had an appointment at a hairdresser later and would be passing Brian Boru Avenue anyway. But first, coffee.

After a few cups of black and bitter coffee I got dressed and hurried down the road, note in hand. I counted the numbers in Brian Boru Avenue until I found what must be number 86. There was no number on the door, of course. People are secretive around here. It looked like an old person's house with thick dusty lace curtains, a flaking door, a tiny patch of weedy lawn. Old people are often the most aggressive so I wasn't looking forward to the encounter, but I rang the bell anyway and waited. Then I rang it again. There was an almost imperceptible twitch of the lace curtain but whoever was in there was not going to open the door. I started to walk away, not sure if I felt deflated or relieved.

The next-door neighbour was leaving her house. I knew her to see and had often exchanged a few words in the street with her when we met walking our dogs. Her little terrier always barked at me. The woman yanked the lead. 'Stop it! Stop it, Prince!' She sounded as if she didn't mean it. It made the dog bark more. Over the yapping, I asked her did she know anything about the rubbish supposedly dumped in her neighbour's garden.

'Somebody dumped two bags of rubbish in poor Dymphna's garden,' the neighbour said, 'and she an elderly woman. She was very upset. Her son got the notes out.'

I held up the note. 'Did the whole neighbourhood get a note like this?'

'Oh no, not everyone! Only the foreigners, the Polish families around the corner and you! Aren't people awful?'

I scrutinised the woman's face. Was it 'Aren't *foreigners* awful?' she meant? But there was no sign of the passive aggression that is the speciality of people here. The way they smile crooked and look at you sideways and lob the insult into you. And you jump up like a well-trained dog and catch it and stand there not knowing what to do with it, so you just walk away with it between your teeth. But there was nothing but innocence in the woman's face. I agreed that people are awful. Also agreed that it was nice that the rain had held up and yes, another fine day by the look of it. The terrier started barking again and hurling itself at me, nearly choking itself.

I went on my way down the avenue and turned the corner. Coming towards me were three Nigerian women that I often see walking together in the area. Today they were all dressed up in colourful African fabrics and artfully tied headscarves and laughing and talking loudly. They were probably on their way to a party or to church. Much as I admire them, I find them strange. Like teenage boys they seem to think that a person on her own has to give way to three persons walking abreast. I wondered would they drop into single file just for once. I didn't think they would so I flattened myself against the railings and let them pass. I smiled and nodded. One of them smiled back. They walked on and I looked at them from behind. They were like fully rigged galleon ships, wide hulls bouncing. I envy them the way they occupy their space without apologising. They are big and proud of it and they don't give way. *They* don't flatten or diminish themselves like I do all the time in every way. I fear attention in case my foreignness attracts hostility. They glory in being noticed. I bet that when they ask 'Does my bum look big in this?' what they want to hear is 'Yes, your bum looks huge in that!'

We are the *dubhghaill* and the *fionnghall,* the 'dark foreigners' and the 'fair foreigner'. Those words are two of a handful I know in Irish. Most Irish people don't know many more. They grieve the loss of their language, but most of them won't learn to speak it.

The *dubhghaill* will do better than me because they will happily integrate but not assimilate. They are here for a good reason. They have decided that life is better here. There is probably less corruption here than in Nigeria and more opportunities. Their choice makes sense. While I was thinking this, one of the women looked back at me. It was the one who had smiled at me earlier. Now she was laughing. I raised my hand to give her a wave but instead I blushed and looked at the ground pretending I had dropped something. Then I turned around and walked on and thought of the folly of me being here in Ireland. I left a perfectly good place that was far better than here even though it was in the mess that is Mitteleuropa. My homeland has always had armies trampling over it, coming from the east and going west and coming from the west and going east. Tatars, Ottomans, the Swedes came and looted and left, then Hitler, Stalin, you name them, they have all been. The borders have shifted and changed. Nowhere could you put a spade in the soil without digging up cartridges and sword blades and cannonballs, bullets, all the bits and pieces from the warmongers' chests.

Best left buried and forgotten now. Many displaced peoples have made their home in that region. It shows in their faces: a hint of the Hun here, the sly eyes of the Slav there, broad Baltic faces, a touch of the haughty Magyar, the hard-headed German physiognomy also in evidence. All rubbing along, all blow-ins who have made their home there, kept the peace, traded, intermarried.

But I became infatuated with this island and its easy-going people (as it seemed then, how wrong I was!). There is something special about islands: utopian Atlantis, Durrell's idyllic Corfu, all the Greek islands really – and magical Ireland in its splendid isolation and the mist to hide in. The Dutch and the Germans especially are suckers for the Irish magic. They drive around the Wild Atlantic Way in their Mercs until they find the perfect damp falling-apart cottage looking out over the sea. It is so *echt*, so genuine. But it needs a new bathroom with a proper shower and a big kitchen with Shaker-style cupboards and an energy-efficient turf-burning cast-iron stove to sit by and look out of panorama windows and admire the view of the sea. That's when the disenchantment sets in. Nothing works here, they complain. The plumber plumbed the washing machine in back to front, the tiler tiled the tiles in crooked and then they fell off the wall, and the electrician never turned up because he only works for local people and friends of relatives, not random strangers. And the locals break your windows because you bring too many friends in from Berlin one after the other and they think you have orgies. Go home, you big eejits, if you're so homesick for order and efficiency and good workmanship. You won't find it here because you can't just buy it, it has to be bartered for and you have nothing to barter with. You will never be included in the 'we' that islanders call themselves.

But I have my own reasons to feel aggrieved. My husband left one evening to go for a pint. 'Just the one,' he said, but he never came back. I had an inkling where he had gone but I wasn't going there looking for him.

Without a husband I was nothing. I had nothing, no Residence Permit, no work permit, and all the utility bills were in his name. Without a utility bill in my name I had no identity. I had never imagined that a household bill was valid as ID. I had neglected these things because I had been at home having two babies, twelve months between them. And now all I had were the children that I clung to as to life itself. They were life itself!

I thought back then I should get the Residence Permit sorted first. I didn't want to go to the 'Aliens Office' up at Dublin Castle, where it was then, where the Gardaí didn't have much to do and often amused themselves by playing good-

humoured cat-and-mouse with the aliens. Good cop, bad cop
– that sort of thing.

Instead I went to see a solicitor and asked him to make
enquiries on my behalf about my status without mentioning
my name. A week later he had an answer for me: 'Your reasons
for residing in the State have ceased.' I was stunned. I wouldn't
get a Residence Permit even though there was no divorce
in Ireland, and I was still married. And I couldn't apply for
passports for the children without my husband's signature. He
had already told me 'I'm signing nuttin'.'

I went to the embassy of my country to ask could I leave
Ireland with my two children. Could the embassy help me?
The official stroked his narrow tie while he scrutinised me.
Then he told me coldly that the embassy could not interfere
with the rights a father has over his own natural children. My
question seemed to have touched a nerve. 'So in a country that
doesn't recognise divorce, a husband can have his foreign wife
deported and keep the children?' He told me he didn't make
the laws here.

So I just stayed on without a Residence Permit and waited
for a knock on the door but nobody came to deport me. I was
left to make my own arrangements. At least the children and
I had a roof over our heads. When the electricity was cut off
because I hadn't paid the bill, we sat in bed under a duvet and I
read them stories by candlelight. I said isn't this fun, to pretend
we are survivors after a nuclear disaster? They said no, it isn't.
So I sent word to their father to pay the bill but he answered
he had just paid the month's mortgage on the house. He wasn't
going to pay for all my outgoings as well because he couldn't
afford to run two households.

That's when I had the idea for a newspaper column, 'A Stranger in a Strange Land', where I gave a foreigner's account of Ireland under a pen name. I managed to get it published in the *Dublin Eagle* on a weekly basis. It became quite a success. My wit was described as wicked and people kept guessing who penned the column. Some said it was all stuff that everybody knew, it was what everyone had thought some time or other. But they read the column anyway. Some said one could tell it was a 'women's libber' by the way the columnist kept harping on about women's issues like contraception and divorce. Others knew it was a 'Japanese guy'. Some said the column was obviously a Myles na gCopaleen-type skit written by some local wit pretending to be a foreigner.

I was just too gormless to be a suspect. I don't know how the editor managed to keep my identity under his hat in this city where nobody can keep a secret. There was no fear of running out of material before the EU dragged Ireland out of the Middle Ages. And even after, I had enough to keep it going.

But I needed more income so I started writing romantic little vignettes from Ireland, pure paddywhackery. The pieces were syndicated for papers and magazines abroad. It was, and still is, hugely enjoyable to write these little stories. I invented a whole village where I supposedly live and where my stories are set. It is full of local 'characters' and gossiping women and quaint customs and cute donkeys that carry crates of turf. Not like the neglected animals crippled by overgrown hooves that you see in the west of Ireland. And the sheep are washed and sleep in curlers like Marie Antoinette's pet lambs. That sort of thing.

Sometimes I type away and stifle my giggles until the tears run down my face. I got into the habit of writing after midnight when the children were small and I had to wait until they were asleep. Now I can laugh out loud in my empty house, I could cackle like a witch to my heart's content, but I would frighten myself if I did.

I call my idyllic vignettes 'Postcards from the Celtic Mist' and 'Ireland, the Magic Island' and 'Backside to the Wind'. They are translated into German and Dutch, Italian and Swedish. They can't get enough of Ireland; long may it last. The German translator rang me to ask what is 'Celtic mist'. 'Mist' means 'dung' in German. That's what my vignettes are, pure shite.

When I got to the hairdresser my regular 'stylist', as they call themselves, was off sick and I was told that another stylist could fit me in. I was tempted to leave but then I would have to come back another day and I had already wound myself up for the appointment. I suffer anticipation anxiety. The dentist, the doctor, the chiropodist, they all hold their own horrors, but hairdressers are in a class of their own. They have special powers to make you feel bad about yourself: the way they make you sit in front of a mirror staring at yourself with the hair dripping and answer probing questions. So I was led to the basin to have my hair washed by a teenager on work experience. She asked was the water too hot and I said no even though it was. And then I was taken to the seat in front of the mirror. I avoided looking into it. I started to describe how I wanted my hair done, the same as before, I said, no layers, blunt here, a sloped line here, I indicated a sloped line from my neck to my chin with my hand. I accidently caught a glimpse of the stylist in the mirror. Her eyes had glazed over.

'Where do you come from?' she asked. I said that I came

from the Czech Republic. 'Originally,' I added, although it isn't strictly correct but I didn't want her to think I had come off the boat that morning. I couldn't bring myself to say that I am Czech-Slovak-Hungarian. It would have been like trying to explain the Holy Trinity to her. It would be too much. I am a mongrel, a piece of many parts, my homeland is in my head. She told me she had been on a package holiday somewhere in Eastern Europe. She couldn't remember the name of the place. The food had been crap there but drink was real cheap. 'Sounds nice,' I said, and nodded approvingly.

'I love your accent,' she said. 'Why did you come to Ireland? Are you married to an Irish guy?' Now the questions were getting harder. 'I came because the grass is greener here,' I said, and grinned so that she would know it was meant to be funny. A wrinkle appeared between her perfect eyebrows. I began to feel panicky, thinking of the unkind cut she must have in mind now. I had to repair relations fast. I said, 'I love it here, I love Ireland!' I stared at myself in horror. Or a mirror image of myself, me reversed, because what you see is not what others see. They see your face the right way round. That's why people hate their passport photo. The photo is not what they think they look like. I couldn't bear to look at my mirror image, my false face, much longer.

I declined tea or coffee and closed my eyes to indicate that I was ready for the cutting to commence.

Who's-Dead McCarthy

Kevin Barry

You'd see him coming on O'Connell Street – the hanging jaws,
the woeful trudge, the load. You'd cross the road to avoid him
but he'd have spotted you, and he would draw you into him.
The wind would travel up Bedford Row from the Shannon to
take the skin off you and add emphasis to the misery. The main
drag was the daily parade for his morbidity. Limerick, in the
bone evil of its winter, and here came Con McCarthy, haunted-
looking, in his enormous, suffering overcoat. The way he sidled
in, with the long, pale face, and the hot, emotional eyes.

'Did you hear who's dead?' he'd whisper.

Con McCarthy was our connoisseur of death. He was its
most knowing expert, its deftest elaborator. There was no
death too insignificant for his delectation. A ninety-six-year-
old poor dear in Thomondgate with the lungs papery as moths'
wings and the maplines of the years cracking her lips as she
whispered her feeble last in the night – Con would have word
of it by the breakfast, and he would be up and down the street,
his sad recital perfecting as he went.

'Elsie Sheedy?' he'd try. 'You must have known poor Elsie.
With the skaw leg and the little sparrow's chin? I suppose she

hadn't been out much this last while. She was a good age now but I mean Jesus, all the same, Elsie? Gone?'

His eyes might turn slowly upwards here, as though in trail of the ascending Elsie.

'She'd have been at the Stella Bingo often,' he'd reminisce, with the whites of the eyes showing. 'Tuesdays and Thursdays. Until the leg gave out altogether and the balance went. She used to get white-outs coming over the bridge. At one time she took the money for the tickets below at the roller disco. Inside in the little cage. Of course, that wasn't today nor yesterday.'

'Ah no, Con. No. I didn't know her.'

In truth, he might have no more than clapped eyes on the woman the odd time himself, but still he would retreat back into the folds of the overcoat, like a flowerhead closing when the sun goes in, and he was genuinely moved by the old lady's passing.

Con McCarthy's city was disappearing all around him.

———

He had a special relish, it seemed to me, for the slapstick death. He'd come sauntering along at noon of day, now almost jaunty with the sadness, the eyes wet and wide, and he'd lean into you, and he might even have to place a palm to your shoulder to steady himself against the terrible excitement of it all.

'Can you believe it?' he said. 'A stepladder?'

'Which was this, Con?'

'Did you not hear?'

'No, Con.'

'Did you not hear who's dead?'

'Who, Con? Who?'

'Charlie Small.'

'Ah, stop.'

'The way it happened?' he said, shaking his head against what was almost a grin. 'They hadn't painted the front room since 1987. Now it isn't me that's saying this, it's the man's wife is saying this, it's Betty is saying this. She could remember it was 1987 on account of her uncle, Paddy, was home for his fiftieth. He was a fitter in Earl's Court. Since dead himself. Drowned in his own fluids, apparently. Betty was a Mullane from Weston originally. They were never toppers in the lung department. Anyhow. Charlie Small says listen, it's gone beyond the thirty-year mark, we'll paint that flippin' front room. Of course Betty's delighted. We'll get a man in, she says. No, Charlie says, it's only a small room, I'll have it done before the dinner if I start after the nine in the mornin' news. Betty strides out for a tin of paint. She comes back with a class of a peach tone. Lovely. Calming, that'll be, she thinks, not knowing, God love her, what's coming next, the stepladder being dragged out from under the stairs, Charlie climbing up to the top step of it, and the man ate alive from the inside out by type-2 diabetes and weakish, I suppose, on account of it, and the next thing the dog's let in when it shouldn't be let in, and that little dog is saucy now, she always has been, and she goes harin' through the front room, a spaniel breed, unpredictable, and the tin of peach-coloured paint is sent flying and Charlie reaches out for it but the ladder's not set right and wobbles and next thing he's over and off the back of it and the neck is broke on the man.'

He shook his head with a blend that spoke curiously of tragic fate and happy awe.

'Dead on the floor before they got to him,' he said.

'Jesus Christ, Con.'

'The day nor the hour,' he said, and he walked away happily into the persistent rain.

———

He had about forty different faces. He would arrange his face to match precisely the tang or timbre of the death described. For the death of a child Con McCarthy's woe was fathoms deep and painfully genuine. An early death in adulthood brought a species of pinched grief about his temples, a migraine's whine its music. He avoided eye contact if it was a drowning that had occurred – he had an altogether dim view of the Shannon river as an utter death magnet, and he was all too often to be found down in Poor Man's Kilkee, looking out over the water, wordlessly but his lips moving, as if in silent consultation with the souls that hovered above the river, their roar at the Curragower Falls.

———

His role as our messenger of death along the length of O'Connell Street and back seemed to be of a tradition. Such a figure has perhaps always walked the long plain mile of the street and spoken the necessary words, a grim but vital player in the life of a small city. But Con McCarthy's interest in death was wide-ranging, and it vaulted the city walls, so to speak, and stretched out to the world beyond to gorge intimately upon the deaths of strangers.

'Here's one for you,' he said, leaning into me one day outside the George Hotel. 'Man in Argentina, I believe it was. Cattle farmer. Impaled on his own bull. And didn't the bull go mental after it and charged in circles around the field ninety mile an hour and the poor farmer still attached to the horns with the life bled out of him. An hour and a half before a neighbour was got over with a shotgun, that long before they shot the bull and got the misfortunate corpse off the horns. Can you imagine it? The man's wife and children were watching, apparently. Roaring out of them. They'll never be right.'

Another day, creeping up behind me, and with a soft little touch to my elbow, and then the lean-in, the soft whisper, and here was news of the famous dead . . .

'Zsa Zsa Gabor,' he said. 'Gone. Though I suppose it was nearly a release to the poor woman for a finish. Did you know she'd been five year on life support?'

'That I did not know, Con.'

'Five year. Heart attack at the end of it. Sure the poor heart would be weak as a little bird's in the woman's chest at that stage. I believe it was ninety-nine years of age she was. They're after plantin' her in a gold box outside in California. No woman deserve it more. A former Miss Hungary.'

———

Had he been exposed to death early? I wondered. Was it that some psychic wound had been opened at first glance into the void? Whatever the case, I believed that his condition was worsening. He began to move out from actual occurrences of death to consider in advance the shapes it might yet assume. Walking down the street now he was reading death into situations. He was seeing it everywhere. He had the realisation we all have but that most of us are wise enough to keep submerged – the knowledge that death always is close by. He might stop to consider a building site. He'd look up. The long, creased face would fold into a hopeless smile, and as you passed by, he'd lean in, the head slowly shaking.

'Are you watching?' he said.

'Which, Con?'

'See that scaffold above there? Are you not watching the wind on it? If that winds gets up at all, the whole lot could come down. A pole could go swingin'. Open your head and you walking down the road as quick as it'd look at you. And that would be an end to it.'

———

He walked the circuit of the three bridges every night. If you idled anywhere by the river of an evening you might take the slow rake of Con McCarthy's worried eye. He would try to have a good read of you. I met him one night on the far side of the river. He was on a bench, the water moving slowly past, the traffic scant but passing its few lights across the falling dark. Maybe it was the September of the year. That sense of turn and grim resolve about the days, the evenings.

'Did you not hear?' he said.

'Ah, which was this, Con?'

'Did you not hear who's dead?'

'Who, Con? Who?'

But this time he just grinned, as if he was playing with me,

and he let the weak-tea smile play out loosely across the river
a few moments.

'Ah, sure look,' he said. 'We're all on the way out.'

'I know, Con. I know.'

'Isn't that the truth of it? For a finish?'

'Can I talk to you seriously, Con?'

'Hah?'

'Can I ask you something?'

'What?'

'Why are you so drawn to it? To death? Why are you
always the first with the bad news? Do you not realise, Con,
that people cross the road when they see you coming? You put
the hearts sideways in us. Oh Jesus Christ, here he comes, we
think, here comes Who's-Dead McCarthy. Who has he put in
the ground for us today?'

'I can't help it,' he said. 'I find it very . . . impressive.'

'Impressive?'

'That there's no gainsaying it. That no one has the answer
to it. That we all have to face into the room with it at the end
of the day and there's not one of us can make the report after.'

I became morbidly fascinated by Con McCarthy. I asked
around the town about him. I came to understand that he was
in many ways a mysterious figure. Some said he came from
Hyde Road, others from Ballynanty. The city was just about
big enough to afford a measure of anonymity. You could be
a great familiar of O'Connell Street but relatively unknown
beyond the normal hours of the day and night. We might know

broadly of your standing, your people and their afflictions, but the view would be fuzzy, the detail blurred. So it was with Con. He did not seem to hold down a job. (It was hard to imagine the workmates who could suffer him.) His occupation, plainly, was with the dead. It was difficult to age him. He was a man out of time somehow. The overcoat was vast and worn at all seasons and made him a figure from a Jack B. Yeats painting or an old Russian novel. There was something antique in his bearing. The rain that he drew down upon himself seemed to be an old, old rain. One night on William Street, I spotted him sitting late and alone in the Burgerland there over a paper cup of tea. That cup of tea was the saddest thing I ever saw. I sat in a few tables from him and watched carefully. As he sat alone his lips again moved and I have no doubt that it was a litany of names he was reciting, the names of the dead, but just barely, just a whisper enough to hoist those names that they might float above the lamps of the city.

———

And maybe he was truly the sanest of us, I sometimes thought, on those nights in October when I could not sleep, and I took to driving late around the streets and the bridges and the town, and I knew that it was passing from me, and how remarkable it was that we can turn our minds from that which is inevitable – Con McCarthy could not turn from it. As cars came towards me at pace on the dual carriageway, sometimes for just the splinter of a moment there in the small hours I wanted to swerve and jolt into their lights and bring the taste of it on to me, the taste of its metal on my lips. Bring forward the news even if I could make no subsequent report of it.

When Con McCarthy died it was, of course, to a spectacular absence of fanfare – suddenly, unexpectedly, and rating no more than a brief line in the *Chronicle* 'Deaths' of a Tuesday in November.

Almost laughing, almost glad, I went along O'Connell Street in the rain with it; I leant in, I whispered; and softly like funeral doves I let my handsome eyes ascend . . .

'Did you hear at all?' I said. 'Did you not hear who's dead?'

The Downtown Queen

Peter Murphy

I was the proverbial young-dumb-and-full-of-cum – mine and half of Cleveland's – but I did two smart things in my life. One was pack a suitcase and board a Greyhound to New York in the summer of '72. The other was, no matter how fucked up I got, I kept records. Boxes and boxes of records. Plus audio cassettes, handwritten notes, transcripts, Polaroids, Super-8 footage, bootleg tapes. I couldn't play an instrument or dance or sing for shit, but for almost a decade I was the downtown scene's resident recording angel. I knew everyone: Warhol, Cale, the Dolls, Debbie, Patti, Richard Hell – a lifetime later I still repeat their names like some sort of rosary, some old queen recalling her suitors from years gone by.

Nine years and all that wild energy evaporated into the Manhattan sky. We were overnight passé. Those of us who survived, who didn't drink ourselves to death or OD or end up joining some macrobiotic cult, we limped back to the 'burbs and asked ourselves if it hadn't all been some beautiful hallucination. Some of us took respectable, got married, had kids, worked boring jobs, got old, got slow, got fat.

Then, somewhere around the turn of the century, rich-kid

musicians and fashionistas started copping our licks, our look, our attitude. They called it *vintage*, like we were from the 1950s or something. Max's and CBGB's T-shirts everywhere. Me, I wasn't going to miss that train. I started pitching scripts. I put together a treatment for a documentary proposal. I got some bites. HBO expressed an interest and an exec put me in contact with a script editor named Scott and together we started going through my archive. There was so much stuff in there, boxes of materials I'd kept in a lock-up in the Bronx.

Me and Scott spent a couple of weeks brainstorming and sifting through the debris searching for some kind of narrative through-line. We speed-read biographies and pored over old issues of *New York Rocker* and *Punk*. Then, late one night as we were reviewing live footage of Richard Hell from, I think, '78, Bob Quine ripping one of those splintered-glass solos without even breaking a sweat, Scott all a sudden hit pause and leaned forward in his seat and said:

'Who's *she*?'

And there you were, arrested in freeze-frame front of stage, raven-haired, dancing with those delicate bird hands like a willow in the wind. Jesus, it almost hurt to see your face again, your dark eyes and alabaster skin, trapped inside the monitor. I nearly put my fingers against the glass to touch your face.

'It *is* a *she*, right?'

And then I spoke your name for the first time in fifteen years.

———

Maxine, queen of the leather bars. Maxine who haunted the sex shows and the fist-fuck pantomimes, moving like some feline animal, so graceful, so precisely tuned. Dangerous too. You'd stalk the city like a leopard. You'd pull a knife on anyone who got too close.

First we met, you were holding court in the back room at Max's, spring of '73. Weeks in town and already you were embedded with the Jackie Curtis crowd. You'd crawled from some cored-out fuckhole town in Michigan, but soon as you got off that bus you shed that history like skin. This is America.

That's you in the Polaroid, eyebrows arched, cigarette holder between long fingers, immaculately poised, whispering to Cale. The Velvets had split by then, Lou was in hiding somewhere, John was making the rent as a record producer and A&R man. No matter what, those boys always made the rent. Andy too. Andy came on like everyone's weird fairy godmother, but he was sharp. I can still hear him in my head. *Hey, the thing that makes money here is silk screens, and if I want to make film, I better sell some more silk screens. Maybe I should make more contacts. Maybe I should have Edie in the film, that would help. Maybe the band needs a blonde bombshell as the focus for a lead singer.*

The blonde bombshell in question was a six-foot German model who spoke seven languages and had impressed Fellini enough to score a part in *La Dolce Vita*. Her name was Christa, Christa Päffgen, better known as Nico, and it was Andy's idea that she front the Velvets. John and Lou didn't like that much, but they knew who was signing the cheques, so they gritted their teeth and made a deal. She'd feature as guest vocalist. Nico had nothing much to offer beyond a harmonium she couldn't play, much less hear – she was deaf in one ear – but she wasn't going to let anything get in her way. She didn't want to be a model anymore. Andy knew how to manipulate image to everybody's benefit. That was his speciality.

So Lou wrote 'Femme Fatale' and 'I'll Be Your Mirror' for Nico to sing – if you can call it singing – and they recorded that first album, and it was amazing, mind-blowing, except it didn't sell shit, then Nico jumped, or was pushed, and then John jumped, or was pushed, and he produced a couple of albums for her, *Chelsea Girl* and *The Marble Index*. We played those albums to death. You'd never admit it, Maxine, but you idolised Nico: the shades, the white suits, the haughty stance. But you would never be so gauche as to cop her style. You had your own thing going on. Just watching you get ready to go out for the night was pure kabuki. The nails, the eyebrows, the hair . . . We could never go *anywhere* in a hurry, you were like some old lady, needed three hours' notice to leave for the liquor store.

I wasn't your closest confidante – I don't know if you ever really let anyone get close, apart from that Limey prick – but I think you liked me more than most. You used to call me Miss Ohio. That night in Max's when we met, though, you were ice-queen cold. Maybe you felt threatened. You looked me up and down and asked Andy if I was man, woman or child, and Andy just blinked and said, in that spacey, far-off way of his, *Child, definitely child*, and that was his signal for you to just be cool.

Cool was everything back then. Cool was currency and philosophy and holy grail. None of us belonged where we were born so we came to New York City looking for that elusive element of cool, searching through the thrift-shop glamour and the sleaze and the noise. We dug the glitter groups. We dug the girl groups. We dug the garage bands. Most of all we dug the Dolls. Oh, how we loved the Dolls, our Barbie Rolling Stones. Johansen's eyes even crinkled like Jagger's when he smiled. David was smart. And I don't mean book-smart, I mean street-smart. They'd taken over a room in the Mercer Arts Center, then all these freaks started showing up, photographers and painters and fashion designers and wannabe actors and journalists, this giant prom of freaky underground people, the band acting as a social catalyst.

If Max's was our Camelot, and the Bowery was Brassaï's night-town repainted as blue neon noir in shots by David Godlis, then CBGB's was our speakeasy, our version of that piss-smelling cesspit Verlaine and Rimbaud used to haunt, the Café du Rat Mort – except instead of young Arthur jumping on to the table to take a dump and then paint his masterpiece in this *powerful impasto*, you had Hilly's dog crapping everywhere, or the Dead Boys in the kitchen jerking off into the chilli.

It all started when Television's guitarist Richard Lloyd and manager Terry Ork were scouting a location for a residency something like the Dolls' Mercer stint – this was, like, March of '74 – and they came across this dive bar in the East Village that served food and featured old hippy music. Terry promised Hilly that if he booked Television he'd get people in and buy drinks for the house, to prime the pump. First gig they played, they all made a dollar, one buck, after they'd paid for a cab to get the equipment. It was more like an insane asylum than a club. There was a flophouse overhead and the wine was dripping through the ceiling and Tom and Richard were getting sparks off the microphones. But it was the beginnings of the mythology. That night Maxine cracked open a bottle of champagne she'd liberated from some secret stash in the Factory and toasted the new year zero and we drank it to the dregs.

Back then the term punk – as in punk rock – didn't exist yet, it was still slang for a wise-ass or a hustler. MC5 guitarist Wayne Kramer was serving a four-year stretch for dealing coke when John Holmstrom and Legs McNeil sent him a copy of their new magazine, *Punk*. Wayne flushed the newspaper cuttings down the john in case somebody got the wrong idea. Or maybe the right idea – I mean, Jim Carroll and Dee Dee made the scene tricking with me and Maxine and the rest of us hustling our tushies on the corner of 53rd and 3rd, getting blown or giving handjobs for forty bucks a pop. Dee Dee even wrote a song about it.

Word of mouth on the Television shows got Patti Smith's attention, and they booked six co-headliners that filled the place. Patti was this sort of slam poet who'd learned how to obliterate all competition in places like St Mark's Church. Watching her doing 'Piss Factory' or 'Hey Joe', it was like she'd been struck by lightning, all that raw energy, words pouring out of her mouth like she was speaking in tongues. Which she kind of was, I think her folks were Jehovah's or something. Cale said producing her first album was as much a literary gig as a musical one.

Then there were the Ramones, who were just adorable: four guys from Queens playing this totally gonzo version of rock 'n' roll, all these fast, loud, sawn-off songs that began with the words *I don't wanna*. And Suicide, who were Maxine's favourites 'cos they were the dregs of the dregs, true pariahs, this vocal/synthesiser duo when such a thing was unheard of.

That was the big difference between me and Queen Maxine. I had a pop heart; she was into darker stuff. She said Suicide was ultimately the only true punk band because even the punk bands hated them. The shit people used to throw at them: axes, knives, chairs, tables, glass, bottles, you name it.

Then there was our beloved Richard Hell, who was so smart and so well read and looked like a matinee idol and was the first to spike his hair and rip his T-shirt. Richard left Television before they recorded the *Marquee Moon* album, and to be honest none of us were too surprised – he was always rubbing Verlaine up the wrong way. He started the Heartbreakers with Johnny Thunders – a match made in the infirmary – and then his own band, the Voidoids. But forget all this stuff about Richard being a nihilist. 'Blank Generation' was about *us*, the young and fucked up at the end of the twentieth century, we who had infinite licence to create something new because we had no history to betray. The Pistols wrote their own version, 'Pretty Vacant' – now *that* was nihilistic. The Pistols stole a lot from Richard. McLaren knew what he was doing. He took Richard's look and Television's musical energy and The Ramones' drive, coupled it with Johnny's swagger and there he had the Sex Pistols. We saw it happen right before our eyes.

The prophet is not without honour except in his own country, Maxine would say when she saw pictures of the Sex Pistols and the Clash and the Damned in the English weeklies. I asked her where that line came from and she said the Bible and I wondered was she from Baptist stock or something, so I asked her straight and she told me that her family were dead to her, they were just some larval shell to be discarded once you'd found your own identity.

'All that's important,' she said, a scowl etched into her brow, sewing lines she'd later curse, 'is who we are right now.'

One of the grand ironies of the downtown scene? Blondie and Talking Heads, who a lot of people regarded as the runts – no matter what they later claimed – became the biggest of any of those bands. I mean, Debbie was a star, anyone could see that. She was beautiful and smart and funny and self-aware and I hated her. Then Maxine told me she was really nice and I felt like such a shitheel for bitching behind her back. They were friendly for a while, she and Debbie, they'd been in some off-off-Broadway thing together. She said Debbie used to take the piss out of the whole sexy-starlet Marilyn Monroe thing, she would sometimes come onstage dressed as a housewife and make herself look kind of funny and kitschy. And sometimes she wore a wedding gown that she'd tear apart during 'Rip Her to Shreds'. Debbie always had this campy performance-art stuff going on, it wasn't just a beautiful girl singing with this combo in the background.

But the clock was ticking. You could feel the rising chill. Maybe Debbie felt it first, and that's why she and Chris were pushing so hard to make it. Debbie had been around for a long time and she probably felt like, this is the last shot I've got. There was a hardness to the New York thing, everyone locking sunglasses with the rest of the club, everyone trying to out-cool everybody else. Some of the older ones who'd been around for a while, they'd never admit to being impressed. Some nights in CBGB's it was like some Fellini movie, all shades and poker faces, no one lifting an eyebrow. Maxine said it used to get on Debbie's nerves a lot, that people were very territorial. For a while Blondie couldn't even get booked at CBGB's because of the Television/Patti mafia, who were trying to keep it very arty, snobby in their own way, and they didn't want to let this kind of rinky-dink garage band in. And look what happened. Me and Maxine took heart from that. Deep down there was always this nagging fear of being left behind, that once the scene imploded we'd be nothing more than casualties. I remember arguing one night as we drank off the adrenaline of whatever show we'd been to. I was starving and scared for the future and spoiling for an argument.

'What are we celebrating?' I said. 'Our own demise? We're just hanging around on the sidelines watching everybody else do their thing. Nothing more than voyeurs. Leeches. Except nobody's getting fat.'

Maxine laughed and shook her head.

'Honey, you couldn't be more wrong. Without us there *is* no scene. The audience is just as important as the band.'

'If that was true,' I said, 'we'd be getting paid.'

Then Maxine drew herself up to her full height, six-three in her stilettos, nails like talons, the faintest shadow of facial hair showing through the geisha mask, and man, she was terrifying.

'Look at me, Miss Ohio. Do I look like a parasite to you? A groupie? I don't write songs or make movies because I don't *have* to. I *am* a work of art.'

———

Once any scene becomes conscious of itself – even one already as self-conscious as CBGB's – the end is in sight. By '79 the wind had changed. Punk was now new wave, which then became no wave. Toerag hardcore bands and skinheads blew into town from DC and California. New sounds were coming from the clubs. We'd go see Brit bands like the Slits or the Gang of Four, or Bronx acts like Funky 4 + 1, or Afrika Bambaataa DJing, playing Kraftwerk. He'd also play 'Mickey' by Toni Basil – he would cut that beat up for like ten minutes, in front of thousands at the Roxy. It was insane.

First I heard Grandmaster Flash was when the Furious Five opened for the Clash at that casino residency in Times Square in February 1980. All the punks booed, scared of the new. How's that for irony? It was even a point of conflict between me and Maxine. She was so stuck on that romantic junkie white-boy squalor shit, hated it when Talking Heads started using Afro rhythms, never understood Tom Tom Club or any of the ZE label stuff.

'It's just bad disco,' she said. 'Monotonous.'

'You're such a WASP,' I said, and for a moment I thought I saw a flash of raw nerve, like I'd cut her, and I felt like shit, but when I apologised she just laughed it off.

'Truth hurts, Miss Ohio. That is a fact.'

By now Max's was closed and Studio 54 had taken over from CBGB's as the place to be seen. I went one time only. It wasn't my thing. I wasn't on coke and I didn't know anyone, so I didn't really get the full experience. To tell you the truth, I was kind of bored after a while. I figured I'd stick with the downtown clubs, even though the scene as we knew it was dying.

But you, Maxine, you almost got clear of the blast zone. Right about when it all started coming apart, you began dating this British guy, Donald something-something, a hot fashion photographer turned movie director. You were so crazy about him. He even set you up with your own apartment and line of credit. Can you imagine that now? An industry insider dating one of us freaks? We were so happy for you. And you carried it with grace, never crowed or lorded it over us. Until one day the rich Brit decided he wasn't queer anymore and dumped you for some society chick. Just cast you out. I'll never forget that awful night you were screaming at him in the Mudd Club 'cos he'd cancelled your cards. Oh honey, you were devastated.

That was a bad time. Friedkin was shooting his hustling movie with Pacino on the Lower East Side and I heard you'd been cast in a speaking part but at the last minute got bumped, and you swore it was that Limey bastard's machinations. Then I just lost you in the slow dissolve of time passing. Last I remember hearing, someone said they saw you in the Village in the eighties, soon after Andy died, said you were wearing shades and had gotten scary-thin, nothing left of you but those cheekbones. And I remember wondering if you'd caught the bug or were on the pipe.

Years went by. I thought of you sometimes in a vague way, but never enough to act on it. Then came the day Scott freeze-framed the footage, and there you were, our Queen Maxine, preserved behind the glass. We did a search on your name but nothing came up. I even thought about hiring a detective to find out if you were still alive. Then the network pulled the money – some big-shot showrunner had pitched a similar idea to ours. Move on, said Scott. If it matters that much to you, write a book. And that was that.

Until a couple of weeks ago this writer friend of mine, Peter, he took me to one of those exclusive gentlemen's clubs between 5th and 6th, one of those places you pay ten grand membership just to have a quiet place to drink, where they take your coat and your phone at the door. We were in the Admiral's Room, sipping a white wine that cost more than my rent, when out the corner of my eye I caught a glimpse of this figure, this – *creature* – quite old and fragile but very elegant, very magnetic, something about the movements, the shape, seemed hauntingly familiar. And in that moment I saw you again in the back room at Max's, and I remembered you dancing on the tables at CBGB's, flicking cigarettes at the Dictators, and I remembered how beautiful you looked even as you swept out of the Mudd Club that terrible night – it all hit me in a volley of images, and I felt suddenly dizzy, and Peter's voice faded to a drone as I rose from my seat and tried to make my way across the room, but by the time I'd manoeuvred around the waiter and his drinks trolley you were gone, just disappeared, like you were never there.

Gérard

Lisa McInerney

Our friend C told us she had started seeing legendary French actor Gérard Depardieu. Naturally this surprised us, to the extent that we assumed she was lying to us, or had suffered some sort of catastrophic mental break. C was born in 1991 and we learned that Gérard Depardieu was born in 1948; the only thing you could say of that, really, was that they were both post-war babies. Of course then we had to argue over what was meant by *post-war*. War with a capital W, we decided, World War, though then it was pointed out that there was always a war going on somewhere, which made us mope. C and Gérard Depardieu had created temporal chaos, an overlapping of incongruous time frames. We doubted ourselves. We furrowed our brows and scratched our upper arms.

C had moved to Paris that April, though she did not speak a word of French. We did not know this until after she had gone. We had assumed she had privately learned to speak French because how could you presume to live in Paris without speaking French? The French had a reputation for being hostile towards English-speaking monolinguals. We thought one would have to be extremely mad to move to France without being able to speak French. We learned this about C when she mentioned that she was looking for a waitressing job and we asked how confident she was about being able to deal with customers – did she know the correct culinary terms, how would she deal with complaints or large groups insisting on splitting the bill? She blithely said she had no French at all. In fact, she could not even say, *Désolée, je ne parle pas français*. One should at least have enough of a language to admit to being inept; we were adamant that that was the bare minimum in terms of self-respect and respect for the foreign other. C wasn't troubled by that sort of thing. C was very rarely troubled by the kinds of things that caused us to mop our foreheads or sprout hives. We assumed that C assumed all of her customers at the cafe would be English-speakers – in fact, that they would be more comfortable speaking English than French. We assumed that C assumed she could find a job bringing sad, milky coffees to Britons and Americans. Else her intent seemed a little arch, and we disagreed with archness in every respect. It wouldn't be like C to be arch.

Gérard Depardieu spoke English, we learned, but not well. We read an interview with him from 2011 in which he stated that he understood English better than he spoke it, though he spoke it in a rather slapdash way that further galvanised the hypothesis that he was mad as a sack of ferrets. We imagined C speaking with Gérard Depardieu, her in her wily Hiberno-English, him in excited malapropisms, constantly misunderstanding each other. They would find it hard to argue because they would not be able to correctly state their stances. Their conversations would be characterised by frustrated gestures. Possibly Gérard Depardieu was being truthful when he told his interviewer that he understood much better than he spoke, and so possibly he thought of C as a sort of zippy innocent, possibly he was toying with her. We did not like this idea, and cursed Gérard Depardieu, and swore never to give him the benefit of the doubt on this or on further issues.

It occurred to us that such a language barrier might be exploited by someone who was not, in fact, legendary French actor Gérard Depardieu, and after all we were all of us young, and C particularly blithe, therefore was it not possible that she was not *au fait* with the output, reputation or indeed *visage* of legendary French actor Gérard Depardieu, and so open to the machinations of imposters.

C told us not to be so stupid, she had vetted Gérard Depardieu thoroughly.

We had to admit that this was somewhat more likely because even though C was very blithe, she was also very clever.

You're so ridiculous, she told us. There's nothing at all wrong with dating Gérard Depardieu, you are acting as if dating Gérard Depardieu is a terrible thing.

It's at least ill-advised, we said.

Why? she said.

We found this *Why?* very irritating because C was goading us with it, for she knew well why we'd find her seeing Gérard Depardieu objectionable. He was much older than her, much richer than her, and he understood English better than he spoke it, and so there was no parity of power in their relationship; he could so very easily make minced meat out of her. Overcooked, under-seasoned, Irish minced meat. This was one of the moments in our lives where we thought of our nationality as an impairment. We were not necessarily correct, but we experienced flashes of inferiority, which we thought must have been very common or else where would we have gotten them? They had to be contracted and passed on; these things aren't natural.

They may have come through from our recent ancestors, who had emigrated because they had no choice, who had not learned the languages of their intended hosts beforehand because there were few ways to do so. We had once read about learned trauma, which applied to human communities and also to crows. C liked crows so much. She left scraps out for them in the hope that they would pass on that we were a good bunch, in the hope that many future generations of crows would come to the spaces we'd made, having remembered beyond all reason that we were their friends. C told us that crows had been found to have accents: crows sounded different depending on where they came from. She imagined that Donegal crows sounded more melodious to their neighbours, Dublin crows harsher, Kerry crows disingenuously lilting.

Is he at least kind to you? we asked of Gérard Depardieu.

At least? she laughed. At least? Like you'll all be sated if I tell you he doesn't beat me or humiliate me in front of famous directors or tell me I'm disgusting and fat? You must have a very low opinion not just of Gérard Depardieu, but of me too.

We told her it wasn't that. It was because we loved her and it was surely understandable that love made people anxious and even unreasonable. We said this very pointedly, so that we might persuade her that she was perhaps not thinking straight due to her own infatuation with Gérard Depardieu, something she had shown no signs of when she was home with us, researching corvid society. She had shown no signs of being obsessed with anyone. She had shown no signs of being the kind of girl who had her head turned at all.

It's all very sudden, we said. This interest in Gérard Depardieu.

I have never been interested in Gérard Depardieu, that's why, she said. When I first met him I simply thought he was an imposing Frenchman. I was not inspired to date him because of his reputation. In fact, I barely knew who he was, even after he introduced and explained himself. So please don't suggest I'm up to something.

Crows were always up to something. C said they learned tricks, or rather, they learned how to manipulate their environment to get the things they needed. They used tools, they pulled insects out of tree bark with sticks, or they raised water levels with stones in order to access some tasty morsel, or they used bait to catch fish, or they dropped walnuts at traffic junctions so that the cars would crack the shells. Ravens played with toys. Magpies liked shiny things. Always up to something, and that was why C loved them so much.

We said that we were not suggesting that C was up to something, rather that the novelty of being with legendary French actor Gérard Depardieu had blinded her to the many drawbacks of being with any legendary French actor, not least one of a certain age and girth.

Do you not find him cumbersome? we asked.

How I find Gérard Depardieu is between me and Gérard Depardieu, C said.

We had gathered at C's mother's house on the morning she went to Paris; we brought her mother chocolate; we gave C gifts and cried. When C and her mother left for the airport we spent some time around the swings in her back garden, tearing at blades of grass, talking about her, what on earth she was doing, how to get her to come back. It was plain that we were all shaken but reality hemmed us in. We couldn't scream or panic, for we'd have looked mad. We were never wilfully ignorant about how we might look to outsiders. We could do nothing but scold C in her absence and talk through where we'd gone wrong.

It wasn't the fact that C had partnered up with someone either, because it wasn't as if we didn't see people. We always had boyfriends on the go. We encouraged boyfriends. Girlfriends not so much. The problem with girls was permanence; we understood how attached girls got to each other. Maybe if one of us was retreating altogether, taking off into an exile either self-imposed or dictated. Maybe if one of us was *retired*, as such.

C had not suggested retiring herself, nor had she ever been put forward for retirement.

How I find Gérard Depardieu is between me and Gérard Depardieu, C said, again, more slowly.

Maybe we should come to Paris, we said. To see for ourselves.

I'd rather you didn't.

Don't you think we miss you? Don't you miss us?

Of course I miss you, she said. But I feel that if you came to Paris now it would be to pick apart Gérard Depardieu.

Outside, sheets of rain moved across the countryside. It was forlorn weather and we were damp to our bones. We wondered if C had figured out how to manipulate the weather. Maybe she didn't need to learn French, because she had access to wilder, more ancient arts than language.

But we miss you intensely, we said. We feel it like a gaping wound in our chests. We feel it like a cracked skull. Like an amputated—

That's so very clichéd, she said. You're being so arch.

Fine. We feel as if we're being haunted.

Better, she said.

We think we should come to Paris.

I don't want you to, she said. Besides, it's practically impossible in a group who are all so highly strung. There were fifty French teenagers on my flight over. They were all screaming at one another. Their teacher clutched her chest. The captain had to come out of the cockpit and berate them.

We're not teenagers anymore, we said. We know how to ferry ourselves. D has been to Tunisia, remember? B was born in Brooklyn.

It'd be too difficult, she said. The dynamics of it. Aren't you afraid that once you're in a new place the whole contrivance will fall to pieces? It seems to me that any fractures caused by my taking off can be blamed solely on me. Isn't that so much safer? If things are stretched now it could easily be the fact that I'm the bad tooth in the mouth.

Don't say that, we said.

I've done enough to challenge this thing we've got going, C said. You don't have to risk yourselves just to see what happens once you spill sunshine on it, or apply smog.

We said, Please come home. If you come home, we can all take a trip together.

C said there was no point in that, because she was already in Paris. What was the point in coming back just to go somewhere else again? No, she was a willing martyr. As

338

a pool of mercury struck and split apart, she said that we needed to see if we all came back together naturally. This is what her absence was all about.

It's not about Gérard Depardieu? we asked.

Well, it wasn't to start with. It was for our own good, to start with. Maybe it is now. Maybe I'm insanely in love with him. Maybe I can't be doing without Gérard Depardieu.

We wondered what we were meant to do. We sat on the floor of our parlour and held hands or leaned into one another. D wanted to light candles but we thought that would be arch. We were not the candle sort. What C had said required analysis, because she wasn't being consistent. She had moved to France because she was blithe and had taken up with Gérard Depardieu because she wanted to, because evidently there was some quality in him that was not cumbersome. At the same time, she was suggesting that she had moved to Paris in order to test us as a unit. On that basis, was Gérard Depardieu a means of forcing our hands? Was Gérard Depardieu nothing but an improbable concoction? Unbeknownst to Gérard Depardieu, was he playing a bogeyman's role?

A asked whether it wasn't immediately obvious that we should ignore C's stated wishes, and all of us go to Paris to meet her and Gérard Depardieu.

F asked about the projects we had on the go, whether all of us leaving wouldn't let a bit too much air in? She was pretending to be concerned on our behalf but we knew that she had been struggling a bit with the boy she was seeing. She had jumped into things with him too quickly and she was finding it tough to maintain a level of interest. Consequently he was beginning to think that she was rather ordinary. We really wanted to leave her to it; she hadn't asked for help. And there was nothing particularly nourishing about him. Still, F was stubborn, and she had never abandoned a project.

E said that it wasn't just that, but work as well; much as she hated to say it she had responsibilities in the outside world. She had just recently started in a veterinary surgeon's office and spent much of the day logging cattle blood. She wasn't sure her boss would be pleased if she looked for time off so soon.

Is this a crisis? B asked.

If he was a guy called Gerard who lived in Ireland, A said, we wouldn't think twice about it. So maybe he's just a guy called Gérard who lives in France?

But specifically Gérard Depardieu?

He's so old.

And horribly rich and accomplished.

And cumbersome.

D asked if we were all considering that C had invented this affair with Gérard Depardieu solely to stir us into coming to Paris to retrieve her. That way, we made the decision to remove her from Paris, and she could offer insincere objections, and she wouldn't have to admit she'd made a mistake.

We decided Gérard Depardieu was the worst possible person C could have taken up with in Paris, and so obviously his name was a sort of incantation, or if we wanted to be ordinary about it, a *cry for help*. C, being blithe, was not always terribly responsible. Being known as the blithe one, she felt that she couldn't be seen to identify problems herself. She had always obligated us to solve things for her.

We downloaded Gérard Depardieu's English-language films

and watched them for clues. *Green Card, Hamlet, The Man in the Iron Mask, My Father the Hero, Life of Pi.* They were mostly terrible and led us to believe that Gérard Depardieu was very easily led. We watched some of his French-language films, with subtitles, for balance: *Cyrano de Bergerac, Le Dernier Métro, Jean de Florette,* even *Astérix et Obélix.* These painted a much more flattering picture of Gérard Depardieu but the problem remained: in French he was intense, focused, charming or sympathetic and in English he was a giant, flamboyant oaf and C, of course, C could not speak French.

Outside, sheets of rain made dangerous weather, the kind that turns the sad lonesome.

We read more about Gérard Depardieu. We approached him as if he were the subject of a school group presentation: we assigned ourselves reading pertinent to his career, upbringing, romantic liaisons and children, and were set to bullet-point and pool what we had learned, but almost immediately we discovered that Gérard Depardieu did not live in France anymore.

It was said that he chose to live in Belgium or Italy or Belarus as a way to avoid paying French taxes. In fact, he had taken Russian citizenship after clashing with the French authorities about his views on taxation, which were that, being a larger-than-life national treasure, he shouldn't be subject to it.

We sat in a misshapen circle and in a sort of misshapen chorus said, Meaning he is not in Paris and therefore unlikely to be dating C.

We knew it! we shouted. We, with our blood magic, with our binding spells, with our stacking of each other's secrets, with our careful arbitration. We, with our private names, with our rules and canon, with our chapter and verse. We founding members of a new civilisation, we who knew we'd be eulogised and immortalised one day.

We thought it kindest not to tell C we were coming.

We went to Paris dressed the same; we did not always dress the same, in fact, we thought that dressing the same was arch, but we thought the occasion called for it. Actually what happened was that we looked like poorly groomed cabin crew, a collective but the wrong sort of collective, one that did not give off energy or a sense of power. And so when we arrived in Paris we had to collect ourselves, and were therefore delayed.

At school we had dressed the same, of course. We were allowed only one accessory and it was meant to be elegant, but we coordinated and all wore the same pendant of plastic fruits; when challenged we tucked them into our blouses. The fruits were so garish, almost neon. Bananas, pears, red apples, purple grapes. This was not symbolism, not at first. We retconned it. We looked back and said it was about ripeness, audacity, fertility, juice. Really, though, we had chosen the pendants for being cheap. Six euro fifty each.

We found C's apartment easily enough. It was over a cafe in the 5th arrondissement, which later we found out was the obvious place for her, but we didn't know much, then, about Paris. We stood back on the street and watched the windows on the first floor, because we wanted to make sure that this was the right place, and we wanted to draw the right distance between what we thought might be the correct door and what we thought might be the correct window, for we had to get this right, we could not ask for directions if the wrong person came to the door, we had no French except *Désolées, nous ne parlons pas français . . .*

The windows on the first floor were open and we moved towards the door when we heard C's voice, because at first we were overjoyed to hear her, and naturally we moved best together, and here we were, so close to being together again. We realised C was speaking in French. We stopped moving. Her accent was still strongly of the Irish south-east, she pronounced the French crudely. *Comment oses-tu dire ça?* said C. *Imbécile! Stupide!*

A man appeared between the curtains, looking towards C with his hands up. We peered and murmured. D took a photograph and zoomed in on the screen. We weren't sure. We waited for one of our number to rush away and bang on the door. We huddled and glared at each other. We willed one another to break rank.

Then came C – no, the fist of the person we assumed to be C – in a flurry at the window, landing hard on the arms and chest and skull of the man companion, who seemed to be ill-equipped to manage what was happening to him despite his considerable girth.

Jesus, B said. Is that Gérard Depardieu?

Is it, though?

It doesn't matter, the rest of us said. It doesn't matter when that's definitely C, with the air gone to her head, with her bent out of shape by the wind. It doesn't matter who it is, it matters who we are. Who we are and how we could let this happen.

There was a flash of artificial light as a large hand jerked the curtain back and an honest face with small round eyes and a large nose looked out, and saw us, opened its mouth, opened the hand, palm upwards.

There was a cry, a fuss, then silence at the window, as if C had realised we were there and had clamped her thin white hand over Gérard Depardieu's soft, mournful mouth.

We stood around the window in a semicircle, our shoulders hunched.

We allowed her tools and toys, we whispered. We let her spread her wings.

C, we called. Enough of this nonsense.

C stuck her head out of the window. She leaned on the balustrade.

Oh, can I not have a moment's peace? she said. Can you wagons not let me live? *Allez vous faire foutre!* she said. Before I set the bodyguards on you.

Notes on Contributors

DARRAN ANDERSON is the author of *Imaginary Cities* (Influx Press/University of Chicago Press) and the forthcoming *Tidewrack* (Chatto & Windus/Farrar, Straus and Giroux). He has given talks on cities at the likes of the V&A, the LSE and the Venice Biennale, and has written for the *Guardian*, *The Atlantic*, *Wired* and *Frieze*, among others. He grew up in Derry and lives in England.

KEVIN BARRY is the author of the novels *Beatlebone* and *City of Bohane* and the story collections *Dark Lies the Island* and *There Are Little Kingdoms*. His work has been translated into more than twenty languages. His stories have appeared in *The New Yorker*, *Granta* and elsewhere. He edited *Town and Country: New Irish Short Stories* for Faber in 2012. He also writes plays and screenplays. He lives in County Sligo.

LUCY CALDWELL was born in Belfast in 1981. She is the author of three novels, several stage plays and radio dramas, and a collection of short stories. Awards include the Rooney Prize for Irish Literature, the George Devine Award, the Dylan Thomas

Prize, the Imison Award, the Commonwealth Short Story Prize (Canada & Europe), the Irish Playwrights' and Screenwriters' Guild Award, the Edge Hill Short Story Prize Readers' Choice Award, a Fiction Uncovered Award, a K. Blundell Trust Award and a Major Individual Artist Award from the Arts Council of Northern Ireland. She was elected a Fellow of the Royal Society of Literature in 2018.

JAN CARSON is a writer and community arts facilitator based in East Belfast. Her debut novel, *Malcolm Orange Disappears*, and short story collection, *Children's Children*, were published by Liberties Press, Dublin. A micro-fiction collection, *Postcard Stories*, was published by the Emma Press in 2017. Jan's most recent novel is *The Fire Starters*, published by Doubleday in 2019. Her stories have appeared in journals such as *Banshee*, *The Tangerine* and *Harper's Bazaar*, and on BBC Radio 3 and 4. In 2018, Jan was the Irish Writers Centre's inaugural Roaming Writer-in-Residence on the trains of Ireland.

JILL CRAWFORD is from Maghera, County Derry. Having attended a mixed-religion school, she studied English and Modern Languages at New College, Oxford, trained at the National Youth Theatre, and became a professional actress. She has lived in South Africa, France and America, as well as in the UK. She began publishing her writing in 2017, prior to receiving the John Boyne Scholarship at the University of East Anglia, where she has since completed the MA in Prose Fiction. Her stories have appeared in *The Stinging Fly*, *n+1* and *Winter Papers*. An essay on language was published by *Boundless*. She is writing a novel about acting, supported by the Arts Council of Northern Ireland.

WENDY ERSKINE lives in Belfast. Her debut collection of short stories, *Sweet Home*, was published by The Stinging Fly Press in 2018. Her writing has also appeared in issues of *The Stinging Fly*, in *Stinging Fly Stories* (2018), *Winter Papers* (2018) and *Female Lines: New Writing by Women from Northern Ireland* (New Island Books, 2017), and on BBC Radio 4.

NICOLE FLATTERY's debut story collection was published by The Stinging Fly Press in 2019. She is the recipient of a number of bursaries from the Arts Council and the winner of the 2017 *White Review* Short Story Prize. She is from the Midlands of Ireland.

YAN GE was born in Sichuan Province, China, in 1984. She is a writer and a PhD candidate in Comparative Literature. Publishing since 1994, she is the author of eleven books. Her work has been translated into English, French and German, among other languages. She was named by *People's Literature* magazine as one of twenty future literature masters in China. The English translation of her latest novel, *The Chilli Bean Paste Clan*, was published by Balestier Press. She has recently started to write in English. She lives in Dublin with her husband and son.

SINÉAD GLEESON's essays have appeared in *Granta*, *Winter Papers*, *gorse* and *Banshee* and the journal *Elsewhere*. Her short stories have been published in the anthologies *Looking at the Stars*, *The Broken Spiral* and *Repeal the 8th*. Published poems have featured in the anthologies *Autonomy*, *Reading the Future* and *Washing Windows? Irish Women Write Poetry*. She is the editor of three short anthologies, including the award-winning collections *The Long Gaze Back: An Anthology of Irish Women Writers* (2015) and *The Glass Shore: Short Stories by Women Writers from the North of Ireland* (2016). Her debut book of essays, *Constellations*, was published by Picador in 2019. She is currently working on a novel.

DAVID HAYDEN's writing has appeared in *Zoetrope: All-Story*, *Granta*, *The Stinging Fly*, *gorse* and *Winter Pages*. His short story collection, *Darker With the Lights On*, was published in 2017. Born in Dublin, he has lived in the US and Australia and is now based in Norwich.

ARJA KAJERMO was born in Finland and grew up in Sweden. She has worked as a cartoonist since the late 1970s and contributed cartoons to *In Dublin* magazine, the *Irish Press*, the *Irish Times*, the *Sunday Tribune* and many other Irish publications. She draws a weekly cartoon for Swedish daily *Dagens Nyheter*. Her short story 'The Iron Age' was one of the six prize-winning stories for the 2014 Davy Byrnes Short Story Award. Her debut novel of the same name was published by Tramp Press in 2017, and included on the 2018 Walter Scott Prize Academy's Recommended Reading list of historical novels. Arja has lived in Dublin for forty years and has given birth to two fine Irishmen.

EIMEAR MCBRIDE is the author of two novels: *The Lesser Bohemians* (winner of the James Tait Black Memorial Prize) and *A Girl is a Half-formed Thing* (winner of the Baileys Women's Prize for Fiction, the Kerry Group Irish Novel of the

Year Award, the Goldsmiths Prize, the Desmond Elliott Prize and the Geoffrey Faber Memorial Prize). In 2017 she became the inaugural Creative Fellow at the Beckett Research Centre, University of Reading, and she occasionally writes for the *Guardian, TLS, New Statesman* and the *Irish Times.* She lives in London.

LISA MCINERNEY's work has featured in *Winter Papers, The Stinging Fly, Granta,* the *Guardian,* various anthologies and on BBC Radio 4. Her story 'Navigation' was longlisted for the 2017 *Sunday Times* EFG Short Story Award. Her debut novel, *The Glorious Heresies,* won the 2016 Baileys Women's Prize for Fiction and the 2016 Desmond Elliott Prize. Her second novel, *The Blood Miracles,* won the 2018 RSL Encore Award.

BELINDA MCKEON is the author of two novels, *Tender* (2015) and *Solace* (2011), which won the Geoffrey Faber Memorial Prize. Her fiction and non-fiction have been published in *Granta, The Paris Review,* the *New York Times, Harper's Bazaar* and elsewhere. She is also a playwright. She lives in New York and teaches at Rutgers University.

ADRIAN MCKINTY was born in Belfast and grew up Carrickfergus, County Antrim. He studied Philosophy at Oxford University before making his way to New York, where he found employment as a barman, salesman and construction worker. He eventually became a high school English teacher in Denver, Colorado. He is the author of ten crime novels and has won the Edgar Award, the Anthony Award, the Barry Award and the Ned Kelly Award.

Notes on Contributors

DANIELLE MCLAUGHLIN's stories have appeared in newspapers and magazines such as *The Stinging Fly*, the *Irish Times*, *Southword* and *The New Yorker*, and have been broadcast on RTÉ Radio 1 and BBC Radio 4. Her debut collection of short stories, *Dinosaurs on Other Planets*, was published in Ireland by The Stinging Fly Press in 2015, and in the UK (John Murray), US (Random House) and Slovakia (Inaque) in 2016. She was UCC Writer-in-Residence 2018–19. Together with Madeleine D'Arcy, she co-runs Fiction at the Friary, a free monthly fiction event in Cork which takes place at the Friary Bar, North Mall, on the last Sunday of every month.

PAUL MCVEIGH's short stories have appeared in anthologies and literary journals, been read on BBC Radio 3, 4 and 5 and commissioned by Sky Arts TV. 'Hollow' was shortlisted for Short Story of the Year at the 2017 Bord Gáis Energy Irish Book Awards. He is Associate Director at Word Factory, the UK's national organisation for excellence in the short story, and is co-founder of the London Short Story Festival. *The Good Son*, his debut novel, was shortlisted for a number of awards including the Prix du Roman Cezam, in France, and won the McCrea Literary Award and the Polari First Book Prize. Paul McVeigh has written for radio, stage and television and his writing has been translated into seven languages.

PETER MURPHY is a writer and spoken-word performer from Wexford, Ireland. He is the author of two novels, *John the Revelator* (2009) and *Shall We Gather at the River* (2013), published by Faber in Ireland and the UK, and by Houghton Mifflin Harcourt in the US and Canada. Peter's journalism and non-fiction have appeared in *Rolling Stone*, the *Guardian*, the *Irish Times*, *Hot Press* and the *Huffington Post*. He has released two spoken-word/music albums with the Revelator Orchestra, *The Sounds of John the Revelator* and *The Brotherhood of the Flood*. He currently performs live under the name Cursed Murphy, and his first single, 'Foxhole Prayer', was released in 2018.

STUART NEVILLE's debut novel, *The Twelve* (published in the US as *The Ghosts of Belfast*), won the mystery/thriller category of the *Los Angeles Times* Book Prize, and was picked as one of the top crime novels of 2009 by both the *New York Times* and the *Los Angeles Times*. He has been shortlisted for various awards, including the Barry, Macavity and Dilys Awards, as well as the Bord Gáis Energy Irish Book Awards Crime Novel of the Year. He has since published six more critically acclaimed books, including *Ratlines*, shortlisted for the CWA Ian Fleming Steel Dagger, and *The Final Silence*, shortlisted for the Edgar Award.

LOUISE O'NEILL grew up in Clonakilty, a small town in West Cork, Ireland. Her first novel, *Only Ever Yours*, was named *Sunday Independent* Newcomer of the Year at the 2014 Bord Gáis Energy Irish Book Awards, the Children's Books Ireland Eilís Dillon Award for a First Children's Book, and the *Bookseller*'s inaugural YA Book Prize in 2015. Louise's second novel, *Asking For It*, won the Specsavers Senior Children's Book of the Year at the 2015 Bord Gáis Energy Irish Book Awards, and was also voted Book of the Year. It spent fifty-two weeks in the Irish top-ten bestseller list and has been adapted for stage. Louise presented a documentary of the same name – on the subject of rape culture – in 2016. Her first, highly acclaimed novel for adults, *Almost*

Love, was published in 2018. Louise is a freelance journalist for a variety of Irish national newspapers and magazines, and has a weekly column in the *Irish Examiner*. She contributed to *I Call Myself a Feminist* – a collection of essays from women under thirty. Her latest novel for young adults is the much celebrated *The Surface Breaks* – a reimagining of the classic fairy tale 'The Little Mermaid'.

MELATU UCHE OKORIE was born in Enugu, Nigeria, and has been living in Ireland for twelve years. She has an MPhil in Creative Writing from Trinity College Dublin. Her work has been published in *Dublin: Ten Journeys One Destination*, *Alms on the Highway: New Writing from the Oscar Wilde Centre*, *LIT* magazine and *College Green*. Her debut collection, *This Hostel Life*, was published in 2018. Her second collection of short stories is due in 2019.

SHEILA PURDY was brought up in Dublin and now lives in Wicklow. She studied at University College Dublin, King's Inns and the University of Ulster. After attending the Faber Academy in Dublin, she went on to do a master's in Creative Writing at UCD, where she won the inaugural Big Storytelling Competition. Her first published work appeared in Faber's *Town and Country* anthology, edited by Kevin Barry. Sheila received an Arts Council of Ireland bursary through *The Stinging Fly* and Claire Keegan. She writes short stories and is working on her first collection.

ELSKE RAHILL was born in Dublin in 1982, and educated at Trinity College. Her works include the novel *Between Dog and*

Wolf and the short story collection *In White Ink*. Her second novel will be published by Head of Zeus in 2019. She lives in Burgundy with her partner and four children.

SALLY ROONEY was born in County Mayo and lives in Dublin. Her writing has appeared in *The New Yorker*, the *New York Times* and the *London Review of Books*. She is the author of *Conversations with Friends* and winner of the *Sunday Times/ PFD Young Writer Award 2017*. Her second novel, *Normal People*, was published in 2018 and longlisted for the Man Booker Prize. She is the editor of the biannual Dublin literary magazine *The Stinging Fly*.

KIT DE WAAL has won numerous awards for her short stories and flash fiction. Her debut novel, *My Name is Leon*, won the Kerry Group Irish Novel of the Year Award and was shortlisted for the Costa First Novel Award, the British Book Awards Debut Book of the Year and the Desmond Elliott Prize. In 2016 she founded the Kit de Waal Scholarship at Birkbeck University for a disadvantaged writer to study creative writing. She is also the editor of an anthology of working-class writing, *Common People*, published in 2019. Her new novel, *The Trick to Time*, was published in 2018 and longlisted for the Women's Prize for Fiction.